JANET OLEARSKI

was born in London and studied languages and linguistics at the University of Edinburgh, and later at the University of London Institute of Education. Her short fiction has appeared in *Wasafiri, Litro, Bare Fiction, The Commonline Journal,* and elsewhere. She has authored several children's books, among them *Twins, Mr. Football,* and *The Sunbird Mystery.* Her short-story collection, *A Brief History of Several Boyfriends,* was published in July 2017. She is a graduate of the Manchester Writing School at MMU and the founder of the Abu Dhabi Writers' Workshop. She has lived and worked in Italy, Poland, Oman, and the United Arab Emirates, and is now based in Central Portugal. Read more at: www.janetolearski.com

Also by Janet Olearski

Short Stories

A Brief History of Several Boyfriends

Children's Books

The Sunbird Mystery

Three Fairy Tales

Mr. Football

Twins

As Editor and Contributor

The Write Stuff

A TRAVELLER'S GUIDE TO NAMISA

A NOVEL

BY
JANET OLEARSKI

Copyright © Janet Olearski 2020

The right of Janet Olearski to be identified as the Author of the Work has been asserted by her in accordance with the Copyright, Designs and Patents Act 1988.

All rights reserved. No part of this publication may be reproduced, stored in a retrieval system, or transmitted, in any form or by any means, electronic, mechanical, photocopying, recording or otherwise, without the prior written permission of the copyright owner.

ISBN: 9798620966431

This book is a work of fiction. Names, characters, places and incidents are a product of the author's imagination or are used fictitiously, and any resemblance to actual persons living or dead, events or locales is entirely coincidental.

Cover Image: ebooklaunch.com

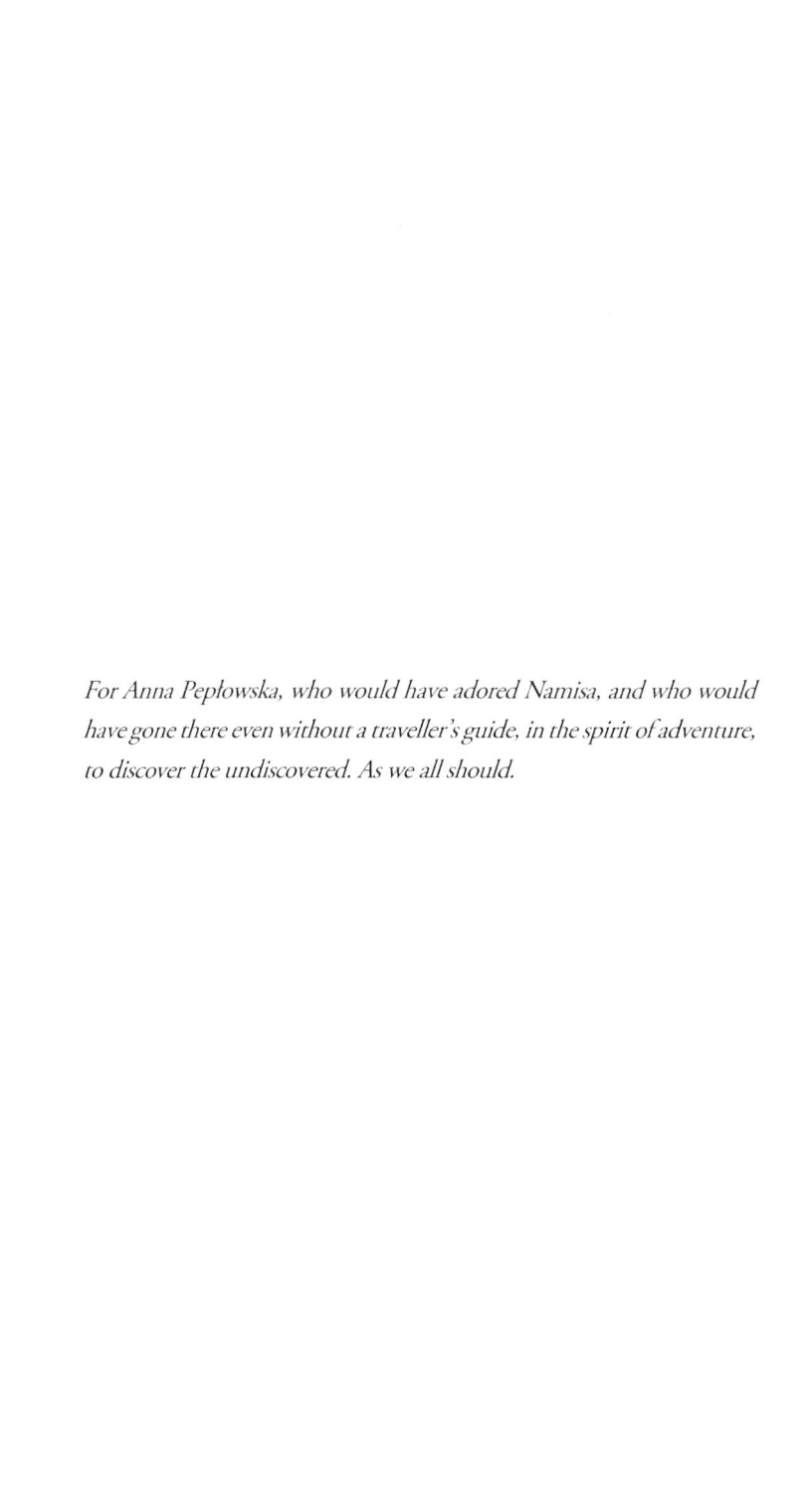

For Anna Pepłowska, who would have adored Namisa, and who would have gone there even without a traveller's guide, in the spirit of adventure, to discover the undiscovered. As we all should.

Contents

PART ONE *LONDON*   1

1 AGE OF ENLIGHTENMENT   3

2 A HUSBAND WAITING TO HAPPEN   18

3 A TALE OF TWO EMBASSIES   32

4 THE EXCESSES OF BAGGAGE   47

PART TWO *TRINAMISA*   55

5 THE COMFORT OF STRANGERS   57

6 STAKEHOLDERS AND OTHER GOURMETS   69

7 A GOOD MEDICAL   92

8 OF FLIES AND COLD MICE   108

9 THE IDES OF AUTUMN   119

10 THE POWER OF THREE   129

11 GREAT BRITONS   139

12 THE GOOD, THE BAD, AND THE TERMINATED   146

13 AMAZING GRACE   161

14 THE FORGOTTEN   170

15 A WORTHY CASE   178

16 LINGUISTIC CONSIDERATIONS   185

17 THE STRAIGHT PATH   197

18 THE IVORY TOWER OF BABEL   209

19 DISCOVER NAMISAN   224

20 THE WISDOM OF THE BABBIGALL   238

21 THE CAMEL DANCE   249

22 THE MATTER OF DIVORCE   259

23 THE BENEFITS OF TEAMBUILDING   270

24 THE SHORT LIST   280

25 THE VANISHING   291

26 FLIGHT FROM TRINAMISA   303

PART THREE *PRAPUNDAR*   311

27 PUNDARI NIGHTS   313

28 CATALOGUES OF DESPAIR   327

PART FOUR *WUNAMISA*   337

29 HOME ALONE   339

30 THE NAMISAN *AUTUMN-AUTUMN*   355

31 GRIKAGRAKA'S REVENGE   367

32 THE *PLIGHT* OF SHAME   381

33 WHILE THE DINNER IS HOT AND THE KNIFE SHARP 395

34 NEW TROPHIES FOR OLD 409

AUTHOR'S LANGUAGE NOTES 418

ESSENTIAL GLOSSARY OF NAMISAN 420

***

Words differently arranged have different meanings,
and meanings differently arranged have a different effect.

    Blaise Pascal, philosopher and mathematician
    (1623-1662?)

PART ONE

LONDON

1

AGE OF ENLIGHTENMENT

We have only one guidebook to our island, and it was a foreigner who wrote that. We have few visitors and for that reason there is not a great deal of demand for guidebooks. In fact, there is not a great deal of demand for visitors either. Setting that aside, I am of the opinion that foreigners should indeed be the ones to write guides to countries that are not their own. And foreigners – not Namisans or Pundaris - should be the tourist guides to our islands too. Only they can see what the places, the customs, and the people mean. Only they can understand what it all represents.

Those of us who were born here cannot see it. We do not understand the culture. To understand the culture, you need to live outside it. You need to make comparisons. Otherwise you are a fake, an imposter, a hypocrite. I am sure there must be a more suitable word, but I do not know it. What I suppose I am trying to say is… how can you evaluate your own country without ever having seen someone else's? And how can you presume to judge other countries without knowing your own?

These are the thoughts that I am committing to paper, that I am writing, rather than saying. Who would I tell otherwise? Perhaps one day I will speak of all this to someone who understands, or who might like to understand.

*

Notes to self:
1. supermarket, library, bookshop - approach woman - make proposal.
2. Soulmates newspaper columns - select woman - phone, write.
3. contact thru friends, relatives, FB, Twitter, etc.
4. advertise - local papers - corner-shop.
5. phone boxes?

He considered this last option for a moment, then put a line through it. He needed to avoid additional complications. He also put a line through option 2. This might generate touchy-feely stuff. He had no time or patience for any of that. He was a practical person, he believed. Perhaps the word for it was 'pragmatic.' He would Google it when he had time. Right now, he *didn't* have time.

This woman needed to be reasonably bright and of pleasing appearance so as to be capable of moving in the elegant circles in which he hoped to find himself. Correction. The elegant circles in which he *expected* to find himself. She – the chosen one – needed to be entirely self-sufficient, since he had no intention of spending time entertaining her. And he could not have a 'wife' who might compromise him. She needed to have an occupation that would keep her both absorbed and out of trouble, an occupation such as knitting, or perhaps painting – even painting by numbers – or writing poetry, which was harmless enough. Anyway, whatever it was that women did in their free time. Not shopping. He'd have to be careful of shopping. Shopping could ruin a man.

He paused for a moment of reflection and self-justification. It wasn't that he was mean. He was just safeguarding his future career. A diplomat, for that was what he would be, needed a partner he could rely on. This woman – this rather attractive, poised, and elegant woman – would not be someone who went in for nightclubs, dancing, and hellraising. That would not do at all. He put down his pen and warmed his hands on his teacup. It wearied him to think of all the things that the wife he did not have should and should not do.

*

The Downing Foundation London

From: Neil Bryant
To: Lady Downing
Date: 10 January
Subject: Recruitment – Officer of Culture and Education, Namisa

In haste, as per our telephone conversation, all confirmed. Will expedite hiring action asap for married status candidate. Go ahead for standard Foundation pep talk as agreed. See you anon.

    Yours

    Neil

*

'The Namisans are a gentle people, Philip,' said Lady Downing, her fulsome lips pulled into a reassuring smile. 'They are islanders, detached – shall we say – from the real world. They are of a delicate sensibility. I cannot stress enough how crucial it is for you to understand this. As a representative of the Downing Foundation...' at this she glanced up – regretfully, it seemed to Philip – at the portrait of Lord Downing on the opposite wall, 'it is of the utmost importance that you respect their customs, their beliefs, their standards of morality. For, as they comport themselves, so should you. Remember this. Your behaviour should be as exemplary as you will find theirs to be. You will discover the Namisans to be kind, welcoming, and generous. You will also find them to be hungry for knowledge and experience.'

Lady Downing blinked as if awakening from a pleasant trance. She smiled at Philip. 'Diplomacy at all times, Philip, even in the face of the most tiresome requests. And always study your Robinson-Smith.' Saying this, she tapped the laminate cover of the well-fingered travel guide that lay in front of her.

Bryant inclined his head towards hers, his eyes all the while remaining on his notepad.

'Should we ...' he said *sotto voce*, though Philip did indeed hear him, 'should we say anything to him now about Bogadan?'

Lady Downing continued to smile. 'And you will find, Philip, that your experience, and that of your wife-to-be, will be quite delightful.'

It occurred to Philip that he should respond at this point to express his gratitude and that of his fiancée for his selection, but the joy of his unprecedented success had clouded his memory and he still could not for the life of him remember her name. He thought it might begin with an "H." Helen? Holly, perhaps? Or Hattie? Hope? Happy? Yes, it was something like Happy, he decided.

Bryant cleared his throat. 'So, Philip,' he said, 'I take it that you can make yourself ready to take up the post as soon as we have secured your visas. Visas for you and…' With spindly fingers he rustled through the various forms in front of him. 'For you and Diane.'

'Felicity,' said Philip.

Bryant looked up as if caught unawares. 'Felicity?'

For an uncomfortable moment he fixed Philip with a suspicious stare.

'Yes,' said Philip, returning his scrutiny. 'Felicity.'

'Ah. Diane Felicity,' concluded Bryant, returning to riffle through the paperwork.

'Felicity Diane,' said Philip.

Bryant paused again and appeared to evaluate Philip, his eyes dark and narrowed. 'Yes, well, we seem to be missing some of the documentation.'

'We'll have Emma sort that out later,' said Lady Downing. 'Philip, I'm sure you'll want to call Diane and tell her the good news.'

'Felicity,' said Philip.

'Or indeed, both of them,' said Bryant.

*

I should say a word or two about the Namisan character. People say we are gentle, and so we are, but our gentle exterior is a manifestation of a national tendency towards hypocrisy. In that, are we so unlike other peoples?

*

Philip curled up in bed with Robinson-Smith, not with the wife whose name he could only occasionally remember.

According to Namisapundar legend, the rebellious folk hero Fella Breekaya defied the wishes of his aged parents by deserting his village, along with his filial responsibilities, to seek his fortune on the craggy isles of the ancient Nagapardar region. There he found the wretched inhabitants enslaved by the great and ferocious sea beast Grikagraka, who resided in the deepest of underwater grottos. One such rock formation, which can be accessed from the shore, has become a popular attraction amongst visitors, and bears the name Grotty Cave of the Young Fella's Ear.

It is said that, while exploring these caves, this courageous young man disturbed the slumbering monster who, on awakening, tore Fella's ear from his head as he ran from the grotto. Today the ear symbol figures extensively on Namisan coats of arms, on governmental documents and on the facades of public buildings. Young Fella's Ear souvenir key rings are a popular buy amongst tourists, as are decorative mugs, tea towels, and fridge magnets.

(Extract from 'Popular Myths and Legends,' (p.52)

in *Namisa – A Traveller's Guide: from tradition to tourism and back*, by Michael Robinson-Smith.)

And he dreamt. This was his destiny… like T. E. Lawrence, like Wilfred Thesiger, like… Michael Palin. Namisa would be his portal to the world, his escape. He would escape with a wife but, fortunately, she would be brief.

*

One week earlier.

It was 5:30 in the afternoon. Philip had reached the dismal little landing of a rambling house in Ladbroke Grove, its interior walls painted in a cream gloss, yellowed with age or nicotine. He paused to catch his breath before starting up the last tract of grimy stair carpet to Flat Four. He was not a smoker, but his sedentary office lifestyle had not prepared him for this unscheduled ascent.

He was motivated by a certain nervous anticipation. He would go up a bachelor and descend a husband-to-be. This was a crucial piece in his complex career jigsaw puzzle. A necessary sacrifice. And once the bride was in the bag, he would be en route for three idling years in that sleepy island paradise, a prelude to something much, much better. There would be no more icy London winters, no more standing at bus stops, no more queuing for *lattes* at Starbucks or Pret á Manger. May the best married man win, he thought… and *he* was that man.

Hugo Danvers, the other hopeful candidate, was

single, and who would have him anyway? Was Danvers about to find himself a spouse? No, Philip thought not. He and only he was poised to break through the invisible barriers, and there would be nothing and no one to stop him. Not even his Auntie Peggy, who even now preyed on him via the numbed buzzing on his mobile phone.

The staircase creaked at his every footfall. He thought affectionately of Diane. Already he could imagine her elation at his news… that he would take her away from all this. This… creakiness. Her life was going nowhere and now it would be going somewhere rather nice. With him. What more could a simple teacher like her hope for? He halted again halfway up the last stretch of staircase. He was only mildly surprised that she had not replied to his message. It was some time since he had been in touch. This he admitted. Two weeks. Perhaps three. In her life, though, precious little would happen even in three months, and now, within the next few minutes, her destiny would be changed forever thanks to him.

He stopped in front of the heavy oak door at the very top of the stairs, and then clung to the banister as he rapped with his knuckles on the scratched varnish.

'Diane,' he called. 'It's me, Philip. Diane, get your coat. We're going to Namisa.' He chortled at the lightness of his own swift wit.

From inside the flat he heard the shuffle of slippered feet and then the door was wrenched open. A woman stood before him on the threshold. She was tall – taller than him – with a hedgerow of ash-blonde hair held in thrall with an array of pink and yellow sponge curlers. From the side of her mouth hung an unlit cigarette and in one hand she held a glass of something whisky-like. A blue silk kimono, which reached just below her knees, was draped around her body and tied with a loose sash. Through red-rimmed eyes, she looked Philip up and down with immense disdain.

'Who are you?' she said.

'Who are you?' said Philip.

'What do you want?' she said, her face contorted with annoyance and perplexity.

'Diane,' he said. 'I want Diane. Where is she?' To his own ears his plea was distinctly pathetic, as though he were asking a mother to let her child out to play. He added as an afterthought and by way of explanation, 'I need her because… because we're going to be getting married.'

The woman stared at Philip for a moment. 'I doubt it,' she said. 'She's long gone.' And she shut the door in Philip's face.

Philip hammered vigorously on the door. 'No, you don't understand,' he said.

'Oh, just go away!' said the woman's muffled voice.

*

An unfortunate turn of events had scuppered Philip's plan. Destiny was punishing him for taking his life into his own hands. On the subject of women, Robinson-Smith provided no consolation: Philip regretted that, clever and insightful as Robinson-Smith undoubtedly was, he must be mistaken.

While foreign males are generally regarded with suspicion in Namisa, foreign females are a subject of fascination as much for Namisan women as for their male counterparts. Female visitors to Namisa who excel in the arts are especially prized and held up as role models. It is in the nature of the Namisan woman to embrace culture and seek fulfilment through the attainment of knowledge. Female writers, philosophers, artists, and scientists are thus sought after, and are greatly admired.

(Extract from 'Women and the Arts,' (p.117) in *Namisa - A Traveller's Guide: from tradition to tourism and back*,' by Michael Robinson-Smith.)

*

On Portobello Road, Philip felt sudden compassion for a *Big Issue* seller and bought two copies. After all, he reasoned, this could have been him, though luckily it was not. As a precaution against the fickleness of fate, he already had a third issue on his coffee table at home.

In his favourite café he ordered a cup of tea and sat by the window, staring out at the street, with his briefcase on his lap. Then he opened the case and removed his *Looney Tunes* exercise book. There was no need to panic. He would work this out on paper, try to figure out the pluses and the minuses. Mostly minuses.

It was actually very simple. All he needed was a wife. Surely that could not be too much to ask of Providence? He didn't actually need to marry her. He just needed her compliance, her willingness to play the part. She must surely exist, but where would he find such a woman? He took out a pen and wrote, 'Notes to self …'

*

Felicity was 'the one' but she didn't quite know it yet. Felicity Manning, romance novelist in a world devoid of romance, thirty-something, but that something was on the darker side of the thirty. No, she was not on the rebound, she told herself. She was beginning a new phase in her life, a mature and knowledgeable phase, the kind embraced by women who are not going to be taken for a ride or taken advantage of, or taken for granted or, indeed, taken anywhere, probably not even taken out for dinner or a night on the town. Slumped in front of her computer screen, Felicity did not look or feel like someone who might become 'the one.'

On the desktop display in front of her there were many files, all with unusual and inspiring names. These were the books she had yet to write. Some arrived at perhaps fifty or sixty pages and were divided up according to plot points, all the highs and lows of her imagination. Others stretched no further than a few paragraphs, a description, a setting, and then nothing. There was no more room in her bottom drawer for abandoned novels.

She had enjoyed some minor successes, fifteen minutes here and there of fame, but of late… She readjusted the seat of her blue upholstered executive chair, sank down unpleasantly, then bounced up again. Now that it was all over with him – and she supposed it was all over – she was definitely going to write this novel. No ifs or buts, or clichés. It was a project close to her heart and it would be her breakthrough, breakout, blockbuster… or similar – her trilogy, a spectacular work of heartrending something or other.

No one, especially not her, could write through heartbreak. She was trying, but her troubled brain had misdirected her. She sipped her whisky and found it a little flat. She was alone. Even Diane her tenant had abandoned her, gone to a land of opportunity, where the grass was browner or even non-existent. No excuse then. Freed from distractions, Felicity was now at liberty to create. The extra income had been useful, but not the invasion of her privacy. She had not cared to relate details of her dismal word count to her lodger, however well-meaning her enquiries.

She clicked on the file labelled 'Holland Park.' The page was blank. She scrolled down and encountered a few scattered islands of text. She re-read what she had written. It was mediocre to say the least. Or was she – in her newly mature and enlightened state – becoming more demanding of herself?

She blamed it all on him, his selfishness, his arrogance. He, who could not be named. He, who could be found just down the road, a neighbour. Why, she might well meet him anywhere. In the butcher's, in the newsagent's buying his *Corriere della Sera*, in the supermarket, in the post office, in a restaurant, in the post office again – well, if not in the post office, then somewhere else. She had not yet erased him from her phone. She wanted to be prepared if he called so that, seeing his name, she would not answer. But he had not called. She could *not* not answer, which made her all the more irritated, enraged, and blocked. She needed a holiday. Somewhere inspiring. But did relocating ever solve anyone's problems, or were the problems themselves merely relocated?

A few days before one week earlier.

When the job was advertised, Philip did his research. He borrowed *Namisa - A Traveller's Guide,* from Kensington Central Library, and it absorbed him. There was no doubt in his mind that Namisa was the place for him… a land of myths and legends, an island paradise set in a crystal sea, a tranquil golden land of perpetual autumn, an autumn warm and fragrant like the very best two days of an English summer, over and over again. This was a place where he could live, where the people – the islanders – would take him into their hearts, recognizing in him his very unique… uniqueness. Plus, of course, he had had his fill of living in the nether regions of the Central Line, in his Auntie Peggy's guest room. This was the price he had had to pay for his career in London. But what career?

From outside his office cubicle came the distant rattle of the photocopier, the chatter of his colleagues, the occasional dull ring of a subdued telephone. He placed Auntie Peggy's postcard of Torquay between the pages of the guide and put the weathered volume front cover down on his desk. There were spies about and this was one idea he intended keeping to himself. He had had a run of bad luck it was true: a few business ventures gone wrong. Not failure but feedback, as per the poster by the water dispenser. These things happened all the time. His mother, recently removed to Los Angeles with her new husband Ray, had looked him in the eye on his thirty-fourth birthday and told him quite categorically that she wasn't "doing handouts" any more and how this time he had to grow up and sort himself out. And he would have done – sorted himself out – but for that unfortunate diplomatic incident that caused him to slip in his ascent up the career ladder here at the Downing Foundation. As to the growing up, she had got that wrong. He knew exactly what he was about.

Philip looked around him and drew the job description out from under a buff-coloured folder. For the third time that afternoon he scanned the key phrases: 'manage and provide leadership,' 'establish and maintain relationships,' 'oversee funding schemes,' 'liaise with Namisan partners,' 'be responsible for a significant budget,' etc., etc. Yes, yes, and yes… he could do all this and more.

*

Looking on the bright side, Felicity had a sense that something must change soon. She procrastinated with diligence, thumbing through her most recent issue of *The Author*. She might consider a writer's retreat. Either that, or a nunnery. A change was as good as a rest. At present she was getting more than enough rest. Mental exertion brought on weariness, that I'll-just-lie-here-for-a-moment feeling.

She had always thrived on the exotic. It might be charming to retreat to a flat in Venice, 'just five minutes to the Adriatic.' Better still, a house in the Andalucian mountains, 'secluded, unspoilt,' or a villa with a wide sea view down a Turkish beach. She flicked through the pages. Or maybe she could house-sit for someone. Someone with a delightful little chateau in France. But this business of being a writer in exile – self-imposed exile – was going to be awfully expensive. There were the air fares, and the car-hire charges to consider, the clothes and the duty free. And then there was the cooking for herself, which she was not very good at. It didn't bear thinking about, but she was thinking about it.

***

2

A HUSBAND WAITING TO HAPPEN

Meanwhile, and still a few days before one week earlier.

He focused now on his application form – the application form of Philip Eric Blair, thirty-ish, adventurer, seeker of knowledge, innovator. All the boxes were ticked, all the essential information was in place, and in his best handwriting with nothing missed out. Perfect.

He hesitated. One thing did bother him. It was the small print at the bottom of page 4 of the Guidelines. The section about marital status. 'Applications from married candidates are welcomed,' it said. Reading between the lines, what could that possibly mean, he asked himself. He had, of course, ticked the 'Single Status' box, but what if…?

The faintest of shadows hovered across his desk. Looking up, he saw Hugo Danvers at his elbow, surveying the disordered contents of his work space. Philip maintained a neutral expression, but his hand trembled as he slid his application under a heap of procurement forms.

To Philip's mind, Danvers was a pokey kind of fellow. Not for nothing did he have a long pointy nose… and yes, his eyes were a dark shade of brown, but to Philip they resembled a pair of stale coffee beans, hard and beady.

'Planning a holiday?' said Danvers in that unpleasant nasal tone of his.

'No,' said Philip, his face growing hot under his colleague's scrutiny.

'Only I see that you're reading Robinson-Smith,' said Danvers. He picked up the book, drew out the postcard and regarded it with a degree of proprietorial nonchalance.

'Erm…' said Philip.

'Or maybe you're applying for a job?' Danvers squinted at him.

Philip shuffled the documents that lay in front of him. 'Look, Danvers,' he said, 'I'm trying to finish these technical evaluations.'

Danvers opened his mouth to speak but, mercifully on cue, Philip's desk phone rang.

'Scuse me,' said Philip, his hand resting on the receiver. He gave Danvers a look of challenge and defiance. Danvers stared back for a moment, shrugged, then threw down the travel guide and walked away. Philip muttered under his breath as he lifted the hand handset.

'No, Auntie Peggy, I wasn't swearing at you. Potatoes. No, I won't forget. Yes, everything is absolutely fine. Yes, yes… goodbye.' He slammed down the phone.

He raised himself out of his seat so that he could see over his partition. What was Danvers up to? The man was clearly onto him.

On the far side of the office next to the radiator, which he had been swift to claim as part of his territory, Danvers sat at his desk, head down, scribbling furiously on a document, which, at that distance, might or might not be… an application form. An application form not unlike the one hidden under the heap of papers on Philip's desk.

*

Emma leaned in towards him. In a whisper, she said, 'You're the only two candidates. It's a quick turnaround. The current post holder has, well, moved on. They need to fill the vacancy as quickly as possible… what with the budgetary year coming to a close.' She stopped as the messenger approached. The youth dropped a letter onto her desk. He glanced at Philip.

'All right then, Emma?'

'Thank you, James. Just move along there, will you?'

Philip put his head down and thumbed through the pages of an office supplies catalogue until James was out of earshot.

'You see,' continued Emma, 'they need to get the funding sorted with the bursaries and all that.' She paused again. 'I shouldn't even be telling you this.'

'Just up my street, this job,' said Philip, biting his lip.

'Right. Just up your street in another country,' said Emma. 'Wouldn't fancy it myself. Funny food, you know.' She glanced over Philip's shoulder. 'It won't be easy to get the edge on him.'

Philip turned to see Danvers on the far side of the room, flipping coins into the coffee machine with that know-it-all air of his. So, what had Danvers got that he hadn't? What exactly did he – Philip – have that was going to tip this job in his direction?

Back at his desk, Philip sat chewing at his nails. Danvers had already had the benefit of two foreign postings, one in Lublin, the other in Iloilo City. Now the world was his oyster. Philip hadn't as yet got beyond Brighton.

Philip watched as Danvers – sneerfully, he thought – gathered up his notes and headed off to the weekly meeting of the Recreation Committee. A nice little number, vetting hotels and restaurants for free, prior to Downing Foundation weekend excursions for employees and their spouses. Philip's mind wandered. Employees and their spouses… And then it came to him.

He flicked through the pages of his application and, with a swift turn of his biro, made a minor adjustment about halfway through. Or perhaps not so minor.

*

Sometimes it seems as though everyone has a story – except me. Why is that? Perhaps we have to create our own story and, I suppose, if we don't… someone may create it for us. Or already has.

But then, how do we know if the story we've created for ourselves is the right story?

*

Across the road from the café where he was sitting mid the reassuring jangle of cutlery and the hiss of the cappuccino machine, Philip noted that a stream of not-unpleasant-looking young women were disappearing through the doorway of a bookshop.

Any one of them would do. He was not fussy. But then the thought that ran through his mind was... what kind of a woman would be so perverse as to want to pose as his wife and accompany him to an obscure foreign location? What would he need to do to persuade a woman to agree to that? Would he have to pay her, for example? What if he found someone and he really didn't like her? Well, he wasn't asking her to go to bed with him, was he? He sipped his tea and thought about this.

No, he thought, he probably wasn't. This was true, but... Philip returned to his original idea. He needed a wife and he needed her now, otherwise it would be back to Procurement for him, and a life of endless drudgery. So, where was she? How would he find her? He thought on.

She wouldn't have to have any hangers-on. That ruled out single mothers, cat or dog owners, etcetera. He wanted no relatives, mothers, aunties, grandparents or the like, and – especially not any boyfriends – showing up on his doorstep. Having to support one person was quite enough.

On reflection, this was all rather troubling. It meant, in short, that he was going to be dealing with some kind of warped, anti-social orphan.

Also, as he had already observed and kept reminding himself, there was a time constraint here. He needed his home-loving femme-fatale misfit now. He couldn't go to an interview and not know the name of his spouse.

Or could he?

He could invent a name for her and say she was coming, but then at the eleventh hour he could confess that they had had a significant disagreement and that, unfortunately, the engagement or the marriage was off and he would have to go to his new post alone.

He threw down his pen, pressed his clenched fists into his cheeks, closed his eyes and groaned. In times of crisis, he found a certain solace in melodrama. He knew he must soldier on through… adversity. 'Adversity' was a good word. He stared down at his notes. What, then, would seal it for her – this Facebook silhouette, this outline without a face? He jotted down some ideas: exotic location, diplomatic perks, villa with a pool, company car with chauffeur. He picked up his pen and added: alcohol allowance. Why not? Perhaps in Namisa he would find some jolly drinking companions. His melancholy eased. That pretty much summed it up, this ideal job of his. From her point of view, what was there not to like?

Three cups of tea later and with an urgent need to head for the Gents, he folded a sheet from his notebook into an oblong of paper with the dimensions of an index card. In his tidiest handwriting – the kind reserved for application forms – he transcribed his advert. It carried the title:

Charming career diplomat (male)
seeks intellectual travelling

companion (female) for tropical island sojourn.

*

'What's this island then?' said the woman. Her tone was diffident and accusing.

The phone enquiries started just after the Touchstone Bookshop opened at 9:30am the following morning, a Saturday. Their 'Way of the Enchantress' workshop began at 10:30am, time enough for those gentle and enchanting participants to peruse the notice board and make a life-changing decision.

'Namisa,' said Philip now tumbled, still sleep-numbed, from his bed. He caught sight of his own gaunt and pasty face in the bathroom mirror.

'Namisa?'

'Yeah! That's the island's name. Namisa.'

'Never heard of it. Where is it?'

Well how did he know? She could Google it like everyone else. 'It's sort of… it's sort of, you know, flying distance from Singapore. Or thereabouts.' He had never excelled at Geography. Why bother when you just get on a plane and arrive wherever it is that you're going? It was becoming apparent to him that he might have to put in some work.

'This is some kind of scam, isn't it?' said the woman. 'What are you doing, selling people or something?'

'No,' said Philip. 'It's…' But the woman had already ended the call. 'Your loss!' said Philip.

The phone rang again almost immediately.

'Yes,' said Philip.

'I'm calling about the holiday on the tropical island.'

'Right,' said Philip, 'only it's not exactly a holiday. It's for three years.'

Silence at the other end of the line. Had that sounded too like a prison sentence?

*

As is often the case in closed and very traditional societies, family life plays an important role. Within Namisan society, it is entirely normal for sons and daughters to remain in the family home until they are married. It should be understood that they do so for cultural and not economic reasons. A close relationship is maintained among siblings long after they marry and have children of their own. Family gatherings are incomplete if a full quota of aunts and uncles is not present. It is customary for children to be sent for instruction, recreation, and safekeeping to the homes of their aunts and uncles. This has been known to cause some disorientation and confusion among the youngest of family members and, in cases where family members are especially numerous, instances of mixed or swapped identities are often reported. In real terms, this practice of 'child-sharing' means that an auntie effectively enjoys the same respect and authority as a mother and, similarly, an uncle enjoys the same respect and authority as a father. As is typical the world over, mothers and aunties make it their business to enquire about the acquaintances and activities of the children in their care, even when those same children may be well advanced in years.

(Extract from 'The Family,' (p.13) in *Namisa - A Traveller's Guide: from tradition to tourism and back*, by Michael Robinson-Smith.)

*

It was in the middle of the eleventh call that Auntie

Peggy shouted for Philip to come down for his lunch. By now he had some indication of how it might feel to be a travel agent. He pulled off the bookshelf his mum's old copy of *The Oxford Home Atlas, Third Edition*, and carried it downstairs with him.

'Is there something I should know, Philip?' said Auntie Peggy.

Philip picked up his knife and fork and began to eat.

'You don't normally get quite so many calls.' She gave him a quizzical look. Auntie Peggy could instil guilt with the merest twitch of a facial muscle.

'It's a date,' said Philip, and feeling the weight of her stare, he turned to the *Gazetteer of the World – Malta to Nasik*.

Auntie Peggy raised her eyebrows and poured tea into his cup.

'You don't think I can get a date?' said Philip. He prodded at the cauliflower cheese with his fork.

'You might want to smarten yourself up a little, darling. A new jumper. A haircut. Sometimes I wonder what they taught you at that university.'

Philip sniffed. 'I did psychology, not haircuts.'

'Yes, I wonder what would happen if you tried to put it into practice?' She sipped her tea. 'On yourself, for example.'

He couldn't talk to her when she was like this, nor could he find Namisa in his atlas. He put the book aside and ate in silence, waiting for her to try a different tack, something along the lines of, 'When your poor father passed away…'

'You know, Philip,' said Auntie Peggy, 'when your

poor father passed away and your mother was on her own up there in Edinburgh, I promised myself I would do my best for the both of you. But there are times when I could do with just a little more cooperation from your side.'

Philip buttered himself a slice of bread. Her next tack would be to establish who, if anyone, he was seeing. He kept himself to himself for good reason. At thirty-something it was just plain embarrassing to reveal to your auntie that you have a love life. He kept his head down and buttered right to the corners, like the sometime perfectionist that he was.

'What happened to that nice girl Delia?'

'Diane.' He tugged at the bread with his teeth – the alternative to gritting them in times of stress.

'Diane, then. What happened to her?'

'No idea. Must have met someone else.' Saying this left a bitter taste in his mouth.

His phone rang.

'Yes, hello,' said Philip. 'Yes, that's right. Dengue fever? No, I don't think so. Okay. Bye.'

Auntie Peggy stared at him, her pale blue eyes filled with pity.

'It's a club we're going to,' said Philip.

'Well, good for you,' said Auntie Peggy. 'Fruit salad?'

*

Do not be misled by the very genial nature of the Namisans. They will certainly come across as friendly and communicative, keen to establish rapport and exchange confidences. Remember at all times that underlying this hearty liberal exterior is a strongly conservative heritage that is home to the Namisans' prying and judgemental character.

(Extract from 'National character,' (p.75) in *Namisa - A Traveller's Guide: from tradition to tourism and back,' by Michael Robinson-Smith.)

*

Philip excluded Karen. Tall, sinewy, with a curtain of glossy auburn hair falling across her face. He excluded her after consulting his Robinson-Smith. Not that he had taken it upon himself to be either prying or judgemental, but he needed to keep Namisan sensibilities in mind. She had a boyfriend.

He excluded Daisy.

'This place… Narnia,' she said.

She was blue-eyed. 'Namisa,' he corrected.

'Whatever. Does it have nightlife? You know, music, events, clubs… stuff like that?'

'Oh yes, it most certainly does,' said Philip. 'There's a lot happening over there in Namisa, a real… hotspot.'

'Just I need to know what to take. What clothes, shoes and so on.'

'And you are…?'

'Daisy. Daisy Adams.'

He wrote down her name. What he needed was a trusty nursery school teacher, not a good-time gal. She was craning her neck to read his notebook.

'Yes, but that's Dayzee with a 'y' and a 'zed' and two 'e's.'

He made adjustments. 'So, Day-zee, what do you do?'

'I'm a nursery school teacher, Philip.'

Many candidates later, he was weary. He had excluded all his possibles but, if nothing else, the exercise would keep him in dates and phone numbers for the rest of the year. After five o'clock that day there were no more calls, no more appointments. Radio silence. Philip sat with his phone in front of him. His job interview was set for Monday morning. Now it was Saturday evening and he still had no wife.

*

It was at the Touchstone Bookshop, while the author Felicity Manning was checking whether or not her last book – a romantic spy novel set in wartime London – was still on display, that she saw the advert.

It might just work for her, she thought. It might just revive her wilting inspiration. An overseas location that was guaranteed to elicit envy, a place far away enough to discourage take-me-back cold calling. She would do it also for revenge. There would come a time when he would be at a loose end, when he would find himself at her front door, his finger on the doorbell, and he would find her gone. And she would experience such satisfaction at his devastating disappointment – except that, as she reminded herself, she would not be present to see it. She would have to hold the imagined moment, trust that it would be so, and relish it.

She searched for Namisa on the Internet and found several sites 'in construction.' But, then, it did not matter to her if she went to Namisa or Namibia or Nantucket. It was important to have a new life, a fresh focus – to cast *him* from her mind, to live cleanly with renewed purpose, steering clear of temptation and bad influences – one bad influence in particular.

She did not have to be in Shepherd's Bush to write about Shepherd's Bush or in Notting Hill Gate to write about Notting Hill Gate. She was, after all, a writer. What she had started, she would now finish. In Namisa.

*

The phone call Philip had been waiting for came at 7:35am on Sunday morning. He was burrowed in beneath the covers fast asleep. He heard church bells ringing in the distance. Maybe they were wedding bells. They clanged in his ears at three-second intervals, until he rolled over the edge of the mattress and picked up his phone. The time and place rendered it almost impossible for him to assume the air of charming career diplomat. He answered the call under the steely glare of his childhood companion Bruno the Bear. Philip's eyelids were superglued together with sleep, his hair ratched up and anxious against the headboard of his bed. The woman's voice was gravelly and urgent, like someone speaking under duress.

'It's about the trip. Can we meet this morning? Say… 8:30?'

'No, I can't do that,' he said. To traverse half of London in that short window of opportunity would have challenged even the most driven, especially the ones who were still asleep.

'You can't?'

'No.'

'Why not?'

'I'm busy.'

'Lunch then. Early lunch. 11:30.'

'No, can't do that either.' He heard the woman give a sigh of irritation. 'Well, all right then,' he said. '12:30. Not a moment earlier.'

*

When he arrived back at the Portobello Road café, there were very few people about, just a few mini-cab drivers and, in a far corner, a woman reading *The London Review of Books.* He approached with care. She was vaguely familiar. Then he remembered a blue kimono, a confusion of ash-blonde hair, curlers, a glass of whisky, someone slightly deranged. His blood ran cold, or at least lukewarm. The woman put down the paper suddenly with a rattle, as if she had felt his stare.

'But you're…'

'Felicity Manning. Yes. Don't tell me you're Philip Blair.'

'I'm Philip Blair.'

She looked him in the eye and then spoke slowly, articulating her words very clearly. 'Philip Blair. The scoundrel who mistreated, misled, and abandoned my poor tenant Diane.'

'The very same,' he agreed. A series of thoughts flashed through his mind. Was this someone he wanted to spend his invented life with? Whatever could have provoked her to call? Could she really be that desperate? Maybe she was not. But he was.

***

3

A TALE OF TWO EMBASSIES

'All right. I've got the picture,' said Felicity, tapping commands into her phone. 'When do we leave?'

'Leave?'

'When do you start your posting? Your posting in Namisa? When do *we* have to be there?'

Philip never imagined this could be so easy. She actually wanted to come. He watched in awe as she scrolled through her calendar. She looked quite attractive in an aggressive kind of way, but he wasn't struck so much by her looks as by her manner, her determination, her assertiveness. This was not a paint-by-numbers woman. The fact that she wrote would be sure to keep her out of trouble. As he understood it, writers were quiet, reclusive people. That would suit him down to the ground. A couple of months should do it, until he got established… and then he could off-load her, divorce her – in a manner of speaking – or send her home. Whatever worked. He'd think of something when the time came.

'Hello? I'm asking a question.'

'Sorry?'

'When do we leave?' She rolled her eyes.

'I don't know,' he said.

'They haven't told you? Not even an approximate date?' Her grey eyes shone fiercely.

'Now, that would be because…'

'Because?'

'Because I haven't got the job yet.'

Felicity shut her eyes and gave a sigh of exasperation. She put down her phone, looked directly at Philip and said, 'Are you a complete half-wit, or what?'

'What?' said Philip.

'I've just been sitting here for half an hour…'

'Twenty minutes.'

'Twenty minutes, then. I've been sitting here for twenty minutes planning my new life in Namisa and you're telling me you haven't even got the job.'

'No, but I will have.'

'I have to say, Philip, it's painfully clear to me now why Diane packed her bags and left.'

'She missed out,' said Philip.

'*Au contraire.* She did herself a favour.' Felicity rose to her feet. 'Diane knew an idiot when she saw one.'

'Steady on,' said Philip.

'You've got my number. Call me when you've got the job and I'll give some thought to your offer. Otherwise…'

'Otherwise?'

'*Adios.* Don't waste my time. I've got…' She hesitated. 'I've got books to write. Goodbye, Philip Blair.' She stepped away from the table and strode towards the door, the edge of her scarf slapping him in the face as she threw it over her shoulder.

*

Your life can turn around in a day. That's what they say and I'd like to think that it can, that you can be doing what you normally do, that you turn a familiar corner and the unexpected happens ... or what you secretly hoped for happens, or what you tried to visualize happens.

Is that destiny, or do we get a say in the matter?

*

And now.

A Japanese couple were descending the stairs from Flat Four when Philip arrived. The man gave a rapid practised bow as they passed. Philip felt a pang of disappointment. Did this mean – and he supposed it did – that Felicity had taken him at his word and was letting out her flat in advance of her imminent transfer to Namisa? When he called with the news of his successful appointment, she gave the impression of being less than thrilled, or was that just her way? He had just had a run of good women and if Felicity was having second thoughts, he wouldn't be shedding too many tears. Now that he knew the way, he would happily head back to the Touchstone Bookshop and give it another shot.

'There you are!' said Felicity. 'Mind the plant pots and put this box over there by the door.'

Philip cast a look behind him to see if she was addressing her request to him or to some unlikely passer-by up there on the top floor. 'Are you talking to me?' he said.

'Indeed, I am,' she replied.

After twenty minutes of rigorous box shifting, Philip felt like a hapless elf.

'Good,' said Felicity, 'that should do it. Some of this will stay. Some will go into storage and the rest...' She paused, making some silent calculations, and drumming her fingers on the kitchen table. 'The rest I'll ship out.'

'Ship out where?' said Philip.

'To Namisa, of course. Where do you think?'

'You're just accompanying me. No need to bring your life with you.'

'I *am* your life,' said Felicity, 'or had you forgotten? We are newlyweds. You adore me and we are starting out in a new country and with a new job... and I am jolly happy about all of that, just as you should be.'

Philip was struck dumb. How could he have got himself into such a mess? He had sold his soul to the Devil.

'Well, say something, Philip,' said Felicity.

Now that Philip's wish was fulfilled, he wanted to unwish it. All he could think was that if he had held out, if he had waited for the right Karen or Day-zee, he could have been on his way to Namisa with delight – and minus the complications.

'You see, Philip, when I decide to do something, I do it. That's how I am. Now this is what's happening.' As she spoke, she moved around the kitchen, shifting and re-ordering objects and utensils inside the cupboards. 'Professor Yamamoto and his lovely wife Yumiko will be renting the flat while I move to Namisa with my new husband. That's you, by the way. There in that blissful island paradise I will find financial and emotional security, which will bring me the peace of mind I need to complete my work-in-progress.'

Philip bit at his lip. This, then, was his failing. He saw it now – the inability to fight his corner. He felt himself in a very tight corner indeed. This was, after all, his idea.

'There will be ground rules, naturally,' said Felicity.

'Ground rules? I think I'm the one who decides the ground rules. Especially since it's my island.'

'Sit down, Philip,' said Felicity, and she cleared a miscellaneous array of cutlery, crockery and cooking implements from Philip's side of the table. She spoke slowly and patiently as if to an unteachable schoolboy. 'In Namisa,' she said, 'I will have a room of my own. You will not disturb me when I am writing – not even to give me a cup of tea.'

'Ha! No worries there.' Philip tapped his foot on the floor and watched with increasing annoyance as Felicity selected a single mug from the kitchen cupboard and dropped a tea bag into it.

'I'll also have my own bedroom and, naturally, you won't disturb me there either.'

'I'd have to be desperate.'

Felicity filled the mug with boiling water from the electric kettle. She jiggled the tea bag up and down, and added a touch of skimmed milk. Then, warming her hands on the mug, she turned to face him.

'And please don't bring any women home, or I'll be obliged to report you to the authorities.'

'What?'

Felicity flipped a chunky pamphlet across the table to him. 'Try a little background reading,' she said.

Philip picked up the booklet. It was entitled, *Morality rules: tips and guidelines for business travellers to Namisa, a publication of the Namisan Cultural Authority Department (NaCAD).*

Felicity strolled away into the lounge and, settling her mug on the coffee table, she made herself comfortable on the sofa amongst a nest of cushions. She yawned and stretched her arms to the ceiling rotating her wrists and hands in the air. 'Oh, I'm so looking forward to Namisa,' she said.

*

A word of warning to visitors and particularly to those taking up residence in Namisa. Should you need to process documentation relating to services governed by official policies, always be prepared for unexpected procedural changes. Indeed, it is not unusual for policies to change from month to month or even from week to week. If you are caught unawares by the law for some minor oversight, bear in mind that the authorities will hold you responsible for the transgression notwithstanding your claims that you were misinformed. No attempt has been made here, therefore, to provide step-by-step guides to obtaining driving licences, car registrations, visas, telephone and internet installation, setting up bank accounts, and water and electricity accounts for the precise reason that the steps may change and the procedure must be re-started. In the face of the unfathomable stubbornness of Namisan bureaucrats, visitors are advised not to overreact.

(Extract from 'Officialdom,' (p.38) in *Namisa - A Traveller's Guide: from tradition to tourism and back*,' 18th Edition, by Michael Robinson-Smith.)

Editor's note: this edition of the Robinson-Smith guide was recalled by the Ministry of Information and pulped. A handful of copies are still available from Amazon. The section on 'Officialdom' is omitted from subsequent editions.

*

A man with a creased and sun-weathered face held the door open just a few inches.

'Yes?' he said, 'What you want?'

'Is this the embassy?' asked Philip.

'So?'

'Well, is it or isn't it?'

'Yes.'

'Can we come in?' said Felicity, pushing forward and trying to see over the man's head.

'Why?' said the man. He opened the door just a few more inches. He was wearing a pink polo shirt, an olive-green sarong and a pair of heavy-duty brown leather sandals.

'We've come to get our visas,' said Philip venturing in a little closer.

'Why?' said the man, closing the door a fraction.

'Because we are coming to visit your lovely country,' said Felicity. 'Now just let us in, will you?'

'Stop,' hissed Philip. 'You're going to cause an international incident. You'll get us deported.'

Felicity gave him a withering look.

'I know how to handle this,' Philip told her quietly. 'Just step aside. I'll do the talking.'

Felicity turned to face the man. 'Come on,' she boomed. 'Make it snappy. We haven't got all day. Open that door now.'

Philip gasped and froze.

The saronged man swung the door open immediately and stood as if rooted to the ground.

'We'd like to speak to your ambassador,' said Felicity.

The man looked at her in awe. 'Ambassador in US,' he spluttered. 'Come back Friday or maybe next month.'

'You don't seem to understand. We are going to Namisa and we are going very soon. We cannot wait until next month. Please take us to your leader right now. Your deputy Namisan Ambassador, or someone like that.'

The man stared at her for a moment. Then his face twisted into a spiteful grin.

'I told you,' said Philip. 'You've ruined it now.'

'This not Namisa Embassy,' said the man, who was now looking very pleased with himself.

'Namisa Embassy next house. This Embassy of Pundar. And goodbye.' The door was closed with a heavy thud.

*

'How could you have made a mistake like that?' said Felicity. 'You're going to have to sharpen up a bit, Philip, if you want to keep this job.' As an afterthought, she added, 'Don't forget that you have a dependent now. We call it "having responsibilities."' Then she muttered, 'I suppose "responsibility" may be one of the rather underused words in your limited vocabulary.'

Philip ground his teeth and sat with his arms folded. They were seated side-by-side in a large cavernous room on blue regulation chairs that were ranged with others in rows opposite a line of interview booths. In the booth directly opposite them behind a glass screen, a man in a brown suit was reading a copy of the *Daily Telegraph*.

'What's our number?' said Felicity.

'Ninety-seven,' said Philip.

Above the single-manned booth, a number clicked into place on an electronic board: fifty-two.

Felicity and Philip sat in silence. Philip jiggled his foot up and down. Felicity studied the stucco designs on the ceiling. From outside came the sound of footsteps approaching and then fading into the distance down the adjacent corridors. The walls of the room were decorated with a variety of colourful posters of Namisa, interspersed with official notices, mostly warnings and instructions about governmental policies, laws and health hazards. The number on the electronic board changed to fifty-three.

'Oh, look,' said Felicity. 'The man on that poster looks like you. Only he's missing an ear, and there's blood running down his face.' Felicity indicated a poster of a primitive wall painting. A monstrous creature with teeth bared and bloody was shown looming over a tiny male figure who held his hands before him in a futile attempt at defence. The side of his face was indeed bloodied and in the grass at the monster's feet was an outsized ear from which dangled meaty threads of flesh.

'Nothing like me,' said Philip, who was watching as the number changed from fifty-six to fifty-seven.

'The ear is definitely yours,' said Felicity.

They continued to sit without speaking as the numbers clicked forward to fifty-eight.

'Have you ever thought that you might have been reincarnated?' said Felicity.

'No,' said Philip.

'No,' said Felicity. 'I suppose not.'

Philip was relieved to see the number change to sixty.

'If one of your ears ached from time to time, you'd know,' said Felicity. 'That would be a sign.'

Philip continued to watch the numbers on the board.

'Or you might go slightly deaf in the ear that, in the distant past, had been ripped off by the monster. You could go deaf metaphorically, like turning a deaf ear as opposed to turning a blind eye. Do you know what I mean?'

Philip sighed.

'Of course, if he's just a mythical or folkloric character, then you can't be a reincarnation of him, can you? But in primitive societies people read a lot of importance into symbols. There are signs all around us,' said Felicity, 'but so many people choose not to read them, or not to hear them.' She looked around her at the empty room. 'I mean, did you by any chance notice that there's no one else in this room? Or maybe your eyes were gouged out in a previous life.'

'Just shut up, will you,' said Philip.

'How charming,' said Felicity.

'Is it really too much to ask? We've only another twenty numbers to go.'

'But there's no one here, Philip.' Felicity rose to her feet and strode across to the booth.

'Felicity, don't…'

She rapped on the window. 'Hello? Can you do our papers now, please? We've been waiting a very long time.'

The man put down his newspaper.

'And what is your number?' he said.

'I don't know. I can't remember. What is our number, Philip?'

'Ninety-seven.'

'Our number is ninety-seven,' said Felicity.

'Then I think you must still to wait,' said the man. And he licked a finger and turned a page of his newspaper.

'No, I will not still-to-wait,' said Felicity, 'Don't you know who we are?'

The man looked first at Felicity and then at Philip. 'No,' he said.

'We are with the Downing Foundation,' said Felicity. 'We are practically diplomats.'

'That is very good,' said the man. 'Now please to sit and wait.' He gestured towards the blue chairs.

Back in her seat, Felicity folded her arms and went into a huff.

There was a click and the number ninety-seven showed on the board.

Philip stood up, walked to the booth and took up his seat in front of the Embassy official. 'Good morning,' he said.

The man folded his newspaper and put it to one side. His face spread into a radiant smile.

'Good morning,' he replied. 'How may I help you?'

'I've come to apply for some visas.'

'Very good,' said the man. 'May I see your number?'

Philip pushed his number under the glass screen.'

'Very good,' said the man, examining the printed number. 'It's just that we must to be careful. Sometimes people try to push in.'

*

'Mmm…aha…mmm…very good…mmm…yes…' The man in the brown suit worked his way with great diligence through the visa applications. Philip and Felicity followed his page-by-page deliberations like spectators at a poker game, with a sense of tension and anticipation. As he reached the final page, Philip relaxed. Felicity sat back in her chair. The man opened a buff-coloured folder and took out a typed document that looked like a checklist.

'Now, let me see,' he said. 'Passport photos? He fingered the two sets of pictures. 'Yes. Very good.'

'Good grief,' said Felicity, leaning across to scrutinise Philip's photos.

Philip shot her a fiery look. The man checked a box on the sheet.

'Passport copies?' He flipped over the corresponding sheets. 'Yes. Very good.' He checked another box and stamped each of the photocopies with unnatural energy. 'Letter of employment?' He glanced over a page bearing the Downing Foundation letterhead. 'Yes. Very good.' He ticked yet another box, his tongue licking at the corner of his mouth. 'And… Wedding Book.' He shuffled through the pages in front of him, then looked up. 'Wedding Book,' he said. 'Where is your Wedding Book?'

Felicity looked at Philip and he at her. 'Philip,' she said, 'where is our Wedding Book?'

The man stared at Philip with furrowed brow. His pen was suspended over the check box.

'Erm... I cannot say. Perhaps it is ...'

'Yes?' said the man.

'I suspect it is...'

'At home, on the kitchen table,' said Felicity. 'That's where it is. I said to you, if you remember, darling, "Philip, don't forget our Wedding Book since we'll be needing it at the Embassy," and what did you do? You left it on the kitchen table.'

'Ah yes... so I did,' said Philip.

'There you are,' said Felicity to the man. 'Our Wedding Book is safely at home. All the necessary documents are in place, so you can go ahead now and issue the visas.'

'But I must see the Wedding Book. It is not allowed to give the visa without to see the Wedding Book.'

'Look. Just do one thing,' said Felicity. 'Just tick the box, issue the visa, and I will pop home, collect the Wedding Book – that my husband absent-mindedly left on the kitchen table – and bring it to you here.'

The man's eyes narrowed. He sat immobile for what seemed like a very long time, fixing Felicity with a probing stare. Felicity returned his glare, but then as Philip watched, her face softened into a picture of extreme sweetness. Something registered in the man's eyes. He blinked, looked down and ticked the box.

'Very good,' he said.

*

From: nbryant@downingfoundation.nm
Date: 11 January
To: peblair@downingfoundation.co.uk
c.c.: titikamee@downingfoundation.nm
Subject: Welcome

Dear Philip,

It gave me great pleasure to meet you at your recent interview in London. I would now like to take this opportunity to welcome you (virtually!) to the Downing Foundation in Namisa. Over the coming months, I look forward to a fruitful working relationship with you as you develop your new and important role as Officer of Education and Culture.

I understand from the London office that all the necessary documentation is now in place and that you should shortly be on your way to join us here in Trinamisa. The matter of the missing 'Wedding Book' has, I believe, been satisfactorily resolved and the Namisan ambassador has graciously admitted responsibility for the loss. He has agreed to waive the embassy's normally stringent regulations in this respect. What actually happened I cannot say with any degree of accuracy although I endeavoured to investigate the situation from the Foundation's side. Your wife, it seems, left the Wedding Book in good faith with an official, but embassy staff deny all knowledge of its existence. I did, of course, point out to the Ambassador that this was extremely distressing for Mrs Blair. Not only has her word been questioned, but she has also lost a valuable document that was of great personal significance to the both of you. You will be pleased to learn that, in the interests of maintaining good customer relations, at least one of the embassy's staff has been relocated for further training to the Namisan Embassy in Baku. Let us now put this incident behind us and look forward instead to your imminent posting with us in Namisa.

The provisional plan is as follows. Your departure from Heathrow will be scheduled for a date (TBA) as soon as is convenient after 24 January. On arrival in Namisa, you will be met by a Foundation representative and delivered to the Shangri-La Hotel in Trinamisa. We will transfer you and Mrs Blair to your accommodation as soon as it has been made ready.

Should you have any 'housekeeping' queries, please do not hesitate to contact my secretary Tiki, who will be very happy to help you. I very much look forward to seeing you next on Namisan soil.

>   Yours
>   Neil Bryant
>   Director – The Downing Foundation, Namisa

***

4

THE EXCESSES OF BAGGAGE

Philip needed his things. He had spent three wretched evenings removing items from his suitcase and substituting smaller or lighter versions. He had made sacrifices. He needed his lucky ties, his lucky socks, his miscellany of lucky charms, but a great many of his lucky things had to be let go of in the last sweep, unluckily for them.

'Look at *my* case, Felicity,' said Philip. 'If I've got everything I need in there, then why can't you get your essentials into *your* case?'

Felicity regarded him with what he would have described as a sneer. 'If you've got everything you need in there,' she said, indicating with a toss of her head Philip's new, medium, powder-blue GlobeTrotter Travelbag, 'then your life must be very bland and shallow indeed.'

This, Philip thought, was a very low blow. 'I am well-organised. I prioritise,' he sniffed, though he was aware his argument was particularly feeble.

'It's like this, Philip,' said Felicity, 'you will arrive over there in Namisa and discover that you desperately need all those things that you probably spent a very long time removing from your suitcase.'

'You can get everything in Namisa,' said Philip, but even as he spoke, he thought with great anxiety of the jar of lemon curd and the tub of Marmite, both of which he had first lovingly wrapped and then – a day later – had taken out of his case.

'I've packed my supplies,' said Felicity, 'and I don't intend leaving without them.'

It was time for Philip to revert to a higher authority. 'We're allowed one suitcase each,' he said. 'One *normal*-sized suitcase. Those are the rules.'

'What rules?' demanded Felicity. 'Let me see those rules. Pardon my incredulity but I'm talking to someone here who probably doesn't even know how to manage his in-flight entertainment.'

Philip resented this last accusation deeply, in part because he did indeed have some difficulty navigating his movies and games some years back on a mini-break package to Miami.

As they spoke, a bulky, sandy-haired man made his way past the other passengers, weaving his trolley around their suitcases. Seemingly oblivious to Philip's presence, he manoeuvred himself to a halt right in front of Felicity.

'There you are, darling,' he said as, with evident ease, he added Felicity's oversized case to the other two on the trolley. 'Need anything else?'

'No, that's lovely, Bill. You're a darling yourself.'

'Safe journey, then. Miss you.' He leaned forward and gave her a lengthy bear hug followed by a lingering kiss. 'See you next holiday,' he said, giving her a playful tap on the cheek with his fist, after which he headed off towards the exit.

In his distraught state of mind, Philip could quite easily have flung himself at the man and slapped him around the head, but this fellow Bill was evidently an escapee from some convicts' gym and was not to be messed with.

'Who's that?' said Philip.

'None of your business,' said Felicity.

'Someone hugging and kissing my wife *is* my business.'

'Yes, well, consider me *La femme infidele* and deal with it.' And with that she took her place in what remained of the queue.

*

'Three suitcases?' asked the ground hostess.

'Four, including his,' said Felicity.

'I'm afraid you're going to be well over your weight allowance,' said the woman, scarcely looking at them.

'I told you,' said Philip. Then to the hostess he said, 'I told her, but she wouldn't listen.'

'Over the allowance? Surely not,' said Felicity. 'We're travelling Business Class all the way to Namisa. We're with the Downing Foundation.' Then, in a confidential whisper, she said, 'We're practically diplomats.'

The hostess suddenly came to life. 'Oh, you should have said. I'm sure we can sort something out. How long are you going for?'

'Oh, a couple of years, most likely.'

'How wonderful! I am just so envious. We get a lot of Namisans passing through here on their way to Dubai or Paris. Lovely people, island people. Untouched by corruption. Not like us. You'll be wanting to take your supplies with you, I suppose?'

'Exactly,' said Felicity.

'Good idea. I'll never forget the day I ran out of moisturiser in Rajasthan...'

Philip looked about him and spotting an abandoned newspaper on a nearby seat, retrieved it and settled down to read until he was called. From the Business Class check-in desk, he could hear the hostess reeling off an inventory of must-take items for exotic foreign travel: 'Weetabix, Marmite, Bakewell Tarts... maybe even Lemon Curd. Hope you packed a good conditioner, or your hair will turn to straw; and tampons, to tide you over till you find out where to buy them; paracetamol or similar... I should imagine settling in will be one big headache, and you'll need carbon tablets for while you're coping with the peculiar food, and mosquito and fly repellent; toilet paper of course; a bug spray – you never know what you'll find in the bathroom...'

*

As he studied the cloud formations from his window seat, Philip had a passing thought, a very fleeting thought, something unsettling. He now had more or less what he wanted, and he had had it almost instantly. He had the job he wanted, the salary he wanted and a wife into the bargain, though not specifically the wife he might have wanted. But wasn't it possible that all this was just a little too easy? He had given up an evening of his favourite television programmes to mug-up on the information he thought might impress the interview panel. They *had* been impressed, or at least they seem to have been, but now he felt an uneasiness. They had been impressed, it seemed, even before he had entered the room. The interview had been short. How could they have evaluated his potential quite so quickly and on the basis of so little information? He cast a glance at Felicity, who was unconscious in the seat beside him. In her sleep mask, she looked like Zorro without the eyeholes. Philip knew that she would know the answer to this conundrum, but she was the last person on earth he would ever ask. As she slumbered, she gave out a gentle purring sound, like a giant kitten ready for the cuddling. Two bottles of Australian Shiraz lay empty on her seatback table. Even if he hadn't much enjoyed himself so far on this momentous adventure, he had brought happiness to at least one person in this world.

From a plastic folder on his lap, he pulled out his job description, by now grubby with coffee stains and the evidence of various lunches and dinners. Philip had studied it inside and out. It contained nothing especially difficult or demanding. There were a few notes about previous award recipients. One name in particular – I. Bogadan – appeared more than once. Philip thumbed through these pages, wishing there might be more case studies of candidates. Much was made within the job's Person Specification of the importance of problem solving, the ability to distinguish between when to take a decision and when to defer, the ability to establish facts by carrying out appropriate enquiries, the ability to maintain good working relationships with 'our foreign partners.' It was easy enough to read between the lines … or even just to read the lines. Obviously, he had to take care not to upset anyone. He had to keep the Namisans happy and he had to see to it that Lady Downing and the Governing Board in London were satisfied that the Namisans were happy.

But, if he was the candidate of choice, why then did he feel this sense of foreboding? And why had such a desirable post come vacant at short notice? Why indeed had it been advertised internally rather than through a recruitment agency or in the Appointments section of the leading broadsheets?

The answer came to him. It must be, he thought – with a degree of contentment and relief – that the Foundation sought the kind of expertise that only an experienced Downing Foundation employee could offer. Philip stared out again at the clouds. Then with a start, he looked down at the document in front of him. If the truth were known, and he hoped it would not, he had no expertise – none whatsoever. So, how on earth did he get this job?

*

At home I have everything that is most precious to me, but now there are new things that I've become accustomed to. I've developed an appetite for things that previously I never knew about and never needed. Will I find them in

Namisa? Possibly not. My life used to be so simple, but now I have new needs. This could be very frustrating.

*

In her dream Felicity was trying to save her most precious belongings. Something awful was happening. She had a sense that her house was burning down and that she had a limited amount of time in which to salvage her valuables. Where would she start? What would she save? She started to fill suitcases. She seemed to have an endless supply of them, brought to her on a trolley by a man she could not identify, but it occurred to her that she was saving things that had little or no importance to her. She searched for her laptop, which she had put in a place of safety… of which she had now forgotten the location. She searched for her flash drives, which were entangled with wires and cords in a drawer of her desk, and as she untangled them, smoke filled her room and the flames roared. She grabbed her files and hurled them from the window, though she wondered if opening windows might embolden the flames, and as her notes and documents hit the ground outside, she imagined or dreamt that an army of looters lay in wait to gather them up and run away with them. And then she was in a house that she did not recognise with a series of men she did not know and did not care to know though they demonstrated an unnatural fondness and familiarity towards her. And when one of them was so impertinent as to lean in towards her, placing his face so very close to hers, she reached out and slapped him with all her energy and determination.

It was after this unfortunate slapping incident that Philip decided it best to relinquish his window seat in favour of easier access to the toilets.

***

PART TWO

TRINAMISA

5

The Comfort of Strangers

A point of interest for the benefit of my British readers: Namisa has approximately the same dimensions as Scotland. My small but loyal following of American readers may be interested to learn that Namisa is close in size to Rhode Island or perhaps a little smaller than South Carolina. Namisa is not an especially varied country. It is bordered for the most part by sandy beaches except on its Northern coast which is peppered with a series of rocky coves, many of which I have visited personally (see the author's stunning photographs on page 212). Across the water from Namisa sits its sister island of Pundar, the mountainous contours of which are altogether more dramatic than the orderly brown-green plains of Namisa when seen from above. For the geographers amongst you, I would refer you to *The Namisapundar Region: A Geographical Companion* (The Namisan Ministry of Information, 1982) for details of the respective latitudes and longitudes, about which I admit to understanding very little.

Though it is but a short flight from Namisa to Pundar, one would advise the visitor to resist a sojourn on this melancholic and atmospheric isle in favour of the less interesting shrub lands of Namisa and its many minor offshore islets. On multiple occasions in the past (see the section on 'History'), Namisa has laid claim to Pundar, but without success (see also my short chapter on 'The Pundexit Debate). For the historians amongst you I would recommend *The Pundarnamisa Region: An Historical Overview* (The Pundari Ministry of Information & Telecommunications, 1983).

(Extract from 'Geography,' (p.49) in *Namisa - A Traveller's Guide: from tradition to tourism and back*,' by Michael Robinson-Smith)

*

In the dying glow of the evening, Felicity saw below her the dark, formidable mountains of Pundar. The plane drifted on through cloud and then emerged to hover over a multitude of beige-coloured islands and one huge, apparently flat area of olive green, criss-crossed with roads, dotted with red-roofed villas, interspersed with intermittent patches of blue. The plane wafted lightly through the air, up a bit, then down a bit, like a small car negotiating a series of steeply undulating country roads. Felicity was beginning to feel a bit woozy and, as she reached for the sick bag, the very profound thought occurred to her that a holiday was merely a state of mind.

She had only the vaguest recollection of her arrival at Trinamisa airport and her transfer to the hotel. She recalled that Philip absented himself for what seemed like a very long time to go in search of the Gents, always a tricky enterprise when you are ignorant of the language and cannot rely upon visuals because the locals wear skirts. A monstrous bear-like man had ushered them through immigration. There was some mention of the tiresome Wedding Book, but after what sounded like a minor altercation, Felicity found herself comfortably installed in the back of a Mercedes and, in the torpid state induced by alcohol and travel sickness pills, she noted only the blurred sight of the back of the driver's head and the fierce smell of his body odour. She made her observation about Philip's absence shortly after they had left the parking lot, after which they did a circuit of the airport and re-entered. She had a sense that the driver was not amused to have to pay a second parking charge.

*

After Paris, how difficult it is to return to Trinamisa. Mon Dieu! And I'm wondering what use, if any, I will have for French in Namisa.

*

Light filtered through the gold brocade curtains of their room. Outside, Felicity heard a chorus of Namisan birds, their chirping, she thought, not unlike that of a chorus of British birds. As awareness overtook her, she remembered that she had spent the night with a stranger. She sat up in bed. The room was vast – a suite – and, thankfully, she was alone. Her suitcase lay open on the floor, its contents tumbling out onto the carpet, evidence of a rapid and unsuccessful search for her face cream and her electric toothbrush. She had, however, found her brown silk pyjamas with the cream lace trim. Overlooking the unruly hair and bloodshot eyes, in these lavish surroundings she might have resembled someone from an advertisement for a luxury chocolate bar. All was silence except for the birds and the low rattle of the air-conditioning in the adjacent room. She started her reconnaissance of the suite. If she could find the room service menu, it would be a very good thing. She stepped past the curtains and onto the balcony, where she gasped with joy and delight for here were date palms and coconut trees, here were swimming pools and cocktails and pool bars and white white sand, and here too was the proverbial azure sea. And here *she* was, every bit a part of her environment. For what previously seemed a risky decision now demonstrated its worth. How right she had been. She had made a sacrifice, but the reward was significant. She must certainly find the spa menu in addition to the one for room service. With new resolve, she headed in the direction of the defective air-conditioning unit and found that the rattling sound was Philip, fast asleep on the sofa.

His eyes flickered open. His face warmed into a smile. 'Nice, isn't it?' he said.

'Yes,' she agreed. 'Very nice indeed! Thank you, Philip.' The words spilt out involuntarily and she blushed at her own blithering thankfulness.

*

Hello, Philip!

I hope you're reading your messages. All is well with us. Ray and I are in Hawaii. Quite pretty – surfers and all that. I hope your move to Namisa went well (where is Namisa by the way?) It must be a very important job since you now have a secretary. Fancy that!

I expect Auntie Peggy kicked up a fuss when you left, but then it's only because she worries about you. (And is most likely jealous of your secretary.) She will probably have told you to wrap up warm and eat sensibly. My advice is the same as always – don't spend all your money, get a financial advisor, and always use a condom. A few other tips … Don't get involved with local girls. Join the local dramatic society or take up a sport. Golf would be good. Don't eat too much at buffets. Drink lots of water. That's all.

Love,

Mum

PS Can Ray be your friend on Facebook? He sent you a request but you haven't replied.

*

Mio carissimo Francesco,

I am in a place where you will never find me. It is useless calling or sending e-mails. I am long gone. I wonder if you even feel just the slightest hint of remorse…

Felicity clicked Save and closed the document. Below her balcony, children frolicked in the pool. Namisa was a very fine place and it would be even finer during the Happy Hour, in which she was about to participate. She opened another document.

Dear Franco,
Perhaps you think it strange that I have not returned your calls. If you dropped by and rang my doorbell then you would have discovered that I am no longer there in the flat.

Felicity saved and closed this document also. She had not had any calls that she had been able to *not* return and, evidently, *he* had not passed by the flat because the Yamamotos would surely have told her. The awful truth, which she would have preferred to ignore, was that he hadn't even missed her. Could there be anything worse than indifference? It was as though she had said to him, 'Look, my suitcases are packed. Look, I'm going now. Look, I'm reaching for the door handle. Look, I'm dragging my suitcase down the stairs.' And from him... nothing.

*

At the hotel bar, Felicity met a tall, wan stranger, a thin gangly fellow with a superior aspect. He wore a cream-coloured fedora and an off-white, over-sized linen jacket, and through a straw he sipped a frothy aqua-blue mixture from a very tall glass.

'You don't mind if I sit here?' said Felicity. The piano

lounge was empty except for the two of them.

'I'm flattered you should choose me,' said the man.

'Felicity,' said Felicity proffering her hand.

'Mike,' said the man, doffing his hat, which he then removed to reveal fine silver blonde hair combed back severely from his high forehead. He took her hand in his and, with great delicacy, raised it lightly to his lips. 'Felicity,' he said, 'have a cocktail,' and he signalled to the barman.

'It's so exciting. Don't you think?'

'What?' said Mike.

'Being here in Namisa. So exotic, so special, and so unusual.'

The man's brow wrinkled slightly and he continued sipping.

'Are you on holiday here?' insisted Felicity.

'Ah, no,' said Mike coming up for air. 'I'm a resident. An ex-pat. Been here for years.'

'Oh, my goodness,' said Felicity. 'Lucky you. What do you do, if I may ask?'

'I suppose I'm a sort of anthropologist. Research, you know, that kind of thing.' He swung around on his bar stool and looked Felicity squarely in the eyes. 'And what do you do, my dear? Are you here on business or pleasure?'

'Both I should hope,' said Felicity. 'I'm a writer. That's what I do.'

Felicity's cocktail was placed before her, a phosphorescent blue in its long, frosted glass.

'A very worthy profession,' said Mike. 'I do so admire writers. Let us toast them.'

They raised and clinked their glasses. 'And, you are

here with your husband, I assume.'

Felicity paused for several beats. 'Yes,' she said.

'In Namisa, when one pauses before a "Yes," it means, "No."'

Felicity averted her eyes and sipped her drink.

'Forgive me,' he said, 'I personally have difficulty separating business from pleasure. Indeed, I am not at all sure that they should be separated. Consider it as a little cultural tip. You may find it useful.'

'No offence taken,' said Felicity.

'So, you are new to Namisa…'

'Yes, it's absolutely wonderful,' said Felicity.

'How long have you been here?'

Felicity looked up at the ceiling and made a few calculations. 'About eighteen hours,' she said.

'That is more than enough time to evaluate the hotel,' said Mike. He drained his glass. 'Though you will need a little longer to get the measure of Namisa.'

*

'What a good line this is!' said Auntie Peggy. 'It's like you're in the next room. And how is the weather over there? A bit chilly is it?'

'Yes,' said Philip, who was standing under the air conditioning vent.

'Well, good job you took my advice and packed a jumper,' said Auntie Peggy.

'Anything new at your end?' said Philip. 'Won the lottery? Anything like that?'

'No, dear, nothing new, but there were some young

women asking for you. And I've popped you a few things in the post. There were a couple of letters… one from the bank, two from the Reader's Digest, and there was some kind of girlie pin-up magazine.'

'You're a darling,' said Philip.

'Heaven knows where they get people's addresses from. I put the magazine in the bin.'

'Oh,' said Philip. 'Okay.'

'Now about the holidays,' said Auntie Peggy. 'I was just thinking I might come over and visit you.'

'The accommodation's really not that good, Auntie Peggy. Just a little bachelor flat. I could probably put you up in a hotel but it might be a bit pricey.'

'Well, maybe I can get a package. I'll think about it. How's the food? Is it awful?'

'Yes, pretty grim. Very spicy. You wouldn't like it.'

'You poor boy. I wish I could do something for you. Can you not get them to send you somewhere else?'

'You know, I think I'm just going to have to sit it out.'

*

Philip leaned in towards the honey-skinned girl. 'And you are?'

'Sylvie,' she said, pulling a strand of fine blonde hair from her eye.

'From?'

'France.'

'Lovely. France. That's delightful. *Je suis Philip.*'

'Oh, but you speak French. *C'est formidable,*'

'*Mais oui,*' said Philip. He was taking the last of the

afternoon sun, lying on a lounger by the pool with his new friend. As Sylvie lowered herself gingerly into the water, he reflected on how much he admired the French.

'And you are working for ze Downing Foundation?' called Sylvie as she bobbed in the water.

'*Oui*,' said Philip.

'In ze place of Monsieur Jonathan?'

'*Oui*,' said Philip.

'*Alors, bon chance*,' said Sylvie, before she dived beneath the water and glided to the other side of the pool.

*

'No,' said Felicity. 'There must be some mistake. You have brought us to the wrong place.'

The man mountain looked affronted. 'This right place.' He held in front of her a limp piece of paper that was crisscrossed with folds. 'Here your name,' he said and pointed.

It now seemed to Felicity that the transition from Heaven to Hell had been short, swift and very brutal. 'No, you don't understand,' she said. 'We were supposed to have been allocated a villa.'

The man looked blank.

'A villa,' repeated Felicity. 'Not bungalow. Not very small house.'

The man looked cross.

'This,' said Felicity, waving her arm towards the offending edifice, 'not villa, absolutely not.'

'Yes, this villa,' said the man.

'No, it is not! Where's the swimming pool? Where's

the roof terrace? Where are the balconies?' Felicity turned to look for Philip, who was crunching his way across the dried earth in the front garden. 'Philip, will you talk to this man, please?'

'Swimming pool at golf club,' said the man.

'No, no. We were supposed to have our own swimming pool.' And turning again towards Philip, she said, 'I'm not happy about this, Philip. This is not what we agreed.'

Philip stood looking up admiringly at one of the trees. 'Look, Felicity, we've got a banana tree in our garden.'

'Philip, we have a situation here. This man…' Felicity looked about her. The man had gone. He was now with Philip.

'This tree,' said the man, 'we call it *yellibellee* tree and it give fruit we call it *yellibellee* fruit.'

'We call them "bananas,"' explained Philip. 'What about these? They look just like daisies.'

'No, no,' said the man, 'this it is *baysee* flower.'

'Oh, for goodness sake,' wailed Felicity, 'this is not Gardeners' Question time, Philip. Can you just sort out the problem?'

'*Baysee*. I see,' said Philip. 'And do you say, for example, "a bunch of *baysees*."'

'Yes, yes. Good,' said the man. 'And some ladies we are calling them "*Baysee*." Very nice name.'

'Is there a song too?' said Philip.

'Yes, yes.' The man's face lit up. 'You very clever, Mr Pilip. How you knowing that? Song is about man wanting to marry girl she is called *Baysee*, and he say to her

"*Baysee*, give me answer quick or I kill myself."

'I suppose that's just an approximate translation,' said Philip, examining the tree nearest to him.

'No,' said the man with an air of great confidence. 'That is *pinga panga* tree. And here is *chicalika* plant…'

The two men moved away into the shade of the *dingamalee* bushes. Felicity slumped into a wicker chair on the porch of the bungalow. She closed her eyes, took deep breaths and counted from one to ten and then on to twenty, then thirty and when she reached forty, she felt strangely transformed and heard only the crickle-crackle of the garden, the lulling buzz of invisible insects and the croaking of alien reptiles. All else was silence. A light breeze rustled through the *pinga panga* and the *yellibellee*.

Felicity opened her eyes and at that moment she knew, for better or worse, that she was home.

***

6

STAKEHOLDERS AND OTHER GOURMETS

Philip observed that Tiki was very small, rather like her name – Tiki. She wore a pale blue linen dress with a frilled neckline and short-capped sleeves. She was like Peter Pan, without the tights.

'Is there something wrong?' asked Tiki, her dark, slug-shaped eyebrows meeting in a frown. She might be petite, but she was also confrontational and Philip was ill-prepared to deal with secretaries of her intimidating calibre. He feigned blankness and looked around the room. It was not how he imagined an executive office, but it was an indisputable improvement on the cubicle that was his in London.

'Is this it? I mean is this going to be my office?'

'You don't like it?' said Tiki. 'It was the office of *Om* Jonathan and he liked it very much.' She glared at him and started to say something but stopped herself.

'Yes?' said Philip.

'I just wanted to say ... that we are all very sorry that *Om* Jonathan is no longer with us. Everyone liked *Om* Jonathan.'

There was a moment of silence between them, then Tiki said, 'Your name is on the door.' She indicated the open door that was pushed back against the wall. A name plate was screwed to the wood. It read, 'Pilip Blair, Officer of Culture and Education.'

'It's..,' began Philip.

'What?' said Tiki looking him straight in the eye.

'It's very nice,' said Philip.

'I'll leave you to get on,' said Tiki. 'I'm sure you must have a lot of work to do.' She stepped out of the room and closed the door behind her. Through the internal window on the corridor side of the room, he saw her make her way back towards her own office. Her manner of going suggested a degree of irritation. The moment she was out of sight, he started to open drawers and cupboards, of which there were many. There was nothing, except for one book on the bookshelf opposite the desk, a copy of *Namisa - A Traveller's Guide*. Certainly, a volume that no one, especially not a newcomer, can be without. Otherwise, the place had been cleared, swept clean. Philip was not sure what he hoped to find. He just had an idea that you understand a little more of your surroundings if you find some remnant of its past. On the desk were three hefty ring binders, filled with papers. Tiki had taken care to provide him with ample background reading, which – since he was slow to take in the written word – would most likely keep him busy until old age overtook him. He sat on the old beige office chair and tested its swivel. Not bad. Then he measured one file against another and lined them up in a row: medium, large, very large – or, he thought, he could classify them as thick, thicker, thickest. He wondered if he should read the medium thick one first or go straight to the very large thickest file and read that – eat the frog as it were. It would be far better if someone could read them for him and simply give him a summary. He wanted the abridged version. Very abridged. He rearranged the files, and as he did so, he heard a tapping sound at the internal window. The man mountain, bearded and sweaty, was hunched over and peering in. This, Philip had learned just this morning, was Ratni, the Foundation's driver and local fixer. His jaw moved rhythmically and in one hand he held a half-eaten sandwich to which he pointed, smiling. Bread and something meat-like stuck between his teeth.

'No,' mouthed Philip, 'thank you.'

Ratni stopped smiling, stood up and walked away.

Too bad, thought Philip. His circle of friends had just grown smaller. He had not arrived at the best of times. Some of the Namisan admin staff were on holiday and the Foundation's remaining ex-pat staff members, Ronny and Alan from Finance, were away on a course. Philip's points of contact were Ratni – too touchy; Tiki – too assertive; and Bryant – too other worldly, too gone-native, and too … tall.

Philip opened the right-hand desk drawer. There he found one pencil sharpener, one eraser, a tiny pad of Post-It notes, one biro, one pencil, one thumb tack, and a pair of children's scissors. Tiki was frugal as well as assertive. He opened the left-hand desk drawer and found it empty. He pushed the drawer closed and he heard something rattle.

He opened the drawer again and stared into it. It was empty, but he slid his hand to the back of the drawer where his fingers found a small rectangular object. He pulled it out. A matchbox. Flipping it over he read the words, 'The Sleepy Hollow Nite Club,' and next to the words was the tiny image of a cocktail glass complete with a cherry on a stick. If this job did not work out, thought Philip, there was a career for him in the police. He fiddled with the matchbox, opening and shutting it, watching its small waxy matches appear and disappear ... until he pushed the box all the way through and flipped the tiny matches onto the floor. And then, stooping to pinch them up, he saw something very curious. Directly below the right-hand arm of his chair there was some kind of organic matter resembling animal droppings. What could have produced these? A mouse? A rat? A lizard perhaps? He had no idea what lizard droppings might look like. He lifted his feet from the ground and reflected that you can never feel comfortable knowing that some invisible evil lurks in your workplace. Tomorrow, he decided, he must wear thicker socks. He was not yet ready to make complaints to Tiki.

He took Jonathan's copy of *Namisa - A Traveller's Guide* from the shelf and returned to his desk, flicking through the pages and passing by the section on rodents and other animals that were sand-coloured and boring, just as he used to do when he visited Edinburgh zoo with his dad. He looked instead for lizards, wondering if he should look at snakes too. Did snakes produce droppings like this? Did snakes produce droppings? He had no idea. He heard something rustle in the air conditioning vent. He held his breath. Yes, he had seen those movies too.

The huge mother lizard is disturbed, its babes slither out into the world, into the office where an innocent sits working at his computer – Philip being the innocent – and then they attack. The creatures, tiny teeth snapping, cover the man so that his head becomes a live mass of wriggling slime. Philip shook himself to disconnect his over-wired imagination, but his mind wandered all the way to Australia. What an awful place that must be, he thought, with little spiders that crept out from dark places and bit your bottom when you were on the toilet. Could there be equally lethal creepy crawlies like this in Namisa? If so, then he could not stay. It would be just too awful. Felicity had reminded him just that morning to buy an insect spray. Heaven knows he had tried finding one before but, unable to read the product description in Namisan, he had brought home a room freshener, mistaking the insect on the cylinder casing to be a pest when it was merely an innocent bee perching on a flower. Was he to have difficulties with the language too? In this moment of unexpected weakness, he asked himself why he had left behind him the comfort of home and the intellectual delights of the Touchstone Bookshop. He heard the patter of miniscule feet distance themselves in the vent and exhaled. Any immediate danger had passed. Anyway, there was nothing in Robinson-Smith about droppings. He needed an altogether different reference book for that area of research. He looked down at the matchbox. If Sleepy Hollow was good enough for Jonathan, then it was good enough for him. He scooped up the largest of the files and set off to locate his driver.

In the forecourt of the Downing Foundation offices,

Ratni was fondly polishing the wings of Bryant's Mercedes.

'Ratni,' said Philip with a certain boldness, 'I'd like you to drop me off over at the Sleepy Hollow.'

Ratni stopped his work, stood upright, and scowled, his huge frame casting a shadow over Philip. 'Drop? You mean take?'

'Yes,' said Philip. 'Like you used to take Jonathan?'

Ratni resumed his work. 'I no take *Om* Jonathan Sleepy Hollow,' he said.

'Never?'

Ratni was silent.

'Ever?'

Ratni continued polishing as Philip waited. 'Well, maybe to Funny Hour – maybe one time, or maybe two time,' he conceded.

'Okay. Good,' said Philip.

Ratni lurched around to face Philip. He wiped his sweaty forehead and then his mouth and beard with the polishing cloth. He made as if to speak and then stopped himself and stared over Philip's shoulder. Philip turned to see Tiki, home-bound, making her way towards them carrying a large black tote bag, its handle looped over one arm.

'Ratni will drive you home, *Om* Philip.' She faced Ratni and fixed him with a severe gaze. 'And no stopping at that place, *Om* Ratni. You will go direct. Do you understand? *Kappi shay?*'

Ratni's nostrils twitched and the black shiny hairs within them flexed. '*Bunga, Imee* Tiki,' he said and he turned to continue his shining of what already shone more than adequately.

'And make sure you take the other car,' said Tiki.

'*Jej*,' muttered Ratni.

'*Adoo*,' commanded Tiki, and she waited.

Ratni screwed up his polishing cloth and stuffed it into his pocket as if it were a large handkerchief, which it probably was. '*Jej, jej*,' he said.

'*Jinkooranipa*,' said Tiki as Ratni set off towards the opposite side of the car parking area.

'You really must be very firm with him, *Om* Pilip,' said Tiki turning to face her ward. 'He is Pundari, you see. If you are not firm, he will walk all over you.'

'Oh,' said Philip.

'The only thing we can be thankful for is that he is not in favour of Pundexit.'

'Erm…'

'You are new here, *Om* Pilip. You will find out in due course how politics work here. For now, you are best staying out of it as *Om* Jonathan should have done. But didn't.'

'I see,' said Philip.

'Yes,' said Tiki. 'Exactly. So, as I said, be firm with *Om* Ratni. I am telling you this for your own good.'

'Thank you,' said Philip.

'And don't worry,' continued Tiki, 'we will make sure you always get home in time for your tea.'

'Super,' said Philip and, in his pocket, he fingered his Sleepy Hollow matchbox with a sense of yearning and regret.

*

'Now,' said Felicity from her control point in the centre of the room, 'this is my workspace and that – over there – is *your* workspace.'

Why did a traffic policeman come to mind as he followed her gesticulations? 'This is our dining room,' said Philip.

'What is?' said Felicity.

'This room, where you've put all your stuff.'

'It's not stuff,' said Felicity. 'It's research material, books, files, writing implements.'

'We need a dining room. We'll have to host dinners for our foreign partners.'

'Will we now? You'll be cooking those, will you?'

'No, you will.'

'Ha!' said Felicity. 'In your dreams.' She strode across the hall into Philip's workspace. 'This looks like a dining room to me.'

'This is my study,' said Philip. Philip had turned the scratched and ridged kitchen table into a desk, across which an unruly mess of papers was scattered.

'Oh, I see, and what are you going to study?' Felicity tried Philip's chair out for size.

'Just don't touch anything,' said Philip. Leaving Felicity alone all day to claim her territory, he realised now, was asking for trouble. He walked back into her space to weigh up the competition. There was a certain order to it, as though she had done this before. There were neat heaps of printed pages on a bookshelf. Near to her huge desk, which bore a close resemblance to a dining room table, there was a shelf of reference materials. On the table itself was a printer and a laptop. There was clearly a large amount of work-in-progress going on here. Philip bit his lip. She had appropriated his intellectual space as well as his personal space. He felt badly done by. He walked, sandals flapping on the floor tiles, back into *his* room. It was bare by comparison, and there at his rickety old kitchen table, Felicity was engrossed in his private papers, his fat, possibly soon-to-be-read-providing-he-had-time file.

'What did I just say? Didn't I tell you not to touch anything,' he growled.

'Have you read this?' she said, turning pages at a rapid rate, pausing from time to time to read a line here, a paragraph there.

'That's classified. You're not supposed to mess with those reports.' He reached out to take the file and she snatched it away, spinning around on his office chair.

'They're like case studies. I could use these. Develop them into characters.'

'You can't do that.'

'Why not?'

'It's unethical. It's a breach of …' He knew it was a breach of something or other but he could not think what.

'Of what?'

'It's an invasion of privacy. These are real people.'

'I would fictionalise them. That's what I do.'

'Come on. Give me the file,' said Philip.

Felicity launched the chair towards the door, hit the ground running and disappeared into her room. Philip hurried after her.

'You know I could probably give you a few tips here,' said Felicity, now sitting at her desk and tapping one of the pages with her pen. 'This is how I see it, Philip. This chap Bogadan keeps showing up for handouts, bursaries and the like. It's not as if he's a pauper, is it? What's that all about?'

Philip sat down at the table and ran his fingers through his hair.

Felicity continued. 'Typical attention-seeker behaviour. That's what it is. No self-worth. He wants to be appreciated. Maybe he's also got a problem with his mother. A bit like you, Philip.'

Philip sighed, as he often did of late.

'You should get on fine with him. You've got so much in common. My advice is to reassure him and let him know that his cause is in good hands and is being attended to.' Then she added, 'It's a lie, of course, but we'll keep that between ourselves.'

Philip held his head in his hands and puffed out his cheeks.

'You should also flatter him,' said Felicity. 'With types like this, flattery always works. It helps to distract them from their original objective, i.e., in this case, appropriating funding from the Downing Foundation.' She looked up at Philip. 'Would you like me to write some notes, or do you think you can remember all of this?'

*

I'm not sure if it's true but they say that foreign men cannot come to work here unless they are already married and come with their wives. Why would anyone not want single expat men coming to Namisa? It must be some kind of Namisan urban myth. Namisa simply isn't that medieval.

*

'Ito Bogadan. Ito Bogadan.' Philip mouthed the name like an incantation. As far as he was concerned, it could have been the notice on the door of the toilet at Trinamisa Airport, except that – as he now recalled only too well from that first night – there were no toilets at Trinamisa Airport. There were bushes. Foliage was lush in Namisa. In Namisa you stocked up with carbon tablets and trusted in God and in scrupulous cafe owners, of which there were few.

'I'm sorry,' said Bryant, 'did you say something?'

'Ito Bogadan,' said Philip. He shuffled clumsily through the papers in the ring binder he had in front of him, the binder he had nicknamed the Bogadan file.

Bryant coloured slightly. 'Yes, well, no doubt you'll be meeting him very shortly,' he said. He blew his nose and polished it with a voluminous white hankie. Philip had a sense that the Namisan dust – and probably much else – got up Neil Bryant's nose.

'It's just that his name seems to come up rather a lot – this Bogadan.'

Bryant coughed. 'We've assigned him to you, Philip. It'll get you started, give you a taste of what it's all about…'

'Oh, all right,' said Philip.

'You'll soon get the picture,' mumbled Bryant.

Philip had been doing his best to show enthusiasm for the task at hand. He wanted to get things right, but he still wasn't at all sure what the rules were. Back home, occasionally Auntie Peggy would come out with gems of good advice, like the one he was thinking of now: 'When in doubt, look wise.' So, he adopted a wise stance. As he continued to remind himself, the rewards for successfully completing this Namisan assignment could be immense. All those glamorous foreign postings. All those glamorous foreign women even.

'It wouldn't surprise me if you met him tonight,' said Bryant.

'Who?' said Philip.

'Bogadan.' Bryant riffled through his own documents and then mumbled again, 'The fellow seems to wangle his way into most of our functions, even the S and Ts.'

'The S and Ts?'

'Science and Technology.' Bryant cast an evaluative glance in Philip's direction. 'Our FFs,' he said. 'Foundation Functions.'

'Of course,' said Philip.

'We hold a little event for academics and professional people once or twice a month. Bit of finger food, a couple of crates of wine. Does wonders for our relationship with the Ministry of Higher Education.'

Bryant sniffed again, then sprang to his feet and lurched to the window. He was a long-limbed man. He reminded Philip of a giraffe, but minus the grace … and anyway, the colouring was different. 'Yes … Ito Bogadan,' he said. He raised his head and took in a deep air-conditioned breath. 'Ah,' he said, closing his eyes, 'Nam-i-sa in the autumn. The Nam-i-san autumn.' He pronounced the vowels with relish. 'You have the Namisan winter to look forward to, Philip.' For once he seemed more cheerful.

'It's February,' said Philip.

'Yes?' Bryant looked irritated.

Philip did not as yet have the measure of his new boss and was wary of erring.

'I thought that Namisa had no seasons.'

'Oh, quite, quite,' confirmed Bryant, 'but you see, Philip, the mention of a season here and there helps to chunk down the time, if you see my meaning. One day is much like the next.'

Yes, thought Philip, this was true. In this the beginning of his second week in Namisa, as he continued to work through his copy of *Namisa - A Traveller's Guide*, he had concluded that Robinson-Smith, in some areas of his descriptions, had been economical with the truth. Could it be, he wondered, that the map was really not the territory after all? This being the case, he was disoriented. What he needed was a point of reference, something to hang on to, something to believe in and measure things by. Namisa, he felt, was pleasant, but limited. Or was it just that he had not met any Namisan women yet?

According to his calculations, there remained two years, eleven months and some fifteen days of service still to complete before his transfer to an altogether more glorious place. Rome perhaps, or Paris, or … His mind was a blank. He would need to consult an atlas of glorious places. He felt a sudden surge of panic, the kind often prompted by the counting of unhatched chickens. His three-year plan would be guaranteed to reach maturity providing nothing unexpected happened …like that rather unfortunate incident back in London with the Minister of a certain country that he preferred not to even think about, the incident that propelled him from rising star in Public Relations to Junior Administrative Officer in Procurement. But all this he had put behind him along with Hugo Danvers.

'Now, what are your thoughts, Philip?' said Bryant.

Philip blinked.

'On the Bogadan situation?' said Bryant. 'We really do need some help with this one and, with your degree in psychology, I was hoping you might just be the person to sort Bogadan out once and for all.'

'Well ...' said Philip.

'Of course,' interrupted Bryant, 'I realise that you may need some time to acclimatise yourself to the Namisan mindset. Very important here to get out and about and understand the islanders. Get a grasp of the language and culture and ... all that. *Tika tika takeena*, as they say.'

'Oh, absolutely,' said Philip, secretly marvelling at Bryant's facility with the local tongue and wondering when he would have a chance to understand the islanders at the Sleepy Hollow Nite Club. He was sure he could grasp something there.

'So,' said Bryant, throwing himself heavily into his chair and viewing Philip through narrowed eyes, 'what are your initial thoughts on the approach to take with Bogadan?'

'Well,' said Philip, thinking that sometimes you just have to start and the rest will follow. 'I understand that he is quite well-placed ...'

'Mmm ...' concurred Bryant.

'He is in a position of some power at the University.'

'Ah, yes, indeed, Philip. Absolutely. His mother, Grace Shoon Bogadan, is the founder. The University of Trinamisa is a fairly young institution and it runs rather like – shall we say – a family business. Nepotism of the highest order. Hardly a model for a world-class institution.'

'So, not good then,' said Philip.

'Quite true, but as I'm sure you will appreciate, we are not here to pass judgement, simply to support. We must be seen to assist our Namisan hosts in every way possible. However, there are many demands on us and we are often restricted by the guidelines on the distribution of our budget. Bogadan is not our only potential beneficiary but, as you will discover, he may be our most persuasive.'

Somewhere deep in Philip's subconscious a lightbulb flickered on. 'I think I have a grasp of the situation,' he said. 'I've dealt with characters like this before.'

Bryant leaned forward, lips pursed, his elbows resting on the desk, his hands clasped.

Philip continued. 'Basically, they are attention-seekers. They need to be acknowledged … to feel that they are of worth … that they are appreciated. They need to know that their cause is in good hands and is being attended to. Some degree of flattery is also of assistance in these cases and it very often helps distract the subject from his or her original objective.' At this point he paused, holding his breath, hoping that Bryant had bought this.

Bryant's eyes darted up towards the ceiling as he considered Philip's response.

'Yes, good. Very good,' he said.

Philip breathed again.

'Yes, very good. That should be enough to get us started. Now, before you go, Philip, just a couple of *pointeez*.'

'*Pointeez?*'

'Points, points, a couple of points, Philip. In your capacity as our Officer of Culture and Education, you realize, of course, that you have quite a large budget.'

'Yes, I'm absolutely fine with that,' said Philip. And as he spoke, he briefly recalled a time when he had set aside small amounts of money each week out of his pocket money and with these accumulated proceeds, he had bought a pair of Nike trainers. It reassured him to remember that he was good at managing money.

'What it amounts to,' continued Bryant, 'is that you inherit a portfolio of scholarships and awards that were doled out to worthy recipients by your predecessor Jonathan. That task now falls to you, Philip, and, naturally, you will be entirely responsible.' Bryant paused and looked directly at Philip. A small nerve seemed to flicker on one side of his left eye. 'It is a very onerous responsibility, you understand,' he said, 'I mean, you *do* understand …?'

'Oh yes,' said Philip, 'not a problem. I feel quite sure I can fill Jonathan's shoes, and I've every confidence I can take over where he left off.'

Bryant's head was bowed and his lips appeared to move in an obscure murmur, something along the lines of, 'Spare us.'

'Pardon?' said Philip.

'That may well be,' said Bryant. There was a moment's silence while Bryant gazed into the middle distance as though recapturing some obscure memory. Then, emerging from this momentary lapsus, he refocused, looking Philip up and down. 'So, the word to remember, Philip, is RAT.'

'Sorry?'

'R – A - T.' Bryant spelled out the letters and slapped the desk as he spoke. A teaspoon balanced in the saucer of his teacup bounced onto the oak surface and somersaulted onto the floor. 'R for Responsibility,' he continued. 'You – and only you – sign on the dotted line. A for Accountability: you are accountable to the Foundation, and you monitor the outgoing of funds.'

Philip's heart pounded faster with every thump of the desk.

'And, finally,' said Bryant, 'T for Timeliness. As you will learn, everything has a deadline. A missed deadline means lost funding and lost opportunities … and, heaven forbid, a loss of credibility on the part of the Foundation. So, you need to remember, Philip: RAT at all times.' With this last assertion, Bryant leaned across his desk and held Philip again in one of his piercing stares.

'Right!' said Philip, 'Got it. RAT. Will do!'

Bryant sprang to his feet. 'Very good. *Bunga, bunga*! Don't waste a minute, Philip. *Hela pala, traka traka*. Strike while the iron is hot. Good man! Now, off you go!'

Philip gathered up his Bogadan file at speed and headed for the door.

'Oh, and don't forget …' called Bryant.

Philip turned on his heel.

'Don't forget to bring your lady wife to the Medical tonight,' he said. 'We're all so looking forward to meeting her.'

*

Returning home late that afternoon to his bungalow in downtown Trinamisa, Philip was overcome with despondency. Bryant and the others were to meet his wife. His credibility, his career, hung on this. He held out little hope for his other half. As the past two weeks had proved, she was a wild card, a loose cannon … and she had a lot of very insightful ideas, which made Philip as mad as hell.

Philip closed himself in the bathroom before he could be intercepted. He had yet again omitted to bring home the insect spray and he knew he would pay dearly for his error. Insecticide or homicide – he was sure it would all end in tears. It was not enough to say that he had had a busy day and had forgotten. Now he had responsibilities for which he was ill-prepared. As a single man, he was swiftly coming to the conclusion that he was not suited to married life.

There was a sudden violent rapping at the bathroom door.

'I know you're in there, Philip,' said Felicity. 'Come out and face me!'

Philip turned on the taps and a deep visceral groaning ensued, followed by a consumptive spluttering.

'And you can't drown me out,' said Felicity, 'Do you hear me, Philip? Do you hear me? Because there's no bloody water.'

A glass smashed and the porch door thumped. A certain someone was a bottle of Chardonnay too far. Philip was beginning to understand how people on foreign postings might well take to drink and lose their mind. Here was the proof. Felicity – home alone all day with just her laptop for company, no knowledge of the language, no transport, no friends. It was cabin fever, all right. Never mind fictional characters. If Philip had been an academic, a doctor perhaps, he could easily have done a case study on the subject.

He gave a sigh and sat down on the edge of the bath. On the floor, a few random ants wove their way in and out of the grooves between the tiles. In many ways, Philip considered himself fortunate. He could have found himself somewhere far worse than Namisa. Papua New Guinea, for example, or Dallas, or Kuwait, or… he strained to think of places in the world of which he had heard disgruntled friends speak ill… of which Felicity would most certainly speak ill. She was, after all, a writer and, as he had come to learn, she could not survive without the creation of adequate conflict in her life. It was unfortunate for him that the limitations of Namisan society obliged her to direct that conflict at him.

Measure for measure, Namisa was actually not so bad. Indeed, for the purposefully employed male, it could perhaps be a place of divine distractions. Namisan females, he had decided, were most pleasing to the eye. True that they could only be viewed from a distance and with great caution, but nevertheless, this was a risk he was willing to take. And what was more, after the bustle and the claustrophobia of London, the idea of spending long leisuresome hours in this haven of peace was not as awful as some would like to make out. There would be time to gather one's thoughts, time to plan a career, to catch up on reading, on TV soaps, on sleep. And for some – one person in particular – there would be time in abundance to complete that novel. As Philip saw it, Felicity should count herself fortunate.

There were moments when he berated himself for being so partner-dependent, but it was indisputably a matter of no bride, no job. A partnered Philip was to the critical Namisan eye preferable to the un-partnered Philip. He became less of a cultural liability. Namisans liked their foreigners married. Thus it was that when, back in London, Philip was short-listed, in that list of two, alongside that nauseating little rodent Danvers, and the fellow had smugly pointed out to him that he – Danvers – had completed two hardship posts in a row and got 'above expectations' on each of his last three appraisals, Philip was able to pull out his ace card. He remembered back to the day of the interview. Peering over Danvers' shoulder at his Suitability Profile, he commented with immense satisfaction and feigned innocence, 'Oh, I see you've ticked the single-status box. Isn't this post only for married candidates?'

What bliss it had been to see Danvers' face darken. 'You're not married,' he had said with a mixture of shock and disgust.

'Is that a question or a statement?' said Philip.

'But you're not married,' said Danvers. A statement.

'Engaged,' said Philip. 'And, if all goes well, we'll be honeymooning out there in Trinamisa.'

Philip was the panel's choice.

'On the understanding, of course,' Lady Downing had said at the briefing, 'that this ...', she had rifled through Philip's application papers, 'that this Miss Manning, is your permanent partner and that you'll eventually be tying the knot, preferably – of course – before you arrive in Namisa.' And, at this comment, she had looked around at Bryant and given a coy little laugh.

So, for Namisan purposes, with or without the existence of the Wedding Book, Philip and Felicity were '*lakati, bunga bunga*' – well and truly married, or in the literal translation, which Philip had copied neatly into his vocabulary notebook, 'spliced good good.'

After her initial enthusiasm, it had taken Felicity a little time to appreciate what she had let herself in for. Her creative juices were not in full flow. She had moved country, she had acquired a husband, she had fought for territory, she was struggling to survive a camping-out cooking experience. What she needed were lattes, a dry cleaner's, M & S ready meals, Portobello Road, Pret á Manger, Chinese take-aways and the camaraderie of the Society of Authors.

'It's like this, Philip,' she had told him with infinite patience. 'My novel-in-progress is set in Ladbroke Grove. I am having some difficulty writing Namisa into the plot. I could, I suppose, have the characters fly out to Trinamisa to buy camels.'

Blame for the imminent West London Trilogy disaster was being batted back and forth between the two of them. Philip was happy. Felicity, it seemed, was not… and Philip was beginning to feel unhappy in direct proportion to Felicity's apparent unhappiness. When night fell, they each closed themselves in their respective bedrooms and slept on the disagreements of the departed day. Felicity's light would remain on until the early hours. Philip would extinguish his immediately, after which he would fall into a deep sleep in which his dreams were inhabited by images of box files, of undulating girls and of fast-moving long-legged insects.

Felicity had all the characteristics of a neglected wife, ignored by a selfish and wayward husband. But did Philip think that Felicity could have improved with the kind of TLC that came with married life? No, he did not. In truth, marriage would have been the last thing on his mind. He wanted to keep his career flowing and his options open. His faux bride, too, was in it for the exotic locations and the diplomatic perks. In this sense he saw that they were of like mind but, in addition to her damaged plot, Felicity hadn't counted on the flawed Namisan scenario. There was no Merc, only a green Cinquecento. There was no villa with a pool. There was only this regulation bungalow with hand-me-down furniture and intermittent running water. She was bound to have been disappointed. Philip was sure that she would mellow once she had done some restructuring of her plots. But the bugs and the humidity were getting to her. Her keyboard was sticky and her notepads were moist.

Philip left early for the Medical on the understanding that the disgruntled author would follow on after she had finished negotiating the plastic jerry cans and pans of water and had emerged refreshed and sober from the bathroom. In the interests of risk limitation, he had already given her strict instructions not to circulate without him, or even to initiate conversation. He left a note on the kitchen table while she was in a huff outside, peeling dead fronds from the *yellibellee* tree.

See you at the Medical.

Ratni will pick you up at 7:00pm.

Cheers, Philip

With luck, water would flow again at midnight when the plastic containers would be refilled and the toilet would be flushed.

***

7

A GOOD MEDICAL

'Namisan met Pundari on flight to London,' recounted one of the male doctors. '"Why are trees tall and people small in your land?" Pundari asked Namisan.'

The doctors were freeze-framed around their stand-up colleague. Bryant hunched above them, leaning in for the punchline like an eager bloodhound.

'Replied Namisan, "For same reason are trees small and people tall in your country."'

The company burst into raucous laughter. Tears of mirth rolled down Bryant's reddened face. '*Ah jej bunga. Joga mumba mumba!*' he exclaimed. He slapped Philip heartily on the back and he too laughed. They were standing in the middle of the huge salon that represented the focal point of Bryant's residence. It was this very room that had featured in the February edition of *Namisan Homes and Gardens*, more than one copy of which graced the glass and wrought-iron side-tables that framed the space.

Philip had a sense that his absorption into Namisan society might be more difficult than he originally thought. It was not so much the language that would obstruct him, he felt, but after this initial period in Namisa – and whatever the merits of his degree in psychology – he was no wiser as to the intricate workings of the Namisan mind. What made Namisans tick? Indeed, what hidden insight made *them* laugh and left *him* stony faced? Perhaps this shift, this upheaval, the transfer to Namisa, the overwhelming responsibilities of married life, had changed him … made him old and humourless.

Bryant lurched from group to group indiscriminately, his long arms flailing, his voice booming and cackling at the Namisan jokes that were contributed excitedly by his invitees. Philip set aside his concerns and allowed himself to be heartened by this merriment. Watching Bryant circulate with such competence, he felt his mood lift. Glass in hand, he joined to listen in.

*

Felicity scoffed. She flicked through the pages of the guide. This was absolute tosh.

When young ladies are taking up residence alone, for work or study, in a new

country – and Namisa is indeed a new country, having gained its independence just a few years ago in 1961 – it is always advisable for them to consult a publication of some authority, such as this volume of 'The Lady Traveller's Guide to Namisa.' It goes without saying that observing correct behaviour ensures acceptance by the host country and guarantees a trouble-free sojourn on the island.

(Extract from 'Introduction,' (p.vi) to *The Lady Traveller's Guide to Namisa: understanding etiquette,'* by Michael Robinson-Smith.)

Yes, granted that this particular volume was an old edition, but she had seen later editions and they could hardly be said to be improving. It seemed to her that Robinson-Smith had just kept churning out the same old nonsense. She could easily have written something a great deal better than this herself – and with her eyes shut – and *she* had only just arrived. Robinson-Smith was a prat and a charlatan, and if she ever met him, she would tell him so. There were no other writers of guides to Namisa. He had the monopoly and he seemed to have had it for a very long time. It looked as though there was no one within Namisa or without, except perhaps for the representatives of the Ministry of Information, who might dispute his words. She and other hapless visitors had to take it that his blather was correct. Like her, this Robinson-Smith was writing fiction. Yes, perhaps on this score they had something in common. What Namisa needed now was a new-generation travel book, something that respected the intelligence and independence of modern travellers, be they male or female – but particularly female. Robinson-Smith and his ilk were relics of the dark ages of tourism.

Felicity walked to the kitchen waste bin, stepped on its yellow pedal and made to drop the book inside, but then it occurred to her that there might be some morsel of meat in this volume, something to feed her imagination… and anyway she did not like destroying the printed word. That was the truth of it. It seemed like a form of murder – bookicide. She let the lid drop and she carried poor old Robinson-Smith, circa 1965, back to her worktable. She browsed more slowly this time, thumbing through this archaic and weathered copy of *The Lady*

Traveller's Guide to Namisa, bought second-hand for 5p in the Portobello Road. She became engrossed, stopping at the sections on 'Cultural Sensitivity' and 'Dress Code'. She studied at length the glossy colour illustrations of Namisan women in a range of unalluring outfits. What Namisa needed in addition to travel writers were fashion designers, unless they had moved on since this book was published, which was highly likely, though how could she possibly know since she had scarcely seen a Namisan woman, let alone discussed the meaning of shoes or handbags with one. Without going out into society herself, she was seriously disadvantaged. For all she knew – despite her accusations – Robinson-Smith may just have got some of this right, and if that were the case, she would be seriously annoyed. Earlier Internet searches had brought to her attention the fact that a very recent revised edition of this text, *The Woman Traveller's Guide to Namisa*, was available, and she had ordered a copy on Amazon. She regretted depositing her money in the bottomless pockets of Robinson-Smith, who must certainly be one of Namisa's major beneficiaries as well as one of its oldest. Come to think of it, he must be ancient by now. She should feel sorry for the old codger. Anyhow, she was curious to see this new edition and to ascertain whether or not Robinson-Smith had recalibrated his understanding of women. There was no indication how long it might take for international mail to reach this backwater. For now, she must grit her teeth and depend on the old edition to provide her with a few elementary guidelines on matters of dress and manners. Better to be safe than sorrily deported.

*

Travellers, tourists, whoever you are that come here... I agree that you shouldn't believe everything people tell you about Namisans – especially our Namisan women. Perhaps you will read these things in your guidebook, but truly that is not where you will find the answers and the explanations. You will need to go and find out for yourself, though I can understand that it is easier to find one version of the story and make it your own, and say, 'The Namisans are like this and this and this.' Once you know that, then you have your bearings and you can tell your friends and family all about it when you get home. If that is what it pleases you to do.

I'm not so young that I can't work this out for myself. I've been there myself and what I've found out is that the guidebook is not the territory.

*

The Medical was a jovial affair. Philip learned from Bryant that the doctors and leading practitioners of the Trinamisa School of Medicine and the Namisan Society of Apothecaries were always keen to attend this prestigious event. They relished the cocktails as much as Philip now needed his. The salon buzzed with their voices and reverberated with laughter.

'Philip!' cried Bryant, whose cheeks glowed with colour, 'come and meet Dr. Jonnan.' He presented an elf-like man, short and broad, with a goatee beard.

Philip shuffled forward. 'A pleasure,' he said, bowing

in the Namisan way, as he had been instructed at his all-too-brief induction in London. The doctor mirrored the bow and Philip secretly rejoiced that in the matter of manners at least he was making some progress.

'Dr. Jonnan is one of TSM's most renowned specialists,' said Bryant as though singing the praises of a favourite son.

'Really?' said Philip. 'And what do you specialise in?'

'Haemorrhoids,' said the doctor grinning.

Philip recoiled.

'You are British, *na na*? Most clients expats from your embassy. Here my card,' said Dr. Jonnan, offering it up to Philip with two yellow-stained thumbs. 'You will need,' he said with disturbing confidence.

Philip looked to Bryant for reassurance but saw that he had already darted to the opposite side of the room and was chortling at a new series of jokes. Philip winced and took the card graciously. He mumbled a smiled excuse, bowed a parting Namisan bow and moved in the direction of a neighbouring group, leaving Dr. Jonnan to explain a new medical procedure to a colleague. It was then that Philip spotted Ratni, who was hovering by the finger food with all the air of someone who is about to rob a bank. Ratni looked up and their eyes met. Philip tapped his watch and moved closer. '*Om* Ratni,' he said. 'It's time to go back.'

Ratni cast a soulful glance at the buffet table. Philip selected a plump canapé, sank his teeth into it and munched.

'Now listen carefully, *Om* Ratni,' said Philip as he enjoyed his snack. 'Go to the house. Get the *Imee*. Bring the *Imee* here and bring her directly to me. Do you understand? Come and get me, but don't let the *Imee* out of the car until I arrive.'

Ratni looked angry. 'I knowing my job,' said Ratni. 'I taking *Imee* in car, then out of car, then in *Om* Bryant residence.'

'No,' said Philip, 'Just listen.' He selected another canapé. 'You take the *Imee* from the house. You arrive at the residence. You call me. I come and I take the *Imee* from the car into *Om* Bryant's residence. On no account let her leave the car before I arrive.'

'Ok,' said Ratni, 'I let she leave car before you arriving.'

'No!' said Philip, 'What I said was "on no account let her leave the car."'

'What account? You need account?'

'Look,' said Philip, 'you drive. *Imee* in car. You arrive. *Imee* in car. You come find me. I come to car. I take *Imee*.'

'*Bunga*,' said Ratni more incensed than before. '*Imee* wait in car. Why you not say this before? Now I late.' He turned on his heel and headed out towards the car park.

'Right. Good,' said Philip and he loosened his tie to let air circulate around his reddened neck, and then waited to regain his composure. He didn't feel like any more snacks. He needed some quiet time. Taking in the rest of the room, Philip now noted that the male doctors lingered with the male doctors, and that the female doctors, glowing and sparkling in their gold and finery, hovered with the other female doctors. Everyone was busy. He wasn't missed. Replenishing his drink seemed to be the best course of action. He altered direction and made his way to the liquor table. Scanning the room, as he quietly enjoyed a glass of aromatic Namisan punch, he concluded that Namisans were a trifle plump, not especially tall, and a sort of nut-brown colour. In some cases, they had goatee beards or little moustaches. The men, that is, not the women. He thought about this for a moment or two, then decided to discard any attempts at ethnographic research until he had a wider sample of subjects and a few more swigs of punch.

His plan was to keep a low profile, make a few more detours via the drinks table and then quietly disappear until Felicity's arrival. He could relax in the garden, or find a little nook where he could put his feet up and read the newspaper. But, while returning through what he expected to be a secluded corner of Bryant's lavish residence, he stumbled upon a group of older female doctors seated in an arc of comfortable lounge chairs. His cover was blown.

'And so you are *Om* Pilip,' said one of them. 'We have been looking forward to your arrival ever since we heard that *Om* Jonathan would not be returning.'

'Yes, that was very disappointing,' said another. 'It is so important to the medical profession for the Foundation to have a presence here in Namisa.'

'Quite true,' said another of the doctors. 'You see, *Om* Pilip, Thanks to the Foundation's connections, our Namisan specialists have been travelling the world over. Let me be introducing myself,' said the doctor, 'I am Dr. Roopata.' She was a large-faced woman, with droopy eyes. She resembled, or Philip thought, a cross between a basset hound and an oversized turnip … but she was pleasant nonetheless.

'I am Director of Namisan National Institute of Alternative Therapy,' she told him in a breathy voice. 'I am founding member of Institute.'

'Amazing,' said Philip. 'I had no idea you used alternative therapies here in Namisa.'

'*Ah jej*,' asserted Dr. Roopata, 'Namisa has very rich heritage of unique remedies for many ailments: Pundari donkey sickness, tree rash, and now new mobile phone- and Internet-related maladies … like empty head and blank-eye sickness. I think you must know them, *na na*? Many parents they are bringing children to us. Also, depressions and sadness, common among ex-pats, love sickness – mostly illnesses of ladies – and of course jealousy, being great *bushkil* for our Pundari brothers. *Om* Pilip, you must visit us sometime.'

Philip was intrigued, but also a little worried about 'empty head,' from which he was now certain he must have suffered intermittently since childhood. Too late, then, to take preventative medicine, but perhaps there were other courses of action. He was chewing this over, wondering if he should seek advice and treatment, when there was a sudden disturbance at the entrance to the main lounge.

Across the room, Bryant raised his head in the direction of the fracas and assumed a serious and troubled demeanour. Philip made the humblest of Namisan bows and excused himself from the presence of Dr. Roopata and her colleagues.

'Oh, *bummer,*' mumbled Bryant as Philip approached. 'I should have expected as much.'

A short rotund man, wearing a neatly-cut grey double-breasted suit and a red tie, was standing in the doorway, his pathway into the busy area blocked by a lofty Pundari security guard. The new arrival had a dark, oily complexion, and the flickering generator-controlled lights of the residence reflected off his bald pate. Philip noted his thick, broad neck and the fine growth of black hair at his temples, neatly trimmed in the Namisan style. The man's face was bent into a frown and his thin, black moustache pointed down in glumness at both ends. As soon as he saw Bryant striding across the room towards him, his face shone, and he gave the guard a brisk tap on the arm and pointed with the open palm of his hand at his host as if to say, 'See!'

'Ito, my dear boy! What a surprise!' exclaimed Bryant, looping his arm through the man's. 'I had no idea you were in town. We were expecting you next week.'

'*Om Baadumba* Bryant, you know I cannot resist a Medical, and to see my friends at the Foundation gives me the pleasure of a thousand peacocks.'

'You must forgive us, *Om Baadumba* Bogadan … my dear friend Ito, this was an oversight for which I shall shed a month of tears. The problem is that we have a new Officer of Culture and Education and he was lacking in his reading of our Honoured Guests' book.'

Philip had not misheard. Wasn't *he* the new Officer of Culture and Education? And what was this about reading an Honoured Guests' book?

Bryant signalled to the guard. '*Bis bis*', he said sharply. 'Bring me the Guest List.'

'You will see, my dear Ito, that the mistake will be corrected and our Officer will pay dearly.'

Philip shuffled backwards into the shade of a large potted plant.

Bryant drew a black and silver pen from his breast pocket and, with a flourish, he added Bogadan's name to the typed list of eminent physicians that the guard held before him in an embossed leather folder.

'This fellow who is lacking,' said Bogadan, surveying the room, his brow crinkled, 'Where is he? He must learn who's who. This could have been making a highly embarrassing incident.'

'Come,' said Bryant, 'I have some excellent Pundari Cabernet Merlot.' He directed Bogadan towards the table of fine wines at the rear of the salon, distancing him in haste from thoughts of the Foundation's lacking-ness.

Philip watched as Bryant, towering over his guest, engaged in animated conversation with him. He knew he would need to make himself known to Bogadan at some stage whatever the risks, and there was no time like the present. Philip approached through the clustered Namisans, but as he made visual contact with Bryant, he noted his superior's violent eye movements and the tic-like jerking of his head.

'No,' mouthed Bryant. No, this was not the time for join up.

Bogadan, meanwhile, glass in hand had begun a routine inspection of Bryant's new acquisitions – an ancient Namisan vase here, a primitive Pundari miniature there.

Philip stepped out onto the terrace and into the humid evening air filled with the diverse aromas of *pinga panga*, *perribinda*, *chikalika*, and *dingamalee*. He closed his eyes to absorb the sounds, the sounds of the Namisan night ... hooting, clicking, croaking, hissing. He opened his eyes. From the shrubbery, someone was hissing at him.

'Hello?' said Philip.

'I am Ratni,' said a voice.

'Yes, Ratni, is something wrong? Did you bring *Imee* Felicity?'

Ratni emerged from the undergrowth. 'I bring, but maybe you check she okay. She very strange lady. She go now main entrance.'

Philip hurried around the side of the building, all the while cursing under his breath. How could Ratni have been so stupid as to let her out? And as for Felicity herself, why couldn't she follow a simple directive not to go anywhere or to speak to anyone without him? The last thing he wanted was for Bryant or for the Foundation staff to hear two conflicting accounts of his and Felicity's past life together. He couldn't have her fictionalising their relationship without being present to hear and correct her. He did a circuit of the house, arriving breathless at the main entrance. Felicity was nowhere to be seen.

He re-entered the building in a blind panic and came face to face with Bryant.

'Ah! There you are, Philip,' said Bryant. 'I was wondering where you'd got to. I've just this minute met your wife and she really is quite enchanting.' With a nod of his head he indicated a group of diminutive Namisan doctors at the back of the room. A tall woman in a floor-length crushed velvet dress stood in their midst holding court. Over her head was a length of black gauze, giving her the appearance of an escapee from an obscure religious order.

As if detecting his stare, she turned, smiled at him – rather smugly he thought – and gave him a little wave. She had not heeded the female-with-female protocol and held these men in thrall. Philip noted with troubled fascination that she was a giant among men.

'She can be a bit outspoken at times,' said Philip.

'Oh, can she?' said Bryant, viewing Felicity from afar and looking very pleased with himself.

'And, as yet, she's not up to speed with cultural expectations, dress code and so forth, so if there's a problem, I can take her home.'

'Goodness, no,' said Bryant. 'She's getting along brilliantly. If anything, she's exceedingly charismatic.' He continued to watch for a moment, his face full of admiration. 'I have to say she's proving quite a hit with the boys.'

The sound of Felicity's laughter reached them from across the room. Philip was at a loss to understand why *he* wasn't such a hit with the boys, or the girls for that matter.

'You'll excuse me for a moment,' said Bryant. 'I need to attend to Bogadan. I'll catch you later.' Again he looked admiringly at Felicity. 'There are so many questions I want to ask your wife.' But with that he was gone, disappearing into the throng of guests.

A sense of rejection overwhelmed Philip. He picked up a copy of the *Daily Mail*, and with a heavy heart, went back through the French windows, hiked to the rear of the garden and sat on a lounger by Bryant's illuminated swimming pool, imagining that it was his house and his garden and his pool. And, he decided that, as soon as he had finished reading the newspaper he would return to the fray and continue where he had left off. For the moment, his charming and charismatic wife would represent him. He tugged the newspaper open with force and ripped the page.

*

Replenished and informed, Philip returned to the reception barely thirty minutes later. Bryant was accompanying Bogadan around the room, integrating him into this group and that, and plying him with Namisan Shiraz from the newly established Dilla Vineyards. It was only a question of time before the two found themselves face-to-face with Philip at the now much-depleted buffet table.

'Philip Blair, the new Officer of Culture and Education,' explained Bryant.

Bogadan looked Philip up and down with distaste and appeared ready to launch an attack.

'Philip will be dealing with the arrangements for your summer attachment,' said Bryant.

Bogadan lightened almost instantly. 'Ah *jej*,' he exclaimed, 'this is very good news. Then, with your help, *Om* Pilip, I am most certainly looking forward to the summer.'

Philip looked to Bryant for guidance.

'The attachment, Philip,' he said, his eye twitching, and then, 'You must excuse me, my dear Ito. I do believe Dr. Niwari is leaving. Give me a minute while I see him off.' And with that he darted away.

Bogadan gazed at Philip with an enigmatic smile on his lips. Philip gazed back. A moment of quiet contemplation passed between the two of them.

'Would that be …?' proffered Philip, 'would that be your summer or our summer?'

'Your summer. Which is a little like our winter,' said Bogadan, as though the question were not unexpected.

From the far side of the salon came Felicity's laughter. She had melted into a sofa and was surrounded by admirers. Philip stood opposite Bogadan, feeling a certain incomprehension.

'In the hills,' said Bogadan by way of explanation. 'Our winter in the hills. *Dillabinso. Binso*, winter – *dillabinso*, hill winter. In your country you have *dillabinso* in the summer so to speak.'

'Do we?' said Philip. He looked around for Bryant, but he was nowhere to be seen.

Bogadan smirked. 'Yes, you do,' he said. 'I can see, *Om* Pilip, that we have much to discuss, and that you will certainly enjoy to learn about our most beautiful country.'

A peal of laughter reached them from the sofas.

Bogadan looked over his shoulder and Philip saw his eyes narrow in a flash of predatory thought.

Almost distractedly Bogadan said, 'I am hoping that *Om* Bryant will be introducing me to that doctor that I am not seeing before.'

Philip followed the direction of his stare and watched as Felicity flipped back her gauze veil so that she could look in her bag for her pack of Galloises. She tapped open the pack, selected a cigarette and pushed it between her lips. An array of cigarette lighters shot out from members of her entourage.

'That,' said Philip, 'is not a doctor. That is my wife.' He looked Bogadan directly in the eyes. Bogadan did not blink. He smiled and continued sipping what was his third glass of Namisan Shiraz, before remarking, 'Your wife, *Om* Pilip, she is very fine and exceptional woman and, I am sure, intelligent also – very *baadee* – for selecting man such as you. May I compliment you on your choice of woman?'

*

Philip drove himself and Felicity home that night, after having prised the keys of the Cinquecento from Ratni's iron fist. Sitting next to him in the passenger seat, Felicity hummed far too happily for his liking. He hardly wanted her developing a taste for gatherings of this kind. He reflected on three facts that had emerged. Firstly, that Bogadan was going to be sticking to him like glue now that he knew for sure he was to have a summer attachment and that, potentially, he might have much more. Secondly, he was coming to the realisation that he was going to be on his own in dealing with this responsibility. It was clear from Bryant's behaviour that he had rather too swiftly dumped Bogadan into the lap of his new Officer of Culture and Education. Thirdly, it occurred to him that he was going to have to safeguard his wife from the unwelcome interest of third parties. As the Cinquecento bumped its way along the potholed road to the bungalow, Philip gave Felicity a cursory glance, and for a moment it seemed to him that he saw her in a new light under the pale Namisan moon.

'What?' she said, ceasing her humming.

'Nothing,' he said.

***

8

OF FLIES AND COLD MICE

In the weeks that followed the Medical, Bogadan saw to it that his relationship with Philip was duly consolidated. For his part, Philip found it difficult to ascertain to what extent Bogadan's flattery was spontaneous and to what extent it was calculated for the purpose of personal gain. How genuine, for example, was Bogadan's interest in Philip's immersion into the Namisan culture? And, in continuing to sing Felicity's praises, after just that one sighting at the Medical, was he showing a true appreciation of Philip's good taste, or pandering to Philip's own vulnerable vanity? Fortunately for Philip, Felicity was not aware that he had gained kudos for wisely selecting her above all others as his companion.

Philip still had his wits sufficiently about him not to forget his original mission on behalf of the Foundation. He needed to establish Bogadan's intentions. But … Bogadan's intentions about what, he asked himself? At this point he was flummoxed, since it appeared to him that Bogadan had no intentions. Bryant had put forward the unexpected proposal of a summer attachment and, having latched onto that, Bogadan seemed entirely satisfied. Was all this anxiety about Bogadan, fed to him by Bryant, a product of paranoia accumulated over too many years in the same obscure foreign location? Philip had been given the impression that he would be dealing with a greedy and manipulative individual and what he found was a caring and indulgent friend.

*

At Bogadan's insistence, the two met regularly in Bogadan's favourite watering spot, the Shangri-La Bi Dillin, Trinamisa.

'I know it very well,' said Philip.

'Ah, but no. I can tell you now that you are knowing very little,' said Bogadan. 'The name, for example. *Bi*, it is meaning "among" or "between,"' explained Bogadan. '*Dillin*, of course, comes from *dilla*, meaning "hill"… *dillin* is "two hills." The hotel is "between two hills."'

'Fascinating,' said Philip, his eyes glazed as he sipped his second Blue Namisan Moon cocktail. 'But, in fact, if I'm not mistaken, I believe there are three hills around the Shangri-La, two on one side and one on the other side.'

Bogadan looked concerned. 'You are right, my friend *Om* Pilip, there are indeed three hills and the name should rightly be *Bi dillinda*, *dillinda* being "three hills," but you must know, and this is most important, that "three," the number *da*, is not a propitious number in Namisan folkloric culture. Interestingly, we find that the third wife is never a good wife, which is perhaps why Namisans try to – let us say – 'know' at least three women prior to their marriage. The number "four," *tree* in Namisan, is most propitious. Of course, I am talking to you of our ancient beliefs and customs. You will not find much of this now in Trinamisa. A wife is thankful for not being number *da,* but she will be annoyed for eternity to know that she is number *tree.* So, the excellent proprietors of the Shangri-La are most wise to acknowledge this fact of the numbers in the naming of their hotel, correct?'

'I think I'll have another cocktail,' said Philip.

Time spent with Bogadan could be as delightful as this. Philip, when he was adequately sober, saw that his friend – for Bogadan was now most certainly his friend – had a keen wit and a natural talent for imparting knowledge. The fact that the knowledge was not always received at Philip's end was no reflection on Bogadan's ability to transmit. Philip felt that the money spent on Bogadan's upcoming summer attachment would be well-spent. Bogadan, whilst a heavy drinker, maintained an air of sobriety at all times. His moods were reflected in the movement of his small hairline moustache, which, Philip learned, was immaculately trimmed and threaded weekly at the Thrifty Hair & Chin Fashion Saloon. As Philip studied this moustache, he was reminded of the smiley icons on his computer. Bogadan himself had a jolly smile that could change like the wave of a Namisan sand dune. The Thrifty Hair & Chin Fashion Saloon must also have been responsible, Philip decided, for Bogadan's olive-coloured baby skin. Some men in these parts displayed a heavy growth of facial hair and a rough complexion, but Bogadan's flesh appeared smooth and oily.

'*Om* Pilip, are you well?' remarked Bogadan. 'You are seeming a little tired today.'

It was not so much the pressure of the job that was getting to Philip, as the culture, and the beguiling range of Namisan cocktails. In fact, both the culture and the cocktails were beguiling. In Philip's mind, both were inextricably linked to Bogadan.

Philip was seriously considering a visit to Dr. Roopata for a little alternative therapy to get him back on the straight and narrow. He could not, he had concluded, be suffering from empty head, but possibly from full head, which to his overloaded mind must be far worse than empty head if left untreated.

Colleagues might well have assumed that Philip relished the company of his new friend above the companionship of his own delectable and *baadee* Felicity. But it was through Bogadan that the mysteries of the Namisan mind were being revealed to him with the same velocity that he found himself initiated into the intricacies of the Namisan language. At last he was even beginning to enjoy some facility in the use of Namisan proverbs.

'It is a shame,' commented Bogadan, casually examining the label on his Armani tie, 'that *Imee* Felicitu does not join us here at *Bi Dillin*.'

It hadn't really crossed Philip's mind. It was, after all, a boy's night out. 'I thought,' he said, 'that she might feel a little uncomfortable in the presence of two men, one of whom was not her husband.'

Bogadan appeared a little disappointed, but after a moment's thought he nodded wisely and said, 'Indeed, for a fly knows more than a cold mouse.'

'Exactly,' said Philip, 'and … a cold mouse knows a lot less than a donkey.'

Bogadan's expression turned to one of immense surprise.

'But, my dear *Om* Pilip,' he said, 'we have no donkeys on Namisa.'

Philip remained poker-faced. He had been misinformed. There was an eternity of silence.

Bogadan's brow wrinkled in puzzlement.

'Horses,' said Philip.

'Ah,' said Bogadan, newly enlightened. 'That's absolutely right, absolutely right-right! Let me get you another cocktail.'

*

Does the man select the woman or does the woman select the man? Females in Namisa still seem to think they are lucky if they are 'chosen' like some commodity displayed on Nam-eBay. Do they really believe that their lives will only be complete once they are selected? And what if they're letting themselves in for a life of drudgery?

*

Felicity, it is true, had started out with the best of intentions. She saw this cohabitation as an opportunity to find her inner domestic goddess, which she supposed must reside somewhere deep within her. She owned one cookery book: *Delia Smith's Complete Illustrated Cookery Course*. When she removed it from one of her boxes, it was a little dusty from previous non-use, but in pristine condition. Occasionally when she had nothing to do, which was quite often, or was stuck for ideas, which was also quite often – increasingly so – she thumbed through it, smoothing her fingers across its thick glossy pages, and from time to time she imagined herself appearing in the doorway of her rustic Namisan kitchen, posing with some steaming dish of amazing culinary perfection. This was for the future. For now, she turned to the page on 'boiling an egg.' She would start small and perhaps dedicate half a day each week learning those specialist techniques that your average cook could not even imagine. This was how one achieved mastery. A typical scene illustrative of domestic bliss might run as follows:

> Philip returns from a not-especially tiring day at the office.
> Philip: What's for dinner tonight, darling?
> Felicity: Don't darling me.
> Philip: What's for dinner tonight?
> Felicity: Boiled eggs with mayonnaise.
> Philip (expressing hope): Home-made mayonnaise?
> Felicity (with a sneer): Hellman's.
> Philip: Oh good.

It had fallen to Felicity to seek out and identify the local amenities, a task which in those early days she did in good part and with energy and determination.

'There is good news and bad news,' she told Philip on the day that she first found the supermarket. Locating the supermarket and then finding her way back from it down the potholed road was the good news.

'The bad news,' she told Philip, 'is that there is no Marmite, no Shredded Wheat, no Bakewell Tarts, no Lemon Curd.' She marked with an asterisk in red biro all the items on Philip's list that she had been unable to find.

Philip buried his head in his arms. 'Oh God,' he said.

'I know what you're thinking,' said Felicity. 'You're thinking, "I can't survive out here without my treats."'

Philip shook his head back and forth without coming up for air.

'Philip. Listen to me, Philip. This is what living overseas is all about. Where is your sense of adventure?'

Felicity had – at that time – been a beacon of hope.

*

Felicity was not a little dismayed to see Philip tottering home after midnight several times a week in a state of alcohol-induced merriment. Her *West London Trilogy* was floundering and it was Philip's fault. He was having fun. She was not. She called him to order.

'Didn't you once think that I might like to come out partying too?' she asked him. 'Can't you see that there's nothing happening for me here? "Come to Namisa," you said, "you'll have a lovely time. It's a paradise out there!" Well, maybe it's a paradise for you, sitting around in that office chatting to all your ethnic friends and doing clever things, but have you any idea at all how it is for me? I don't have any friends, unless you count *Imee* Malitee from Number 66 and I can't count her because I don't speak the language and I don't know what she's talking about. I don't have any transport. Sometimes I don't have any electricity, and if I manage to get down that road to the supermarket – and yes, thank God they have a supermarket – if I manage to get down that road without falling into a hole, I can't read the labels on the food once I get inside the shop.'

It was a rant by any other name.

'I really think you're exaggerating,' said Philip, helping himself to Felicity's marmalade. 'You can't blame your writer's block on the supermarket. You see, Felicity, a bad workman blames his tools.'

Felicity gave him an icy stare. 'A supermarket is not a tool,' she said, 'and I am not a workman.'

The only satisfactory service Felicity had found so far in Trinamisa was the family-run dry cleaners at the bottom of the road. It was a very long road. In the window, unlike the other small shops, they displayed signs in Namisan script together with translations in English. Next to the signs were racks carrying swathes of neatly pressed multicoloured chiffon and, next to these, a row of Namisan turbans, skilfully wound and folded from those same materials. Every time she passed the shop, Felicity was transfixed by the array of elaborately woven garments hanging in orderly fashion inside. In the end, she could no longer contain her curiosity and, setting aside her linguistic apprehension, she carried in five of Philip's best shirts, a couple of pairs of his shorts, and her own most unfavorite skirt. Better to err with Philip's possessions than with her own. A young woman wearing a pair of heavy black-framed glasses greeted her with a traditional Namisan bow. With great delicacy she received Felicity's cleaning, and then requested that Felicity sit in a comfortable brocade-covered armchair while she brought her a freshly brewed pot of *cha cha*. This put Felicity, weary from her most recent supermarket foray, into a delightfully soporific state. The young woman, dressed demurely in a green sarong-like garment, sat at a desk and, pen in hand, she took considerable trouble to write out Felicity's dry-cleaning docket in a fine ornate Namisan script. At the top of the receipt, as Felicity noted when she later removed it from her purse, were the words 'SnowWhite Dry Kleen Shop.' In smaller letters below this were the words, 'Incorporating The SnowWhite Dry Kleen Coffee Circle and The SnowWhite Sandal Repair Service.'

Returning three days later, Felicity was greeted by a much older woman, well-padded around her middle, yet elegantly dressed in the European manner. She wore a pair of elaborately fashioned gold earrings, three gold rings, and two or three gold bracelets in different designs on both wrists. She jangled like a child's toy as she moved about behind the counter. Felicity rummaged in her bag, but the SnowWhite Dry Kleen Shop receipt could not be found. The woman waited patiently as Felicity removed all manner of objects from her bag: a herbal tea bag; half a tube of peppermints; a flash drive; three biros – one red, two blue; a notebook; keys; a stapler; a TV remote – picked up in error instead of her mobile phone; a pocket Namisan-English dictionary – edited by Robinson-Smith; miscellaneous scraps of paper; a lipstick; a weathered toothbrush; another notebook. Felicity grew increasingly flustered.

'Just one moment, my dear,' said the woman. 'Please take a seat.'

Felicity gathered her knick-knacks and sank into the familiar armchair. The woman disappeared amongst the racks of clothes, leaving them swaying and swishing. A minute later she re-emerged with five shirts, two pairs of shorts and Felicity's one unfavourite skirt, all of them impeccably cleaned and pressed, and presented on white enamelled hangers.

'There you are, my dear,' said the woman.

'My goodness,' said Felicity. 'How clever you are! How did you know this was my cleaning?'

'Well, my dear,' explained the woman. 'It's just that so very few Namisans wear safari shorts.'

*

For his earlier transgressions, Philip was put on food-shopping duty. He agreed to the task as a matter of honour, to prove that he could do anything that Felicity could do, but with greater proficiency. In the supermarket, he tipped boxes and tetrapacs this way and that, trying to fathom out the meaning of the curly Namisan script on the labels. Some letters, in less ornate script, he managed to decipher and he mouthed these slowly in sequence, hoping he would not be taken for a half-wit, and that he might recognise a familiar word or two … but it was all Dutch to him. How he had taken Tesco's and Waitrose for granted! It was, of course, to the credit of the Namisan nation that they were well able to produce so many of their own foodstuffs and cater to their own needs.

Philip noted that while the Namisan shoppers were adept at filling their trolleys, they navigated them poorly to the check-out. This was less to do with the mechanics of the trolleys than with the incompetence of their drivers. Trolleys would veer recklessly towards him from the other side of the aisle only to divert and skim past him at the last moment. As it was on the roads of Trinamisa, so it was in the aisles of the Trinamisan supermarkets. It was only after a number of near misses that Philip succeeded successfully in bringing home the bacon.

Felicity, however, was quick to spot the flaws in Philip's shopping techniques.

'What's this on my toast?' Philip asked one morning at breakfast.

'Lard, my dear, lard. I'm told it's the new butter!'

With food shopping under his belt, Philip was better able to survive cohabitation. However, it was just a few days after the lard incident that some unexpected elements of change began to enter his life.

***

9

THE IDES OF AUTUMN

'So, Philip, how are things going with Bogadan?' asked Bryant. Philip noted that it was one of his boss's off-days. He was slumped in his chair, looking dejected.

'Extremely well,' said Philip. 'He's invited me to the University. I thought I'd pop up there and take a look next week.'

'Mmm …,' said Bryant.

'You know … to get a handle on the situation, see how the tertiary sector works around here.'

'Or not,' mumbled Bryant. He stared ahead, tapping his fingers on the desk. 'Well, I suppose if you're going up there, you'll need to see the paperwork.' He opened a drawer and pulled out some documents. He looked through them, selected a pink folder and tossed it across the desk. 'It's Jonathan's,' he explained. 'Now that Jonathan's moved on, you'll need to start reviewing how far he's got with his various projects. No doubt Bogadan will have told you about Jonathan's role in TUDI.'

'No…,' said Philip hesitantly. 'TUDI is …?'

'Short for "Trinamisa University Development Initiative,"' said Bryant, staring long and hard at Philip. 'You'll see, Philip, that Bogadan keeps his cards close to his chest. Do not be surprised by anything you learn here on in, and bear in mind that Bogadan is not as transparent as he seems.'

A chilling thought occurred to Philip. 'When Jonathan left…?' He paused not knowing how to phrase his question.

'Yes?' said Bryant.

'I mean, did his going have anything to do with TUDI?'

Bryant pursed his lips and looked pained. 'I can only say that Jonathan and Caroline have been posted to Tblisi.' There was a brief silence.

'I see,' said Philip.

'He was relocated – shall we say – in some haste.'

'Oh,' said Philip.

'Yes,' said Bryant, 'and therefore he was unable to dispose of a number of his possessions prior to leaving. Since he won't be coming back and you are his successor, I suggest that you take these over along with the contents of his filing cabinet and his desk drawers.' Bryant rose from his chair and stood at the window staring out. Nothing was to be had from Jonathan's desk drawers, as Philip was well aware. Unless he counted the Sleepy Hollow matchbox. 'If you should come across any personal items,' said Bryant, turning away from the window, 'then, of course, we can arrange for them to be sent over.' Avoiding eye contact, Bryant took out his handkerchief and blew his nose. 'Ratni has a few items in safekeeping, which he'll bring over to you later on today.'

Philip took his cue. Picking up the TUDI folder, he said, 'Well, must go. Lots to do. Catch you later,' and hurried back to his office.

*

At 3:30 on the dot, Ratni brought him the cage and the rubber squeaky toys. 'He is belonging to *Om* Jonatan,' explained Ratni, 'and now you are take him.'

Philip looked aghast at the contents of the cage. 'I don't think so,' he said.

'My wife not want no good *Babbigall* bird,' said Ratni. He slammed the cage down on the floor and left the room.

Philip peered into the cage. A large bird stared out at him. Its grey feathers puffed out and then flattened as though he had been inflated and then deflated by an invisible bicycle pump. A ragged piece of beige card, once a luggage label, dangled from the top of the cage. It read, 'Parrot Wordsworth.'

'Hello,' said Philip. 'Who's a pretty boy then?' The bird sat hunched on its soiled perch. 'Hello … Parrot,' ventured Philip.

The bird uttered a low fearsome growling sound and then wings flapping like a prehistoric raptor, it squalled, 'Stop it! Stop it! I said stop it!' After which it gave out a high-pitched never-ending scream.

'Stop it!' said Philip.

'Stop it!' said Parrot.

The door of Philip's office burst open. Tiki stood in the doorway. 'That's quite enough,' she said. 'Will you two please try to keep the noise down? Some of us have work to do!'

Philip and Parrot fell silent.

*

Fitting Parrot's cage into the Cinquecento seemed plausible at the outset. Philip opened the door and fiddled with the front passenger seat. Then, as Parrot lunged violently at his fingers, he attempted to edge the cage in through the door. No joy there.

'Stop it!' said Parrot.

'Oh, shut up,' said Philip and continued to push the cage where it would not go. He stopped for breath. His encounter with Parrot was becoming stressful. He tried again. This time he tipped the cage on its side. Parrot fell off its perch and screeched loudly. Then as Philip tried to right the cage, it said, 'You bastard. I hate you!' and it clamped its beak onto Philip's left index finger.

'Okay, that's it,' said Philip.

Parrot came home to Felicity, its cage tied and knotted to the roof rack of the Cinquecento. Philip emerged grimly from the car, a paper hankie wrapped around his bloodied finger.

'You bastard,' squawked the windswept parrot. The voice was distinctly female. 'You bastard. I'll get you for this,' it said.

*

When Philip later reflected on the events of that evening, he realised it was all the fault of Parrot. He had looked upon his visit to the Shangri-La as being a necessary recuperation from the trauma of the afternoon. Bogadan appeared unsurprised by his account of the Parrot delivery.

'Yes, a parrot is a good idea,' said Bogadan, 'but really *Imee* Felicitu should be having babies, not parrots. She is not getting young. She is getting old. She is alone in house. She is not doing good works. She has much time given to thinking and thinking, and this can only bring problems. Too many *bushkilat,* in fact. Now, before time is finish, is good time to take action. In Namisa, we say *Hela pala, traka traka, Om* Pilip. I think you know what I am meaning.'

He and Philip were in their favourite spot next to the poolside bar. Philip's choice this evening from the cocktail menu was a Namisan Incantation. He had been feeling weightlessly blissful until this mention of babies.

'This is not possible, *Om* Bogadan,' said Philip blinking to regain focus.

Bogadan looked at Philip with pity in his eyes.

'You cannot *traka traka*?' he asked. 'But today there are cures. And you know yourself that here in Trinamisa we have the Institute of Alternative Therapies, which has many specialists in these area.'

'No, no,' said Philip. 'It's not about *traka traka*-ing. It's just that Felicity …'

'Yes?' said Bogadan, closing his eyes as he sipped pinkish liquid through a straw.

'Well, you see, Felicity is not *Imee* but *Imiteenee.*'

Bogadan gave a gasp and opened his eyes wide.

Philip felt only elation at that moment. In cocktail veritas. 'If she's *Imiteenee*,' he reasoned, 'and we are not *lakati*, then my guess is that we shouldn't be doing any *traka traka*-ing until she is *Imee*. Am I right?'

The olive baby skin on Bogadan's forehead furrowed. He put down his drink. 'Well, it all depends for the length of the string,' he said. 'Namisan law it is for Namisan and can be flexible. For example, important *om* has plans for big family, so good to know before *laka* ceremony that babies coming easy. But you are British, *Om* Pilip, and ...' Bogadan stopped to think for a moment, 'and you are with the Foundation, and you are in position of trust, and you are being one thing but you say you are being another thing.' He paused. 'This is not honest, *Om* Pilip. Why you not say anything about this to me?'

'So ... how big a *bushkil* is this?' asked Philip.

'Too big,' said Bogadan.

Philip saw that he was troubled.

But then his expression changed, and he smiled a slit of a smile. 'But I promise you, *Om* Pilip, that, with me, your secret is safe. As safe as inside the belly of the Sharra Fish.'

*

Flocky, the central character in Felicity's *West London Trilogy*, was now contemplating a transfer to a remote and exotic island.

> Her melancholic walks in Holland Park had led her to re-evaluate her life and the misguided choices she had made to date. An opportunity had arisen. A friend had offered Flocky the use of his villa overlooking a shore of undulating sands on the coast of a secluded island. She could stay for as long as she needed to recover from her recent acrimonious break-up with Roberto, an angst-ridden and narcissistic Italian professor.

Felicity thought she might delete either 'angst-ridden' or 'narcissistic.' She stopped to thumb through her thesaurus, but it was more difficult for her to find the words she was looking for … now that Jonathan's *Babbigall* bird had shredded so many of its pages. In the stillness and silence of the night, while Philip was Shangri-La-ing with Bogadan, Felicity felt uneasy alone in the bungalow with the bird, otherwise named Parrot. In the evenings Parrot was at its spookiest. Uncanny voices emanated from its immobile throat, deep distant voices and shrill squealing laments in alternation. It was as though the bird were possessed by the lost souls of previous owners, who were imprisoned within it for eternity to atone for their wickedness.

She continued to elaborate her story outline.

> Wandering down the narrow streets of the village one day, Flocky comes across a small café run by Mrs …

Mrs. Somebody or other. Felicity's fingers hovered over the chipped keys of her laptop. In addition to the lower blue plastic scroll button, Parrot had nibbled away the left-hand shift key. Felicity revised and deleted. It was fortunate for Parrot, she thought, that he or she – she was not sure which he or she was – had not completed his or her nibbling of the computer cable while it was still connected to the mains.

"Flocky comes across a small café," she wrote, "where she is befriended by Katrina, an elderly artist, a flamboyant character, an outsider.' Felicity liked outsiders, but was aware that she might have a few too many in her novel. Perhaps she should delete 'elderly.' Wasn't that a bit too ageist? Well, she would worry about that later. She continued, "Flocky is attracted by Katrina's insights and her very forthright opinions." She deleted 'very.' "… and her forthright opinions. It is in Katrina's company that she meets Charles, a mysterious stranger who, ironically, reminds her so much of the man she is trying to forget …"

Felicity looked up.

Parrot stared at her from its perch as she sat motionless in front of her computer screen. She looked back at Parrot. Then Parrot whistled at her.

'You very bad boy,' it said to her in a cute little Namisan voice. Then it whistled again, and laughed a very deep and manly laugh. 'Ha ha ha.'

Felicity shivered in the warmth of the Namisan night. A series of muffled voices, some high-pitched, some grunt-like, some almost eerily familiar, came at her as do the murmurings of bickering couples through the walls of a cheap hotel. Clearly now she heard a woman's voice. It spoke gently. It whispered, 'Darling, darling.' Felicity tensed. Parrot twisted its head sideways, giving her a weird and penetrating look with one beady eye. Its beak opened and then closed again as it uttered an almost imperceptible intake of breath followed by the sound of heavy breathing.

There was the sudden creak of a door.

'Hello! I'm home,' shouted Philip.

'Hello! I'm home,' shouted Parrot.

*

Now that I've travelled, now that I've lived abroad, now that I've come home and made some comparisons, I'd be more inclined to trust a foreigner than a Namisan. Let me make it clear that I'm talking here about men.

*

It was partly out of her concern for the safety of Parrot, and partly because of her fear of Namisan brown-outs that on one adventurous foray into the Trinamisa Tuesday market, Felicity saw fit to buy herself an old Olympia Splendid 33 – possibly abandoned by some equally tormented writer before her. Outside the Trinamisa Typing Centre, she came face-to-face with her fairly newish friend Mrs. Mitzee Katraree, she of the SnowWhite Dry Kleen Shop. Mrs. Katraree, who it transpired had strong reservations about the Pundari typewriter vendor, did not manage to dissuade Felicity from the purchase, but she did secure her promise to attend a future meeting of the SnowWhite Coffee Circle. There, Mrs. Katraree assured her, she would receive 'good advices about cultural matters as well as the purchasing of all things.'

For now, the possession of a typewriter, together with the presence of Parrot, she felt gave a more Hemingwayesque feel to her writing. So it was that under the slowly revolving ceiling fan, in the wavering light of the undecided electricity supply, and with her shirt sleeves rolled up to her elbows, she pounded at her typewriter keyboard with renewed energy and inspiration. West London shifted to Trinamisa, and Notting Hill Gate became but an indistinct memory.

***

10

THE POWER OF THREE

The early morning train from Nanamisa station was full of executives in elegantly cut suits made by the cream of Namisan tailors. Namisa was famous for its tailors, just as Pundar was famous for its taxi drivers. To Philip's relief, Ratni had not been free on this occasion to convey him to the University of Trinamisa in the outer regions of the city. Instead of journeying a long distance hunched up in the green Cinquecento with this permanently disgruntled employee of the Foundation, Philip could now look forward to another unique and enlightening cultural experience.

There had been no suitable opportunity as yet for Philip to broach the subject of TUDI with Bogadan. There had perhaps been too much talk of parrots, cocktails and babies. Today, though, was the day when Philip would take the bull by the horns and, using his favourite phrase in Namisan ... possibly the only one: *Hela pala, traka traka.*

Comfortably lodged in his seat, he began reading through Jonathan's paperwork relating to the University of

Trinamisa. Page 1 was headed, 'The TUDI Project, Innovation in Developmental Planning for Student, Faculty and Staff Welfare in Trinamisa – A Study of Impact, by Jonathan Wordsworth and Caroline Wordsworth.' This was a major piece of work, thought Philip. What clever people Jonathan and Caroline were! It was definitely worth reading ... and just before he slipped into a deep sleep, it occurred to him that somebody really ought to read it. Last night, from the bar menu, Philip had chosen a Namisan Shooting Star, probably more than one, and now as the train's movement lulled him to sleep, he had a sense that the shooting stars still circulated in his blood, and as they twirled their way through his veins, he heard them jingling and singing and clinking.

On board the express train to the rural suburb of Wunamisa, the air rang with the tones of mobile phones, a flock of mechanical birds from the urban centre. Voices rattled in the guttural, flapping Namisan tongue. Philip opened his eyes and noted that it was *snek* time. Close by, a minute Namisan opened a plastic container of pinkish rice speckled with chopped seafood, fish entrails and squashed mixed vegetables. He whispered a Namisan blessing over his food and offered the container to each of his travelling companions in succession. Each in turn gave a quick inclination of the head and muttered a ritual Namisan phrase declining the offer. On his limited travels Philip had never as yet seen anyone accept.

Philip gave a nod as his turn came and mumbled a polite refusal under his breath: '*Na na taka.*' The man stared at him in horror. Philip's neighbours, disturbed, turned to look at him. Philip perspired in the cool of the

Namisan air-conditioning. He quickly corrected himself: '*Na jej taka,*' he said, and for good measure, '*jej jej.*' Here it was … further proof that his Namisan was nowhere near up to scratch. The man looked relieved and his face spread into a wide smile. His teeth flashed. Philip's neighbours also smiled and laughed and chatted merrily amongst themselves. Philip smiled, reprieved, he realised, from a nasty diplomatic faux pas.

Throughout the rest of the journey Philip continued to thumb through the TUDI Project report. He sighed at the enormity of the task. He remembered how his mum had always told him never to read the end of a book before the beginning. He immediately turned to the back of the report, where he found a 'Questionnaire for TUDI teachers,' a 'Project Framework,' a chapter on the 'Ripple Effects of TUDI' and a section on 'Financial Guidelines and Projections.' From this last section he gathered, firstly, that the Foundation was paying a very large amount of money to the University and, secondly, that the purpose of this money was to maintain to a high standard the pay and conditions of the University's faculty, staff and students. By the time Philip stepped off the train, he understood everything, and a warm benevolent feeling washed over him. He was a representative of the Foundation, and the Foundation was sending a very positive, sustainable message to its Namisan partners.

On this day of his visit to the University of Trinamisa, Philip was met off the train by a university driver, to be conveyed to the university in a comfortable – though battered – Daewoo Lanos.

*

It is a known fact that the vast majority of Namisa's taxi drivers come from the neighbouring mountainous island of Pundar. It should be remembered that, whilst Pundar is a land of vertiginous crags and precipices, Namisa has only three hills, which in fact are counted as just two hills for the purpose of traditional beliefs. This means that the Namisans, through lack of opportunity, are generally considered to be less skilful in the art of driving. Initially, of course, driving as such was limited to the management of donkeys or horses – horses only in the case of the Namisans, since there are no donkeys on Namisa. There are, however, both donkeys and horses on Pundar.

For centuries, the Pundaris perfected the art of driving their animals fast and furiously along the narrow and treacherous paths of their mountainsides. Many a fine man and animal were lost, falling to their death from these lofty escarpments. In more recent years, the attempt by the Pundari government to impose speed restrictions or compulsory stopping points did little to lower the accident statistics. The Pundaris are a rough, tough race, and the speed and recklessness with which the menfolk traverse these rocky tracks have always been seen as a mark of manhood and bravery. It was this aptitude for driving in difficult conditions, honed over generations, with skills passed down from father to son, that made the Pundaris into a nation of taxi drivers par excellence.

While there exists a small cadre of Namisan taxi drivers in Namisa, these are by far fewer in number than Pundaris, who were quick to realise that driving cars in

Namisa brought greater riches than driving animals in Pundar. By contrast, there are no Namisan taxi drivers in Pundar, where there is little or no demand for taxis. Pundaris continue to come to Namisa for a better life and, in recent years, to exploit the influx of foreign expats to Namisa. In short, in Namisa there is a constant demand for Pundari drivers, be it in the state taxi sector or as private family or company drivers. Namisa has a thriving economy and it is well within the financial reach of even average families for them to be able to afford a Pundari driver.

The Namisans, who are for the most part a gentle folk, have suffered hardships in the past and are well able to deal with the fickleness of the short-tempered Pundaris. This is a feature of the Namisan character that often surprises foreigners. An otherwise mild-mannered Namisan can confidently silence a temperamental and troublesome Pundari with a few sharp and well-chosen words. These contrasting character traits of the Namisan and the Pundari are a key consideration in the recruitment of drivers by foreign nationals. As a rule of thumb, one can say that Namisans are generally calm and drive slowly and carefully, while Pundaris drive fast, heedless of the hazards of the road. Namisans arrive when they arrive, but Pundaris arrive at their destination ahead of time, though often the worse for wear. The same applies to their passengers.

(Extract from 'Transportation,' (p.123) in *Namisa - A Traveller's Guide: from tradition to tourism and back*,' by Michael Robinson-Smith.)

*

It's so easy to get into serious trouble if you are not aware of a country's customs. If anyone is visiting, though admittedly not many people do, I always refer them to Robinson-Smith's travel guide. I think we should be immensely grateful to him for explaining to outsiders about the importance of our traditions and superstitions. If visitors don't read up on Namisa before coming, well, then, they only have themselves to blame if they end up shamed, or even in jail.

*

Philip felt strangely exhilarated by the enjoyment of his journey and the anticipation of visiting a new place. As the car sped along the narrow roads of Wunamisa, he marvelled at the lush vegetation and the vast areas of green land. They passed large villas and attractive houses. Some were older more established buildings, having a certain antique grandeur, while others were newer, more adventurous constructions. Wunamisa was favoured by Namisa's professional classes.

Philip noted that many of the very large houses had lesser adjoining buildings, evidently for the purpose of housing staff. There was little or no crime on Namisa – or if there was – the newspapers did not report it. Nevertheless, every house they passed had its own security guard, who was to be seen either sitting comfortably outside the gates in an armchair or enclosed in a sentry-style box to one side of the gateway. High walls surrounded most of the houses and a variety of exotic plants and trees peeped above these boundaries, giving a hint of the garden paradises within.

The road began to slope upwards until it reached a more level plain from where greater expanses of land, less verdant now, could be seen. As the car's velocity increased, Philip's view of the land became a sandy blur. The engine growled and juddered and then the forward motion of the vehicle pinned Philip back against his seat. Seized by panic, Philip's language skills failed him.

'*Na! Bis bis,*' he shouted above the roar of the engine.

'*Bis bis? Ah, jej!*' shouted the driver ecstatically.

'*Na! Na!* screamed Philip, immobile now in his seat as the scenery shot past him and a fine stream of sharpened air cut through the top of his passenger window.

'*Jej jej!*' shouted the driver, his foot pressed down hard on the accelerator.

Philip scanned his numbed brain. Where was the word he needed? Where was the word he needed when he needed it? And then it came to him.

'*Sutti!* he screamed. '*Sutti sutti!*

'*Sutti?* said the driver.

'Yes, *sutti*!' screamed Philip. 'Now!'

The driver lifted his foot and the blur outside the car window turned to the texture of brown earth and sand.

The driver took his eyes off the road, reeled around in his seat and grinned at Philip. 'What you think my driving, *Om? Bunga?*

'Yes, *bunga*. Thank you,' said Philip. 'Very *bunga*.'

'Okay, *bunga,*' said the driver, and still grinning, he leaned forward and maintaining a modest pace, he hunched himself over the steering wheel as though taking up some irregular sleeping position.

In the distance, across the flat landscape, a vast sweep of constructions could now be seen. They entered a wide avenue shaded by tall Namisan date palms and approached a security checkpoint. A uniformed guard waved them in. Minutes later they drew to a halt outside a massive grey building above which was a sign that read, 'University of Trinamisa.'

It is customary when taking leave in Namisa to make a parting statement, wishing well on those from whom you are parting. Philip had learned this from his Robinson-Smith. Before leaving the car, he had checked his notebook for an appropriate phrase, which – due to its complexity – he had written in English not Namisan. So it was that, having climbed out of the vehicle, he turned and said to the driver: 'Thank you, *Om*. May you have at least four sons, but not just three.'

He noted immediately that the driver's eyes were growing small and black and that he had clenched his jaw, and that his nostrils had begun to flex and change shape. In the split second before he burst forth with a violent stream of invective in his own garbled tongue ... only then did Philip catch sight of the small golden symbol of the Number Three dangling above the driver's dashboard.

*

An important difference between the character of the Pundari and the Namisan, which has already been touched upon, is that the Pundaris can be hot-tempered and violent to an extreme, while the Namisans are cool and law-abiding. Pundaris frequently encounter problems with the Namisan authorities and regularly break the law. Take, for example, the car number plate issue. Since the Pundaris are more attached to tradition and superstition than the Namisans, they are inclined to doctor signs, symbols, anything in fact that runs counter to their beliefs and that can be interpreted as inauspicious. So, the Namisan authorities have taken to issuing car number plates that contain neither 3s nor 4s. A hard-line Pundari will refuse point blank to drive a car with the figure 4 on its number plate and will even go so far as to change a 4 into a 3, which obviously causes a great deal of difficulty for the police. While the less dogmatic Namisans tend not to make a fuss about 3s, they are not especially happy about driving cars with this figure on the number plate. Pundaris, however, take their hatred of 4 to even greater extremes and it is not unheard of for a Pundari to change the totals on his electricity or mobile phone bill so that all 4s become 3s and the amount payable is therefore reduced. The authorities have not as yet resolved this conundrum. The question of mobile phone numbers is another matter, which is discussed in a later chapter (See p.156).

(Extract from 'Belief and superstition,' in *Namisa - A Traveller's Guide: from tradition to tourism and back*, p. 76)

*

It was Bogadan who, emerging a deus ex machina from the university foyer, rescued Philip in the nick of time from yet another ugly cultural misunderstanding. He smartly moved Philip aside, out of the reach of the driver's now flailing arms. He leaned in through the car window and, without hesitation, barked a tirade of obscure Namisan at the occupant. The man fell silent almost immediately, put the car into gear, and drove away without another word. Here was a side of Bogadan that Philip had never seen before.

***

11

GREAT BRITONS

Bogadan was clearly not in the least concerned about Philip's encounter with the Pundari driver. This and experiences like it were part of his friend's initiation into Namisan life. Rather, Bogadan was entirely focused on enlightening his guest about the merits of the university on this his first visit.

Philip was ushered across the glistening white marble floors of vast foyers. He passed through mighty automatic glass doors that opened abruptly with a fearsome whoosh. He was signed in and out of embossed leather guest books. He was given visitor's badges for this building and that, though never for Building Three. He was swept down echoing hallways, directed past bubbling fountains of crystal water, and led around spacious sparkling classrooms. He padded through thickly carpeted departmental libraries and across the squeaky-clean floors of communal dining rooms. Very occasionally he saw a student or two. In the faculty corridors he noticed doors labelled with grand titles such as 'Dr Eliot Jaffar, Professor Emeritus, Department of Physics,' or 'Dr Tobias P.

Roberts, Research Fellow, Social Sciences.' There were doctors to the left of him and doctors to the right of him.

On entering the newest block on the university campus, Bogadan guided Philip to the end of a wide corridor. Above a set of double doors of rich imported oak was a sign that read, 'The Sharwarmiyya Lecture Theatre.'

'You have heard of Sharwarmiyya of course,' said Bogadan.

'Erm ... you know, I can't quite place him ... perhaps you could refresh my memory?' said Philip.

'Dr William Sharwarmiyya,' said Bogadan, raising his eyebrows.

'Of the ...?' Philip was struggling.

'Of the Oil and Gas Institute ...'

'Of course,' said Philip, 'so, Dr William Sharwarmiyya, most impressive. I take it he is one of your benefactors.'

'He is indeed,' said Bogadan, glowing with pride. 'There are two lecture theatres like this one. The third – let us call it the fourth – you will see, is under construction,' explained Bogadan.

The tour party moved on.

'There!' said Bogadan as they arrived outside lecture hall Number Two. Philip cast his eyes upwards at the sign above the double doors. It read, 'The Wordsworth Lecture Theatre.' Philip lightened. Here at last was something he could relate to, a gesture towards the great contribution of Britain to world literature.

'Oh, William Wordsworth,' said Philip in delight, 'very good!'

'No! Jonatan!' corrected Bogadan, 'Jonatan Wordswort!'

'Jonathan? Our Jonathan?' asked Philip.

'Come, come,' said Bogadan, 'there is more.'

He directed his bewildered companion to a small open doorway that was draped with a large piece of plastic sheeting. The two men passed under this to enter a huge dusty worksite. Men in paint-splattered overalls crisscrossed the floor area, carrying tools and building materials. The air resounded with hammering and drilling.

'Our new lecture theatre. Number Four,' said Bogadan.

Philip's mind was elsewhere – somewhere in the region of lecture theatre Number Two. What he was asking himself was exactly how and why Jonathan had a state-of-the-art lecture theatre named after him.

'This,' said Bogadan, waving his hand with a flourish in the direction of the work in progress, 'this, I think, we will name it the Blair Lecture Theatre.'

Philip could not recollect that any British Prime Minister had ever been credited with having made a contribution to Namisa.

'Tony Blair?' asked Philip perplexed.

'Pilip Blair!' said Bogadan, and he gave a deep guttural laugh, 'Ha ha ha,' and slapped Philip on the back.

A pretty little Namisan jingle rang out from Bogadan's pocket. 'Excuse me,' said Bogadan, pulling out his phone. Philip looked about him as Bogadan chattered rapidly to his caller. Far to his left, a man in a baggy, maroon t-shirt was leaning against the wall of an open balcony area, smoking a cigarette. Sunlight shone in through the balcony opening, which overlooked the terrain at the back of the campus. From where Philip stood, he could see the shaggy tops of the date palms.

'Sorry, *Om* Pilip,' said Bogadan, snapping shut his phone, 'just five minutes and I am coming.'

'No problem,' said Philip.

Bogadan hurried away and exited through the plastic drapes.

An unusual calm descended upon Philip as he stood in the middle of the construction site. The workers seemed to have disappeared, though he could still hear the hum of drilling in the distance. He picked his way across packing materials and debris towards the balcony, watching the trees loom as he moved closer. From the height of the building, he looked down onto an expanse of land, the palms in the immediate foreground but, behind them, a mass of lush vegetation untended and grown wild. Birds flitted from tree to tree, whistling and twittering. Unseen creatures rustled and croaked in the undergrowth. Philip saw that a tract of the greenery had been cleared and several rows of abandoned shacks filled the area.

'Nice view,' said the man in the baggy, maroon t-shirt.

Philip gave a start. The man had been so silent, standing there smoking his cigarette, that Philip had scarcely registered his presence. 'Sorry,' said Philip and he held out his hand, 'Philip Blair.'

'Frank Gibson,' said the man. 'You must be the new bloke from the Foundation.'

'That's right,' said Philip. 'You teach here?'

'English,' he said. 'Six months more and I'm out of here. But some of those poor buggers are locked into rolling contracts and they're not going anywhere.'

'Oh, is that so bad?' asked Philip. 'It all looks so idyllic around here, and the campus... well, it's just perfect.'

Frank gave a brief mechanical grin. 'Sorry,' he said, standing up straight, 'got to go.'

'Just one thing,' said Philip. 'What are those shacks down there? Is that a little Wunamisan village or something? Might be nice to go and visit it.'

'Faculty compound,' said Frank sourly and, with that, he threw down his cigarette end, squashed it with the heel of his sandal, and walked away.

Philip stared down in horror at the shanty town below. Surely not, he thought. In the distance he could see some small figures moving about between the shacks. He narrowed his eyes against the sun. Could it be, he wondered, that they were carrying plastic water buckets?

*

We all need a purpose in life. I'm considering my options, and they are not thrilling. Pappee *is more openminded than most. She'd like me to marry and have children – that's true – but more than anything she would love me to take over the business from her. I don't feel that it's in my heart to do that. That would be Option 1.*

Option 2 would be academia. Plenty of opportunities there, but to my mind it would be as horrible as going into the army. You get a rank, and you get promoted. Then if you're lucky, you get to see the world by presenting at overseas conferences, where no one is in the least bit interested in what you're researching. Working in a university is prestigious. It's also stressful. Perhaps I've been spoilt, but I want my freedom.

Option 3 is the most depressing. Option 3 is marriage. Did I really spend all that time studying and improving myself only to end up being told what to do by a lazy Namisan husband? It would have to be a Namisan. Who else is there? As far as I can see, the husband pool here is very limited, and when I hear what boys like Ushri get up to, my heart sinks.

I need more options.

*

Felicity was working on the backstory of her book. Her central character, Flocky, was a survivor of an *amore non corrisposto* – unreturned love. This had a tragic ring to it, which she rather liked.

Roberto – the angst-ridden and narcissistic Italian professor – took her with him to Denpasar, where he took up a post as Visiting Professor of European literatures. He had begged her to come. He couldn't be there without her. He had said: *'Amore mio, vieni con me.'*

Felicity thought it might be intriguing to the reader if she peppered her text with phrases like this. She could always put a little glossary in the back of the book. A good USP, she thought.

Installed in the Balinese capital, the couple passed themselves off as man and wife. Flocky assumed that marriage would soon follow but, unbeknown to her … unbeknownst to her – Felicity would check this in her dictionary – Roberto had secured the post by falsifying his application and indicating that they – he and Flocky – were in fact a teaching couple. But, thought Felicity, did Flocky really aspire to marriage? She didn't seem the type, but then … this was fiction. What did she care? She pressed on.

Flocky, herself an author, therefore – since she was so jolly clever – took up a lectureship in literary fiction, and her lectures eventually proved to be even more popular, of course, than Roberto's own series of seminal lectures on, 'An Introduction to 19th Century European Literature.' Roberto, however, was the star player whose high-earning post – the revenue from which was sent home forthwith to pay for the renovation of his hillside property in Siena – was dependent on the presence and contribution of his 'wife.'

Felicity considered that this was a fair assessment of Flocky's potential situation, though she had spontaneously enhanced her original story. Looking up from her Olympia Splendid 33, she noted that Parrot had gone silent on her as he or she or it often did in her moments of total absorption. For the sake of convenience, Parrot was today a 'he.' His head was tilted to one side in his characteristic pose, and he was studying her with that eye of his. Felicity waited to hear his judgement. He opened his beak, then closed it … then said quite clearly, 'I love you.'

A single warm tear rolled down Felicity's cheek. These were the words she longed to hear. That bastard Francesco had exploited her, and she would make sure that never ever happened to her again.

***

12

THE GOOD, THE BAD, AND THE TERMINATED

Bogadan made his preamble.

'As you all know, we are here today thanks to my mother *Imee Baadeeyyumba* Grace Shoon Bogadan who, in her infinite wisdom, obtained decree from the Government to set up TU, and drew up first TU statutes.'

Philip gazed down at the meeting agenda. It was long, very long. He was to say a few words about the Foundation and its links with the University, but he found his name at the very bottom of the agenda, between the item about faculty appraisals and the procurement request for new blinds in the Building Four second-floor kitchen.

'When I first joined TU,' continued Bogadan, carefully adjusting his favourite red Armani tie, 'I was based at the University of Prapundar. The post it was an extremely prestigious one and, in coming here to TU, I accepted salary that was at least 43 percent less than what I was receiving there, but I was having absolute faith in my mother's vision for TU, and I accepted this job with pride and anticipation.'

Bogadan's voice droned on. Philip's stomach was like an empty cave inhabited by a discontented whining beast. He had not had any *sneks* today, he realised. The deep rumbling down in his gut was echoed by a similar vibration emanating from the insides of the learned professor seated next to him.

Looking around the boardroom table, Philip noted with surprise that Frank Gibson was amongst the members of this elite assembly. He sat slumped in his chair, doodling on his agenda. His legs were stretched out in front of him, crossed at the ankles, and his lumpy unpedicured toes were sticking out of the same dusty brown sandals that he had been wearing when Philip first saw him on the balcony. He still wore his maroon 'Having a spicy time in Tobago' T-shirt.

Hunger and fatigue, together with the stress of his encounter with the Number Four, made it difficult for Philip to keep his eyes open.

'And for the benefit of our guest from the Foundation *Om* Pilip, let me just introduce the members of our Committee …'

Philip was roused temporarily at the mention of his name. In his semi-conscious state, he registered the words … Doctor, Professor, Acting Head of Social Studies, Acting Head of Mathematics, Department Head, Acting, Acting … there seemed to be a lot of acting going on. His head bounced onto his chest. He opened his eyes as wide as he could and stared up at the light flooding in through the opposite window. He bit the insides of his mouth and he breathed deeply so that the influx of oxygen would revitalise his tired blood supply. He felt his eyelids droop.

Must not sleep, must not sleep, said his inner voice, and then once again his chin bounced onto his chest. His eyes opened to see an attractive young woman in a multicoloured Namisan sarong take the floor.

'*Imeetinee* Fatt, the new Acting Head of Health and Safety, will now tell us about…' Bogadan put on his glasses and leafed through the pieces of paper in front of him.

'About *Safety in the Home*,' said *Imeetinee* Fatt.

Philip regained his senses at the sight of this beautiful and elegant creature. She did not appear in any way fat to him. In fact, she seemed just perfect. He sat up, arms folded, in order to pay better attention.

'Yes, *bunga*,' said Bogadan. 'Please go ahead, *Imeetinee*.'

'Why is *Imeetinee* Fatt Acting Head of Health and Safety?' interrupted Frank. 'Yesterday Jim Miller was Head of Health and Safety.'

Imeetinee Fatt blushed. She looked at Bogadan.

'Regrettably,' said Bogadan, '*Om* Jim had an accident in his home, and we have assisted him to return to his country.'

There was a pause as Bogadan stared at Frank over his glasses, and Frank stared back defiantly at Bogadan.

'Last night,' added Bogadan. 'He left last night. *Imeetinee* Fatt has kindly agreed to take over his duties until a suitable replacement can be found.'

'This wouldn't have anything to do with his HSE report on the faculty compound then?' said Frank.

Bogadan stared at Frank, and Frank stared back at Bogadan. Philip noted that a great deal of staring was going on.

'No,' said Bogadan. And then he gave a curt nod to *Imeetinee* Fatt.

'Safety in the home…' she began.

Delightful though *Imeetinee* Fatt was, the subject of her PowerPoint was not sufficiently engaging to hold Philip's attention. He drifted off from time to time as her voice twittered in the background.

'… and we advise lock windows, so babies not fall out,' she warbled.

'Actually,' said Frank, 'if I may interrupt a moment…'

Imeetinee Fatt appeared confused. Bogadan had been busy sorting papers. He looked up over his glasses.

Frank continued, 'I don't have any babies, and I can't open any of my windows, so if there were a fire, and let's say I had to escape quickly, then I'd be in big trouble.'

'Fire not a risk now,' said *Imeetinee* Fatt assertively. 'Last week we have talk on fire safety. Everybody know what to do. Now I may continue?' asked *Imeetinee* Fatt.

'Oh, all right! *Jej jej*,' said Frank, and he ticked off an item on the handwritten list that he had in front of him.

Philip looked at his watch. Various questions were unanswered, such as *How long was it to lunchtime? Would the meeting end before too long?* and, *What was for lunch?* When it was his turn, he decided, he would keep it very short, and he would perhaps throw in some statement to indicate that he was happy to be here as a guest and to have been invited to lunch … something like that … something to move the proceedings on.

Next up were 'faculty and staff pay increases.' There was a brief rustle of attention amongst the committee members.

'Faculty and staff pay increases,' said Bogadan. This was his show. 'Now, it's like this,' said Bogadan removing his glasses. 'Good employees – maybe they're faculty and maybe they're staff – they're going to get pay rises.'

'When?' said Frank. There was a sharp intake of breath from the ranks of the professors and heads of department.

'I'm sorry, I didn't catch that,' said Bogadan.

'When?' said Frank more loudly. 'We want to know *when* employees are getting their increases.'

'That hasn't been decided yet,' said Bogadan. 'I have to consult.'

'Oh, I see,' said Frank, 'you have to ask your mum. When will you ask her?'

'In due course,' said Bogadan. 'Now the thing is that I have to be sure that people deserve what they get. The people who they are going to get pay increases – they're good employees and they're the ones who deserve what they get.'

'I don't understand,' said Frank. 'What is a good employee?'

'Well, that's easy,' said Bogadan smugly. 'It's someone who he works very hard, and who's being here early in the morning and late at night. This is kind of person we want at TU. It's someone who he is coming on time, someone doesn't take long lunch breaks, for example.'

Frank put up his hand. 'We don't have lunch breaks,' he said. 'We're not allowed to.'

'*Jej*, correct,' said Bogadan. 'It's somebody who if they were having them, would have no intention of taking them, because they are focused on their work, and working towards the betterment of TU is their one objective.' He stopped abruptly and looked around the room. There was silence. 'Any questions?'

'I was just wondering ...' said Frank, and all eyes turned towards him, 'what percentage increase these *good* employees could expect?'

The eyes of the Committee turned towards Bogadan.

'That will be communicated,' said Bogadan.

All eyes were again on Frank. 'How about communicating it now?' said Frank.

The Committee members braced themselves. Bogadan put on his glasses. He sifted through the papers in front of him, and pulled out one sheet, which he scanned quickly as the Committee sat in silence.

'For the cost of living, good employees will receive 3 percent.'

'Well, according to the recent Ministry of Labour report,' said Frank, 'the cost of living in Namisa rose this year by 8%, so the *good* employees would still be short 5%. What about the bad employees?'

'Most probably they will no longer be with us,' said Bogadan, pausing to glare at Frank. 'As for the good employees, on basis of their appraisals they will get between 1 percent and 5 1/2 percent.'

For a split-second Frank seemed undecided as to how to continue.

'Next point,' said Bogadan. 'Faculty appraisals.'

'Wait a minute,' said Frank. 'We haven't finished faculty and staff pay increases yet.'

'I believe we have,' said Bogadan.

'No,' said Frank slowly. 'What you're doing is merging cost of living increases and appraisal increases.'

'What I am doing,' said Bogadan, 'is giving employees – they are faculty or they are staff – good opportunity to prove their worth through performance, and if performance is good then employees' living standard will improve, and better performance from faculty and staff means TU maintains reputation as world-class university. Those people they are underperforming are having to shape up or ship out. I think this is clear, *na na?*'

There was some coughing and clearing of throats amongst the assembly.

'All appraisal forms to me please by the 22nd of this month,' said Bogadan. 'Now, *Om* Pilip will tell us about cooperation between TU and the Foundation …'

*

I don't want to marry an empty head, or an airhead for that matter. Namisan mothers seem to think that appearance is more important than brains, so when they go matchmaking for their daughters, they're looking for men who are bungaoomumba. *I'll admit it. I'd like a man who's both attractive and smart, but I think I'd be happy if I could just find someone who was kind, truthful, and had a sense of humour. Namisan men take themselves far too seriously in my opinion. And then there's all that looking in the mirror to see how lovely they are …*

*

Mrs. Katraree's coffee mornings in the SnowWhite Dry Kleen Shop often extended to late morning, to early lunch and sometimes to late lunch. A team of family members dealt with the day-to-day affairs of the shop, taking in laundry and dry cleaning and then, within twenty-four hours, returning the immaculately cleansed and carefully pressed garments to their owners. From time-to-time, Mrs. Katraree made an appearance at the front desk to ensure that work was being carried out correctly and that her clientele was satisfied. Felicity's own expectations were exceeded. Mrs Katraree had seen fit to invite her to join in with the activities of the Coffee Circle so that she could contribute her 'expertise' and her 'oversights.'

'Perhaps you mean "insights,"' said Felicity.

'*Jej*. Those too,' said Mrs Katraree.

As well as leaving their laundry and their drycleaning, customers were able to take advantage of the new SnowWhite Sandal Repair Service, which was currently managed by a disgruntled and soon-to-be-replaced Pundari. Mrs. Katraree had purchased most of her dry-cleaning machinery and her shoe repair equipment from Singapore, and the increased efficiency of the shop left her free to develop her social and cultural interests. She believed fervently that happy personnel attracted happy clientele and happy clientele would return again and again, often bringing gifts and favours. This was why she intended to let go of her Pundari cobbler.

'Ah, *jej*,' she explained to Felicity in one of her Friday morning coffee sessions, 'Pundaris should be driving taxis, not cobbling. Here in Namisa, fortunately for us, it's not a lot of Pundari cobblers.'

'You mean there *aren't* many Pundari cobblers,' corrected Felicity.

'No, there isn't. Correct,' agreed Mrs. Katraree.

In addition to discussing the poor fashion sense of Pundari diplomats' wives, the question of the suitable pairing of young Namisan singles often arose. Felicity took note, for data of this kind, she thought, might prove useful for her book.

'Today we will talk of matchmaking Namisan-style,' said Mrs. Katraree. 'I know that *Imee* Felicitu is very interested in how we find husbands and wives for our young people here in Namisa, and I am sure you will think of many *snippeez* of information that we can pass on to her for when she is writing her book.'

'Snippets,' said Felicity.

'Correct,' said Mrs. Katraree. 'In English, snippets. In Namisan, *snippeez*.'

'Ah, a loan word from English. How very intriguing!' said Felicity.

'Correct,' reiterated Mrs. Katraree, 'we loan it from you and thank you.'

'Borrowed,' said Felicity.

'*Ah, jej*, also borrowed,' confirmed Mrs. Katraree. 'And, by the road, we are preferring to speak in English here at the Coffee Circle, and much often in Namisa, because it is an *easy-easy* language.'

'Super,' said Felicity.

'So, to continuation,' said Mrs. Katraree, 'finding *husbundeez, etset.*'

The SnowWhite Dry Kleen Shop was, without doubt, a leader in the field of matchmaking.

'It started like this,' explained Mrs. Katraree.

The ladies from the SnowWhite Coffee Circle always enjoyed this story, especially when it was retold to a newcomer. The gentlemen cared less to hear it again, and tended to return to the reading of their newspapers whenever they heard those familiar words, 'It started like this …'

'It started like this,' explained Mrs. Katraree, ignoring the background rustle of Namisan newspapers. 'I sent Babli to deliver three ladies' gold-edged sarongs and one gentleman's suit to a house over in Dilamisa quarter. He was a very long time. When he came back, I said, "*Looka looka,* Babli, why are you so long in Dilamisa?" He said, "*Imee* Katraree, I took tea with the gardener and you know it was not possible to refuse. Then, while I was there, I saw two young girls who were the most *trikee* I have ever seen and, *ah jej*, according to the gardener, not *lakati*, though their mother is *searching-searching* for a long time." So, I said to Babli, "Babli, go about your business and do not trouble me with these stories of *imeetinee na lakati*." Now, just a month later, I sent Babli to deliver three *shala kanz.*'

'What are *shala kanz*?' asked Felicity.

'They are like shirts, my dear *Imee*, but they are below the waist or to the knees and only men wear them … though I note that now ex-pat ladies are wearing them.'

'Maybe I should get one, then,' said Felicity.

'I strongly advise you against it,' said Mrs. Katraree. 'Now, Babli delivered the *shala kanz* and was away a very long time. Then when he returned, I said to him, "*Looka, looka*, Babli, why are you so long delivering the *shala kanz*?"

Felicity stifled a yawn.

'... and he said to me, "*Imee* Katraree, I took tea with the driver and you know it was not possible to refuse. Then while I was there, two young men – very *mumba*, I thought – came and sat with us, and I said to the driver, 'They are *lakati*?' and he said to me, '*Na lakati*, can you believe it?' and he told me that their mother also is *searching-searching* for too long."'

There was a buzz of anticipation. This was the part that the ladies from the SnowWhite Coffee Circle enjoyed the most.

'And what do you suppose I did next?' said Mrs. Katraree.

'Well,' said Felicity, but she was quickly hushed by the lady sitting next to her. This, it seems, had been a rhetorical question.

'I went *bis bis* to the house of the *shala kanz* delivery,' continued Mrs. Katraree and there I found *Imee* Djosi, the mother of the two young men, and I said to her, "*Imee* Djosi, you looked everywhere, but did you look in Dilamisa? If not, I think your *searching-searching* is over. I think I found for you two brides." Now to cut long story *shorty*, *Imee* Djosi and two sons went to visit. The young ladies were indeed *trikee*, and *baadee* also, but not too much. So, the two families they started marriage discussion.' Mrs. Katraree paused at this point. Then, looking directly at Felicity, she explained, 'Marriage discussion in Namisa very complicated and I am-will tell you about this.' She paused again, looking around the room for signs of animation at the possible introduction of this topic. There was very little movement. The ladies sipped their coffee and the gentlemen read their newspapers. Then she said, 'But I am-will tell you about this another day.'

*

'That's all I have,' said Bogadan, 'I believe that concludes the meeting. My thanks go to *Om Baadumba* Pilip for attending today, and …'

Frank had his hand up.

'Yes, Frank,' said Bogadan.

'AOB,' said Frank. The learned professors, who had already risen to their feet, took their seats again.

'What is it?' said Bogadan sharply.

'Water and electricity,' said Frank. 'Those of us who live on the faculty compound had very high utility bills this month, and we want to know why.'

Bogadan leaned across the table, his weight on his right elbow, waving his glasses at Frank.

'You see,' he began, narrowing his eyes, 'what is happening is that you people over there on the faculty compound, you are used to wasting huge quantities of water in your own countries. The same applies to electricity. These are precious resources that we respect here in Namisa. You people have televisions and computers and music centres, and these appliances they are plugged in and on standing-by at all times. It is hardly surprising that your bills are above those of the average Namisan.'

'Well,' said Frank, 'since we don't have any water coming out of the taps in our accommodation, we get our water from the decorative fountain at the entrance of the compound.' There was a murmur amongst the professors. 'Maybe *Om* Pilip ought to know about this,' continued Frank, 'since you'll well remember that the purpose of the TUDI Project was to maintain our pay and conditions to a high standard. Maybe he'd like to know what kind of a high standard the Foundation money has been maintaining. Electricity? Well, the lights go off at 8am and they come back on again at 5pm, then they go off at 11pm and come back on at 5am.

'With the electricity I cannot see the problem,' said Bogadan. 'You are teaching from 7 to 4, so there is really no need. But the water, *jej*, I will look into it.'

He slammed shut his diary and stood up. A traditional Namisan war chant rang out on his mobile phone: '*Ullulah, ullulah, ullulah mumba! Traka!*

'*Om* Pilip, please excuse me for a moment,' he said, 'then we will go for lunch.' He hurried out of the room.

'*Bummer!*' said Frank, whom Philip noted had not yet ticked off his complete list of action points. The professors were filing out of the room as quickly as was respectful. Frank made his way to where Philip sat, but he checked over his shoulder before he spoke. 'We need help here,' said Frank. 'I have reason to believe that …' He looked around the room again and spoke in hushed tones, '… that Foundation money is being misappropriated.'

'That's a rather strong accusation,' said Philip whispering, his eyes darting towards the doorway. 'Are you sure that you've got your facts right?'

'Look,' said Frank patiently, 'how do you account for the fact that we're living in abject poverty on the faculty campus while we've got two new professors Emeritus who've been given a villa each in the diplomatic quarter, and a limousine with a Namisan – not a Pundari – driver. You won't see them queuing up to fill their jerry cans at the ornamental fountains. We're talking big money here.'

Frank lowered his voice still further. 'Not only that, he's talking about merit increases and cost-of-living increments, but he hasn't said anything about how he's finding excuses to cut salaries.'

Philip could hear Bogadan out in the corridor, barking into his phone.

'What do you mean? How is he cutting salaries?' said Philip.

'How come I'm Acting Head of English?' hissed Frank.

'I don't know,' said Philip. 'How are you Acting Head of English?'

'Because the bloke before me resigned. That's why. I came in on a lower salary. And he's doing this in all the departments. Somebody resigns or is terminated and he just promotes someone else up into their place at a fraction of the cost … and that way he gets to impress his mum.'

'Look, if I'm going to take this any further, I think I need to hear more from the faculty … or the staff,' said Philip.

'You think anyone's going to talk to you about this? It's a dictatorship. One word out of place and …'

Just outside the door, Bogadan could be heard winding up his phone call with the required Namisan farewells.

'Got to go,' said Frank.

*

Bogadan ushered Philip quickly across the university campus towards a large and elegant colonial-style house on the west side. Colourful blooms sprang forth along the pathways, their petal faces turned towards the spray of water that reached them from the automatic irrigation lines embedded in the topsoil of the campus gardens. Philip took note every time they passed a fountain, large or small, placed as a centrepiece in the midst of a miscellany of exotic flowers.

'I hope you did not find the meeting too tedious,' apologised Bogadan. 'There is always someone who tries to lead the discussion off topic.'

'Like Frank, you mean,' said Philip.

Bogadan was unfazed.

'This man Frank,' he said, 'he is a rough sort. We got him through the *Times Educational Supplement*. Naturally, he will not be with us much longer.'

Bogadan led Philip up the steps of the house, which were framed by two lofty Corinthian pillars. 'When she is not away on official business, my mother lives here,' said Bogadan. 'You are very lucky. Today she is home.'

***

13

AMAZING GRACE

'You are most welcome,' said *Imee Baadeeyyumba* Grace Shoon Bogadan, greeting Philip in her lavishly furnished sitting room.

She was a small woman and, not unlike her son, distinctly on the tubby side. She wore a Harrods twin set in marshmallow pink and, around her neck, a set of precious grey Namisan pearls. Her skin was crinkly but soft. The fingers of her hand, which she extended limply in Philip's direction, were plump and squidgy. Her nails were immaculately manicured, and she wore varnish of a dark and indecent fuchsia.

Imee Grace was just returned from the International Conference for Power and Innovation, hosted by the Oil and Gas Institute of the fast-developing state of Abu Nar.

'I was the guest of Professor William Sharwarmiyya,' she explained, looking directly at Philip with dark piercing eyes. 'You know him, I believe.'

Philip returned a weak smile.

'He said to me, "*Imee* Grace, this is one conference we could not have staged without you. You are our lucky charm." My keynote address was entitled, *Research and its Potential for Diversification: A Namisan Perspective*.'

'Ah, yes,' said Philip, 'yes …' Philip had – for a split second – known what to say, but in another split second he had forgotten.

Grace and her son waited to hear his judgement.

'Yes, indeed,' said Philip. 'This is a fact that is … easily forgotten.'

'Too true,' said *Imee* Grace. 'You see how well *Om* Pilip understands my theme, Itotee. You must understand, *Om* Pilip, research is most important, and sponsorship for research is essential. I give funding to you. You give rewards to me. The long-term benefits we enjoy them both.'

Philip agreed with all of this, mainly because the only benefit he was most interested in right now was lunch.

*

'Research, research, research,' said *Imee* Grace Shoon Bogadan. 'First and foremost, research.' She passed a plate of strong-smelling Namisan delicacies across the table to Philip. 'Eat, eat, *Om* Pilip,' she urged.

Philip ate, though he had been hoping for something less spirited.

'The Foundation has been most generous,' continued *Imee* Grace, 'and we will be showing our appreciation through the naming of the rooms in our new lecture hall building.'

Inside his mouth, Philip's tongue began to sizzle, and he cursed himself for his unbounded greed.

Bogadan had little to say for himself. With the tips of his fingers, he selected some fried leaf-like flaps of green vegetal material. He carefully placed a minute bundle of red-speckled rice in each, and then fashioned the leaves into moist little parcels which he popped rapidly into his mouth and devoured with a prolonged movement of the jaw. As he chewed, his eyes closed very slightly.

'Here at TU we are still in our infancy,' said *Imee* Grace. 'There will be plenty of jobs for the boys – of that I have no doubt – but what of the girls? We must think of them.'

'Quite so,' said Philip, loading his fork with meatballs in yellow gravy.

'This is *kwa kwa,*' explained *Imee* Grace, 'which we make from monkey liver. It is high in cholesterol and helps to maintain the smoothness of the skin.'

Too late for second thoughts, the *kwa kwa* was already on its way down Philip's gullet, coated in its fiery sauce.

'I am thinking in particular of my granddaughters Tumik and Sokee … Itotee's nieces. They will marry, of course, but they need a good purpose in life, a good grounding. To be honest, I do not like what I see at the Oil and Gas Institute. For the boys, it is very fine, but I am not inclined to send my daughters to do a man's job. We are very much ahead of the times here in Namisa, however we draw the *liney* at certain occupations when it comes to the upbringing of the young Namisan women. I cannot see Tumik and Sokee setting foot on an oil rig.

This is not acceptable in our culture. Perhaps Pundari parents would allow their daughters to do this, but even that I am not sure it will happen.'

Philip cooled his tongue with a spoonful of green-tinted yoghurt.

'That is very fine *bulbi* juice,' said *Imee* Grace. 'It is not really juice, of course, but we call it that since we make it in the liquidiser. It is local cow's yoghurt mixed with skinned filleted *bulbi* lizards, quite a rarity since these are found only in the forested interior of Namisa.'

'Delicious,' said Bogadan. 'Try it with a little grated tree bark.' And he handed Philip a small dish of dark wood shavings. 'We smoke the bark first to give it its distinctive taste. Try it.'

Philip took a spoonful and emptied it onto the side of his plate, then very delicately wiped the excess perspiration from his forehead with a paper hankie.

'What I am thinking,' said *Imee* Grace, 'is to introduce a degree in wedding planning. I feel there is a great deal of mileage in this idea and I am certain it would attract many female students, even from the most distant regions of Namisa … and they could also do research.'

'First and foremost, research,' added Bogadan.

'Now that I am thinking about it,' said *Imee* Grace, 'we could also offer a degree in the culinary traditions of Namisa. What do you think, Itotee? I could teach a module on this, *na na*?'

*

Philip could not manage the desserts. He had made the classic mistake of complimenting *Imee* Grace on the fried *chikoko* meat and was obliged to eat a second helping.

'*Chikoko* – it is a small animal, native to Namisa. How do we say this in English, Itotee? I think it is "hamster," *na na?*'

'No, I do not think so,' said Bogadan. And then, addressing Philip, he said, 'It is bigger than a hamster, you see, and darker in colour and it has a very long tail, but we cut the tails off when we fry them, which is why they maybe look like hamster.'

'It is a pity you are not able to try our desserts, *Om* Pilip,' said *Imee* Grace. 'Never mind. Tuki will wrap them for you and you can take them back for your dear wife, *Imee* … *Imee* …'

'*Imee* Felicitu,' said Bogadan, with an expression on his face that resembled a smirk. Or so it seemed to Philip, unless it was some perverse manifestation of the intestinal discomfort that he himself was now experiencing.

'She will enjoy, I am certain,' continued *Imee* Grace. 'And remember,' she instructed, 'that our *hura* fruit has a very strong smell and needs to be consumed within the day. Otherwise you will need to dispose of it, preferably outside of your house.'

'*Pappee* … *Om* Pilip, please, will you excuse me?' said Bogadan, rising from his chair and giving a quick bow of the head. 'I have some business to attend to. Please take your time, *Om* Pilip. We will meet later in Building One. I will send the driver.' And with that he took his leave.

Imee Grace seemed delighted to have Philip to herself. 'Come, come, *Om* Pilip,' she said, 'let us take tea and talk.'

*

Wait a minute! I think I'm missing something here. If relationships with husbands and partners are so restricting, why does Namisa have so many baadeeyyumba *women, strong, intelligent women who have made a success of their lives?*

All around me I hear young women, women of around my age, whining that life isn't fair. 'I can't do this. I can't do that. There are no opportunities for women. Men walk all over us.'

Haven't they seen what's going on? Haven't they seen that they are the ones who keep reinventing glass ceilings, their insurance policy for failure? Meanwhile, these businesswomen, academics, doctors, scientists have been around for generations. They took it as their duty in life to try and design a grand future for themselves. They just got on with it. Very baadee, *very* smaartee.

*

'Now you see, *Om* Pilip,' said *Imee* Grace, 'Itotee has worked very hard to make TU a world-class university, but soon we will come up for international accreditation and, personally, I do not rate the University of Prapundar very highly.'

'Prapundar?' said Philip, struggling to make the connection.

'It is the state university of Pundar and not a very good one at that but, you see, they were established before us. This is where Itotee studied for his BA and his MA, and where he commenced work on his PhD. I did tell him at the time that he should go to Cambridge, but he felt the degree there was too long. He said to me, "*Pappee*, give me a good reason why I should spend three or four years at Cambridge when I can finish everything in under two years at Prapundar?" Young people!' exclaimed *Imee* Grace. 'This is the way they think, but you understand it will count for very little in the academic environment for which Itotee is destined.'

She came now to the purpose of her discourse.

'So please, *Om* Pilip, do your best to help him obtain his scholarship. We are not fussy. He could go to Cambridge, perhaps, or Luton, or maybe Oxford. What is important is that he has British as well as Pundari qualifications. This will give him some street *credee* in the academic world. Professor Sharwarmiyya would most certainly take him at TOGI, but between you and me, they are not yet world class in the arts and social sciences. Added to that, I would not wish him to leave us. His duties lie here with us at Trinamisa. We are also not yet quite world class, but not to worry. Itotee will be fixing that when he comes back from UK.'

*

In Bogadan's Lexus, with a large package of assorted desserts in his lap, a bothered and bloated Philip made the cross-campus return journey to Building One. Approaching the faculty compound, it occurred to him to dismiss Buba the driver and take a small detour on foot, as much to clear his head as to avert an unpleasant attack of colic. Once past the landscaped gardens and the marble courtyards, he found himself picking his way awkwardly over uneven ground and negotiating puddles of muddy water leaked from the gurgling irrigation pipes. Soon, though, he reached an area where the dust flew into his face and settled on his clothes and shoes. Chickens ran loose in the shrubbery surrounding an odd collection of shacks and outhouses. A lone goat followed Philip as he circled the buildings looking for some sign of life, but there was none. He thought better of it and retraced his steps.

On his arrival at Building One, Philip was directed to a lift that chanted the floor numbers from one to six in Namisan – with the obligatory omission of the number three – and, when he stepped out at the sixth floor, a security guard escorted him down a lushly carpeted corridor to Bogadan's spacious business suite. The door to the inner office was closed, but in the lounge that served as an anteroom, Philip could hear Bogadan's muffled voice escaping through the panelled woodwork. He took stock of his surroundings. To his left, a window of panoramic proportions overlooked the campus and a section of the faculty compound. On the opposite wall was a full-length portrait of Bogadan wearing a green silk *shala kan* over which was draped a black robe with a white lining. In his right hand he held a scroll. His eyes stared out at Philip menacingly.

Philip moved to the window to take in the view, but with an inexplicable sense of foreboding. He noted some degree of movement below. A Jeep was now parked outside one of the shacks, and beside it stood a blue-uniformed security guard. Philip could see that there were three suitcases heaped roughly inside the vehicle. Another man – given his mode of dress, Philip guessed him to be the Pundari driver – leaned on the bonnet, smoking a cigarette. As he watched, a man emerged from the shack, carrying a large cardboard box piled high with files and books. The maroon T-shirt was unmistakeable. When man and box were safely loaded, the Jeep started to move off. In the distance, Frank's gaunt white face turned in the direction of Building One, seeming to identify Philip as he stood and watched in consternation from the window above.

The door to the inner office opened.

'Ah, there you are, *Om* Pilip,' said Bogadan. 'So sorry for keeping you waiting. You will no doubt be wanting to catch your train. If you are ready, then Buba will take you back to the station. There is much here to see, of course, but time enough for that on your next visit.' At this point, Bogadan looked down at Philip's shoes. Philip followed his gaze until his eyes rested on the sheen of powdery dust that had deposited itself on the surface of the leather. Bogadan's mouth stretched into a pained smile and his upper lip quivered almost imperceptibly.

'Indeed, you will already have seen,' he said, 'that our faculty compound is still very much under construction.'

***

14

THE FORGOTTEN

Felicity's novel was temporarily on hold as she moved ahead with her research. Her notebook bulged with useful observations about Namisa, its inhabitants, and its language, all of which could profitably be incorporated into her writing to add that touch of realism that was essential to work of any significance.

All this talk of matchmaking and marriage discussions had refocused her on her protagonist, the mysterious and enigmatic Charles. Felicity searched her mind to place him. She had him as a friend of Katrina, the flamboyant artist type who was Flocky's self-styled mentor. Concerned by Flocky's pointless and unnatural bitterness towards Roberto, Katrina determines to pair up the two. *Flocky meet Charles. Charles meet Flocky.* Yes, thought Felicity, because Flocky is all eaten up with bitterness. She is living in the past. She is letting her relationship with Roberto dominate her present and her future. Felicity liked this rather dramatic slant. Flocky was nursing a deep hurt, and that hurt was set to direct her life. Set to direct her life … somewhere. She would sort that out later.

In Felicity's novel, Flocky would come to learn that Charles was ruthless and determined, but she would find this strangely attractive. Felicity herself would have liked Charles to be everything that Roberto was not. Charles would be assertive, while Roberto was not … the spineless bastard. Charles would be uniquely exotic, while Roberto was not. Felicity paused to consider this. Surely, since Roberto was supposed to be Italian, he could not have been less exotic than Charles? Felicity pondered over her choice of names. She could of course change Roberto's nationality – he could be French, for example, except that she holidayed in France and, if the novel were a success, which she certainly hoped it would be, she could not show her face there after it had come out in translation and was displayed in her local village bookshop.

She could make Roberto Iranian, perhaps, and give him a European or American passport, and then his name would have to be …? Here she had a problem since she could not think of any Iranian names. Added to this she also hoped that one of these days she might visit Isfahan and her current plans might result in the banning of her book there.

Clearly there were flaws in her plot of the kind that would not occur in real life. Furthermore, writing her *magnum opus* had become so much more difficult since she had relocated her characters from Notting Hill Gate. How much simpler it had all been before. Felicity sighed. From its beady-eyed vantage point on top of a wooden IKEA dish rack that was accommodated on the kitchen draining board, Parrot also sighed.

Felicity sat at her keyboard and typed.

'I can see you find Charles attractive,' said Katrina, *'but so have others before you. This I can say, though, that one day he will meet the woman he will love above all others and she will be the only one for him.'*

Felicity felt a lump at the back of her throat. She continued,

'And nothing will come before that woman – not work, nor ambition, nor money …'

Felicity resolved that Flocky would meet Charles at the artists' café, where she had taken to sitting and whiling away the hours in conversation with Katrina. Appropriately, Charles would be in the company of another woman, but at Katrina's cue he would bow and kiss Flocky's hand. It occurred then to Felicity that most likely Namisans did not kiss the hands of ladies. She opened her notebook and wrote:

Namisan greetings. Hand kissing?

Parrot watched, nibbling as he did so, a large embossed card that he had fetched from the opposite side of the sink. Rising from her seat at the kitchen table, Felicity lunged at the creature and tugged at the corner of the card.

'Give me that,' she hissed.

Parrot resisted, wings a-flutter, and twirled the card in his gnarled claw, shredding each edge with studied precision. From the fridge, Felicity retrieved two icy grapes which she dangled in front of the raptor's beak. She found this bargaining ritual both tedious and stressful. The card read as follows:

Dr. Neil Bryant

has great pleasure to invite
Imee Felicity Blair
to the Foundation's Autumn-Autumn G & T
RSPV

'Oh, *bunga*!' thought Felicity, and with some degree of nostalgia, she reflected that where she came from G & T had a meaning other than Geophysics and Technology.

*

Red alert! Red alert! I came back early from my run this morning and I caught pappee *rummaging about in my room. She said she thought she had seen a* chikoko *run inside. Very good at thinking on her feet my* pappee*.*

Was she looking for this notebook? I'm guessing she knows that I'm writing a journal and wants to find out what's in it. One of the maids must have said something.

What does it matter to her? What's she worried about? Does she think I'm prey to subversive ideas? She knows I know Bindee Fatt, and Bindee has a bit of a reputation for agitating. Maybe she thinks I'm a Namisan autumn-autumn *sympathizer. That's so absurd.* Pappee *just loves conspiracy theories. She'd be very disappointed to know that it's not politics I'm writing about, but love. Mostly. Maybe I should just tell her.*

No, I won't. I'll leave her in suspense.

*

That afternoon as he travelled home from Wunamisa, Philip was a troubled man. He was only too aware that he was being dragged into Bogadan's circle of trust and being made into some kind of honorary friend. Soon it would be nigh on impossible to deny Bogadan anything.

After the dust-on-the-shoes incident, Philip feared he might have lost credibility, though there was no particular indication of this from Bogadan's side. Returning on the Trinamisa Express with the Industrial Park commuters, Philip tucked himself into a corner seat and took out from his briefcase his Desperate Dan notebook. He nibbled the end of his biro and then, after another moment or two of thought, he began to write.

> *Facts come to light – not anticipated.*
>
> 1 *Foundation pumping money into TU. None of faculty or staff appears to have benefited.*
>
> 2 *Jonathan probably involved – profited from friendship, or maybe some kind of partnership with Bogadan.*
>
> 3 *Bogadan no doubt assuming now that fruitful relationship with Foundation set to continue with my help, and without hindrance.*
>
> *Action:*

What action? Here Philip paused and looked out of the window at the yellowing Wunamisan grasslands. If he had been beguiled by Bogadan, then he only had his own naivety to blame. Bryant had, after all, warned him that Bogadan could be exceedingly persuasive. But, no, Philip thought, he would not be corrupted. He was not like Jonathan. Why would he ever want a lecture theatre in the back of beyond named after him? Was Jonathan so pathetic that he had sold himself for this? Philip closed his notebook. Tomorrow he would give Bryant a full report. Let *him* sort it all out.

*

Gazing out of his Foundation window at the *autumn-autumn* morning – a stance in which Philip most commonly found him – Bryant seemed not to be listening to his account of the visit to the University of Trinamisa. Bryant sniffed, and blew his nose.

'It may seem to you, Philip, that I am not listening, but in fact I am hearing this only too well. All this business with Bogadan is hardly news to me. I cannot comment on Jonathan's going, or on the story of the lecture theatre, but the fact that our funding may be going in unexpected directions needs to be monitored.' He paused for thought and drummed his fingers on his desk. 'Let's take this step by step, shall we?' he said. 'First of all, we have to decide if Bogadan is going to the UK … indeed, if Bogadan deserves to go to the UK. If in doubt, follow the rule book. That's what we shall do.' He looked pleased with himself. 'The important thing here,' he continued, 'is that Bogadan has nothing on you. He can't oblige you to do something you don't have to do.'

'I'm not sure I follow,' said Philip.

'Well, let's say you are … I don't know … a kleptomaniac.'

'Oh, but I'm not,' protested Philip.

'No, but let's pretend that you are, and that every time you set foot in a Namisan shop, you can't resist the temptation of picking something up and popping it in your pocket.'

'Yes..,' said Philip uncertainly.

'And, let's imagine that Bogadan happened to see you doing that one day … or that, for example, you had one too many at tonight's G & T, and it loosened up your tongue and you blabbed to Bogadan about this weakness, this flaw of yours. Well, then, he'd have something on you … and he'd use it. Maybe he wouldn't use it immediately but sooner or later, if he wanted something off you, he'd menace you with whatever it was that he'd found out about you.'

'Oh,' said Philip.

'But, fortunately for you, you're clean.'

Philip looked at Bryant and said nothing.

'Aren't you?' said Bryant.

'Yes,' said Philip.

'Well, there you are,' said Bryant. 'That's why it's always good to bring in new blood.' He pulled out his hankie, blew his nose again and then stuffed the hankie back into his jacket pocket. 'Now, what I suggest is that you nip down and see Alan in the Accounts Department. Since Jonathan isn't able to help us with the procedures for giving people bursaries, Alan is the man to talk to – a bit pedantic, but he knows his stuff.'

Philip remained in his seat, assailed by a feeling that he had forgotten something.

'Off you go, then,' said Bryant.

Somewhere in Philip's subconscious was a recollection of an indiscretion … an indiscretion mixed with Namisan cocktails.

***

15

A WORTHY CASE

'What can I do for you then, *Om* Philip?' said Alan, tearing apart a croissant.

'Is this the Accounts Office?' said Philip, looking about him.

'Yes,' said Alan, 'Why? Is something wrong?' He sipped his cappuccino.

'No ... it's just that it's ...'

'Very tidy. I know. You were expecting Bob Cratchit, or someone similar hidden behind a pile of ledgers. But now, you see,' and he waved his arm around the orderly room, 'we have the paperless office, and, well ... this is it.' He tucked a shred of croissant into his mouth and chewed, 'So, what can I do for you then? Need a management course or something, or maybe you want to bring in a consultant, or is it a conference you're organising? You name it ... Uncle Alan can do it.' He grinned flakes of pastry and took another slurp of frothy coffee.

'Well,' said Philip, 'I need some advice on how to arrange a summer bursary. It's for a chap from the University of Trinamisa.'

'Oh, gawd!' burst Alan, spitting croissant flakes across his empty desk. 'Not Ito again.'

'Well, yes … if you mean Ito Bogadan. Yes, it is Ito Bogadan. Why? Is there a problem?'

'Blimey! I can't believe it!' roared Alan. 'I might as well set up a Direct Debit for him. How much is he getting this time? Or is it for the … Uni-ver-sit-y?' Alan wiggled his head and raised his eyebrows as he said this. 'Here, Ronny,' he called, shouting in the direction of a cream-coloured partition. 'Have you heard this? That Ito bloke's collecting some more of our money.'

A head popped up from the other side of the partition, a thin pasty face topped with wispy, yellow hair.

'You have got to be joking!' said Ronny.

'I kid you not. Ito's definitely having someone on! Nice one!' and in unison, he and Ronny hooted with laughter.

Philip felt his face grow hot and puffy. 'I think I need some advice,' he said.

*

'Now this matchmaking,' said Mrs. Katraree to Felicity and the ladies of the SnowWhite Coffee Circle, 'it does not just apply to the young islanders.'

Two of the men put down their newspapers, and one strode across the room to refill his coffee cup.

'So, it applies to older islanders, you mean?' asked Felicity. 'Who exactly?'

'To older islanders and to younger islanders. As you will see,' said Mrs. Katraree, extending her arm with a flourish, 'many of these islanders they are here now amongst us. Some they are coming all the time to the Coffee Circle. Some just once a month.' She lowered her voice. 'You see, *Imee* Felicitu, it is not uncommon for the older Namisan man to be *na lakati*.'

'*Ah jej*,' whispered Felicity, and she looked in the direction of the newspaper group.

The men were looking up from their reading and smiling warmly in her direction.

'You may be interested to hear the case of *Om Baadumba* Advocate Kimzee,' said Mrs. Katraree.

'Good fortune was upon him!' said the lady seated next to Felicity.

'*Ah, jej jej!*' chanted the other ladies as one.

'I am like this story,' whispered the lady on Felicity's left.

'Sssh!' said the lady on her right.

'*Om Baadumba* Advocate Kimzee started coming to our Coffee Circle in the autumn of before two years,' began Mrs. Katraree. 'He was a very dear *Om Baadumba* and a good husband but, alack, he lost his wife before one year before two years – a tragic taxi accident. She went to visit some relatives in Pundar and she did not return.'

'*Jej sheema!*' said the lady on the left.

'After a long and happy marriage,' continued Mrs Katraree, 'Advocate Kimzee found himself suddenly alone, but he gained some solace here in the company of new friends at the Coffee Circle. It happened at that time that *Imeetinee* Gummu joined us after that unfortunate incident with her husband-to-be-who-was-not …'

There was some murmuring at this point amongst the members of the Coffee Circle.

'However she was a courageous *Imeetinee*...'

'Also *trikee* and *baadee*,' added the lady on the left.

'Correct!' said Mrs Katraree. 'And one *thingy* led to another *thingy*. *Om Baadumba* Advocate Kimzee fell instantly in love with *Imeetinee* Gummu. He asked her mother for permission to marry and so they were united in the auspicious *autumn-autumn* season.'

'How sweet!' said Felicity.

'Correct!' said Mrs. Katraree.

'How old was she when they married?' Felicity had a personal interest in the answer to this question.

'*Imeetinee* Gummu had thirty-one years. A little old, but still possible.'

'And *Om Baadumba* Advocate Kimzee?'

'Ninety-four. He is *pushed-on* now, of course, but thanks to the Coffee Circle all his autumns were *bungaoomumba*.'

*

I suppose I should simply abide by tradition. I should just find myself a husband and be done with it — get married, have some kiddeez *super fast, and then get on with my life. Disturbing thought – by the time I get all that behind me, I'll be ancient.*

Also, I'm not sure I would know where to start. I'd want to avoid matchmakers and matchmaking like the plague. I want to be in control of my life. I don't want others to tell me who would be a good match for me. But where would I find someone otherwise? There are wedding ceremonies, of course. Lots of women meet their partners at other people's weddings. And then, of course, there are places like coffee circles, though, to my mind mostly the old, the divorced, and the widowed go to those. I'm not that desperate. Yet.

*

'The important thing is not to panic,' said Alan. He was leaning back in his swivel chair, his hands clasped behind his head. Philip sat opposite him pale and tense, his pen at the ready so as not to miss clues leading to the solution of this obscure equation.

'You have a number of options,' said Alan. 'Option number 1: you give young Ito whatever it is he's asking for, which is …?'

'A bursary for some kind of summer attachment or other, and then finance for his PhD in the UK,' said Philip.

Alan sucked in a large quantity of air. 'That's one very large packet of money!' he said.

'It's not monkey nuts!' shouted Ronny from the other side of his partition.

'Thank you, Ronny,' said Alan. 'The issue with Option Number 1 is that our mate Ito has been the recipient over an extended period of time of not a small percentage of our Funding and Bursary Budgets. Who's going to sign on the dotted line this time? You? I can tell you that the bloke upstairs isn't going to be signing. So, if you take this on, you are going to have to exercise your justification-writing skills to the extreme! And I mean to the extreme!'

Philip sighed and threw down his pen.

'Now, Option Number 2,' said Alan. 'You avoid giving our cash to Ito Boy by finding someone else to give it to.'

'You can give it to me,' shouted Ronny. 'No problem there!'

'But, you know, it's late,' said Alan. 'It's *autumn-autumn*, and it's coming up for *autumn* and the paperwork's got to go in. If you start touting around for other candidates, chances are they won't be able to get their act together in time.'

'And *he's* going to find out about it,' said Philip.

'That's another story,' said Alan. 'It could turn out bad for the other candidate, or for whoever's representing the Foundation.'

'Me,' said Philip.

'Yes, you in this case. But, you know how this works. I think you've been with the Foundation long enough to know that where money's concerned, you keep your nose clean and you don't let anyone do you any favours. Am I right? Know what I mean?'

'Like lecture theatres, and cocktails, and ladies,' shouted Ronny.

'Thank you, Ronny!' said Alan.

'And,' said Alan, in a confidential tone, 'you need to avoid lunches with his mum. You don't want to end up feeling like you're under obligation to hand over the money because she asks you to help him …'

Philip ran his fingers through his hair.

'Anyway, no harm done as yet. That's the worst-case scenario. Option Number 3, and this is the one I would go for … Education Points. You find someone who has the most Education Points and you nominate them. You know, a worthy case.'

'But isn't that the same as Option Number 2?' said Philip, despairing.

'Yeah, a bit, but this way's more under your control. There's bound to be someone out there who's deserving, but who wouldn't automatically put themselves forward. And, that's a plus for the Foundation too. That way we get someone who'll follow our agenda instead of someone who's self-promoting or on some kind of personal mission.'

'So, let's say I find this person, then I do the paperwork …'

'You write the justification, you commission a set of references, you choose where you're going to send the lucky candidate – so we make some university department very happy in the process – and then you stick 'em on the plane to Heathrow, Manchester, or wherever.'

'And then Bogadan goes ballistic when he finds out.'

'Ah, yes, well – that I can't comment on,' said Alan.

***

16

LINGUISTIC CONSIDERATIONS

The Foundation's archives, where Philip spent the rest of the afternoon, were far from paperless. In this dimly lit basement, there was row upon row of metal storage racks, packed with brown and white boxes. There were sludge-coloured files and pink folders and mottled grey box-files. There were filing cabinets, and there were more boxes on top of the filing cabinets. Philip tried to uncover some kind of order amidst the apparent chaos. He sat on a broken operator chair and, wobbling and rattling, propelled himself up and down the aisles past the metal shelving. He thought that he must be looking for something relatively recent, so, bypassing the older files and the dustier corners of the archives, he turned his attention to any new boxes marked, 'Universities,' 'Applications,' 'Applicants,' 'Bursaries,' 'Scholarships,' 'MA candidates,' and 'PhD scholars.' But this, it seemed, was a life's work.

Delving into the box marked 'Scholarships,' he had some moderate success. He discovered from these records that Bogadan had received finance to spend a summer in

London to attend a course in Phonetics. This would perhaps account for Bogadan's unusually competent command of Received Pronunciation, setting him several notches higher than the average Namisan speaker of English. If all else failed, he might well get a job as a newsreader for the BBC. Philip noted that there had been other candidates for this especially coveted summer scholarship but, strangely, they had all withdrawn their applications. He jotted down some eight or nine names and then cross-checked for them in the 'Applicants' and the 'Universities' boxes. Six of these had worked at the University of Trinamisa but had since left. A seventh had transferred to an admin post in the Maintenance Services Department. An eighth had taken extended sick leave.

Philip chewed the end of his pen. A bad attack of *empty head* was upon him. He gazed at the ceiling and then at the floor. What he needed was a Namisan cocktail. Alas, a symbol of his transgression. He shuddered at that foggy memory.

There was every likelihood that Bogadan would come to tonight's G and T, even though he had not been invited. Philip was assailed by self-doubt. How could he ever make it to Rome, Paris, or Dubai if he could not even deal with Namisa? Could it be that he was simply not up to the job? Perhaps he would not even make Tbilisi? And, what if they sent him to … Alaska? He felt nauseous. His life was flashing before him and his ears were ringing. And then he realised that while his life was indeed flashing before him, it was the telephone that was ringing. With a sigh he stood up and raised the receiver of the grey phone that sat on the shelf between a box marked 'Contracts and Emoluments' and another box marked 'University of Prapundar,'

'Oh ho! Still there?' said Alan.

'Still here,' said Philip.

'Just had a thought,' said Alan. 'I'll bet you haven't considered picking someone from Pundar. No reason why you shouldn't. We do funding for them as well, you know … or maybe you didn't know,' he said. 'That's all. Got to go. Tata!'

Philip replaced the receiver and reached for the box marked 'University of Prapundar.'

*

Half an hour later, and back at his desk, Philip started to examine one particular file in more detail. There was a handful of worthy candidates at the University, but this one was easily the best. Like Bogadan, Professor Shimee Timmaya had completed most of his undergraduate and postgraduate study at the University of Prapundar, but in addition he had an MA from the School of Oriental and African Studies. Philip leafed through the now crinkled pages of Timmaya's CV. His MA dissertation was on *The Cultural Traditions of Modern Namisan Literature*. Unlike Bogadan, Timmaya also had a highly commendable list of scholarly works to his name. This would mean that while Bogadan might have accrued a lifetime of Brownie points, Timmaya had clocked up a healthy number of Education points. Therefore, Philip concluded, Professor Shimee Timmaya, who had previously been unsuccessful in his applications, now headed the list of two prospective candidates for an overseas postgraduate scholarship. Elated, Philip closed the file and prepared to head home, all the while reflecting on how he was really quite good at this job after all.

*

Since I've been back, Pappee has become rather pesky and tiresome. Much as I love her, her curiosity about my studies in the UK and France is verging on the obsessive. She bombards me with questions about places I visited, people I met, books I read, activities I took part it. Obviously, she's concerned about any negative effects on my brain of my immersion in alien cultures.

Now she's saying that she'd like to read some of the papers I wrote. Not a good idea. I can imagine her face if she were to read my last term paper on The Namisan Culture of Entitlement. *Ouch! It doesn't matter that today we're thriving. The foreigners came and enjoyed our fruits. Now they have to pay. It irritates me that so many Namisans have no qualms at all about asking for or taking any privileges they can get their hands on. I never thought about it before I went away, but I do now.*

*

That evening, Ratni came at 7pm on the dot to collect Felicity and Philip in the green Cinquecento. He had left early by mistake and his glum expression indicated he was now regretting his timely arrival.

'Hurry up,' said Philip, standing by the car door and wrenching back the passenger seat. 'We need to get there before seven thirty. Come along. Just pop in the back here.'

'No,' said Felicity.

'No?' said Philip.

'Philip,' said Felicity, 'perhaps I haven't made myself clear on earlier occasions. I don't do Cinquecento rides with Ratni. If you drive, fine – sort of – but not if *he* drives, especially not after the last time.' She fired a disdainful look in Ratni's direction.

'For goodness sake, Felicity,' said Philip, 'what's the matter with you?'

If the truth were known, Mrs. Katraree's monologue that morning at the SnowWhite Coffee Circle, which had been on the subject of Pundari drivers, had made a noticeable impact on Felicity. Ratni, scowling, and understanding only a tiny percentage of the discourse, watched from the Cinquecento's driving seat as the argument unfolded.

*

There are inevitably major similarities between the Namisan and Pundari languages, but nevertheless Namisan is a foreign language for the Pundari and vice versa. Pundari and other languages are taught in Namisan schools as a matter of course, but Namisan is offered only in Pundari private schools, of which there are few. Both Namisans and Pundaris have a strong oral tradition and, when they put their mind to the task, are able to learn languages with some facility. Namisans are, in effect, better language learners, but have not perceived a need to learn languages. The Pundaris on the other hand are driven to learn languages – in this case Namisan – for economic reasons: they need to earn a living. So, in short, out of necessity Pundaris learn Namisan as a foreign language, and in doing so they demonstrate a sometimes extraordinary capacity for language acquisition. A Pundari arriving for the first time in the Namisan capital without a word of Namisan will be conversing fluently within a maximum of one to two weeks. Needless to say, he will speak Namisan incorrectly and often with a distorted accent, but in his new language he will be well able to convey to others his day-to-day needs and the cost of a taxi fare.

('Linguistic considerations,' *in Namisa - A Traveller's Guide: from tradition to tourism and back,'* **p. 104)**

*

Felicity had grown quite red in the face. 'The man is a bad driver and he is also quite disagreeable,' she said. 'I don't know which is worse.'

Ratni sat staring ahead through the diminutive windscreen, his back teeth grinding visibly in his square jaw.

'We'll be late if you don't get in,' said Philip.

'If I really have to go, I'm certainly not getting in the back,' said Felicity. 'I'll sit in the front where there's more room.'

'No, you can't sit in the front,' said Philip.

'And why not indeed?' demanded Felicity.

'It's not culturally appropriate. *Imees* never sit next to a man, especially not a Pundari.'

'I sit next to you!'

'That's different. I'm your husband.'

'No, you're not!'

'Please could you keep your voice down,' hissed

Philip, looking over his shoulder.

The neighbours from Number Sixty-Two had come out to enjoy the row, and the neighbours from Number Sixty-Six, *Imee* Malitee and her husband Tieyik, had already set their wicker chairs out on the veranda and were watching their neighbours instead of their new plasma TV. Tieyik had brought with him the cool box and was helping himself to a can of Golden Lizard beer. This had become a very public argument.

By now, Ratni was muttering under his breath.

'Please, just do this for me, Felicity. Ratni's getting nervous!'

'Never mind about Ratni! *I'm* getting nervous!'

In a momentary break in the proceedings, *Imee* Malitee waved at Felicity to register her involvement. Felicity waved back. '*Salatee, Imee ooh Om*!' shouted Felicity. 'What jolly people the Namisans are!' she said.

'Will you cut that out,' said Philip, finally losing his patience, 'and get in the car?'

'He go, or no he go?' said Ratni, interrupting. 'No he go, I go.

And it was at that moment that Felicity did something very amazing. She turned around, stood face-to-face with Ratni, looked him straight in the eye and said, '*Om Ratni. Huhu taffee bungaj*! *Adoo pawatu sibee combi an wagoopa*!'*

Ratni looked shocked and disoriented, but perhaps not quite as shocked and disoriented as Philip.

> *[* Lit. 'Om Ratni, that's quite enough!*
> *Now you will do exactly as I tell you.']*

'*Eh, bung?*' demanded Felicity.

Ratni was clearly distressed. He said, '*Jej, jej, Imee Baadeeyyumba Felicitu*', and the matter was resolved.

At twenty-five minutes past seven precisely, the Cinquecento rolled up outside the entrance to the Foundation. Philip was in the passenger seat. Ratni was scrunched into the back seat, various parts of his huge body flattened against the glass of the car's windows. Felicity was in the driver's seat. The journey had passed in silence.

*

The relationship between Philip and Felicity remained strained for most of that evening. After his earlier excitement at solving, with considerable brilliance, the scholarship problem, Philip had come down to earth with an unpleasant bump, experiencing a major loss of face in front of Ratni, Felicity, and the neighbours both from Number Sixty-Two and Number Sixty-Six. For one who had been in the country for such a short period of time, Philip had rated his competence in Namisan as above the average. He had read *Survival Namisan* from cover-to-cover and he had listened to the recordings on CDs in the bathroom, and on his MP3 player whilst jogging, but it still had not taught him how to tell Ratni to listen up and show some respect. Either the course was rubbish or his aptitude for language learning was at fault. He concluded that it was the former.

Negotiating his way around the G & T buffet table and enjoying the finger food provided by Namisan Hotel Catering, Philip came face-to-face with Bogadan.

'*Om* Pilip!' he exclaimed, 'I see you are well-returned to Trinamisa. I have been seeking you. I am thinking about my trip to UK.'

'How is your dear mother *Imee Baadeeyyumba* Grace?' said Philip, thinking on his feet. 'I trust she is well and experiences good fortune?'

'*Ah jej*, good fortune is upon her,' said Bogadan, 'and while my thoughts are always with her, I was thinking also about my trip to UK.'

'I trust also,' continued Philip, 'that good fortune is upon you and all your transactions.'

'*Ah jej*, I count myself fortunate under the sun and the moon, and that is also why I am giving some thought now to my trip to UK.'

Philip was at a loss. He looked around desperately for assistance. Bryant was on the far side of the room, clearly enjoying the company of the Geoscientists. Felicity, whom he was prepared to forgive in exchange for some release from Bogadan, was dedicating herself wholeheartedly to Namisan Technology.

It was just Philip, Bogadan and the NHC buffet. Philip hurriedly stuffed three spicy rectangular *samats* into his mouth, an action he would greatly regret later that evening. Seeing that his companion was temporarily incapacitated due to his excessive intake of *samat*, Bogadan rattled on unprompted.

'I am thinking of Royal Holloway for my studies. I understand that it is in a green and pleasant place and that it is very close to London. I like this name Royal. In Namisa, I think you know that we are very fond of your Royals and we like to read of them in *Hello* magazine. I think this 'Royal' will make much impression here in Namisa, but on checking 'Holloway' I find that it is both a place – a market that is now some kind of up-market – and it is also a prison for women, which I am afraid will not be acceptable.'

Philip dabbed his face with an ice cube. 'Oh, my goodness,' he said, 'I suppose you may need to cancel your trip on this occasion if there is no suitable institution to take you.'

Bogadan looked put out. 'Well, no, there are many places, *Om* Pilip. You yourself suggested SOAS.'

'I did?'

'You did. But I have looked at it on the Internet and I have excluded it – for the heavens know this – that it is full of foreigners and it also would be too much like a taxi driver's holiday.'

'You mean like a busman's holiday,' corrected Philip.

'No, like a taxi driver's holiday, since we do not have buses in Namisa.'

'You should go somewhere nice like Bath,' said Philip, in an attempt to get into his stride.

'Bath?' said Bogadan. 'Yes, Bath, perhaps, though the name is not as good as Royal.' He hesitated, 'But this Bath, I think it is very far from Knightsbridge, *na na*?'

At the nearby drinks table, the recently exhausted Californian Shiraz had been replaced with the cheaper yet more potent Namisan Shiraz and the noise level had risen accordingly. Suffering the combined ill-effects of Bogadan and the *samats*, Philip edged away from his companion, and from the company of the now jovial technologists and geoscientists. From the hearty laughter coming from

Felicity's end of the room, it seemed to Philip that he would not be missed, except perhaps by Bogadan.

'Do not go, *om* Pilip,' said Bogadan, still loading his plate. 'I have some questions for you about Harvard.'

*

Philip trekked across Bryant's garden, past the pool and through a low metal gate into the rear of the Downing Compound, then up the steps to the offices, where a security guard waved him in.

In the quiet of his office, Philip pulled out Timmaya's file. There were various numbers typed into the contacts box. One that he recognised as a TU number was scored out. He circled the remaining two mobile numbers. Philip's plan was simple. He would secure Timmaya's interest in a scholarship and then he would set up a telephone interview with him … and then he would get Bogadan out of his hair once and for all by explaining that, though he had been on the short list, Timmaya had more Education points … and for that reason he was the one who got to go to the UK to do his PhD. These were the rules after all.

Philip felt an undeniable sense of power. Perhaps he was even the villain of the piece. But then, this was what Bogadan got for taking it for granted that he could continue to milk the Foundation for freebies, including the countless bottles of Shiraz that he had consumed on these premises. The truth of the matter was that Bryant and Jonathan were way too soft. They had let Bogadan walk all over them. Never in a million years would *he* have let Bogadan simply stroll into the Medicals and the G and Ts or any of the other FFs. Someone of Philip's calibre – like Philip, for example – was needed to sort out this mess and it would have been an even greater mess if he had not been around to untangle it all and put an end to this blind-faced exploitation of the Foundation.

Philip felt a lot better after thinking all this through. Dubai, Rome, and Paris were definitely back on the horizon. He dialled the first number. After three rings, a child answered. In the background, the screams and baby talk of other children could be heard.

'Is your daddy there?' said Philip. 'Your *mammee?*' There was no reply, just the gurgle of a baby, a clatter as the phone was dropped, and then the TV evening news in Pundari carried across the airways.

'*Salam! Salam!*' Philip shouted. He heard a rustle as the phone was retrieved and then, a woman's voice.

'*Salati*, I am sorry,' she said. 'You are searching my brother. He is away. He is in Namisa for the marriage of his cousin.'

A stroke of luck, thought Philip. He would pull Timmaya in and get the full story straight from the horse's mouth or, since he was Pundari, from the donkey's mouth.

***

17

THE STRAIGHT PATH

Professor Shimee Timmaya was a tall distinguished-looking man with silver-grey hair and hazel-green eyes of vivid brightness. He had the height of a Pundari, but not the breadth. A sullen-looking Ratni directed Timmaya to Philip's office and then stood grumpily in the doorway until Philip told him to go away.

Timmaya smiled. 'He is a Southerner, you see, and – I am not sure if you know – there is a long-standing animosity between the inhabitants of the North and the South of Pundar. Or rather, I should say that the Southerners dislike the Northerners, but the Northerners either do not notice or do not care. It is a belief amongst the Southerners that Northerners are in some way privileged and are blessed with good fortune. It is in the nature of the Southerner to believe that his neighbour has more than he has, and this makes him perpetually miserable. Thankfully, I am a Northerner and, although I am sometimes miserable, I am not as miserable as he is.'

On this the third day of his cousin's wedding celebrations, Timmaya welcomed an escape to calmer climes.

'My cousin is nearly married, but we still have some four or five ceremonies to complete,' explained Timmaya. 'If you have time this week, I will invite you, but I warn you that it is a tiring business this getting married. I have published a book on the subject. In the Pundarnami tradition, a correct marriage ensures a lifetime of good fortune. However, our wedding ceremonies are so complex that it is difficult to ensure that they are all carried out entirely correctly. Previously, mixed marriages were unheard of, but now with the economic success of Namisa and the consequent influx of Pundari manpower, it is more common for Pundaris to seek Namisan brides. Have you been to Pundar, *Om* Philip?'

'Er … no, I haven't,' said Philip. He had in truth considered that if all Pundaris were like Ratni and the other drivers he had met, then he did not much want to go there.

'When you do go,' said Timmaya, 'you will see that our ladies are altogether different from the ladies here in Namisa. They are quite … how can I say this? They are quite powerful … in the sense of strong. They are big-boned and muscular. Like the men, in fact. Strong women like these are prized in our society – or at least they were until the Pundari expatriate workers started to bring back their Namisan brides. The Namisan women, to our eye, are quite … quite exquisite. Small, delicate, and caring, with an air of helplessness about them. I have to say that this has brought about a profound change in the nature of the Pundari male. By that I mean, in particular, those who have intermarried. These mixed marriages – Namisan female with Pundari male – have, of course, had both a positive and a negative outcome. There are now, for example, a greater number of unmarried women on Pundar and, of late, the situation has grown untenable, with the result that the Pundari government has passed a law allowing Pundari men to take both a Pundari wife and a Namisan wife. But as yet, Namisan law does not permit residents of Namisa to take both a Namisan wife and a Pundari wife. Hence the perpetual conflict we find ourselves in with our Namisan brothers. You yourself are married once over?'

'Yes, I am,' said Philip with the faintest reddening of his ears. 'Just once over.'

'Very wise,' said Timmaya. 'May the sun and the moon bless you and bring you a multitude of healthy offspring.' He pressed his hands together and bowed his head, as in a traditional Pundari greeting.

Philip was not clear if Timmaya meant that it was very wise to be married, or if it was very wise to be married just once over. He felt, though, that it would be excessive to ask for clarification, just as it would be excessive to be married twice over.

A relaxation of Namisan immigration laws meant that Pundari academics such as Timmaya were free to live and work in Namisa.

'Salaries on Namisa,' explained Timmaya, 'are much higher than they are on Pundar and, as a result, Pundar is experiencing a brain drain … and also a taxi driver drain, although the latter is less of a problem since we do not really need taxi drivers so much on Pundar. For myself I was fortunate to obtain a lectureship at the University of Trinamisa in the Department of Anglo-American Literature.'

'This was before or after you completed your Masters?'

'After,' replied Timmaya. 'I joined with great enthusiasm and hope for the future. There were just a handful of us at that time, and we were at liberty to bring the best of our experience to the construction of the TU academic programme. Those were exciting times, but then …' Timmaya's voice trailed off.

'But then?' asked Philip.

'But then,' said Timmaya, 'Ito Bogadan returned from Prapundar with his MA.'

*

Not a lot going on around here at the moment. Actually, there was never a lot going on around here. There are a few weddings coming up. That should break the monotony. Ushri was supposed to be taking me over to the Sleepy Hollow, but apparently now it's out of bounds. Can cross that one off my list.

I am definitely on the straight path to the sun and the moon. Ha ha! Well, there's nowhere else to go, is there?

*

'We are still very eager,' said Mrs. Katraree, 'to hear about wedding discussions in UK.'

In order that they might hear Felicity's account as clearly as possible, the gentlemen put down their newspapers and carefully re-arranged their chairs and armchairs.

'Oh, but I don't think I'm the best person to talk about this,' said Felicity. 'I mean, you need an expert, maybe an anthropologist or someone like that.'

'*Na jef!*' exclaimed Mrs. Katraree, 'that is not the way of the Coffee Circle. Our approach is much more personal, and our close relationship here permits us all to ask the kind of questions that we would never ask in a public lecture or something of that sort. And after all, you are married, *na na*? Who better than you to provide us an oversight?'

'Well, yes …' said Felicity.

'Correct! You are perfect – *bungajoomumba* – for us. You will tell us in great detail, from your personal experience, about wedding discussions in Britain. We would like to understand, for example, how your husband's mother negotiated with your mother for her son to marry you, and we would like to know how much money changed hands, since some people, like Mr. Nombu over there,' she gestured towards a forlorn-looking little man in a neatly-pressed grey business suit 'have said that it is free, though the wedding sarong and the jam moon are expensive.'

'Honeymoon,' said Felicity.

'Correct,' said Mrs Katraree, 'you see, you know everything. We cannot possibly depend all the time for our information on *Hello* magazine. We need to hear it from the goat's mouth.'

'Horse's ... horse's mouth,' said Felicity.

'Correct!' said Mrs Katraree. 'I hope someone here is taking notes. But, before you begin, I have to say – and this is entirely my own personal opinion so it is not necessarily representative of the views of the Coffee Circle – I have to say that I feel that wedding discussions are probably not as well done in Britain as they are here in Namisa.' Mrs. Katraree fell silent. The entire company looked towards Felicity. Felicity thought for a moment.

'*Ah, jej jej.* Correct!' she said. 'But, Mrs. Katraree, may I ask with great respect why in your wisdom you say that?'

Mrs. Katraree beamed. '*Jej!*' she said.

Felicity smiled back. There was a further silence.

Still smiling Felicity said, 'Mrs. Katraree, why in your wisdom do you say that you feel that wedding discussions are probably not as well done in Britain as they are here in Namisa?'

'I am very glad you asked that question, *Imee* Felicitu,' said Mrs. Katraree. 'You see, I have observed that in Britain and America, and also Hampstead, there is much incomprehension between husband and wife. I would like to relate to you the case of a dear *Imee* who used to come here to the Coffee Circle until quite recently.' There was a sudden squeaking of chairs being moved, and the rustle of newspapers as the members of the SnowWhite Coffee Circle readied themselves – or otherwise – for the telling of this tale.

'This *Imee*,' said Mrs. Katraree, 'whose name I can- will not mention in order to protect her from embarrassment, came from Britain. She came from a place that is called West Hampstead. For those of you who do not know Britain, West Hampstead is a small but very important city with many inhabitants living closely together in very tiny houses. There are houses in the *dillat* and houses in the *waddat*, but each house is touching the next house. There is very little privacy. The city itself has a mixture of people who are *lakati* and *na lakati*, and many of the people – men and women – who are *na lakati* live together like people who are *lakati*.

'*Sheematihutoo*!' cried one of the ladies.

'*Jej! Sheematihutoo*!' cried another.

'I must remind you, *Imeezat*,' said Mrs. Katraree sharply, 'that their customs in West Hampstead are not our customs, and we are here at the Coffee Circle with the aim of discussing current affairs and of broadening our cultural understanding. This we cannot do if we are always crying out '*Sheematihutoo.*' I am sure that you agree, *na na*?'

There was a murmur and a nodding of heads. Apparently satisfied with the response, Mrs Katraree continued her story.

'This *Imee* – exceptionally – worked *longaside* her husband. I will not mention his name in order to protect the *Imee* his wife from even further embarrassment, even she is not here with us more. Many of you – indeed most likely all of you – will remember both of them.'

There was again a murmur of assent. Some of the ladies conferred, and the gentlemen too. Mrs. Katraree raised her hand for silence, then took a sip of coffee.

'This coffee is cold,' she said and waved to *Imeetinee* Petee, her young cousin thrice removed, who sat in waiting by the door, to come and replace the cup. Since the Coffee Circle was a considerably elitist gathering, outsiders were not permitted to join until they had been thoroughly vetted first by Mrs. Katraree. The Circle was therefore serviced – or 'supported,' as Mrs. Katraree would say – by various cousins, nieces, aunties and other family members.

'This working together,' said Mrs. Katraree, 'is a very modern *thingy*, which, *Imee* Felicitu, is discouraged in Namisan society. It does no good at all for the wife to see her husband work, or for the husband to see his wife work. It breeds discontent. The husband notes that his wife is capable of *felicitatious* interaction with others, and the wife sees that her husband often has cause to have private dealings with people she does not know or approve of – *Imeezat* as well as *Omzat*. Imagine a wife who sees an *Imee*, or worse, an *Imeetinee*, enter the office of her husband and then for the door to close with the two inside and the wife outside. This causes much distress. And, indeed, this is confirmed by the *Imee* of my story. In this working-together nonsense, it is often the case that the *Imee* will interfere in the business of her husband, attempting to direct his policies and decisions and, where the *Om* is weak, he will comply. Thus, the *Imee* runs two *workeez*, her own and that of her husband.'

Mrs. Katraree paused as *Imeetinee* Petee brought her a fresh cup of coffee. She took a sip and said, '*Bunga*. This is much better, thank you.' She turned to Felicity. 'This is our own coffee, of course, grown here in Namisa. No need for South American coffee, which is inferior to ours.' This was a cue for others to refill their coffee cups.

'As I was saying,' said Mrs. Katraree, 'on the subject of the *lakati Imee* and *Om* working together, this does not work also for another reason. Let us imagine that the *Imee* suffers a minor injustice at the hands of a colleague, or perhaps not even as much as a minor injustice. Perhaps that *Imee* desires something that is owned by her colleague, but the colleague will not give it up. The *Imee* may go to her husband and say to him, '*Looka looka*, my colleague is not fair with me and gives me *bushkilat,*' and the husband goes to his superior and he said, "There is an *Imee* (or an *Om*) in this department who is a bad colleague and gives much grief." So it is that many a wife has made for a *booting* of her colleague.'

'*Sheematihat*!' exclaimed *Imee* Malitee from Number Sixty-Six, who was seated on Felicity's right.

'Correct, *Imee* Malitee! *Sheematihat,*' said Mrs Katraree. 'And let us not forget confidences or *rumoreenz withinside* the department. An *Imee* may hear something in her department, which is a confidence, but she tells this to her husband who works in another department … and vice.'

'Vice versa.'

'Correct!' said Mrs. Katraree. 'Think how much grief this can-will give. This also is how *rumoreenz* begin, passed from husband to wife, and wife to husband. So, when I tell you that this particular *Imee* worked with her husband, I would like you now to consider the stresses that were upon her.'

There was a short break as the Coffee Circle members thought about these stresses, sipping their coffee and helping themselves to the small button-like *pikapika* fruit biscuits, baked in Mrs. Katraree's own SnowWhite Kitchen.

'Now, as I was saying,' continued Mrs. Katraree. Felicity stretched her arm down the side of her chair, rotated her wrist and took a surreptitious look at her watch. '... the *Imee* came frequently to join us here at the Coffee Circle, but mainly in the afternoons and at weekends since at other times she was doing her *workee*. It was clear that she had many *bushkilat* with her marriage, which were revealed with the passing of time. Not the least of these was the fact that she herself was very *baadee*.'

'*Baadee?*'

'Like you, my dear, *baadee* and *smaartee*. Could she help this? No, she could not. Indeed, she was more *baadee* than her husband was *baad* – and yet her husband had the better *workee* and the better salary. We find this in all societies, even here in Namisa.'

'*Ah, jej jej!* Correct!' agreed Felicity, taking care to write down this observation in her notebook.

There was some low grumbling in the area of the gentlemen's armchairs, however, no one chose to dispute this point. Mrs. Katraree gave a smirk of triumph.

'Now, at that time, a nephew of my brother Dr. Towdi – this *yobbee* his name is Ushri – he visited us on his university vacation from TU in Wunamisa.' Mrs. Katraree looked around the room until she met the gaze of *Imeetinee* Petee, who at that moment had been replenishing a *pikapika* plate. 'I believe *Imeetinee* Petee has cause more than others to remember young *Om* Ushri's visit, *na na, Imeetinee?*'

Imeetinee Petee blushed, lowered her head and returned to her seat by the door.

'It was indeed,' continued Mrs Katraree, 'on these very same steps of the Coffee Circle entrance that Ushri was coming nose-to-nose with the *husbundee* of our *Imee*. Ushri recognised this *husbundee*, and the *husbundee* recognised him. Ushri however was saying *not-a-thingy*, just as the *husbundee* of the *Imee* was saying *not-a-thingy*. But after, Ushri he said to his uncle, "*Looka looka*, uncle, I know that *om* and he is not a good person." And Dr. Towdi asked, "How do you know him and how do you say that he is not a good person?" "Because," said Ushri, "I see him nearly every night at the Sleepy Hollow Nite Club." And, at this, Dr. Towdi swimmed into a great rage, for Ushri was in his care. His sister-in-law, the mother of Ushri – you will remember she is *lakati* with Mr. Shi Sondan, the Editor of our very own *Namisan Times* – she had said to her brother-in-law, "Brother, brother, you are responsible, so be sure your nephew Ushri is on the straight path to the sun and the moon." But the way to the sun and the moon was not, of course, same as path to the Sleepy Hollow Nite Club.'

In the back of her notebook, under the heading, 'Places To Go,' Felicity wrote 'Sleepy Hollow Night Club,' and as an after-thought added two asterisks.

'To cut a long story *shorty,*' said Mrs. Katraree, at a timely moment when Felicity was beginning to understand the importance of coffee, 'Dr. Towdi himself went to inspect the Sleepy Hollow Nite Club. You see, he felt it was necessarily important to see the company his nephew Ushri was keeping. Now, what follows, is not at all pleasant …' Her brow furrowed, Mrs. Katraree looked sternly about her at her companions, several of them paused in the act of enjoying the last crumbs of their *pikapika* fruit biscuits. 'We are *Imeezat* and *Omzat* of the world,' said Mrs. Katraree, 'and generally open-brained people, but I would urge those of you who wish to avoid offence to leave the room now for some minutes. Those remaining of you who are here in the interests of personal development and in finding ways to keep your young ones on the straight path to the sun and the moon, you will find it profitable to stay, but I warn you that what I am about to say may be especially shocking.'

Mrs. Katraree and Felicity together looked around the room. No one stirred.

***

18

THE IVORY TOWER OF BABEL

A tiny, barge-like craft chugged along the murky olive waterway that circled the Trinamisa Super Theme Mall. In the two front passenger seats of the violently lurching boatlet, a batch of chattering Namisan men, clad in white *shala kanz*, were wedged side-by-side. Protecting the trippers from the harsh *autumn-autumn* sun was a woven canopy, striped and variously ornamented in the colours of the Namisan flag: green for the land, pink for the sky, large purple dots for the hills. From the viewing *galley* of the Trinamisa Night Sky Dome, sprinkled with stars of sunlight, Philip and his guest watched the scene as they awaited their order from the *Bungagogo* Food Court.

Philip had seen it prudent to transfer his interview with Professor Timmaya to this new location after growing suspicious of Ratni's extended paintwork inspection of his office door. Timmaya, though unaccustomed to impromptu excursions of this kind, accepted graciously the offer of a free lunch.

'I am not clear,' said Professor Timmaya, 'why you have invited me here today. Certainly, it is an immense pleasure for me to enjoy your company and to share with you, who are new to Namisa, some of the social and educational developments of the Pundarnami region. But, I am concerned that your agenda may be another, and you will understand that I do not wish to commit any indiscretions that may cause harm to my associates, or indeed to myself.'

'Dear Professor *Om Baadumba* Timmaya,' said Philip, 'please rest assured that you are here today to learn something to your advantage.'

Professor Timmaya expressed contained amazement – a raised eyebrow, a twitching foot – when Philip outlined to him the Foundation's offer. His surprise, though, had a tinge of dismay about it.

'I am not sure that I can accept,' said Professor Timmaya.

'Why ever not?' said Philip.

'For political reasons.'

'Goodness,' said Philip, 'I can't see that there's anything political about a scholarship helping someone to study in the UK.'

'*Ah jej*, but it is entirely political,' said Timmaya, 'even the fact that you yourself are dealing with this and not *Om* Wordsworth – your predecessor Jonathan – and, in his sudden absence, his superior, your Director *Om Baadumba* Bryant.'

Philip blushed at his own obvious naivety.

'Let me outline for you some of the facts,' said Timmaya. 'This application of mine for a scholarship – yes, I did make an application, but a long time ago. In those days when I worked at the University of Trinamisa

… in those happy and formative years of the University. Upon the return of *Om* Bogadan, all hopes of receiving scholarships were abandoned.'

From above their heads a Namisan ditty rang out from loudspeakers that were disguised as war drums. Two miniature Namisans scampered past their table en route to the Baskin Robbins ice cream stall.

'I don't understand,' said Philip.

Timmaya waited. A third child danced around them irreverently before sliding across the cool shiny floor to claim his cone. '*Ah, quant'e bella la giovinezza!* exclaimed Timmaya, eyeing the youthful cluster around the ice cream tubs. 'After, I will offer you dessert … but first things first. You need to know about these applications for Foundation scholarships. They were processed through the TU Human Resources office. They were to be countersigned by *Om* Bogadan himself. Initially the documents remained untouched in his in-tray. It was *Om* Jonathan who enquired after the applications and eventually retrieved them, but not without encountering a series of objections from *Om* Bogadan.'

'Objections?'

'He argued that some applicants were undeserving, and that others were performing poorly and were therefore unsuitable candidates. In the case of still others, such as myself, he did not want to release them because they were 'needed' at the university … and so it went on. The rest you know. None of us succeeded in securing a scholarship despite the fact that the Minister for Education that very same year had encouraged the members of the academic community to do their best to profit from offers of overseas bursaries. From a situation in which professional development was supported, we found ourselves in one that positively discouraged any initiatives for personal improvement.'

'But am I correct in saying that no one has ever tried to re-apply?' asked Philip.

'That would seem to be the case,' said Timmaya, and then he added, 'It would not have been in our best interests.'

'How so?' said Philip.

Timmaya hesitated. 'The threat of negative repercussions,' he said. 'In short… revenge.'

*

'Not long after Ushri's startling revelations,' continued Mrs Katraree, 'Dr. Towdi made his way, in disguise of course, to the Sleepy Hollow Nite Club. Naturally, he took with him a pen and a notebook. There in the Nite Club he found, amongst others, an *Om* answering the description of our *Imee's husbundee*. Dr. Towdi followed this *Om* to find out if Ushri had spoken the truth. I am sorry to say, my dear friends, that Ushri *had* spoken the truth. Dr. Towdi discovered that this *husbundee* had taken up with a young Namisan dancer named Fliflee.'

A gasp from the assembled company.

'*Jej jej*, my friends, that very same Fliflee who had earned a reputation for herself, and a very sizeable *eggnestee*, by stick-dancing in Dubai. Her name had been in the Namisan tabloids on more than one occasion, linked to one scandal or another.'

'Erm ...?' said Felicity.

'*Jef?*' said Mrs Katraree.

'Stick-dancing?' said Felicity.

'I hoped you would not ask, my dear,' said Mrs. Katraree.

The gentlemen, remaining silent, gave each other knowing looks and, fixing Mrs. Katraree, they sipped their coffee, waiting for her explanation.

'Stick-dancing,' Mrs Katraree explained, 'it is a form of music and movement, carried out by,' and here she lowered her voice very slightly, 'carried out by scantily-dressed ladies who are swimming around…'

'Swimming or swinging?' said Felicity in the interests of accuracy.

'Swinging, yes, swinging around … correct! Swinging around, and also sliding down a slippery stick.'

'*Ah, kappi skow!*' said Felicity.

*

'Perhaps I should explain to you why I left the University of Trinamisa,' said Timmaya. He was seated opposite Philip in a red and black speckled swivel chair that pivoted on a white stem. Before him, on his plate, the remnants of his *Chick Chick* Caesar salad. The two men had eaten in relative peace, but now there was a fresh blast from the war drums. 'Pap,' said Timmaya.

'Indeed, it is,' said Philip.

'We have our own very fine music, but increasingly this Namisan pap is rammed down our throats. I follow these trends, you see. How could I not? I have *kiddeez* of my own.' And, as if on cue, from beneath the table he drew out a *kiddee* of the Namisan variety and, with a few gentle words of admonition, he sent the boy on his way.

'You see, *Om* Philip, I was the one who set up the TU Department of Anglo-American Literature. I recruited an excellent faculty team including one young Namisan lecturer, *Om* Nadinda, and one Pundari, *Om* Trattat. Both of these I took under my wing and mentored. Both had MAs from the University of Prapundar, but their experience was lacking and their competence in English was extremely limited. I felt that with guidance these deficiencies could be addressed.

'My colleague, Professor Dwinndee, joined the University at the same time as I did, setting up the Department of Language and Linguistics. He too was one of those who applied for a scholarship. When *Om* Bogadan returned from Prapundar, his mother *Imee* Grace gave him free rein to expand the University's representation in the Arts. So it was that he established a Department of Language and Communications, which came into direct competition with Professor Dwinndee's own department. Using the authority vested in him by his mother, Bogadan transferred Professor Dwinndee's best faculty members to his own department. The one or two faculty members who protested were summarily dismissed.

Then something happened that, for me, was beyond the bounds of belief. That autumn, before the end of the academic year, *Om* Bogadan invited me into his office for *cha cha* – and, as you know, in our culture this is something that we cannot and would not refuse. We discussed our health, our families, the weather, and the autumn, which was much as it had been the previous year and through the year. Then he came to the real purpose of the meeting. He advised me that he had been in discussion recently with his mother about changes to the University's infrastructure and its overall objectives. With the aim of opening up opportunities for younger members of faculty, his mother had told him that she wished *Om* Nadinda to take over my position as Head of the Department of Anglo-American literature. What he said to me was, "You have done a good *workee*, *Om* Timmaya, but now it is time to step aside and let someone else have an opportunity to run the department and to adjust the mistakes you made during your term." I cannot say that I was aware of any significant mistakes that needed adjustment.'

'And so, what did you do?' asked Philip.

'What would *you* have done?' replied Timmaya. 'Faced with the ignominy of working under a less-qualified peer, I felt I had no alternative but to resign and return to Pundar.'

'I had no idea.' said Philip. 'I realised you had left but…'

'You have been to TU, *na na*?'

'I have,' said Philip.

'*Om* Philip,' said Timmaya, 'did you not notice that TU is meant to be an English-medium university, but that no one teaching on the main degree program is a native speaker of English.'

'No, I hadn't noticed,' said Philip, 'but surely that is quite normal. One would expect Namisans to teach in their own universities.'

Timmaya remained silent.

'I did notice ...' said Philip, rewinding to the memory of his participation in the TU faculty meeting, 'that no one speaks much in meetings ... except perhaps ...'

'Ito Bogadan. Correct! That is because most of the main program faculty, apart from Bogadan himself, simply cannot speak English,' explained Timmaya, 'not even the Professor of Anglo-American Literature, my successor *Om* Nadinda.'

Timmaya paused for a moment and shook his head.

'Do you know what they call TU at the University of Prapundar? They call it, "The Ivory Tower of Babel." They speak all the dialects of the Pundarnami region, but they cannot speak the language they should lecture in, which is English!'

'What of your colleague Professor Dwinndee?' asked Philip. 'Is he still in his post? I don't recall meeting him when I was there.'

Timmaya gave a sardonic laugh.

'Just a month after my meeting with Bogadan, Professor Dwinndee had the same experience as I had. He too was invited for *cha cha*, and there in Bogadan's office he learned that he was no longer Head of the Department of Language and Linguistics. Like me, Dwinndee is from Pundar, but he is a Southerner and as I mentioned to you earlier, they have an altogether more moronic temperament and a combative nature. Dwinndee is an unhappy man at the best of times. He told Bogadan that he refused to step down. This shocked Bogadan, who thought Dwinndee would go quietly. On the contrary, he had to have my colleague escorted off the premises by security. That was some three months back. In fact,

Dwinndee is still there, and was probably there when you visited. Did you go to Building Three?'

'No.'

'No, of course not. You know about our threes and our fours. No one goes to Building Three. That is reserved for Pundari administrative staff. Professor Dwinndee has a secret office in Building Three. That is where you will find him, working on the outline of his PhD, readying himself for the day when his opportunity will come.' Then, wistfully, he added, 'Perhaps it will never come.'

'Well, that's why I am here,' said Philip. 'That's my job, my *workee*. I'm Officer of Education and Culture.'

Timmaya gave a warm, almost affectionate laugh. '*Om* Philip, you are a good man, I am sure ... but then so was *Om* Jonathan. Remember that we are faced here with a very devious and manipulative character.' He spat out these last words. '*Om* Jonathan came, like you, with the best of intentions, but then he was, let us say, he was corrupted.'

Philip sat back dismayed.

'Yes, I know what you are thinking,' said Timmaya. 'You are thinking, "This cannot happen to me," but, you see, it happens, and it happens when you least expect it.' He paused and looked directly into Philip's eyes. 'Indeed, it may already have happened.'

'I ... I mean ... How could ...?' said Philip.

'How could this happen? Very easily. Bogadan has a way of finding your flaw, or perhaps some secret that you have, or some weakness. Many of us have all of these. In my case, he saw my pride. For as long as the autumn is autumn, I will regret the fault of pride, but it is *withinside* me and probably will remain so. That day when Bogadan told me that *Om* Nadinda would take my place, he knew that I could not ever submit myself to the authority of someone so lacking in knowledge and experience. I say this with the greatest of respect, *Om* Philip, but you should ask yourself which part of yourself you have already revealed to Bogadan that will fuel the fire of his machinations.'

The two men sat for a moment in silence – a silence punctuated only by the joyful squeals of the ice cream *kiddeez.*

'Bogadan is a very powerful man,' said Timmaya. 'Perhaps it does not seem so but, without betraying any confidences in your capacity as an Officer here at the Foundation, can you tell me that you have not as yet come across discrepancies or irregularities in the matters of high finance where Bogadan or TU are concerned?'

Philip hesitated. 'Yes, there are one or two matters that are perhaps a little disturb…' He stopped himself. '… that give some cause for concern.'

'Research money, for example,' said Timmaya.

'Erm … yes … to some degree,' said Philip.

'The research funds that are finding their way into the coffers of a certain Middle Eastern University …?'

Philip's alarm bells were ringing. Perhaps this conversation, which had had an entirely different objective, had gone beyond the boundaries of his present brief.

'In the Pundarnami tradition,' said Timmaya, as though he were changing the subject and beginning a lecture. 'In the Pundarnami tradition, we have built our economic stability on centuries of bartering and exchange. I give you a *pikapika* fruit, and you give me a portion of *kwa kwa.*'

Philip shuddered briefly at this mention of *kwa kwa*.

'If I gave you funds for your research program,' said Timmaya, 'and you were developing your reputation as a world-class institution in a sea of other world-class institutions, what would you give me in return? A stipend perhaps – that would, in fact, be a percentage of the money you had sent my way. Or perhaps I would give you an office with your name on the door, or I could nominate you as a member of an important research team. This would certainly stand you in good stead with regard to your activities *withinside* the world of academia.'

Philip flinched with that increasingly familiar feeling of foreboding, and he registered that a cone-bearing *kiddee* – a Kipkip Cream Whopper perhaps – returning in haste towards them had lost his footing.

'How hypothetical is all this exactly?' said Philip. He could see what was coming.

As the *kiddee's* prone body, arms outstretched, juddered along the marbled floor, his tiny fist opened and the ice cream cone parted company from its owner, soaring softside up through the air and then arching downwards – softside down – to its inevitable landing place, roughly between Philip's hairline and the bridge of his nose. Plop!

'Hypothetical? Did I say this was hypothetical?' said Timmaya.

*

So, Ushri was telling me that there's this woman – Pinga – who works at the Trinamisa School of Languages, and she teaches an advanced class in Namisan, and she's got this horrible man in her class who seems to be obsessed with her. He's always making suggestive remarks, winking at her during lessons, and bringing her gifts. It's so awful, apparently, that now she's only teaching there two days a week.

You hear stories all the time of teachers marrying their students, but no one says much about the students who harass their teachers. I can't imagine anything worse than having an advanced student who's too advanced. Just because a student has paid for a course it doesn't mean he's bought the teacher. That's taking bartering a marketplace too far.

I mention all of this because, after grumbling that I don't get out much, I've been offered a workee *at TSL. Certainly, that would help me re-integrate, but it's not exactly a good career move. As I see it, teaching any language is like painting a very long bridge. You start at one end and when you've finished, it's time to go back to where you started, and do it all over again. People offer you different paint and different paintbrushes, claiming it will speed up the process, but the fact remains that if the motivation isn't there, the job will only move forward at the pace of a* cara-cara.

I'd be wasting my time. I have no passion for it. We have to do the things we have a passion for. I wouldn't accept anyway for political reasons. After investing so much hope in my education, pappee *and* mammee *will think teaching at a language school is unworthy of me. And* pappee *wouldn't sleep at night worrying in case I fell in love with one of my students.*

Yes.
If only.

*

'So, let me see if I have understood correctly,' said Philip, carefully removing the *kipkip* ice cream from his brow. 'If I were bartering with this Middle-Eastern university, I could expect to secure myself a stipend, an office …'

'An office with a golf course view,' said Timmaya.

'And… a place on a research team,' said Philip.

'A very *prestigious* research team,' said Timmaya.

'Anything else?' asked Philip.

'Your research publications would be listed on the university website. Naturally, the team would do the writing.'

'And my photo?'

'And your photograph would also be on the website. Correct! You would be pictured standing in front of your bookshelf, holding an open volume in your hand.'

'So, I would have a role of some kind then?'

'Most certainly,' said Timmaya.

'As …?'

'Visiting Fellow in Communication and Cultural Understanding.'

Timmaya raised his eyebrows, looked at Philip and waited for his response.

'You're not telling me,' said Philip, 'that Bogadan is capable of teaching a course in Communication and Cultural Understanding.'

'Correct!' said Timmaya. 'I am not telling you this. You see,' he said, inclining across the table towards Philip, 'from time to time Bogadan flies in and makes an appearance. He does minimal teaching. A couple of hours at most. What he *does* teach he gleans from … *The Bluffers' Guide to Paralinguistic Behaviour* and various other – what do you call them? – quick-fix texts. And, in addition, he has an array of very excellent PowerPoints.'

Timmaya relaxed back into his chair and studied for a moment the impeccably manicured fingernails of his right hand. 'Yes,' he mused, 'he has a very excellent collection of PowerPoints … that he downloaded from my computer. Bogadan, you see, is a plagiarist par excellence.'

'But that's outrageous!' said Philip. 'Surely they can see through him?'

'The question is,' said Timmaya, 'do they *want* to see through him? And the answer is *na jej*, they do not. Abu Nar has its research funding. Their director has a lecture theatre named after him. Bogadan has his research post and his insurance policy. They are united for posterity: the two universities sealed together in a perpetual academic embrace.'

Not for nothing had Professor Timmaya held the post of Director of the Department of Anglo-American Literature.

Timmaya looked at his watch. 'I'm sorry, I must go,' he said. 'The wedding recommences at six. We have the Dove Ceremony tonight. One cannot miss the Dove Ceremony.'

The two men made their way towards the main entrance through the Nemo Acqua Tunnel, where predatory fish darted about them, and *kiddeez*, their faces pressed flat against the glass, glowed blue and green in the water lights.

'We need to meet again,' said Philip.

'With great pleasure,' said Timmaya. 'And I hope you will find time to come to the wedding. A marriage is a very important event in a man's life as I'm sure you are aware.'

Philip blushed. 'Indeed,' he said, 'and do please give the scholarship some thought. We need to move on this quite quickly.'

'I shall, as you say, give it some thought,' said Timmaya. 'Oh, and one more thing.' He cast a concerned glance at Philip's congealed eyebrows. 'I would advise you to rub that in since it contains many properties that serve to enrich the skin. *Kipkip* ice cream is far cheaper than the lotions they sell in the Trinamisa Galley, and equally effective.' Timmaya gave a brief smile. 'Just a little Pundari tip,' he said.

At their approach, a set of Mall doors slid open. A large bulky figure stood in the entrance, silhouetted against a flood of bright *autumn-autumn* sunlight. Philip blinked.

'Ah, Ratni,' he said. 'What a pleasant coincidence!'

'*Om* Pilip,' said Ratni, scowling. 'You need driver?'

***

19

DISCOVER NAMISAN

'We are beginning with brief history of Namisa,' said the teacher.

Philip thumbed through his new copy of *Discover Namisan – Pre-Elementary*. This first lesson was not what he had anticipated. He had to get on, and time was of the essence. He had heard just one comment too many about Felicity being a natural linguist and having a 'real flair for languages' and a 'rapport with the culture' and, 'wouldn't she have been an asset if she had been working for the Foundation?' Well, too bad, thought Philip. *He* was the one working for the Foundation, not Felicity, and so what if she managed to string a few words together and make herself understood? No *bushkil* there. Philip scratched his pencil up and down the seam of his notebook. The teacher droned on. Philip wanted language not culture, but *Discover Namisan — Pre-Elementary* was going to give him both, whether he liked it or not. What Philip wanted was total proficiency in Namisan. And he wanted it right now. There was not a minute to be lost, especially not on a brief history of Namisa.

'So,' explained the teacher, 'neighbouring islands of Namisa and Pundar they obtained independence from Britain in 1961 after great deal of legal *wranglee-wranglee* about organisation and distribution of government in Pundarnami region.'

With a knobbly bamboo cane, he pointed to a map on the wall that was labelled with indecipherable writing in curly letters.

'Following this,' continued the teacher, 'there was amicable separation of two peoples — Namisans and Pundaris. As you maybe being aware, over centuries Namisans are being traditionally peacemakers and diplomats, while Pundaris they are being very great noble warriors and war-makers. So, you are maybe asking yourselves why when there is having great potential for strife, division was amicable?'

Philip was not actually asking himself that question, but he was going to be obliged to listen to the answer anyway.

'Well, division into two countries is being-been amicable because Namisans is on Namisa, and Pundaris is on Pundar. In 1960s, connection by air and water is-being very poorly, so basically too much trouble to fight war and go, come back, go, come back. Better stay in one place and be friends.'

It had been with a profound sense of regret and failure that Philip had finally signed up for a course in Modern Standard Namisan at the Trinamisa School of Languages. He was prompted to do so by Alan, who went there himself – but only because he particularly liked his advanced-level teacher *Imeetinee* Sprytee. However, for

Philip it was the *Namisan in the blink of an eye* publicity that had sealed it. He saw himself going in one door with next to zero Namisan, and emerging from another door fluent, accurate and with an impeccable accent. If Felicity was sitting at home doing nothing and yet had by far surpassed him in her command of spoken Namisan, then, clearly, this must be a very simple language, which he should be able to master easily … in the blink of an eye.

A quick look around the classroom confirmed to him that he was in the company of a group of people who would undoubtedly struggle with the unique challenges of the Namisan tongue, since they had probably not yet mastered their own. There was Bernardo, the forty-something from the Italian Embassy, who sat with his legs crossed, swinging his foot restlessly back and forth. There was the diminutive Sylvie from the French Embassy – she of the Shangri-La pool – apparently attending her third beginners' course. There was a German, who looked like a Klaus or a Werter, and there was a Lebanese, who looked like … a Lebanese, and who dozed in the corner of the room. There was a cross-looking Pundari, whose name no one knew since he spoke no English, French, Italian or German.

For Philip it had come to this. From cocktails to conjugations.

*

Enough of all this worrying about what to do. I can't expect everything to fall into place immediately, though obviously that's what I'd like to happen. Instead… shopping trip with Bindee coming up. That's what people expect girls to do. I won't disappoint them.

Weird dream last night. I was in a shopping mall and it was full of water, like a whole sea of water, and I was sitting in a boat, bobbing about, and opposite me was a very large babbigall *bird playing a guitar and singing me a song. Somewhere in this dream,* pappee *was sweeping up* babbigall *droppings and complaining they were polluting the ocean. None of this was that surprising. I'd been up in the attic the previous morning sorting through miscellaneous storage boxes, picking out my old schoolbooks to send to a charity for poor children in Pundar. On reflection, I'm not quite sure how these* kiddeez *would benefit from a heap of out-of-date British textbooks, but* pappee *said it was a good idea so I did it anyway, thumbing through the pages, reading bits here and there and looking at the pictures.* Pappee *is doing her* autumn-autumn *cleaning. We all have to be seen to cooperate.*

It set me thinking that it might be fun to have a babbigall *as a pet. As I recall, someone at the Foundation owned one. Bindee says he left in a bit of a hurry so it's likely he didn't take the bird with him, and then she said it was scandalous that people bought or adopted pets and then abandoned them when they grew tired of them or moved on. Ushri said I should get a puppy, which of course set Bindee off on one of her rants.*

I wonder where he ended up – the babbigall, *I mean, not Ushri?*

*

Alan attended the Trinamisa School of Languages only on Mondays and Wednesdays, because on Fridays his beloved *Imeetinee* Sprytee went to stay for the weekend with her mum in Wunamisa. In her place, *Om* Ghettit took the class.

'If I bump into him,' said Alan, 'he says, "Oh, *Om* Alan, why you never come to my class." Poor old *Om* Ghettit. He just doesn't get it.'

And he chortled with laughter, having found himself very amusing. It was Alan who guided Philip through the enrolment formalities and who provided him with words of advice and encouragement.

'What you need to do is hurry up and get into Sprytee's Advanced class. That's what you need to do, because, you see, the longer you stay with Trattat and the beginners, the longer you remain a social outcast. It's like this: Namisan accent good, Pundari accent very bad.'

It was true that Namisans could not much see the point in teaching foreigners their language. It was a tedious and unrewarding job. And, anyway, why open up the secrets of your linguistic code to a bunch of ex-invaders? Far better, surely, to keep them in the dark? The task of filling the demand for language instruction thus fell to Pundaris, who were in effect the least prepared to provide this.

'So that's why my teacher is *bunga*,' said Alan, 'and your teacher is *na bunga*. Give me *Imeetinee* Sprytee any day,' said Alan. 'In fact, give me *Imeetinee* Sprytee.'

Philip concluded that Alan was in Namisa because in any other country he would have been locked up.

'I still don't know what you're on about,' said Philip.

'Well, take your bloke Trattat, for example. Maybe if he'd been Namisan instead of Pundari, he'd still have a job at TU. You see, when push comes to shove, it's Pundaris out and Namisans in.'

'So, what about Equal Opportunities?' said Philip.

'That *is* Equal Opportunities,' said Alan. 'It's just that to benefit from it, you need to be Namisan. Get it?'

*

'Practise, practise, practise … you must always making-practising,' said *Om* Trattat. 'This is key to good language learning. No speak, no learn. You no speak Namisan language and instead you speak your language, you are becoming very good speaking your language, but Namisan nothing, so practise, practise, practise.'

Philip observed that since he had not actually learnt anything in his first lesson, there was nothing yet that he could practise.

'You all have book?' asked *Om* Trattat, looking around the classroom. Everyone had the book, except for the Lebanese, who had had a hard day and had not yet woken up. But, since he was sitting in the corner at the back of the class propped up against the wall, it did not much matter. *Om* Trattat opened the book at Unit One. The class opened the book at Unit One.

'This book,' said *Om* Trattat, 'I not like it much, because it having too many pair works, and not explaining verbs properly.' He closed the book. 'So, we not using book in this my class.' He walked slowly from the left of the classroom to the right of the classroom. All eyes followed him. 'Now, first lesson,' he said, and he walked slowly from the right of the classroom to the left of the classroom. Then he stopped and pulled a small piece of paper out of his pocket. He examined it for a moment and then said, 'Translate please this sentence.' He read slowly and deliberately. "I have come here today to thank you for the lovely flowers that you sent to me yesterday." He walked to his desk, sat down and began reading his copy of the Monday edition of the *Pundari Observer*.

In the silence that followed, Philip heard only Bernardo's sighs and the flutter and flap of rapidly turned pages as Klaus – or Werter – scoured the glossary at the back of his book. Philip thought it best not to panic at this early stage but to approach the task systematically word by word. He put up his hand and gave a quiet cough.

'Yes?' said *Om* Trattat.

'What's "I" in Namisan?' asked Philip.

'Good question,' said *Om* Trattat. 'The word is "*an*." In Namisan, this word is a personal pronoun. Other personal pronouns are: *annee, pa, pa'ee, ut, at, init, nit, nittee, paat, paatee, utoo, atoo*. Very good. Now continue.' *Om* Trattat resumed his reading of the *Pundari Observer*. There were a few moments of silence, then Philip put up his hand again.

'Yes?' said *Om* Trattat.

'How do you say "have" in Namisan?' said Philip.

'This is also good question,' said *Om* Trattat. 'In Namisan, this word is verb. It is "*upa*."'

Philip chewed the end of his pen. He was worried that he did not know the Namisan word for "come" and he felt embarrassed to ask. He looked over at Klaus's exercise book. Klaus quickly masked the page with his Empire State Building pencil case. Sylvie put up her hand.

'Yes?' said *Om* Trattat.

'What iz zee word for "come"?' said Sylvie.

'Good question,' said *Om* Trattat. 'In Namisan, this word is also verb. It is "*gogo*."'

Philip put up his hand.

'Yes?' said *Om* Trattat.

'I've finished the first part of the sentence,' said Philip.

'Uffa!' said Bernardo throwing down his pen in irritation.

'Good,' said *Om* Trattat. 'Read please.'

Philip cleared his throat. '*An upa gogo*,' he read, and then looked smugly around Sylvie in the direction of Bernardo. Bernardo avoided eye contact and sat with his arms folded, jiggling his foot up and down.

Om Trattat came from behind his desk and, looking down at the floor, he walked slowly from the left of the classroom to the right of the classroom. Then he stopped and looked up. 'No, this is incorrect,' he said. 'In Namisan "have come" is another word. It is "*gogot*." So, "I have come" is "*An gogot*"' *Om* Trattat looked up at the clock on the wall above the door. Then he looked at the class.

Philip noted that he had a way of looking at you as though he was not looking at you. He gave the class this vacant look of his and then he said, 'I think now is late so we will take *nappy*.'

There was a brief rustle of activity and, as a body, the newly awakened Lebanese included, the students put down their pens, vacated their seats and headed for the door. *Om* Trattat slowly wandered behind them. He stopped just before he passed Philip on his way out of the room.

'You are not going to *nappy?*' he asked.

'What is *nappy?*' said Philip.

'Like rest,' said *Om* Trattat. 'We take rest for maybe ten, fifteen minutes.'

'Oh, okay,' said Philip, and he set down his pen and followed in the path of the other students, to take his *nappy* in the Trinamisa School of Languages Canteen.

*

The gentlemen's section of the Coffee Circle was almost a full house that afternoon. It was rumoured that Mrs. Katraree was going to talk about the disreputable practice of lip-dancing.

'Some of you will have heard that today I am going to talk about lip-dancing,' she announced. 'In fact, this is incorrect. What I would like to talk about today is the conservation of the Namisan language.'

There was a fierce rumbling as chairs were moved back to their original places, and discontented muttering arose from the men's section.

'Now,' said Mrs. Katraree, 'some people think that APPuL is a fruit, but those of us who are at the know, know that APPuL is "Association for Preservation of Pundari Language." This association is in University of Prapundar but here, based TU, we have UPNaL, "Union for Preservation of Namisan Language." Important to remind you – and to tell to *Imee* Felicitu here – that there is big difference between Pundari and Namisan. Pundari is dialect only, but Namisan is language with long tradition and great literature.'

Felicity took note.

Mrs. Katraree continued. 'Namisan is language of diplomacy, education, law, fashion, but Pundari is dialect of common *om* in the street ... taxi drivers, security guards, plumbers, and – of course – cobblers. And, *Imee* Felicitu, you should-knowing that good words are in Namisan, also long words, but bad words are in Pundari. Who is learning language of Namisapundar Region for social integration and *acception* must be learning Namisan, not Pundari.'

This all seemed perfectly clear to Felicity.

*

Philip found the Trinamisa School of Languages to be a rather grim place. This belief was compounded following his first visit that afternoon to the school canteen.

'*Salami,*' Philip said to a burly fellow wearing a striped apron with frills down the sides.

The man glared at him. 'No *salami* today,' he said, 'Step aside. Next!'

Philip stepped aside and shuffled to the back of what was now a very long queue. Sylvie moved up to the front of the queue.

'*Salati,*' she said sweetly to the man in the apron.

'*Salati, Imeetinee* Sylvie,' said the man. 'What you like today? We got *sanddijez*, different kind, like *chick chick*, *chikoko*, *bulbi patter*, and special today ... *kwa kwa.*'

'*Ah jej, chick chick* ee iz *bunga,*' said Sylvie.

Twenty minutes later when all but the slow snackers had returned to their classrooms and the queue had dispersed, Philip reached the counter.

'*Salati,*' he said.

'Okay,' said the man.

'I would like a *chick chick sanddij,*' said Philip.

'All *sanddijjez* finish,' snapped the man, 'only *krips* is there. You take or you leave.'

'Take,' said Philip, '*Krips* are *bunga.*'

*

On his way back to his classroom after his *nappy*, eating his packet of *krips*, Philip passed the open doorway of a room where an English lesson was just coming to a close. He caught sight of a familiar, baggy maroon T-shirt.

'So, for Wednesday,' said the teacher, 'write me six conditional sentences, and for the Namisans amongst you, no need to write any third conditionals. Okay? Just first conditional and second conditional.'

'Frank?' said Philip. The man turned, and Philip saw the unmistakable, 'Having a spicey time in Tobago,' slogan on his chest.

*

So, Philip concluded, Frank was another TU refugee who had found his way to the Trinamisa School of Languages. Later that evening, Philip was at last happy to find himself seated at the smoke-engulfed bar of the Sleepy Hollow Nite Club. Before the all-nighters took up their places for the floor show, Philip fuelled Frank with Golden Lizard beers in exchange for the latest account of events at that unfortunate establishment.

'That teacher of yours,' said Frank, 'he's the bloke who was recruited by Timmaya.'

'Which teacher?' said Philip as he munched his *chikoko krips* and looked out for stick-dancers.

'You know. Trattat,' said Frank, speaking loudly above the rising rhythms of the Sleepy Hollow *drumsters*. He took a cigarette from his pack of Namisan Lights, and lit up. 'There were two of them … Trattat and Nadinda, both equally useless and both of them hired by Timmaya to work in his Department of Anglo-American literature.'

'Oh! *That* Trattat!' said Philip, shouting. 'You know, I'm finding this all very confusing. I mean, who's Namisan and who's Pundari? And who's from TU and who's from TSL? I'm trying to get it, but …'

'No, not Ghettit,' said Frank, shouting back above the music. 'Not Ghettit. Trattat! Ghettit works at TSL. Trattat was the one from TU who got terminated … then came to TSL. And Nadinda was the one who got Timmaya's job. Got it?'

'I thought you said it wasn't Ghettit,' said Philip, distracted now by the gyrating beat of new-age Namisapundar Rock.

Frank moved in closer. Philip could smell the smoke on his breath.

'The important thing,' said Frank, 'is to know your Pundaris from your Namisans – then no one gets hurt. Trattat and Ghettit and Timmaya – well, they were just unlucky. They got born Pundari.' Frank sniffed, took a swig of his beer, and then swivelled around on his bar stool to watch the first floorshow.

'Well, *looka looka!*' he said, 'If it isn't Fliflee – another of Bogadan's little playmates.'

*

There was a relaxed atmosphere next morning at the Coffee Circle. Since the members had had a real author in their midst for the past few months, Mrs. Katraree was now toying with the idea of starting a book club.

'Those people over at the temple,' said Mrs. Katraree, 'they have a Cha-Cha Circle, you know, for the discussing of books. I find it very preventative.'

'I think that's "pretentious,"' said Felicity.

'*Sahsah!* I think so too, my dear. They discuss literature, but they are a very simple people – very *bassee.*'

Felicity jotted down this word.

'And I understand,' interposed Dr. Towdi, 'that they drink their *cha-cha nitted* with *tiga-tiga.*'

'Is it customary to *nit* tea with *tiga-tiga*? I think I'd like to try that,' said Felicity.

Mrs. Katraree laid her hand on Felicity's arm. 'It is powerful stuff, my dear. I do not advise it,' she said. 'You would get *nitted* very quickly.'

'They are reading Chick Lit,' continued Dr Towdi, who had been over there to take a look.

'Well, I don't think any of us here is interested in agriculture or farming, *na na?*' said Mrs. Katraree. 'With perhaps the exception of Dr. Manyu from the Department of Agriculture.'

Dr. Manyu looked up briefly from the sports section of the *Trinamisa Times*, but thought better of it.

'Actually …' said Dr Towdi.

'What else are they reading?' demanded Mrs. Katraree.

'They have read nearly all the novels of Barbara Taylor Bradford, and they like them very much.'

'Indeed!' said Mrs Katraree. 'Well, if he is someone worth reading, perhaps we should consider him.'

***

20

THE WISDOM OF THE BABBIGALL

Felicity was greatly changed since that day she first set foot inside the SnowWhite Dry Kleen Shop. She had definitely mellowed, becoming more contemplative and less irascible. This was in part due to the calming intellectual climate of the SnowWhite Coffee Circle, and in part due to the presence of Parrot.

After the initial trauma of his separation from Jonathan and Caroline, and his unwanted initiation into the world of *kiddeez* during his temporary residency at Ratni's home, Parrot was now infinitely better off with his adoptive parents in Trinamisa than he would have been in Prapundar or – for that matter – Tbilisi. His sulky feather-plucking days had come to an end when, on the advice of Dr. Manyu, he was allowed to roam free and liberate his inner *babbigall*.

Felicity was in awe of Parrot's remarkable powers of language acquisition. She was more inclined to listen to him than to speak in front of him. Indeed, it was out of consideration for Parrot and his loose grey tongue that, of late, she rarely swore out loud though, subject to extreme pressure – the kind most often triggered by Philip – she might do so under her breath.

Fortunately for Felicity, Mrs. Katraree's daytime Coffee Circle had weaned her onto coffee and off the erratic downing of 'sun-uppers.' Her alcohol consumption was limited now to sundowners, and to the occasional multicoloured Namisan cocktail, all of which could only be deemed a very good *thingy*. Just one further factor may have contributed to Felicity's more tempered demeanour. Some might have said that she was in love.

The mysterious Charles – friend of flamboyant artist Katrina – entered Felicity's novel, displacing Roberto, whom her protagonist Flocky had now recognised for what he truly was: arrogant and self-centred. Yes, it was all coming clear to Felicity now. Although Flocky had separated from Roberto, she had not been able to rid herself of her memories of him … the way he held his cigarette, the way he tossed his hair back from his forehead, the way he buttered his toast, like the perfectionist that he was, smoothing the butter right to the edges of the crust.

Felicity paused for a moment and, with her magic marker, blacked out the last part of that sentence since, as she was well aware but sometimes forgot, fussy buttering habits, like the squeezing of toothpaste tubes, were the stuff of irritation not fond recollection.

Yes, Roberto, in all his composite glory, was gone from Flocky's physical life, but for some inexplicable reason he remained *withinside* her heart. He was unfinished business. Flocky needed … closure.

Felicity stopped typing. Would Flocky need to confront Roberto, or could there be closure without confrontation? Surely, she could not sell the film rights of a novel that contained no dramatic confrontation? How would Flocky realise once and for all that Roberto was an arrogant, self-centred bastard?

Well, for one *thingy*, he had been beastly to her. She was the one who had had to trudge down the pot-holed road to the Two Rivers Co-op to buy marmalade for his breakfast because he was too busy doing his *workee* to go for himself. After all. she wasn't his housemaid, *na na*? Felicity slammed back the carriage of her typewriter. Pulling at strands of her unruly hair, she sighed. Parrot sighed too. They both knew this would not do. Flocky was simply getting all deep and embittered again. Yet it was true that Roberto had cared so little for Flocky that he had left her alone night after night in their little beach house in Nusa Dua. But for Flocky, all that was in the past. Now there was Charles.

Who can ever say if the created character follows or precedes the real character? Felicity, and others like her, would have said that the created character stood alone in his own world of the imagination. Observers from the Coffee Circle might have judged otherwise. As Parrot preened his feathers, Felicity sipped her Namisan Dawn cocktail, mixed by her own hand to a recipe acquired in an informative session led by Mrs. Katraree. On reflection, she realised she had learned much from the Coffee Circle and had greatly expanded her social connections as well as her linguistic repertoire.

Felicity's thoughts again turned to Charles. Flocky was intrigued by him, drawn to him. What exactly did she see in Charles? He was not especially handsome, not at all in fact. He was elegant it was true. It was something about him. He had a certain look in his eyes that she could not define. He was knowledgeable. This man could teach her things she could not even imagine, or maybe she could teach him a *thingy* or two. She took another sip of her cocktail and closed her eyes. Her eyelids fluttered.

Flocky wanted to know who he was in reality. What dark secret was he hiding? And, anyway, why was a secret always dark? Charles had made no mention to Flocky of any woman in his life. Could he have been nursing some deep hurt, some rebuttal, some bitter experience that had caused him to close himself off from his emotions? Was this some kind of forbidden love, a love that was not right for him? Had he refused to accept that this woman, for whatever reason, was unattainable? Was he still seeing this woman? Who was she and what was her name? Felicity took another moment to savour her cocktail.

Appearing now from beneath the table where he had been hanging silent and bat-like in the wrought-iron frame, Parrot hauled himself onto the table top and shuffled his way to the typewriter to dismantle whatever needed to be dismantled.

'This woman,' said Felicity out loud, 'who was she and what was her name?'

Parrot turned his head sideways, looked at Felicity with his beady eye and in a strong masculine voice, said quite clearly and unequivocally, 'Fliflee!'

'Fliflee?' said Felicity.

Parrot replied in a sweet little baby voice.

'Come to Fliflee,' he said. 'Come to Fliflee.'

*

I've had a slight difference of opinion with Bindee. I should have seen this coming. As I've mentioned before, she's always agitating about one thing or another, organising meetings, and talking about staging protests.

At the moment, it's all about Pundexit with her, and she isn't even Pundari. She says that as a nation we are ethically flawed and it's up to people like us to put things right. I told her that if she didn't watch out, she'd get herself into a lot of trouble. Oops! Mistake. She said I was very naïve and I didn't know the half of what was going on in my own country. I said that as far as I could tell everything was going on just fine and people were very happy and had good jobs and a high standard of living. She rolled her eyes and said the best place for people like me was the shopping mall.

Very upsetting. What am I missing here?

*

After the next lesson, in which Philip learned the words, "here," "today," "to," "thank," and "you," Philip cornered *Om* Trattat in his *nappy* and arranged to take him out for a drink at the Trinamisa Tower Café, just around the corner from the school. He felt sure that the sight of Fliflee and her sequined companions would have been too overwhelming for *Om* Trattat, which was why

Sleepy Hollow was not on their itinerary. Also, *Om* Trattat was not really dressed for the part. He came to every lesson in the same dusty old grey suit, which had miscellaneous stains down the front of the jacket. His one treasured possession was a battered brown briefcase with the gold embossed logo of the Oil and Gas Institute on its front flap, a relic from a conference attended by Bogadan, and deposited by him soon after in a campus skip, whence *Om* Trattat had rescued it.

Om Trattat clasped his beer glass tightly in both hands for fear of someone taking it from him. The alcohol loosened his tongue, as Philip had hoped it would.

'So, what happened at TU after Professor Timmaya left?' said Philip.

'*Na bunga. Na bunga,*' said *Om* Trattat, shaking his head. 'This man *Om* Nadinda he was being my colleague, and then he was being my boss. This because *Om* Bogadan wanting to do many changes in Department.'

'What kind of changes?'

'It is happen like this,' said *Om* Trattat, and then he talked.

*

Om Trattat had always considered himself fortunate to have secured a job in a world-class university like TU. In Namisa, under the wing of Professor Timmaya, for the first time in his life there was scope for advancement. He and *Om* Nadinda took up their posts in the Department of Anglo-American Literature at the same time. *Om* Nadinda was the younger of the two, and both had their

MAs from the University of Prapundar. Prapundar was a respected and well-established Pundari university, though its academic reputation was not such that it could compete with similar institutions outside the region. In that sense it could not be considered to be world-class. Nevertheless, it attracted the crème de la crème of Namisan, as well as Pundari, scholars. Many of these remained in Prapundar and took up teaching posts though, for most, the great dream was to transfer to Wunamisa and enjoy Namisan-style benefits.

The post *Om* Trattat held at TU was not Assistant Professor but rather Assistant to the Professor, but this represented to him the poor Pundari man's achievement of the Namisan dream. Both Trattat and Nadinda received the same monthly supplement to their salaries, which meant that *Om* Trattat could at last set aside some money for the future, affording him a comfortable home for his wife and young family in Pundar. The situation though was set to change.

After his unexpected promotion, *Om* Nadinda distanced himself from *Om* Trattat and grew cold, whereas before he had showed warm collegiality. There was no more discussion between them about departmental matters and *Om* Trattat found himself obliged to communicate with *Om* Nadinda via his secretary. Increasingly, he was excluded from departmental meetings. They simply happened, and he found out about them after the fact.

Roughly two months after the departure of Professor Timmaya, *Om* Trattat received his first unexpected and unwanted surprise. His salary cheque showed a substantial deduction, resulting in the overall total falling to that of the wage of an Administrative Assistant. From the starry ranks of honorary Namisan, he had fallen into the dark pit of the impoverished ex-pat worker. *Om* Nadinda's secretary was tight-lipped about the deductions, and the man himself was constantly busy and inaccessible. Looking again at his salary advice, *Om* Trattat felt there must have been some administrative error, some oversight on the part of the Accounts Department. If they had meant to change the parameters of his salary, they would surely have informed him beforehand, leaving open some channel for appeal or negotiation.

Om Trattat sat down at his computer and, in his best and most formal Namisan, he wrote to *Om* Lulli, the Head of Accounts. He explained carefully and with the utmost courtesy how his salary had been so catastrophically reduced from one month to the next and how this was undoubtedly an unfortunate mistake which he would respectfully request them to correct at their convenience. He sent his letter forthwith via e-mail, but it was only after a wait of two days that he received a response. *Om* Lulli's reply was telegraphic in so far as electronic mail can be termed as such. His salary reduction, *Om* Lulli informed him, was as per the instruction of HR Memo AUT 44 874 TRAT. There was nothing more to explain the whys or wherefores of this decision.

Om Trattat wrote again to *Om* Lulli. Could he, he humbly requested, be allowed to see HR Memo AUT 44 874 TRAT? He waited a further day for an even briefer response. He was advised that he should 'revert to HR' for further information. On that same afternoon, as he prepared himself to compose a stronger more specific message to *Om* Lulli, appealing to whatever compassionate side he might have, the word spread that *Om* Lulli had been 'terminated.' He had gone as swiftly as Timmaya, no warning and no explanation. *Om* Trattat passed by *Om* Lulli's office within an hour of hearing the news. He found the room empty and the desk cleared of any record of the man who had previously occupied that space.

This was a very lean month for *Om* Trattat. In addition to the inexplicable deductions for that month and the previous month, a huge and undocumented utilities bill depleted his funds, pruned at source from his salary payment. He contacted the Faculty Housing Department and requested a copy of the original electricity and water readings from DEW. They sent him the figures, but not the bills. Math was not his strong subject, but he managed to add up and take away the various elements of the cost. Their totals did not match up with his totals. He was living as a single man in a tiny flat clocking up the same expenses as a family of six. How could this be? Additionally, there had been no running water in his flat on the Faculty Compound since he had moved in. Like other university employees, he fetched the water himself from one of the ornamental coffee pot fountains on the campus close by the entrance of the compound. Even enduring this hardship, he had considered himself more fortunate than most, for the money he sent home guaranteed a level of comfort and security above that afforded to the average Pundari family.

The deduction of the allowance combined with the unexpected rise in the cost of *Om* Trattat's utilities now meant that almost every last *kola* went home and he struggled to survive on the sparse funds remaining. Driven to desperation, he started to compose a letter detailing his case to *Om* Fredee, Head of Human Resources. Snatching a break from this task to find a scrap of food on some unscraped plate in the cafeteria, he caught sight of *Om* Fredee being escorted from Building Two by a grim-faced Pundari security guard.

*

With trembling hand, *Om* Trattat lifted his glass and drank.

'So, did you ever get your allowance back?' asked Philip.

'*Na jej,*' said *Om* Trattat. 'Who is being there that I am asking? Professor Timmaya he gone, *Om* Lolli he gone, *Om* Fredee he gone. *Om* Nadinda, he gone in his head he gone. And others they afraid they going too. Others they also find surprise in pay cheque and too afraid to go complaining.'

'What about Bogadan? You couldn't go and see him, confront him?'

Om Trattat drained the last of the Golden Lizard beer from his glass.

'I am thinking this and I'm going,' said *Om* Trattat, biting his lip.

Philip waved to the waitress for more beers.

'And …?' said Philip.

'*Na bunga,*' said *Om* Trattat. 'You see, *Om Baadumba* Pilip, that is why I am teaching now at Trinamisa School of Languages.'

*

For some time, Felicity had harboured doubts and suspicions about Parrot and his former owners, Jonathan and Caroline. Now here it was, the walking, talking proof – or should she say, the shuffling, squawking proof? – of Jonathan's infidelity with the shameless Fliflee, who should have been sent back to Dubai forthwith, and of Caroline's presumed infidelity with … with someone … someone who did not have the voice of Jonathan, or Fliflee, or Caroline. In short, Parrot was a parrot – or rather a *babbigall* – that had seen things Felicity could scarcely imagine. Except that, being a writer, she *could* imagine them and, she had decided, would most certainly incorporate them in her book.

She wiped her typewriter clean of *babbigall* droppings and began a new and intriguing episode of her story. She knew she should not, but she felt herself drawn to write about that wastrel Roberto, how he had used her protagonist Flocky, how he had neglected her and betrayed her, and how, once transposed to a foreign soil where no one knew him or could point an accusing finger at him, he had indulged in a life of unrestrained debauchery.

***

21

THE CAMEL DANCE

Philip's appointment was for seven in the evening at the house of Professor Timmaya's cousin Wallee. Philip borrowed Alan's Nissan Sunny for the purpose. The green Cinquecento usually came 'with driver,' but Philip's better judgement told him to leave Ratni out of it for the moment. His first stop had been outside a concrete two-storey building next to the Trinamisa School of Languages, where *Om* Trattat waited for him wearing a violet *shala kan* edged with gold thread, and a pair of loose pale blue cotton trousers that concertina-ed at the ankle. Except for the orange Oil and Gas Institute baseball cap, Philip thought *Om* Trattat looked quite smart in an ethnic sort of way.

Philip himself was well-prepared for the evening ahead, having consulted his Robinson-Smith prior to leaving the house.

> For the purpose of marriages, the men and the women hold separate ceremonies, periodically uniting in a mixed event. Betrothals very often follow in the

wake of these joint functions with the result that one series of wedding ceremonies very often leads to another series of wedding ceremonies, and in Namisa – or indeed in Pundar – one can happily be a full-time wedding guest. In a recent census carried out by the Namisan government it was revealed that, as a general rule, more working days are lost to wedding attendance than to sickness.

(Extract from 'Courtship and marriage practices,' (p.201) in *Namisa - A Traveller's Guide: from tradition to tourism and back*, by Michael Robinson-Smith)

Om Trattat, who was usually expressionless or simply glum, appeared now to be unusually happy and was looking forward to being reunited with his old boss. Added to this was the fact that he and Philip were to take part in the most greatly preferred of all the marriage functions, the Camel Dance. This always took place on day five of the celebrations and it was performed, or so Timmaya had informed him, to ensure that the couple's journeying through life would be safe and productive.

Wallee's 'house' was in reality a small run-down apartment on the first floor of a row of buildings that were built on one of Trinamisa's hillsides. Philip parked outside behind one other vehicle, a small pick-up truck. The door of the apartment was open and there was a hive of activity and light *withinside*. When Philip and *Om* Trattat entered, they found seven or eight young men sitting on carpets, chattering and snacking, with a television playing in the background. A group of children, their ages varying from three or four through to seven or eight, ran from room to room screaming and laughing, and occasionally changing channel when they managed to steal away the TV remote. Young women dressed in multicoloured sarongs, presumably the children's mothers or elder sisters, pursued the youngest of the children and on catching them, force-fed them spoonfuls of mushy, beige food.

The air was thick with a heavy incense that burned in painted ceramic jars placed around the corners of the apartment, leaving the occupants to tread through a ground fog of headily odorous white mist. *Om* Trattat was immediately at ease in this company, joyous to find himself back amongst Pundari compatriots and, as Philip had anticipated, even more elated to be in the company of his ex-Director on this auspicious occasion.

Timmaya had emerged minutes after their arrival, bedecked in his finest marriage regalia. Philip scarcely recognised him. Gone were the elegantly cut suit, the crisply ironed white shirt and the School of Oriental and African Studies tie. Instead, he loomed in the doorway in an imposing turban of yellow, green, and red, its folds twisted, furled and tucked until it reached a great height, and then embellished with the red feathers of the *babbigall* bird. He wore a gold-threaded orange and yellow sarong, not in the usual dyed cotton, but in a glistening brocade that reached down past his hairy ankles to his brown-sandaled feet. His matching *shala kan* was buttoned up to the neck, and at his waist he wore a wide sash in the same chiffon-like fabric as his turban, but additionally decorated with small sea shells looped through a chain of tiny gold-coloured beads. Firmly tucked into the sash was a ceremonial *krot*, an instrument resembling a large hammer with a thick wooden handle, carved and painted in the Pundari fashion and with a weighty sphere-like embossed metallic head. Throughout the war-filled history of the Pundaris and the Namisans, the *krot* had been a fearsome weapon of mass brain destruction. One well-trained blow of a *krot* initiated the recipient's journey to the afterlife.

'Welcome! *Bungagogo!*' exclaimed Professor Timmaya, giving the traditional Pundarnamisan bow and then throwing open his arms to embrace first his colleague and then his honoured guest.

This visit to Wallee's apartment lasted some two hours, twenty-five minutes of which were given over to the *nalungaseesee* ceremony reserved for friends reunited. A further twenty minutes served to introduce Philip to his new companions. Forty minutes or so were given over to miscellaneous eating and drinking from communal vessels. The remaining time was, to Philip's dismay, given over to kitting him out in suitable attire for the evening's proceedings.

Philip lost count of the Pundaris who came and went from the flat that evening. His ears were filled with their easy chatter, and his nose with the overpowering aroma of the incense from the *okaly* tree, some of which he noticed was being rolled into strips of dried *yellibellee* leaves, then lit, and then passed from guest to guest with much pleasurable clucking and humming. When his turn came, his lungs filled with a rush of menthol and cinnamon, edged he thought with an aftertaste of fly spray. His head swam, and lights flashed at the corners of his eyes. The cry of *tika tika takeena* went up as his new friends looked on with immense glee, and then cheered and whistled when the smoke filtered out through his nose.

'*Mumbatipa!*' they exclaimed, slapping him on the head in admiration.

Timmaya, who emerged from the kitchen at that moment holding a glass of *bulbi* juice, witnessed the scene and said in a loud and booming voice, '*Sheematipa-at,*' and promptly removed Philip from this overly ribald company.

Philip regretted that his Namisan was limited mainly to the phrase, "I have come here today to thank you," and that his Pundari was at zero. A more comprehensive understanding of the language would have eliminated surprises and better clarified for him the Pundarnamisan and the Namisapundari agendas. Still a little woozy from his first taste of *okaly*, it took Philip a few minutes to realise that the Pundaris were on the move. Timmaya took hold of his arm and led him to the door. He instructed him firstly that he was to follow the *pikky-up*, and to take with him some of the Pundari *yobbeez* for whom there was no room in the *pikky-up*, and secondly that he was to store in the boot of his car the five trays of *hura* fruit desserts and the *chikoko sanddijez*, which were destined for the refreshments table at the venue.

It was with considerable difficulty that Philip climbed into the driving seat of the Nissan Sunny, since he had never before worn a skirt. His turban brushed against the roof of the car and he had to remove it despite calls from the *yobbeez* in the back seat that it looked especially fine. It may have looked fine, he thought, but for the purposes of the journey it did not feel fine. His *krot* was also troublesome. It pinched uncomfortably at his waist and its roughly pointed handle sat at an angle that made him fear for the consequences of encountering sudden dips in the road. He removed it and stationed it temporarily in the car's cup holder. As he did so, he noticed that *Om* Trattat and one other unnamed Pundari now shared the passenger seat. Philip switched on the engine and lights, and put the car into first gear. Before pulling away from the kerb, he checked his rear-view mirror … in which he saw only turbans. A large quantity of *yobbeez* had squeezed unprompted into his car and now sat in the back seat smoking *okaly* and drinking *tiga tiga*. Being young, they were Pundaris of the smaller variety, but nevertheless the noise and disturbance they were producing was significant. Philip put his foot on the brake. Turning around in his seat, and possibly emboldened by his recent inhalation of *okaly*, he said, '*Looka looka*, I'm having none of this messing about in my car. Understand?' The *yobbeez* fell silent, then looked at each other and appeared to discuss the situation. The doors of the car were opened and they scrambled out, *okaly* joints beween their lips and carrying their bottles of *tiga tiga* with them. There was further discussion and raised voices in the dark at the back of the *pickky-up*, then the rear doors of the Nissan Sunny were again flung open and four substitutes climbed back in. They sat silently while Philip inspected them. Reassured that there was no *okaly* and no *tiga tiga*, he said '*Bunga,*' and the car moved off, heavily, behind the *pikky-up* and proceeded towards its late-night destination.

Philip strained in the dark to follow the rear lights of the *pikky-up*. The vehicle, with its passengers crammed together like sheep for the market, rattled ahead along the highway, tailgating and overtaking other cars, cutting diagonally across lanes. Philip, fearful of losing his guide, swerved in and out of the traffic, blasted by a tirade of angry claxons. Twenty minutes into the journey, the *pikky-up* lurched onto a secondary road and careered into the dark unknown. Philip clung to the steering wheel, scanning the blackness for some indication of the nature of the road ahead. The Nissan Sunny bumped in and out of unexpected dips. Turbans bounced up and down against the car's ceiling. The occupants of the vehicle tipped to the left and then to the right and then to the left again. No one complained except for Philip who muttered obscenities under his breath.

It was much, much later that the convoy arrived in a dimly lit street filled with half-constructed buildings. They rolled through a gateway into an extensive unpaved enclosure where other cars and *pikky-ups* were already parked. The entrance of a large building opposite them was fiercely illuminated, and silhouetted forms in turbans and sarongs were being sucked into it like moths to a flame. Namisan drums boomed from inside the vibrating edifice. The party was in full swing.

*

It's going to be a long night. Bindee definitely not coming. Still in a sulk. Her loss. Ushri told me to go easy on the tiga-tiga. *Look who's talking. As he spoke these words, smoke issued from his nose.*

Patronizing little yobbee.

*

The principles of the Camel Dance were not unfamiliar to Philip. It went something like this. You put your left leg in and then you put your left leg out, then you put it in and then you put it out, then you put it in again and out again and then you shook it all about. You did all this, but rather laboriously in time to the slow rhythm of the drums, and as you did so, you progressed in a rumba-like circle around the room. Having completed one circuit of the room, you then completed another, and another and another, but at the completion of each circuit, the lead dancer, who wore the beige head dress and red ornamental tassels of the symbolic *jimi* or camel, might choose to change step or gesture, thus creating a ripple effect of reversed movement. Hence, the right arm might go in, then the right arm might go out, then – in sequence – the same arm would go in and out and in and out, and then it would be shaken all about. From time to time, the man who followed behind the lead dancer gave a shout, to which the entire company responded with the words, '*Jimi krak, jimi krak, jimi krak*', and then '*Jej mumba!*' Philip fell in with this quite naturally and found that these slow and repetitive movements, the further inhalation of *okaly* and the crescendo of the drumming caused a pleasing trance-like state in which the dancer was lost within time and space.

In something resembling a dream, Philip met a beautiful young Namisan woman. In his vision she entered the hall – all four of her – in the company of a thousand others, but not one as beautiful and as radiant as she. Philip gazed at her dumbstruck, following her movements until he found her seated opposite him deeply engrossed in the chatter of a young *yobbee* multiplied several times over. Then, after Philip had floated slowly to the ceiling and back down again, he engaged with her in conversation. He spoke but heard no words issue forth from his mouth. She answered and he saw her lips move, but he did not hear her voice, which he knew to be as sweet and as delicate as the breeze that blew gently towards him and tipped him backwards so that he could see the million flickering stars that floated above him. The sky slid across the ceiling and down the walls and as Philip watched this magical transition, food appeared in front of him and he ate. There was laughter and he laughed. A metallic goblet was put into his hand and he drank, and then, as he very gradually regained his senses, he recognised his friends Timmaya and Trattat seated next to him on a large woven mat of blue and yellow, and again in front of him a collection of large flat earthenware dishes materialized, piled high with Namisan and Pundari delicacies. Admiring an abundance of *kwa kwa* , he thought that there could surely be no monkeys left in Namisa. The huge room was full now and noisy with the chatter of the guests. He saw in blindingly sharp detail the attire of the other dancers, the colours and the textures, and he heard Timmaya's comment that the bigger the *krot*, the more important the man, and in this illuminating awakening following his first Camel Dance, Philip noted that some men were very, very important and some not important at all.

*

It was when the men and the women came together in the final phase of the Camel Dance that Philip once again saw and recognised that same young woman who was so very *trikee trikee*. They passed like camels in the night. She came towards him in the thick of the dance, and he looked over his shoulder as the circle of dancers carried her away again. On the next circuit, he searched the swell of revellers for her face until she flowed in his direction.

'I do hope you are feeling better now,' she called as the men and women surged towards him.

'What is your name?' he called back.

'Tanita. My name is Tanita,' she said. 'It means "gold star." And what is your name?'

But before he could answer, he was separated from her by a sudden rush of *yobbeez*, shouting and yelling to the accelerated beat of the drums.

Never before had Philip longed so much for a gold star.

Wallee the groom took his place on a small podium at the far end of the hall and gave greetings as the ceremony came to a close with the guests filing past him to pay their respects and to take a spoonful of camel *auda*, a creamy beige-coloured paste which each member hastily swallowed and then washed down with a tiny glass of *tiga tiga* juice.

One of the two – the camel *auda* or the *tiga tiga* juice, or perhaps the two combined – contributed to Philip's non-arrival at the office the following day, thus confirming the findings of the government census on the causes of time taken off from work.

***

22

THE MATTER OF DIVORCE

Admittedly his speech was garbled and his eyes were glazed, but otherwise he seemed like a nice person… or might be.

*

The camel dancing expedition did not go down well with Felicity.

'Have you any idea what you looked like when you came in this morning?' she said. She was dressed and ready to go out.

Philip gave her a pained look.

'You can't tell me that that was official business. People who are on official business simply don't look the way you looked or indeed smell the way you smelt. Is that some kind of new ethnic aftershave?'

Philip stared down at his sandaled feet.

'I mean, who are these people you're hanging around with, and why were you shouting *jimi krak jimi krak jej bumba* when you got out of the car?'

Philip studied his fingernails.

'And whatever it was you had in the boot of that car… if you still have it, please don't bring it into the house.'

Philip wrapped his dressing gown around him more tightly and said nothing. He could not remember what had been in the back of the car, but he thought the odour might at least trigger a memory or two. Parrot stood opposite him, claws splayed on the kitchen table, staring and tilting his head.

'You have to observe the ground rules, Philip. You're behaving like a juvenile playboy … all this going off with your Namisan friends, hanging out at nightclubs, drinking in bars. And then you come back here and expect me to keep house for you. If you think I'm always going to be here running after you, forget it. It's got to stop.' Felicity was pink in the face and almost breathless.

Parrot fixed Philip with an accusing eye. He opened his beak, then closed it, then opened it again and said, 'Naughty.'

'Yes, he is!' said Felicity. She buttoned up her jacket and picked up her notebook. 'If you need your wife,' she said, 'she'll be at the Coffee Circle. But, since you have your own friends I doubt that she'll be required.'

Philip avoided eye contact. Parrot scurried to the other side of the table as he followed Felicity's movement. The porch door banged shut behind her.

'Ba ba,' said Parrot. 'See you later.'

*

Felicity felt she needed to consult with Mrs. Katraree on the delicate matter of divorce. A propos, she jotted down a few *pointeez* in her notebook.

'Today,' said Mrs. Katraree, '*Imee* Felicitu has suggested our subject for discussion. It will be divorce.'

There was a hum of approval from the ladies, but there were cold looks from the men's section.

'Divorce, as you know,' continued Mrs. Katraree, 'is a very sensitive topic, but we will do our best to answer *Imee* Felicitu's questions and reach our conclusions on this important issue.' She turned to Felicity and smiled. Felicity took this to be her cue.

'Yes, thank you, Mrs. Katraree,' said Felicity. 'Now what I want to know is… Is there any stigma attached to being a divorcee? I'm referring now particularly to divorcees here in Namisa.'

Mrs. Katraree stared at her for a moment, and then she said, 'What is stigma, my dear?'

'Well,' said Felicity, 'it is when the divorcee is ostracized by the community.'

Mrs. Katraree crinkled her brow.

'I mean, when the divorcee is treated badly by the community,' said Felicity.

Mrs. Katraree continued to look perplexed. 'Do you mean the *om* or the *imee*?' she said.

'The *imee*,' said Felicity.

'*Ah jej*, now I am understanding,' said Mrs. Katraree, 'because in Namisan language *divorcee* he is the *om*, and *divorceetee* she is the *imee*.'

'I see,' said Felicity, scribbling the words into her notebook. 'In English, "divorcee" I believe must have come to us originally from the French, and I suppose some people still make the distinction between the male and female forms in their pronunciation of the word. In English, however, we use the same word for both the man and the woman.'

'Is that so?' said Mrs. Katraree, taking off her glasses and looking admiringly at Felicity. 'I must ask my daughter about this word since she knows French very well. What you are saying makes perfectly sensible.' She looked around the room. 'We all know these people from the French Embassy, *na na*, and it does not surprise me in the little that this word is from them.'

There were murmurings of assent from the assembled company.

'My brother Dr. Towdi,' said Mrs. Katraree, 'he is telling me these people from the French Embassy and the Sorbum and also Aliens Francaise, they are all the evenings in the Sleepy Hollow Nite Club, and this is a very worrying *thingy*. Many of our young people are thinking *bunga thingeez* are from Kingdom of France, like Yves Saint Laurent, like Shitroyen cars, like long pointy bread, like Louvery …'

'The Louvre,' said Felicity.

'Correct!' said Mrs. Katraree. 'What I am saying is … it is important the setting of good examples, *na na*? People representing Kingdom of France, they are not doing this.'

'Actually, it's not a kingdom,' said Felicity. She was concerned that her favourite holiday destination was being maligned. 'They don't have a king, so it's not actually a kingdom, you see.'

'*Ah jej!*' said Mrs. Katraree in amazement. 'Like us they have no king?'

'No, that's right,' said Felicity. 'They had a revolution, and they beheaded their king… you know, cut off his head.' And just to be sure her meaning was clear, she made a gesture to this effect.

'There you are!' said Mrs. Katraree. 'You see! I am telling you this! They are setting very bad example. They are even revolutioning.'

'Revolting,' said Felicity.

'Correct!' said Mrs. Katraree. 'I'm so glad you are agreeing.'

*

When Alan came with Ratni in the Cinquecento to collect his car later that morning, Philip, pyjama-clad, made the effort to rise from his sick bed to phone Timmaya on his mobile.

'Just calling to thank you for yesterday,' said Philip, putting on a brave voice.

'You are most welcome,' said Timmaya. 'I do hope you enjoyed taking part in our little traditional celebration, even though ceremonies like the Camel Dance are a trifle subdued here in Namisa.'

'It was unforgettable,' said Philip. 'Quite unforgettable.' Philip had forgotten a great deal, but he had not forgotten the girl – the girl with the nut-brown skin. Did she have nut-brown skin? He couldn't remember. And was she with someone? He couldn't remember that either. Perhaps he should just forget her.

'And I trust that the *yobbeez* behaved themselves on the way home.'

'Yes, yes, no bother at all,' Philip lied. From his window he could see Alan sponging down the back seats of the car with a bucketful of Dettol. Ratni stood holding the bucket, his face twisted in distaste.

'Truly a learning experience,' said Philip, 'for which I thank you from the bottom of my heart.'

'Certainly,' said Timmaya, 'for the poet picks figs from the oldest tree.'

'Indeed,' said Philip, 'and the ... the ...

'... pineapple.'

'Yes, good,' said Philip, 'the pineapple grows yellow with age before ... before ...'

'...the beetle,' prompted Timmaya.

'The beetle. Right,' said Philip. 'Before the beetle falls under foot.'

'Correct!' said Timmaya. 'And the fields of autumn in Namisa ...'

'Actually,' said Philip, 'just to change the subject for a minute, there are still a couple of things I would like to ask you about Bogadan.'

'*Ah jej,*' said Timmaya, 'such as?'

'I mean, this business of his qualifications, well ... he has already started his PhD, why on earth would he want to, or need to, start it all over again. Who in their right mind would? It just doesn't make sense to me. Quite honestly I've never heard of such a thing before.'

'*Om* Philip, *Om* Philip,' Timmaya chided. 'We ask ourselves, why does the *spidee snapper* eat its young. Oh, but it makes perfect sense. Remember that Bogadan's ambitions, and those also of his mother, go a long way beyond Namisa. Bogadan may give the impression of being someone who leaves much to chance, but in reality, you will find that where money and ambition are involved, he looks well to the future and has a finely tuned five-year plan. In five years' time, he knows exactly where he wants to be and it won't be Trinamisa, though Trinamisa is still very much part of the plan.'

'If it's not Trinamisa, then where is it?' said Philip.

'I am sure that five years down the road Bogadan expects to be a highly respected academic living in the Middle East – the Gulf to be precise. But,' said Timmaya, 'just as quickly as the fly takes its breath, so it will fall irrevocably into the coconut oil.'

'Ah, you mean there's a fly in the ointment?'

'Exactly so. You should know, *Om* Philip, that Bogadan's Prapundari qualifications will never pass mustard when it comes to US or UK accreditation. The shoots of bamboo may hide by the tallest tree, but blooms are gathered nonetheless.'

'Fascinating,' said Philip.

'Yes, you will see that over there in Abu Nar, where they believe they are building a world-class university, they will not want a third-class academic. I would wager that the university itself is so completely focused on receiving Bogadan's research funds that they are unaware, or perhaps do not care, that Bogadan's qualifications are not quite up to *scratchee*. Under the bark of the *preepree* tree, the sun vole feasts.'

'But, with respect,' said Philip, 'are you saying that your own degrees are not up to *scratchee* either?'

'*Om* Philip,' said Timmaya gravely, 'there are men who savour and men who close their eyes in false sleep.

Let us say that there are those of us who were subject to the judgement of an external examiner and those who were not. If the records are examined, the validity of Bogadan's studies will come under scrutiny, and certain ... irregularities will be uncovered. It is rumoured that Bogadan will be taking up a new position in Abu Nar as Reader in Communication and Innovation, and between then and now he will either have to obtain a new qualification through the normal hard-*grafty* channels, or he will have to buy one. Alternatively, he will have to get someone to study for one on his behalf. Another Caroline Wordsworth perhaps. Indeed, while I am on the topic, I would strongly advise you to look into the activities of both Caroline and her husband Jonathan.'

'Ah yes,' said Philip, 'that's something else I was wanting to ask you about...' Before he could go any further, the line went dead.

'Hello?' said Philip, but he was talking into a void. He redialled the number and got a recorded message first in Pundari and then in English. The number was unattainable, it told him.

*

Mrs. Katraree was in full flow. Clearly it was not so much the quality of the coffee as the quality of the advice that brought together the members of the Coffee Circle. It had occurred to Felicity on more than one occasion that – in addition to the linguistic insights presented to her – there might well be a book to be had in Mrs. Katraree's wealth of thought-provoking revelations. One of the questions now in Felicity's mind was whether or not Mrs. Katraree's observations, transposed to a different cultural ambiance, could impact a foreign reader to the same degree across time and space. To what extent, thought Felicity, is Mrs. Katraree directing the opinions of her audience as opposed to voicing or reflecting their shared beliefs? Felicity chewed the end of her pen and studied the ceiling fan as she considered this question. A small lizard, possibly a *bulbi* lizard, flitted across the polished bamboo struts.

'I am sure you agree, *Imee* Felicitu, *na na*?' asked Mrs. Katraree.

'Oh, I'm sorry. What was that?' said Felicity.

'What I am saying,' said Mrs Katraree, 'is that tall *preepreez* from little *trikitz* grow, *na na*?'

'Very true. *Jej, sahsah*,' said Felicity.

'There, you see!' said Mrs. Katraree to the members of the Coffee Circle. 'Now,' she continued, 'before we are giving *Imee* Felicitu answer to this *vexy* question, "Are *divorceeteez* oscillated in Namisa?" first we must-should consider mistakes that *husbundeez* commonly make that are leading to divorcing. For we all must be remembering that there is no leaves without trees. Best to watch from very beginning if something is wrong in marriage. The *imee* is at fault if she is allowing *husbundee* staying out late with other *yobbeez*, because this leads to mixing with bad people, like people from French Embassy, for an example. This is a *bushkil* from early marriage. Another *bushkil* is when the *husbundee* makes *scuses* about where he being and where he going. Maybe he will be saying, "I am going there for official business," but then he is coming back smelling of smoking and drinking. He is also coming smelling of perfume and incense, but he is saying, "I was in the shopping mall and an *imee* sprayed me with perfume," and maybe even, "I was buying this perfume for you, but then I did not like it," and we know this is not true because – and I am embarrassing to say this – the spraying is going in places that ordinary spraying does not reach.'

The members of the Coffee Circle shifted uncertainly in their seats perhaps recognising something of themselves in these descriptions.

'And another reason for divorcing,' said Mrs. Katraree, 'is when the *husbundee* is not pulling his weight. The *imee* is making the laundry and the ironing – maybe she does not know about SnowWhite Dry Kleen Shop – and he is saying, "Where is my *shala kan*, where is my turban, where is my *undersidewear*?" In *shorty,* he is all the time wanting for something, so that the *imee* is waiting on him day-time and night-time and, resulting, she has no time for herself or for coming to Coffee Circles like this one.' Mrs. Katraree gave a sharp nod to *Imeetinee* Petee, for this was her cue to make a circuit of the room refilling the coffee cups. 'In conclusion,' said Mrs Katraree, 'are people regarding a woman badly if she divorces? *Na jej,* I think not, but people are regarding badly the *husbundee* because evidently he must be making there reasons for *discontinence*.'

'So, Mrs Katraree,' said Felicity, 'would you say that if *thingeez* are not working out, the *imee* should get a divorce?'

'*Ah jej, Imee* Felicitu, divorce is very extreme measure,' said Mrs. Katraree. 'First we must be giving the *husbundee* opportunity to improve. It is important for the *imee* to put her *cardzat* on the table so *husbundee* can be appreciating the situation. If the *husbundee* he is not cooperating, then the *imee* has ace card.' Mrs. Katraree looked around the room to make sure everyone was listening … and they were.

'The *imee* has ace card,' she said. 'She can be withdrawing conjugation rights. Very severe, but very effective.'

***

23

THE BENEFITS OF TEAMBUILDING

When Philip got back to the Department the following day, he was dismayed to see that the surface of his desk was papered with little yellow notes, telephone messages from Bogadan. But there was not a word from Timmaya, who must surely have realised the urgency of applying for a Downing scholarship.

In Philip's inbox, there was, however, a short cryptic e-mail from Bogadan:

Pleese give updates scolarship situasion for summar bursry and phd. Time short. Meet up tonite?'

The man was everywhere, even in Philip's voice mail messages:

'Om Pilip, I am needing to discuss with you the details of my scholarship. It is some time that I am not hearing from you so I am assuming all is in order. Is all in order? Or maybe you are needing other documents? Or maybe some references I can get them for you no worries. We can meet tonight to discuss.'

There was something very unsettling about all of this urgency on his part, especially in the context of Timmaya's sudden disappearance. One minute, there he was giving Philip insider information about Bogadan's activities and the next minute he couldn't be traced. Philip could not solve this conundrum, but he knew a man who could.

*

'I think the answer may be valet cleaning,' said Alan, keying commands into his phone.

'What?' said Philip.

'Especially since there's a funny smell in the boot,' said Alan. 'You haven't had any *hura* fruit in there, have you? You need to go and have a sniff and see what I mean.'

'Very smelly, that *hura* fruit,' shouted Ronny from the other side of his partition.

'Alan, I'm talking to you about something very important,' said Philip.

'I'm glad you appreciate that,' said Alan. 'I'm very fond of that car.'

'We're talking here about the disappearance of a learned professor. I mean, doesn't it strike you as a bit strange that Timmaya is lined up for a scholarship one day and is gone the next, and then I have Bogadan hounding me to give the scholarship to him?'

'So, you think Bogadan's bumped off Timmaya?'

Philip recoiled at the suggestion. 'Well, I don't know. Is he capable of something like that?'

'How long's he been gone then?' said Alan.

'A day?'

'Ooh, that's terrible!' shouted Ronny. 'Call the police.'

*

I made the mistake of telling Bindee about the cute ex-pat yobbee I met at Wallee's wedding ceremony. She helpfully pointed out that many foreign yobbeez lead double lives. 'You have to remember,' she said, 'that they have deserted their own country to come and live in another, just as they may have deserted their foreign wife and taken up with one of us.' At this point she looked at me rather accusingly, I thought. 'What I'm saying,' she said, 'is that a man alone and so far from the comforts of home will be looking for alternative liaisons.' As she rambled on, I'm sorry to say that I dozed off on the sofa... so I've no idea what else she said.

*

Philip was aware that when you are not getting the necessary support from your team, decision-making becomes very onerous. This was not just about Timmaya going missing and Bogadan trying to get his PhD funded. It was the fact that he – Philip, Officer of Education and Culture – was going to end up like the little Dutch boy, sticking his arm in the Downing Foundation dam to block the liberal flow of funds through to Abu Nar. It was true that he had inherited all this as a package when Jonathan left, but Bryant and the Foundation would regard it exclusively as his responsibility and he either had to see it through or stifle it.

In the bathroom as he stared at his troubled face in the mirror and cooled his overheated brow with water from the tap, the word 'scapegoat' came to mind. If there were a scapegoat in this story, who would it be? Surely not, he thought. Surely not.

As the day progressed, he convinced himself that there must be someone around him, or in the office, who was leaking information to Bogadan. If Alan and Ronny were not going to help, then there was nothing for it. He would have to take the matter into his own hands. Through the remainder of the day, he conducted his own investigations. The mole – or its Namisan equivalent – had to be found and silenced.

On the pretext of picking up his post, he sidled into Tiki's office. He studied her through narrowed eyes. She seemed innocent enough, but these were usually the guilty ones. She sat at her computer, intent on a complex piece of cutting and pasting, her bejewelled hands moving confidently across her keyboard, her long dark eyelashes flickering with concentration, her slug eyebrows burrowing into each other. Philip leaned awkwardly against a filing cabinet, re-reading a letter advising him that he had won £50,000 in a prize draw. He observed Tiki between sentences. She was so neat, so precise, the kind of person who would be capable of recording every minute detail and passing it on. As a secretary, she had access to each and every crumb of information that passed around the Foundation offices, from the private correspondence of the Director through to consultancy documents, financial reports, budgets and scholarship applications. It was so clear to him now. Why had he not seen it before, this duplicity? Tiki looked up from her work and her eyes met Philip's.

'*Na jej*! You stop that right now,' said Tiki, 'or I am reporting you for sexual harassment. Who do you think you are, coming in here with your unclean eyes? And you have a wife at home too. *Sheematipa*!'

Philip opened his mouth to speak, but thought better of it. He returned in haste to his office, closed the door behind him and crossed Tiki off his list.

*

Perhaps Philip had overlooked some important clues. He was new to this, so it was entirely understandable. However, there was now little doubt in his mind who the culprit was. He went in search of Ratni and eventually found him sitting in the security guard's room eating an extra-large *chikoko sanddij*. Philip braced himself. What he was about to do required nerves of steel.

'Ratni,' he said, giving a brief matter-of-fact smile, 'where were you last night… and the night before?' He was convinced that whatever had happened to Timmaya must have taken place under cover of night.

'Uh?' said Ratni, taken unawares, the half-masticated *chikoko* revolving in his mouth. 'I at home with wife, watch Pundari Big Brother on new-install *smaartee* TV. Why? You got *bushkil*?' He was standing up, looking at Philip menacingly now. Philip stood his ground.

'No, just asking,' said Philip.

'You thinking maybe Sleepy Hollow Nite Club?' he boomed. Philip backed out of the door and turned to hurry down the corridor. Ratni followed him to the doorway, his voice rising to a crescendo. 'Me is Pundari *bunga, husbundee bunga,*' he shouted, spraying the air with his now spoilt lunch.

*

'Ronny,' said Philip. This was his last shot before heading off to his rendezvous with Bogadan.

Ronny was just a skinny little chap, apparently quite harmless, but these, too, were the ones to suspect. He was sitting at his desk, tapping figures into an Excel sheet on his laptop. He took a sip of milky *cha-cha* from his Wallace and Grommit mug.

'Yes, Philip?' he said.

'I hope you don't mind me asking … it's just to eliminate you, you see, but where were you yesterday evening?'

Ronny took another sip of *cha-cha* from his mug, then sat back in his chair holding the mug in both hands. He thought for a moment, before fixing Philip with a melancholic stare.

'I was at Wallee's house,' he said, 'with Professor Timmaya.'

Philip gave a gasp.

'Yes, Philip. You see, it was me,' said Ronny. 'I did it. I killed Professor Timmaya.' He took another sip of his *cha-cha* and looked unblinkingly at Philip.

Philip stood frozen in Ronny's little compartment.

'Got ya!' shouted Ronny, who then dissolved into a blast of uncontained laughter, which was echoed by the unsympathetic occupant on the other side of the partition.

Philip retreated to his room, the cruel barbs of ridicule reverberating in his ears… or possibly piercing them. There were other potential moles. Alan himself, possibly. Maybe even Felicity. But just now his heart wasn't in it. He was barking up the wrong *preepree*, and it was time to change direction.

*

'Alan.'

'Yes, Philip.'

'The TUDI money. Who originally signed off on that?'

'Jonathan,' said Alan, 'countersigned by Lady Downing … and Imee Grace.' Philip took note.

Alan rummaged in his red metal filing cabinet where, in defiance of his paperless office, documents and files protruded in disarray. He pulled out a thick dusty pink folder.

'There you go,' he said, thrusting the bundle into Philip's arms. Alan, whose mind was like a flash drive, remembered it well. The two women had signed the papers while on a shopping expedition to Harvey Nichols.

'Which is why this is filed under "H",' explained Alan.

Over a good number of years, the two women had forged a bond built on their common interests: Burberry's, Fortnum and Mason, Ascot, and the Royal Academy Summer Exhibition. This much Philip could work out for himself: if Lady Downing had signed in good faith, then the discovery that the money was being channelled elsewhere would be a considerable embarrassment to her. The person who had the answers to all Philip's questions was Grace herself who, more than Bogadan, must be the villain of the piece. Philip was beginning to think that he had maligned Bogadan and that all along Bogadan had been the unsuspecting agent of his own mother's diabolical schemes.

*

Halfway through the afternoon, as Philip scrutinised the funding receipts, the phone rang. It was Bogadan.

'So, *Om* Pilip, I think we are meeting tonight, *na na*? Same time, same place, and you will bring *Imee* Felicitu?'

'No, I think not.'

'*Najid bushkil.* It is better she sits with the *babbigall*.'

Cocktails awaited and … what else? Philip was aware that this meeting could be crucial. As it grew late and the office emptied, Philip sat at his desk in pensive mood and retraced what he had learned so far. He had a collection of pieces from this ornate Namisan jigsaw but, as he was well aware, his powers of logic were so woefully inadequate that it was beyond him to put the pieces in the right places. Bogadan's five-year plan involved securing himself not just a simple lectureship, but the significant position of Head of Research in Communications and Innovation at The Oil and Gas Institute. So, then, could Bogadan have led TOGI to believe that he had a PhD from a world-class university? Yes, of course he could. The fact that his existing academic credentials would never stand up to scrutiny meant that he needed a fast track UK qualification. Bogadan must surely have pots of money, thought Philip, but his personal finances were destined for altogether more joyful, or even illicit, pursuits. Clearly, he needed the support of the Foundation to continue to channel money through to TOGI, but he also needed the Foundation to finance his vacations – or rather, his studies – in the UK.

But what of Jonathan? One minute he was happily signing Bogadan's funding applications and the next he was on the plane to Tblisi. One false step, Philip thought, and he could fall into the same trap … if he hadn't done so already.

Philip took out a sheet of paper on which he wrote:

1) *Sign TUDI funding papers – Result: money goes to TOGI, but no pay rises or improvements for TU faculty and staff = Bogadan happy + I keep job.*
2) *Don't sign TUDI funding papers – Result: no money to TOGI + no pay rises or improvements for TU faculty and staff = Bogadan not happy + scandal because marriage lie exposed – I lose job or go to Alaska.*
3) *Give scholarship to Bogadan – Result: Bogadan goes to UK = Bogadan happy + Bogadan out of my hair + I keep job*
4) *Give scholarship to Bogadan and sign TUDI funding papers – Result: TOGI gets money + Bogadan goes to UK = TOGI is happy + Bogadan very very happy + Bogadan out of my hair + I keep job*

5) *Give scholarship to Timmaya – Result: Timmaya goes to UK if alive to get on plane = Bogadan not happy + scandal because marriage lie exposed – good deed done, but I lose job or go to Alaska.*

This method of working through problems systematically was excellent for clearing the mind and helping one to make the right decisions. It always worked… except, of course, for now. Groaning to vent emotion, sipping cocktails, and simply giving up also helped. Philip threw down his pen and rested his head on his desk.

***

24

THE SHORT LIST

Bogadan was his usual jovial self when the two friends met up by the pool bar of the Shangri-La. Philip had made a mental note definitely not to accept any Namisan Dawn cocktails, the effect of which was similar to *tiga tiga*. He remembered only too well – or thought he did – what *tiga tiga* could do to him.

Bogadan put on his glasses and fingered the cocktail menu.

'How about a Namisan Dawn?'

'Oh, all right,' said Philip.

Philip was well aware that he had limitations but had not yet indulged in sufficient self-help to do anything about them. He was, however, determined this time to take control of the conversation so that Bogadan could not get the upper hand.

'Now, *Om* Bogadan,' he said, 'I've been wanting to know for some time about Jonathan and Caroline Wordsworth.'

'And I also have been wanting to know,' said Bogadan, who was twirling an olive on a stick beween his thumb and forefinger, 'about my scholarship to UK.'

'All right,' said Philip helping himself to a handful of *krips*. 'Let us talk first about the Wordsworths, and then about the scholarship.'

Bogadan popped the olive into his mouth, chewed, and thought about this for a moment. Then he genteelly ejected the stone and waving the cocktail stick in the air, he said, 'You know, *Om* Pilip, I think it is better to talk first of the scholarship, then of Jonatan and his *Imee* Caroline, and then to talk of you and *Imeetinee* Felicitu.' He stared directly at Philip with a kind of impudent defiance as he said this.

The *krips* lodged themselves in Philip's throat and he began to choke.

'Ah here we are,' said Bogadan, beaming at the waitress as she set their drinks on the table.

'Now with regard to the progress of my scholarship,' continued Bogadan, 'I am not hearing anything from you, and the time for signing papers and finalising applications is, I think, upon us.'

His eyes watering and his face still reddened from his coughing fit, Philip said, 'You do realise that a PhD will involve a great deal of work on your part?'

'This is not a *bushkil*,' said Bogadan. 'I have people who can help me. I will supervise and they will write.' Bogadan sat back and sipped his drink. In the background, the gentle chords of a traditional *lingling* melody floated through the warm evening air.

'Now *looka looka*, Bogadan,' said Philip, emboldened now that his cocktail was taking effect, 'Frankly, I have to say that I am not happy with this situation. You want money off the Downing Foundation to do a PhD that you are not even going to research for yourself. Do you honestly believe I can sanction your study grant knowing that the funding will be subject to abuse?'

Bogadan's face changed. He was no longer smiling. 'Are you saying that you are not going to authorise it?'

'It depends,' said Philip. 'Let's say I am considering it.'

'Well, while you are considering that,' said Bogadan, 'consider also that you are here under false pretences. Let us not be beating about the bushes.'

'I don't know what you are talking about,' said Philip assuming what he believed to be an air of nonchalance.

'I am certain that you do,' said Bogadan. 'I refer to your situation with *Imeetinee* Felicitu.' As he stressed the word *imeetinee*, he gave an irritating wiggle of his head.

'What situation with Felicity?' said Philip.

'*Om* Pilip, you are *na lakati,*' said Bogadan. 'You told me yourself.'

'I did? Surely you must be mistaken. I'm sure I didn't.'

'You must realise, *Om* Pilip, that this will not go down well with the Downing Foundation when they find out. My mother is a very good friend of Lady Downing.'

The two men stared at each other for some time. The music had stopped and only the lapping of water on the nearby shore could be heard.

'You're on the short list,' said Philip.

'That is no use to me,' said Bogadan, raising his voice. 'I need to be top of the short list.' He finished his cocktail and slammed his glass down on the table. Then he leaned forward in his chair and spoke in a low and measured tone. 'Be very careful, *Om* Pilip,' he said. 'Remember that I have assisted you and even named one of my lecture theatres after you. I don't want to hear that my scholarship money has gone elsewhere. I am warning you, Pilip, cross me and you will be regretting for the rest of your life.'

'Steady on there, Bogadan,' said Philip.

Bogadan pressed on. 'I want you to assure me that no other applications will be considered. The consequences could be very grave indeed for anyone involved. If I hear anything to the contrary, I assure you I will take the necessary action. And, remember also that Pundaris cannot be trusted. You are still new here, *Om* Pilip, and maybe you are forgetting this. If you have any information and you are intending to act on that information, you need to be very sure that your sources are reliable.'

Philip's blood ran cold or, at least, lukewarm. He had never been threatened in this way before … in fact he had never been threatened, unless you counted Clare Parker in Form 3. 'Yes, well, as I said, you are on the short list, and all I can say about that is … it is very short.'

'Good,' said Bogadan. 'That's what I want to hear.' He sat back in his chair. 'Now I will offer you another cocktail with *tiga tiga* chaser.'

In the matter of exotic beverages, Bogadan showed boundless generosity.

*

Early evening get-together with Ushri and Bindee. Didn't go at all as anticipated. Ushri was already there at Macdonald's Bi Dillin *when I arrived and had already started eating without us. Thanks, Ushri. Namisaburger with extra fillings of* chikoko *and* kip kip, *French fries, followed by waffles and maple syrup. Everything washed down with* bulbi *and* yellibellee *shakes. I think the term is 'greedy so-and-so.' I honestly don't know where he puts it. He's unbelievably skinny. Must have worms.*

I asked him if he could please take off his back-to-front baseball cap – at least while he was eating. He obliged and that's when I saw something glinting on his wrist. I said, 'You've got a new watch,' and he said, 'Yeah. So?' He can be very awkward when he wants. He told me his dad had given it to him. I said, 'Why?' He said, 'He loves me.' So, I said, 'My mammee *loves me too, but he hasn't bought me a Rolex. What did you do, pass an exam?' And he said something like, 'Well, you don't have Sleepy Hollow issues.' That's when Bindee arrived.*

Everything amicable at first, like old times, but then Bindee made some comment or other about the waitress and started on about a minimum wage. I don't know what's got into her lately. She used to be so timid and endearing. Then she got promoted at work and hasn't been the same since. She blames everything on 'foreigners.' I said to her, 'What's your problem, Bindee? She said, 'Open your eyes, Tanita. Do you not realise that for centuries we have been oppressed, by the British, the Americans, the French, the Germans, the Italians, and … and… the Mexicans?' I said, 'Mexicans?' She went red, and she said, 'Yes,' and looked at Ushri, who was having a second helping of waffles. And then Ushri said he thought she was right, and Bindee said, 'There! See!' And Ushri said, 'Yeah, all those foreigners have left us with nothing.'

I lost it. I told them they were both insane. After which, it all went rather badly. Typically, Bindee got up in a huff, left the restaurant, and drove away in her BMW. By then Ushri was downing his third mega-shake. Helpfully he said, 'What she needs is a husbundee.*' He checked his watch and asked me if I wanted a lift back home. He'd brought the Hummer. I had* mammee's *Ferrari so no problem there. I'm starting to wish I never came back.*

*

What crossed Philip's mind at first was that he must humour Bogadan, distract or distance him.

'What I am thinking,' said Bogadan now that he had Philip under his spell, 'is that I will go on a renaissance visit.'

Philip raised his eyebrows, but said nothing. Why the likes of Bogadan might now want to spend a summer in Florence was beyond him.

'I need to see if I like any of these universities that we have talked about,' continued Bogadan. 'To this end, I am planning a little visit to UK to meet with departmental supervisors prior to starting my PhD in the autumn – your autumn. So, *Om* Pilip, tell me, what do you think?'

'Well, I don't know about renaissance visits,' said Philip. 'Are you talking about requesting additional funds? I'm not sure how I would justify that. If you want to go before you start the PhD, then you need to do so at your own expense. That's how it usually works.'

'Oh,' said Bogadan, 'but I do not buy something before seeing if it is what I want. If I buy *kwa kwa*, then I taste it first. That, I think, *Om* Pilip, is how it usually works, *na na*? Also, it's just a *shorty* trip,' said Bogadan. 'I don't see the problem. I have already some invitations.' He reached for his briefcase and pulled out some sheets of paper. 'Here is one from University College. It is a very nice place just opposite Dillons Bookshop and a bus ride from the village of Soho. They are saying that they are very interested in my proposal and that I am welcome to visit when I am in town. You see that it is at the suggestion of the university,' said Bogadan. He handed Philip a letter with a university crest at the top.

Philip sniffed and skimmed through it, hoping that he would find an escape route, and he did. His face lightened. 'Oh, dear me,' he said, feigning concern, though not very well. 'You know, I really don't think you'll be able to go.' Philip was quite pleased with himself.

Bogadan was put out. 'Why not?' he said.

'Well, these dates ..,' said Philip. 'I may be mistaken but it looks to me as though they coincide with your TU Graduation Ceremony.' Just that morning Tiki had sent off a copy of TU's academic calendar to the Downing Foundation in London. 'You couldn't possibly miss the graduation, could you? I mean everyone will be going … the students, their parents, the faculty, Bryant, all sorts of people… and of course, Lady Downing.'

Bogadan picked up the letter and, putting on his glasses, he studied it with furrowed brow.

'It's a shame,' said Philip, 'but I doubt that you'd be able to get away, and if you go any later, it'll be in-between terms in the UK, and naturally everyone will be on holiday then. Basically, your dates and their dates don't match.'

Still studying the letter, Bogadan sipped his cocktail. 'In that case …,' he said looking up. He took off his glasses. 'In that case I will change the dates of the graduation on the academic calendar. The students can graduate late and faculty can cut short their vacation. This is not a *bushkil.* Not at all.' How clever Bogadan was at getting out of tight corners. Philip marvelled. Sparring with him, as Philip now appreciated, could result in the disruption of countless lives and the ruination of family holidays. Philip was considering which it was to be – fight or flight? Perhaps the time had come for him to remove his boxing gloves and admit defeat.

He was Bogadan's captive audience of one. He had seen a surprising volatility in his companion and dared not excuse himself from this meeting lest he re-awaken Bogadan's ire and undergo further grilling and bullying. The entire situation had turned out to be very tricky. Philip felt his face lock into an idiotic half smile. The smile of one who has lost face, and hopes no one will notice the loss. And it came to him that, as Jonathan had failed, so had he.

'And as regards the Wordsworts,' said Bogadan, as if prompted by Philip's random thoughts, 'we found their name most difficult for us to pronounce, so it is perhaps not a bad thing that they are gone. And in addition to that Jonatan's wife was very *trikee.*'

'She was difficult?' said Philip. 'In what way?'
'No, she was *trikee* … beautiful,' said Bogadan.
'Ah, "pretty",' said Philip.

'*Na jej*', said Bogadan correcting him, 'the word is *trikee* not *prittee*. You will remember the film *Imeetinee Trikee.*'

'Oh yes, I do. The one starring Richard Gere.'

Bogadan shook his head and tutted. '*Na jej, na jej*, this actor, a very fine actor, his name is Risho Geredan. He is Namisan, but not a lot of peoples are knowing that.'

'So,' said Philip, 'Caroline was a *trikee* woman. I mean, she was an *imee trikee*. And was she also *baadee*?'

'Ah *jej!* She was, *Om* Pilip, she was.' Bogadan was evidently impressed. 'Now we are talking same language!'

'And what about Jonathan? What was he like?' said Philip.

'Yes, very good man,' said Bogadan.

'And, of course, he did a lot to help TUDI,' said Philip.

'Correct,' said Bogadan, lighting his cigar.

'It was nice of you to name your lecture theatre after him,' said Philip.

'Well, *pa kappi shay*, he was spending a lot of time signing papers,' said Bogadan. 'This was a small gesture on my part.'

'How about his character?' said Philip.

Bogadan inhaled. 'A little jealous.'

'Oh really,' said Philip. 'And why was that?'

'As I said, his wife was very *trikee* and sometimes this was *bushkil* for *Om* Jonatan, causing *shorty* temper. Very nasty. Also, maybe he was a little, *pa kappi shay*, flighty,' he said.

'In what way flighty?' asked Philip.

'I believe he was liking the ladies much,' said Bogadan. 'We went a few times together to the Sleepy Hollow Nite Club. Of course, I would never go myself to such a place, but he insisted. As a friend, I warned him. I said, "Take care, *Om* Jonatan, someone see you here, maybe *Om* Bryant, and Lady Downing will be finding out."' Bogadan shook his head. 'Sure enough, little time after he was refusing to sign TUDI papers, they find out. Very unfortunate. Good for you you are not jealous or flighty, *Om* Pilip. The Foundation must always be above any kind of suspicion, *na na?*' He smiled and his teeth glinted in the dark.

*

Bogadan, who had driven himself to the hotel that evening, now called Buba to drive him home. Confident that he was on a winning streak, Bogadan had worked his way through a repertoire of his favourite beverages. Buba did as he was told and arrived, muttering, on the back of a Pundari *pikky-up* wearing his driver's cap and, over his *shala kan*, a navy jacket with brass buttons. While Bogadan slumbered in the back of the Lexus, Philip was delivered home and let off by the *preepree* tree at the bottom of his potholed road.

On the unpleasantly humid walk back to the bungalow, swatting insects as he went, Philip took a very important decision. He decided he would make an honest woman of Felicity. He would propose. She would accept. They would marry. It was very simple. They were living together anyway. Worse things could happen. The chances of him ever meeting the likes of the lovely Gold Star were remote, and anyway, why re-invent the wheel? Felicity was the devil he knew, and she always got the laundry done on time. Philip was all for the simple life and the removal of horrid threats. He experienced a pang of delight at the thought of thwarting Bogadan, and had in the construction of this plan perhaps the vaguest sense of déjà vu.

***

25

THE VANISHING

After his evening with Bogadan, Philip had one thought on his mind, in addition, that is, to the distressful memory of having being intimidated and threatened by his one-time friend. What bothered him now was that, in all urgency, he must alert Timmaya to the fact that Bogadan, via the as-yet-unidentified mole, might have found out about the imminent award of a scholarship to his Pundari rival. He was duty bound to put Timmaya on his guard.

As he searched his desk for the number of Timmaya's cousin Wallee, Philip had the sudden strong conviction that he had forgotten something that might well be rather important. This feeling nagged at him like a toothache but he cast it aside for later, just as one reschedules dental appointments.

He made ready his copy of *Discover Namisan – Pre-Elementary* and, from his desk at the office, he called Wallee's number.

His new friend was overjoyed to hear from him. 'Hey, *buddeeitee. Nalungaseesee*!'

'*Nalungaseesee*,' said Philip, turning to page 7 and the introductory unit on 'Greetings.'

'*Bungagogo*, Pilipitee.'

Philip ran his finger down the page for a suitable response. '*Bungagogotipa*, Walleetee,' he said.

'*Salati bunga bunga*, Pilipitee.'

This, Philip found a little more difficult. He turned to the glossary at the back of the book, then back again to the Greetings page. At the other end of the phone, Wallee could be heard filling a glass and partaking of a beverage.

'*Oo salatitipa bunga bunga*, Walleetee,' said Philip at last, labouring over the words but also revelling in his own resourcefulness.

'*Alotta* …' replied Wallee in between slurps, '… *mumbatipa*.'

Here Philip was in unknown territory. This sounded like it might well be something from Unit Three. He bit at his lips and thumbed through the pages but found nothing. There were lessons on 'Describing people,' which was good if you needed to report someone to the police, 'Talking about habits,' useful for talking to your psychotherapist, 'Expressing possession,' if you possessed anything worth expressing about, 'Saying where someone is from …' – that would be either Namisa or Pundar. Flicking through the pages, Philip was at a loss. None of this was any use. At the other end of the line, Wallee was blowing his nose. Philip reverted to his Robinson-Smith *Dictionary of the Namisan Language*, searched for *alotta* and lo … there he found it – the complete response. Clever man Robinson-Smith who could predict the language learner's every dilemma and save him from disgrace and embarrassment. 'Got it!' he said.

'Got it?' said Wallee, who was doing something strange with plastic wrappers at his end of the phone.

'*Alotta alotta mumbatipa oo jinkooran*, Walleetee,' said Philip. With that he shut his book, flipped it into the open drawer of his filing cabinet and put his feet up on his desk.

'Ah-ha!' exclaimed Wallee. There was a pause as Wallee popped something into his mouth and began to crunch. Then between munches he said, '*Oo jinkoorantipa, Om Baadumba*, Pilipitee.'

Philip could not believe what he was hearing, and retrieving his dictionary, he searched for a suitable phrase along the lines of, 'That's it, Wallee. I've had enough. Just cut it out, will you?' The nearest he got was, '*Adoo*, Walleetee. '*Huhu taffee.*'

'*Taffee?*' queried Wallee.

'*Jej, taffee.*'

'Okay.' Wallee was not one to complain about errors of protocol.

Philip now understood very well why phone bills tended to be expensive in Namisa. It was difficult to cut to the chase. He had almost forgotten why he had called in the first place. It was that Wallee would surely know the whereabouts of Timmaya. 'Wallee,' he said. 'Walleetee, I'll come straight to the point. Where is Professor Timmaya?'

Wallee had a chain of wedding ceremonies to report, but no news of the professor.

'So, you really haven't heard from him then?' said Philip.

'*Na jej. Not-a-thingy*,' said Wallee. 'For sure I'm calling him but phone is *pushed-on*. So, I think he's maybe going Pundar. He having *alotta* books to write. *Alotta* kids to feed. *Bunga* you call him there in Pundar. Then you come here for drink *tiga tiga* and eat *okaly* cake.'

*

Philip keyed Timmaya's Pundar number into his phone. After five rings a child answered.

'Hello,' said Philip. He eyed his watch and wondered how long it would take to get past the kid.

There was a baby gurgle, then a clatter as the phone was dropped. The line went dead. Philip sighed and redialled. The line was engaged. He waited a few minutes and called again. 'Hello,' he said when the next baby answered. 'Hello, is your *mammee* or your *pappee* there? Or your uncle?' said Philip. 'Or in fact, anyone.'

The little tot cooed.

'How about the tall man with the turban?'

The child began to wail. There was a rustle and the phone was dropped again. In the background, Philip heard distant screams and garbled baby talk. Then there was a further rustle as the phone was retrieved. A woman answered.

'*Toto*,' she said.

'*Toto*,' replied Philip.

'*Tototipa*. How may I help you, *buddeeitee*?' said the woman.

*

Philip was perplexed. It was Timmaya's wife who had come to the phone. Unlike the professor's sister on an earlier occasion, she had spoken to him in impeccable English, raising her voice above the cries of a multitude of *kiddeez*. Her husband had been due back the day before, she told him, but she had not yet spoken to him. All this was not unsurprising to her. He often stayed away for *meetz*, for wedding ceremonies, for courses and for appointments –appointments with whom she could not say. She simply did not know. She was under the impression that he must be at the university.

'My husband is a very *drudging* man,' she said. 'You would be best advised to contact him here at the University ... in the Department of Anglo-American Literature.'

Philip did as she suggested, navigating the University of Prapundar's maze of a switchboard. But he drew a blank. No one had seen Timmaya or heard anything from him since he had left for Namisa. He had gone and he hadn't come back.

*

I'm going to be helping out for a while at the dry cleaners. One of their number is off sick so I'm filling in for her. Let's call it 'minimum wage research.' I shall take notes.

I am abandoned. My buddeez *have both disappeared. Bindee is at the university doing something like promoting world peace, and Ushri is away for a long weekend in Dubai with his fellow* yobbeez.

For want of something better to do, I wandered down to the Perfume Galley, and who should I meet, sniffing fragrances, but Dr. Manyu from the Department of Agriculture. Horror of horrors, he invited me to dinner. I mean, he's a nice man but he's no autumn-autumn chick chick.

He looked so disappointed when I told him I was 'unavailable.' I didn't want to hurt his feelings so I told him it was very fortunate that we had met because my dear friend Bindee had many animal welfare questions that he might be able to help her with.

There you go.

*

'Timmaya has definitely gone AWOL,' said Philip. 'I can't find him anywhere and no one knows where he is.'

'I don't like the sound of that,' said Alan, picking the croissant crumbs off his desk and popping them into his mouth. 'You reckon he's been got at then?'

'Probably off somewhere getting a new identity,' shouted Ronny from his cubicle.

'I'm really not buying into that,' said Philip. 'I should imagine he's holed up somewhere in Prapundar working on his definitive grammar of the Namisan language.'

'Maybe you should let sleeping Pundaris lie,' said Alan emptying an extra sachet of Namcafe sugar into his *cha-cha*.

'If Bogadan thinks that he can frighten me off by talking about spilling the beans to Bryant … or by making a point of telling me that his mother knows Lady Downing, he's making a big mistake.'

'Spilling the beans about what?' shouted Ronny. 'Is there something I need to know?'

Alan was licking the stickiness off his fingers. 'So, what did you tell him?' he said.

'I told him he was on the short list, of course,' said Philip. 'What else could I do? He was menacing me.'

'Aha, so he *did* scare you!' said Alan.

'A bit,' admitted Philip, a flush of colour spreading across his face. 'But I'm taller than he is.'

'Yeah, well, this short list of yours is very short because we haven't had Timmaya's new application yet.' Alan reached for a buff folder and took out a chunky document with multiple layers in yellow, pink, and pale blue. 'We need one of these,' he said. 'London won't give us anything unless we file the proper paperwork.'

'*Bunga*,' said Philip. 'Just throw a little package together, will you, and we'll courier it off to Pundar.'

'I don't think so,' said Alan, tutting. "Fraid we don't courier anything to Pundar.'

Ronny was sniggering on the other side of the partition.

'Why ever not?' said Philip.

'It never arrives. We've tried it before. Everything vanishes without trace. Then we have to courier the courier to get our money back. So, sorry. Company policy: no sending couriers to Pundar.' Alan gave Philip a short, taut smile.

'Well, then,' said Philip, 'we'll have to scan the documents and send them by e-mail, and then he can sign them, scan them and e-mail them back.'

'We can do, but remember that these are people who never read their e-mails. Their inboxes are full and any messages – especially those with attachments – just get bounced back.' Alan looked very pleased with himself and drummed his fingers on the table.

'Faxes?'

'Yup, faxes are possible,' said Alan, 'if their machines aren't out of paper, or switched off.'

'Good grief, Alan, is there no way of communicating with the other side?' said Philip.

'Knock once for yes and twice for no,' shouted Ronny.

'We send Ratni,' said Alan. 'Good excuse for him to pop home and find out what wife number two is up to. They're a very jealous people you know.'

'Pundaris have more than one wife?' said Philip. He had not seen anything about this in the Culture boxes in his copy of *Discover Namisan – Pre-Elementary*.

'No, just Ratni,' said Alan, 'and since the two wives don't get on, it's best to keep them apart.' Alan shifted papers about and produced a pen. 'So, I'll prepare the documents,' he said, 'and Ratni can take them.'

Philip went back to his office and pondered this solution for some time. He checked his e-mails and had a cup of *cha-cha*. He tried to remember that 'something-important' that he thought he might have forgotten. Then as often happens, in the middle of this self-imposed mental workout, he had a flash of inspiration. He turned to the full-colour map of Pundar on page 62 of *Discover Namisan*. He didn't know why he hadn't thought of it before. He dialled Alan's extension.

'How do you get to Pundar?' he asked.

'Just down the road and across the water. Why?' said Alan.

*

The card index in Tiki's office revealed that just one copy of Robinson-Smith's *A Traveller's Guide to Pundar* was archived in the Foundation's Resource Room. Philip found it wedged under one leg of an otherwise wobbly table. However, its dented pages were of little help as air travel was much improved since the publication of this ancient volume. There was no way Philip would be travelling by fishing boat as Robinson-Smith had done in his early pioneering days. Philip returned for assistance to the fount of all knowledge.

'If you'll take my advice,' said Alan, 'you'll just say that you're away for a few days on family business, looking after your Auntie Peggy – something like that. We don't want Bogadan getting wind of this little trip, do we?'

Like a veteran, Alan explained how Philip should travel to Pundar. 'Now,' he said, 'you can fly out of Trinamisa airport. There are two flights out a day, one with Namisan Air and one with Pundari Air Services & Transport. The flight takes approximately fifty minutes to Prapundar's Naga Simmayya Airport. Point of interest, Philip … the airport was named after Pundar's much loved first president, who was assassinated in 1962.'

'One might ask,' said Philip, 'if he was much loved, why was he assassinated?'

'No,' said Alan, 'don't ask that. Pundaris are very sensitive about everything, especially political issues. I would advise you, naturally, to take the Namisan Air flight, which leaves at 07:00 in the morning and gets in at 07:50. Then there's another flight from Naga Simmayya that departs at 19:00 and that will bring you back for 19:50. This means that you can get in and out within the day.'

As Alan spoke, Philip busied himself taping the loose pages back into the guidebook. At this point, he looked up. 'Oh,' he said, 'I rather hoped I could do a spot of sightseeing.'

A cry of derision came from the adjoining cubicle.

'Most business people, Philip,' said Alan in a fatherly tone, 'don't want to spend a minute more than is necessary in Pundar. And very wise too, in my opinion.'

*

The task of booking the flights fell to Tiki, who was sworn to secrecy by Alan. But, despite his best efforts, news of the trip soon came to Ratni's ears. When he heard that Philip was doing the trip instead of him, the Pundari driver went into a sulk for the rest of the day. Just before lunchtime, his great hulk filled the doorway of Philip's office. He had come to give Philip the benefit of his experience.

'Yes, Ratni?' said Philip.

'Pundar,' said Ratni. He was stoneyfaced.

'Yes?'

'Pundar bad place,' he said. 'People go, they don't come back.'

'Thank you, Ratni. I'll bear that in mind,' said Philip.

*

'Yeah, well he came back,' said Alan when he heard of Ratni's miserable rantings. 'And we'd all be a lot better off if he hadn't.'

As it turned out, all Tiki's efforts to find a flight out on Namisan Air were in vain. They were booked up for the next two weeks.

'But, plenty of economy seats on Pundari Air Services & Transport,' said Tiki.

'Don't go there,' said Alan when Philip reported back.

'He means "Don't go PAST,"' shouted Ronny from his cubicle.

'No, don't even think about it,' said Alan shaking his head.

'Look, I don't have a problem travelling economy class,' said Philip. 'I can handle it.'

'If you go out on the PAST flight,' said Alan, trying to reason with him, 'you'll have to stay overnight.'

'So?' said Philip.

'Just that it's not recommended,' said Alan.

Philip was torn between what was not recommended and what needed to be done. He also very much wanted to do what everyone told him not to do. Like the great Robinson-Smith before him, he had a niggling curiosity about the forbidden and the unknown. And he could do as he pleased – and would do – before he became old and infirm. He had no responsibilities, no dependents, no wife … Well, he had a wife of sorts, but she didn't count.

'Book it,' he told Tiki, and just fifteen minutes later when he stopped by her office, the deed was done. Ratni, incandescent with rage, closed himself in the security guard's room and glowered at Philip through the window every time he walked by.

'The PAST flight leaves at a quarter past midnight and arrives at five past one in the morning,' Tiki confirmed. 'I've booked the flights and two nights at the Coral Creek Beach Hotel.'

'Don't they have a Shangri-La?' said Philip.

'Ah *jej*, it's very difficult to get building licences on Pundar,' said Tiki. 'That's the best I can do.'

'Okay,' said Alan when he heard. 'Just don't say I didn't warn you.'

It only remained for Philip to pack a bag and – oh yes – leave a brief note for Felicity.

***

26

FLIGHT FROM TRINAMISA

Philip's a-quarter-past-midnight flight on Pundari Air Services & Transport was not scheduled to leave until three thirty in the morning. Philip waited in the airport lounge, along with a sprinkling of other lost souls, watching an episode of Tom and Jerry in Namisan on the tiny monitor above the cream-coloured bucket seats. From time to time, he dropped off to sleep, awakening rudely just before he slid off the edge of his plastic chair.

It was in one of these brief soporific intervals that he was suspended in dreamland. He had a sense of being at TU, where he was walking down a long dark corridor vaguely reminiscent of the fifth floor of Building One. The lights flickered above his head and a rusty tap stuck out of the brickwork. Huge oil paintings lined the walls, though in the dim light Philip could not see who or what they depicted. He caught only the glint of eyes, not painted eyes, but real ones staring out at him from the darkness. Turning a corner, he saw, in the distance, a large white fridge. At that moment, he was aware only of his immense hunger. First, he was at the end of the corridor looking at the fridge, then he was close up to it, his hand reaching out to tug open the door. A blast of white light blinded him, and he put up his hands to shield his eyes. Blinking, he could discern a dark shape in the centre of the bright glow within, a shape which gradually defined itself into a head. A bloodied severed head. The closed eyes opened suddenly, and he recognised the face of Shimee Timmaya. He slammed the fridge door shut but, in that instant, a hand touched his shoulder and gripped it firmly, pinning his whole body to the ground. Philip saw a large object bearing down on him. He opened his mouth and let out a long piercing scream. A voice – Bogadan's voice – said, 'What's the matter? You no want dinner?'

Philip opened his eyes. A mean-looking Pundari ground hostess, wearing a navy-blue uniform, topped with a tiny pill-box hat, had grasped him by the shoulder. She had thrust a small white cardboard box into his lap and was roughly shaking him awake. His screams had aroused some degree of concern in the immediate vicinity and two or three onlookers or *kureeoserz* with time on their hands had come to look him over. He scrutinised his watch, trying to fathom out the figures on the dial. It was half past one. Bleary-eyed, he looked inside the box and found one *chick chick sanddij*, a packet of *pikapika* biscuits, a *Bulbi* Delight dessert, and a miniature bottle of frothy white *hura* juice.

As Philip munched through his boxful of *snekz*, still in the trance-like state endowed by sleep, he felt profoundly disturbed by his dream. Could it be true that Bogadan would stop at nothing to have what he wanted? Was it possible that Timmaya had paid a dreadful price for his Education Points?

One more *thingy* troubled and tormented him. Trinamisa airport had no toilets, and sooner or later he would need to step outside and into the dense bushes.

That time came at around ten minutes past two. All was quiet when he left the terminal building. He stood for a few moments at the exit, listening to the moan of the thick humid air through the trees and undergrowth. Shadows danced back and forth across the swaying shapes before him. He looked behind him and around him and then stepped forward towards the malodorous foliage.

He had only gone a few paces when the air seemed to still and, in the ensuing silence, he heard only his own nervous breathing and felt the erratic thump of his heart. In the corner of his eye through the blackness, he perceived a movement. He stood still in the realisation that he was not alone. Something, a shape, a figure, was slowly moving towards him.

*

Dry cleaning is not as tiresome a business as I thought. It's very interesting to find out who's wearing what and why. It occurs to me that clothes hold many secrets – hopes, achievements, failures. When you hand your clothes over to a stranger, you are separating from a part of yourself. Show me someone's clothes now after this workee experience, and I'm sure I can tell you who they are.

There is safety in clothing, clothes of the same colour, clothes of the same style and texture. I wonder if this applies to all cultures? Perhaps I should ask Mike. It's time, I think, for him to update his information on dress codes, possibly with the help of someone with insider knowledge, a dry-cleaning expert, for example.

I might even try my hand at writing self-help books, something along the lines of The Clothes Coach, or The Power of Your Clothing, or Change Your Clothes, Change Your Life.

*

It was the familiar 'Having a spicy time in Tobago' T-shirt that now emerged from the bushes. Philip had two thoughts. Being an orderly person, he liked to enumerate his thoughts and, in addition, since he often forgot what his thoughts had been, it helped somewhat to keep track of them. The first thought was that he would not die decapitated by Bogadan that night. The second was that the spicy-time T-shirt must surely have grown rank, unless it was part of a multiple set and there might be hope that the items in the set were being washed and used in rotation.

'It's only me, *Om* Pilip,' said Frank. 'Are you just of a nervous disposition, or could you have been expecting someone else?' He gave Philip's arm a jaunty slap with the back of his hand.

Alan had been right to warn Philip that his PAST experience might prove stressful. His unpleasant nightmare and the earlier talk of assassinations had contributed to the trauma of meeting Frank Gibson now in the Trinamisa Airport bushes.

'You may be a little sad to learn that I have now left the Trinamisa School of Languages,' said Frank.

'Not really,' said Philip.

'But not to worry,' continued Frank, selecting a cigarette from his pack of Namisan Lights, 'I'll still be around if you need me.'

Philip could not imagine why he might need Frank, though it was helpful to have him stand guard while he used the airport facilities.

'You see, *buddeeitee*,' said Frank when Philip had disentangled himself from the shrubbery, 'I'm a bit of an authority on the Namisan scene, though I say it myself. Insider knowledge, familiarity with the leading players, awareness of cultural implications … It all helps you fall on your feet. Robinson-Smith may think he knows it all, but he's got nothing on me.'

As they picked their way through the undergrowth towards the terminal building, Frank outlined the latest amendment to his C.V.

'English Language Supervisor, University of Prapundar. Can't do better than that now, can you?'

He'd been attracted to the job for a number of reasons. Firstly, and rather perversely, he liked Pundar and its unpredictable lifestyle and, secondly, he'd heard that the English Department was in total chaos.

'Well, I mean,' said Frank, 'what else is new? I haven't yet worked in any English department that wasn't in chaos. I expect I'll find them re-writing the curriculum and ditching the course books. *Na bushkil.* All in a day's work. We don't want to make it too easy for the students, do we?'

'I suppose,' said Philip, 'that this is going to make a major difference to your earnings by comparison with what you were getting in Namisa?' He stifled a snigger. 'I expect it means you're going to have to down-size your beer intake.'

Frank rubbed his chin as he pondered this question. 'Well, let me see,' he said, and then looked up towards the night sky as he grappled with a mental Maths problem. 'If you exclude the yearly return air fares to my point of origin, and the accommodation in PU's new mountain chalet complex and, without counting the lump sum furniture allowance, I think I'd be getting roughly ... 30% more than I was at TU.' Frank lit his cigarette, inhaled and looking at Philip, cocked his head to one side as if to say, 'Try that out for size.'

'You see, Pilipitee, things are looking up in Pundar. Even a pile of rocks is useful to someone somewhere. International conglomerates are getting involved, and PU isn't handicapped the way TU is by the likes of TUDI. They need experts and they're prepared to pay for them. So,' he blew a cloud of smoke into the air, 'you know what they say ... *Hela pala, traka traka*. And I did.'

*

Philip scooped a mosquito out of his beer glass at the Fella's Rest Airport Bar.

'At least,' he said, 'I'll have some company on the flight.' His PAST departure had now been shifted to three fifty-five.

'Ah no,' said Frank. 'I'm travelling KLM.'

'To Prapundar?' said Philip, who was beginning to feel underprivileged.

'Via Singapore,' said Frank.

'But that's miles away,' said Philip. 'You might as well be going via New York.'

'Yes, that was the other option,' said Frank. 'The joys of air travel.'

'Economy?'

'Are you joking? Business Class. They're paying. My wish is their command. You could call it a rags-to-riches story. One day I'm at the Trinamisa School of Languages and the next I'm flying KLM Business Class to Singapore. Got to know how to work the system, Pilipitee, my boy.' And with that he drained the rest of his beer and lit another cigarette.

***

PART THREE

PRAPUNDAR

27

PUNDARI NIGHTS

It was not a pleasant flight. As the plane taxied down the runway, Philip toppled from one side of the aisle to the other, trying to find a seat.

'Please to sit down, Mister,' urged the air hostess.

'I would if I could find a seat,' snapped Philip.

'Sit!' commanded the hostess.

Philip had some suitably harsh words at the ready but stopped himself when he saw her indicate the men grouped about her feet, the whites of their eyes glinting in the dimmed aircraft lights. When the hostess said 'sit' she meant sit down ... anywhere, as these men had done. Philip sat down on the floor in the Business Class aisle, his head level with the elbows of those more fortunate passengers. As the plane ascended, he slid backwards into Economy Class, which was his rightful place. The cleanliness of this PAST plane was disappointing. Philip gave in to fatigue and exasperation, and slumbered amongst wayward peanuts, cracked plastic cups and the remnants of old *chick-chick* sandwiches.

When he arrived in Pundar early that morning, Naga Simmayya Airport was enveloped in thick fog. No doubt this was attributable to the mountainous terrain. Either that, or the fact that most Pundaris were heavy smokers and this tended to have a detrimental effect on the atmosphere when humidity was high and the absence of a cross wind prevented the dispersal of tobacco clouds.

Philip found himself herded down the gangway and onto to the airport shuttle bus by a rush of Pundari workers bearing blanket-clad bundles and Namisa Duty-Free plastic carrier bags. From the bus, he was jostled and manhandled and carried along in the tide of souls competing for first place in the passport queue. In error, Philip was delivered ahead of the mob and found himself face-to-face with the immigration officer, wide-eyed and dumbstruck, with cigarette ash in his hair and nut kernels adhering to his jacket.

'Holiday?' asked the officer.

'Yes,' said Philip, who was taken unawares.

'Welcome three times to our beautiful country,' said the man. Then he stamped Philip's passport with vigour and handed it back to him with a smile and the words, 'And now push off.'

Philip's first thought was to exchange some money since he was not sure how nicely his credit card would do here in Pundar, and in any case he needed cash to pay for his taxi to the hotel. It was time for him to consult his aged but recently restored Robinson-Smith guide to Pundar.

Visitors are advised to accumulate Pundari currency prior to their visit. There are no banks in Pundar, but there are many money exchange booths to be found behind the cattle market in the Pundit neighbourhood of Prapundar. Travellers should exchange Namisan currency only. On no account should the traveller attempt to exchange dollars, pounds or any European currency since this will attract the unwelcome attention of black marketeers (please refer to the sections on Health, Insurance, and Medical Treatment.)

(Extract from 'Money Matters,' (p.22) in *A Traveller's Guide to Pundar: easy come, easy go* by Michael Robinson-Smith.)

Fortunately, Philip's Robinson-Smith *Namisa - A Traveller's Guide: from tradition to tourism and back*, 2011 edition, contained a helpful Pundar supplement, which read as follows:

The currency in Pundar parallels that used in Namisa — the main unit of currency being the *kola* — but while Namisan notes are issued by the National Bank of Namisa (NBN), in Pundar they are issued by the Pundari United Bank (PUB). For newcomers to Pundar – and it should be pointed out that most foreign visitors remain newcomers since they rarely stay long enough to become oldcomers – misunderstandings often arise around the expression, 'See you down at the PUB, *buddeeitee,*' which results in Pundaris spending many a wasted hour waiting at the bank for their overseas visitors, while the visitors for their part search in vain for drinking places in which they might find their Pundari friends. This is not to say that there are no drinking places in Pundar. Far from it. These places exist but it is not recommended that outsiders should visit them, given the risks involved. (In this regard, please consult the sections on Entertainment, Police, and Medical Treatment.)

(Extract from 'Pundar - Money Facts for Visitors,' (p.32) in *Namisa - A Traveller's Guide: from tradition to tourism and back***, by Michael Robinson-Smith.)**

*

At the PUB exchange window, Philip again stood in line awaiting his turn to be served. It was because Ratni held the monopoly on trips to Pundar that the Foundation could not supply him with a cash per diem. As he continued to wait, he cursed Ratni under his breath and thumbed through his guide.

The Pundaris are a very assertive people and it is in their nature to take the shortest and easiest route to the solution of every problem. Thus, if you are Pundari and you find someone obstructing your path, you bypass or remove them, if necessary, by force.

(Extract from 'Pundar – Character and Identity,' (p.32) in *Namisa - A Traveller's Guide: from tradition to tourism and back***, by Michael Robinson-Smith.)**

Seven Pundaris, one after the other, systematically edged their way to the front of the line and displaced Philip with a sharp nudge of their elbow or thump of their shoulder. Philip was obliged to take defensive measures.

When the next Pundari boldly sidestepped in front of him, he said in a very loud voice, '*Looka looka*, I have been *waiting-waiting* here for fifteen minutes and now it is my turn. Please go to the back of the queue.' This proved entirely successful, earning Philip some degree of respect. It enabled him to reach the window of the exchange clerk without further interference, but at the same time it attracted a small crowd of *kureeoserzs*. Any hopes that he had had initially of remaining low profile, were now quashed. As he handed over his Namisan notes for exchange, seven or eight Pundaris clustered beside him peering over his shoulder and looking into his wallet, while clerks emerged from adjacent exchange desks to root for his business.

'Good exchange is here,' said the biggest and probably the hairiest of them, gripping Philip by the arm. 'We give you better price.'

'No thank you,' said Philip. He wrestled himself away though the man had a hand like a vice. He collected his receipt and received a hefty wad of notes stapled together in uneven batches. Mopping his forehead with his sleeve, he hurried through to the arrivals lounge, closely followed by the *kureeoserzs*. Behind him, the hairy money-changer, smiling, waved him goodbye with the words, 'You make bad mistake, Mister.'

Philip was dismayed to find that the lounge was lined on both sides with taxi-hire booths. Where to begin? He approached the first of these and peered in through the service window, where he noted a seething mass of bodies, evidently the working members of an extended family of taxi owners.

'The Coral Creek Beach Hotel. I want to go there,' said Philip in the loud voice of someone who is making himself understood to the natives. He took care to keep his money close to his chest, zipped inside an inner jacket pocket. The evil-smelling *kureeoserzs* who had followed him here from the exchange desk had swelled in number and now pressed against him in inquisitive intimacy, staring into his face and kneading the fabric of his shirt and trousers. Within the taxi booth, the inhabitants conferred for a minute or two after which their spokesman, a large man, red-faced and unshaven, named their price.

'One thousand,' he said, and then waited for Philip's reaction.

This figure was the precise amount Philip had received for his Namisan currency at the money exchange counter. Good news travelled fast in Pundar, it seemed.

'One hundred,' said Philip.

'No, no, *buddeeitee*,' said the spokesman laughing. He slapped Philip on the back. 'You very funny man. I telling you what, I give you special price. You first customer from today. Only nine hundred.'

'I don't think so,' said Philip. He thought for a moment. 'One hundred and fifty,' he said.

The man stopped laughing and assumed a solemn air. '*Om*, it not possible,' he said. 'I have many childrens. How I feeding them? Perhaps I feeding one today, then maybe one tomorrow, maybe another after that day. I thinking you joking me.' The man resumed his laughter, which was echoed by the tribe members in his booth. 'I can give good offer. You give me eight hundred. Very good deal and thank you.'

'Two hundred then,' said Philip.

'You not understanding,' said the man sighing. 'We taking you Coral Creek. It costing us go there. It costing us come back. You money not cover cost petrol. You my brother. Brother, give me seven hundred and we all happy happy.'

'I need cash pay hotel,' explained Philip. He wasn't about to be giving his per diem to them. 'Here,' he said and reaching inside his jacket, he fingered his bundle of loot and tore away some stapled notes. He counted them out in front of his new friend. 'Three hundred.'

At every new offer, the *kureeoserz* murmured and commented.

'*Om Baadumba*,' said the man again, assuming a serious manner. 'Night black,' he said sweeping his hand through the air. 'Difficult see.' He pointed to his eyes. 'Need good driver. We give good driver. Good eyes and no drinking. I take rocking bottom price. Five hundred fifty. Price too much good.'

Philip rummaged again inside his jacket and pulled out an additional fifty. 'Three hundred and fifty. Last offer,' he said, fanning the notes in the man's face. 'But I want a good driver. Not a fast driver. *Kappi shay?*'

The man snatched the money from his hand. 'I give good driver. Even driver have licence. No extra charge.' With that he snapped his fingers and growled commands at a group of boys who hovered loose-limbed by the booth. A small black-haired child separated off from the others and raced towards the exit and the airport car park.

By now the night sky had lightened over the Pundari hills. With the deal done, the *kureeoserz* began to lose interest and disperse. The taxi booth man lit two Pundari

Lights and offered one to Philip who accepted in observance of protocol. 'My name Tymm,' said the man. 'But you calling me ... Fred. Fred giving you good driver. He coming now.'

*

It was around five thirty in the morning when Philip, driven in a battered Citroen by a man who might have passed for a serial killer, finally arrived at the Coral Creek Beach Hotel. The mist was beginning to settle, and the decrepit pink stone building materialised before him in the half-light of the dawn. The taxi drew to a halt in a large half-paved driveway, at the foot of a chipped stone staircase. This in turn led to an open porch-like area furnished with four or five wooden deckchairs, some marble topped tables littered with cigarette ends, and a selection of wicker armchairs.

Philip stepped out of the car and did a few celebratory stretches. Any hotel was better than no hotel. The driver deposited his bag and briefcase by the staircase, gave him a half-crazed look, then jumped back into his cab and drove away with a certain urgency into the fog.

'Hey!' shouted Philip. But the car's taillights had already disappeared in the mist. 'Well, no tip for you,' said Philip. The least the driver could have done, he thought, was keep him company until he had checked in and maybe take a cup of *cha cha* with him. He stood there in the semi-darkness. Not a soul stirred. He had seen movies like this before and invariably they did not have happy endings. He felt the need to run for cover. He gathered up his baggage and, as fast as he could manage, he staggered up the hotel steps. On the porch he dropped the bags, looked about him and wondered what to do next.

Somewhere in the distance he heard a door creak. Then came the rattling of chains, and then the thud of monstrous footsteps. A man built like a mountain, with a bushy moustache and a belligerent expression, emerged from behind a full-length velour curtain. Philip froze. The man stared at him for a moment. Then, with single-minded grimness, he strode towards Philip and made as if to strike him. Philip flinched, drawing his arms up over his head to protect himself, but the man was too fast for him. He lunged forwards and, with a firm grip, wrenched down Philip's arms.

'*Bungagogo*,' he boomed and with that he cast a garland of scarlet flowers around Philip's neck and shoulders. Then he snatched up Philip's travelling bag and his briefcase, and made off with them into the dark recesses of the hotel. Philip scurried behind leaving a trail of petals as he went.

*

Accustomed as he was to the Shangri-La, the Coral Creek Beach Hotel – like the PAST flight – was a great disappointment to Philip. There was little or no water in his bathroom and, probably as a result of the high humidity, the air conditioning did not work. Philip struggled to wash himself in a trickle of water from a tap in the wall. During those early hours, he was bitten by a variety of flying insects and come 8:30am, after just a few hours' sleep, he awoke with a jolt, looking like the unmade bed of someone who suffers from nightmares. In a moment of weakness, he reached for his phone and dialled Felicity's number. It was only right, he thought, that a man should seek solace in the reassuring words of his wife. But there were no words of reassurance or otherwise. Felicity's phone rang and rang until the call was timed-out. Here, thought Philip, was a woman who was a Coffee Circle as well as a Chardonnay too far. He felt very sorry for himself indeed.

In search of breakfast he made his way to the hotel porch where he found a plump man of pallid complexion sitting at the reception desk with a large ledger open in front of him.

'Ah, *bungagogo*, *Om* Philip,' said the man, 'let one introduce oneself. I am the manager of the hotel. My name is *Om* Sinlatt, but you can call me Sin. Here at the Coral Beach Hotel one speaks English,' he said.

'Which one?' said Philip.

'Why, me of course,' said Sin. 'I think you're come from Namisa and mostly one does not speak English there. They are very lazy monoglotted people. How is your room by the way?'

'Just the job,' said Philip, which reminded him that he had a very important job to be getting on with.

*

Something I felt bad about. In Edinburgh, everyone seemed to have a part-time workee. *My friend Jane worked in a fish and chip shop. Hamish worked as a bicycle messenger. Keith worked in a pub. Fran worked in a shoe shop. When we were all together one evening, they told me they were working to earn money to pay for their courses and support themselves while they were studying. And Hamish said to me, 'So, Tanita, what is it that you do?' And I said, 'I go to the ATM.'*

And everyone went silent.

*

'A taxi?' asked Sin. 'You want a taxi?' He looked troubled. 'We used to have taxi drivers – many of them – but now they all gone to Namisa. Money is better there. Never fear, *Om* Pilip, one will find you transport.'

Sin was true to his word. After an absence of just ten minutes he led the camel into the forecourt himself. It was harnessed to a wooden cart that resembled a four-poster bed, and that was draped all around in pink chiffon. 'One will bring cushions to make you more comfortable,' said Sin, and an armful of satin cushions, embroidered with images of Grikagraka were brought from the hotel lounge by the angry-looking garland man and thrown unceremoniously into the middle of the cart.

'There,' said Sin. 'One will be a little slow but one will get you to the university by eleven o'clock no problem.' He snapped his fingers at a gaunt, yellow-skinned man, who hopped onto the vehicle and arranged himself barefooted and cross-legged on a narrow wooden bench at its front edge.

Philip climbed into the cart, behind the chiffon drapes, and lolled on the rolling cushions, hugging his briefcase to his chest. The cart lurched forward down the hotel driveway towards the city centre, bumping across potholes and easing itself forward through fetid mounds of manure and mud. From time to time, the animal bellowed out a protest, flapping its tail and looking about it with an air of extreme arrogance. The creature was as ugly as sin, but Philip reminded himself not to make this comment out loud.

*

'What I am thinking today,' said Mrs. Katraree, 'is to speak about two *thingeez*. Now, if there is time, I would like to talk about the matter of coincidences, but I will first start with the very important subject of misunderstandings between *om* and *imee*.

'Oh, my goodness,' said Felicity, noting the early morning missed call on her phone. 'What a coincidence! That's what I was going to ask about.'

'See!' said Mrs. Katraree. The members of the Coffee Circle could not but admit to Mrs. Katraree's uncanny ability to anticipate the direction of their thoughts. 'So, to continue,' said Mrs. Katraree, 'note that I am talking about misunderstandings as opposing to incomprehensions. Now misunderstandings can be happening very easily. Let me see if I can think of some examples.'

'Perhaps,' said Felicity, 'if I may ... a misunderstanding can happen when the *imee* believes something about the *om*, but she is mistaken.'

'Correct!' said Mrs. Katraree.

'Or perhaps when the *om* believes something about the *imee*, but he is mistaken.'

'Also correct! But I am thinking now of the case of *Imee* Laulee. You will all remember this. It was some years back. She came here often to the Coffee Circle.'

'*Ah jej*,' murmured the ladies.

'*Imee* Laulee was a quiet *sortee*, happily married with big children.'

'Oh, she was Pundari?'

'*Na jej*. I am meaning that her children were growed and out of the way.' Mrs. Katraree nibbled the edge of a *pikapika* biscuit and thought for a moment. 'Now what happened was this. She found some credit *cardee* recipes in her *husbundee*'s pockets from the shop of *Om* Savatt the jeweller and from the Perfume Galley in the Trinamisa Shopping Mall.'

'I was just wondering …' said Felicity.

'Yes, my dear?' said Mrs. Katraree.

'Did she always look through his pockets?'

There were murmurings around the room, and the men's section of the room became suddenly animated.

Mrs. Katraree looked a little put out. 'We advise it, my dear, before bring suits to the Dry Kleen Shop. We cannot compensate our customers when they are telling us, "*Looka looka*, I had a *kooka kola* note in my pocket and now it is dissolved." It is true that in the process of the cleaning, much is dissolved but the *kooka kola* note it becomes only a little bleached, so we know they having us under.'

'Having you on,' said Felicity.

'Correct!' said Mrs Katraree. 'So, before the gentlemen over there are having a misunderstanding, they should-can know that *Imee* Laulee was only doing as we are instructing previous to cleaning process.' Mrs.

Katraree sent a glare in the direction of the men's section. 'Now, returning to *Imee* Laulee and the credit *cardee* recipes,' she continued. 'She was thinking "*Shematihut*! He is buying *thingeez* not for me, but for a young *imeetinee* because if he was buying them for me, I would be having them now, *na na*?" And so, this *imee* – normally being so quiet – she goes into big anger, uncontrolling herself, and when *Om* Laulee returns home, she is attacking him viscously with frying pan.'

There were gasps from the ladies at this point.

'Viciously,' said Felicity.

'Correct! Very viscously,' agreed Mrs. Katraree. 'And then she is thinking, "Where am I putting the body?" So, she is dragging him to the cellar and down the stairs. Boompa, boompa, boompa. She was a big *imee* but also her *husbundee* was big *om*, so *workee* of bringing body into cellar not an easy *workee*. Well, then she is sitting in cellar to recover from this *graftee* and she is seeing the red carrying bag of the Perfume Galley, and looking inside, she is seeing her anniversary card and two presents from her *husbundee*.'

'*Ah jej*!' exclaimed Felicity. 'What a terrible tragedy!'

'*Na jej*! Not a tragedy, my dear *Imee* … a misunderstanding!'

***

28

CATALOGUES OF DESPAIR

A long banner, off-white in colour – not unlike a strip of someone's old bedsheets – was suspended from one of the university's boundary walls. Daubed on it in red paint was a message. It read:

> 'The University of Prapundar welcomes
> Professor Philip of Downing Foundation.'

As his Coral Creek cart trundled up the road to the main gate, Philip saw the members of the welcome party from afar, straightening their ties, smoothing down their hair and brushing fluff and dandruff from their jackets. This sizeable group, made up of senior faculty and elite administrators, competed for places in the photo opportunity line-up. Roughly removed from his vehicle, Philip was grasped, spun around, bowed to, his hand shaken many times. He was taken and seated on a gold-varnished chair in the midst of a wisdom of professors, and when the goats were shooed out of the picture, he was blinded by the lightning flashes of Prapundari cameras. He was snapped in pairs, in threes, in groups of four and more. His jaw began to ache with unaccustomed smiles. And then, glistening with perspiration, he faced his audience from behind an ancient CBS microphone. When the clapping subsided, he beamed at his new friends and they at him. There was a moment of pleasant silence. Philip cleared his throat.

'Thank you. Thank you, my friends, for this warm welcome.' Philip looked about him and saw that more was required. 'What I want to say from the bottom of my heart, my friends, is ... I am *happy-happy* to be here and thank you.' He said this with a tone of finality, then placed the palms of his hands together and gave a bow.

There was rapturous applause during which interval Philip, not a little pleased with himself, was whisked away to the cafeteria for a lunch of miscellaneous delicacies and an abundance of *tiga tiga,* and all the while bombarded with questions about the Foundation, about Namisa, about his wife, about his life in Britain, about the US President, about mobile phones, about his recommendations for the Nobel Peace Prize, about student assessment ... Philip himself had only one question, and that he asked of the Provost, a tiny bald-headed man with a shiny nut-brown face and prominent eyes, who spoke with an English accent that Philip found both endearing and reassuring.

'Professor Timmaya?' said the Provost. 'Well, I really don't know. We rather assumed he would be accompanying you from Namisa. To tell the truth we have not seen him since he left for his cousin's wedding ceremonies.'

At that moment Philip experienced the kind of disappointment he had felt at school when some longed-for prize had gone someone else's way, a team selection, a grade, a project evaluation. It was always the other boy who got the cup or got the date with the coolest girl at the end-of-year dance. Had he really come to Pundar for this? Not that he had anything else to do, but he had wasted his time. Instead of pursuing Timmaya, he could have been looking for his Gold Star, his lovely Namisan sweetheart … or similar.

'But I've come all this way. I've got documents for him to sign. Important Foundation documents.'

'And we have essays for him to correct,' said the Provost, nodding in resignation at the Assistant Provost, a slim, elegant woman in her mid-forties. 'We have been expecting him back for some time, but there is no sign of him as yet. Is it not so, Dr. Rashatt?'

'Yes, we think it is a little strange,' said Dr. Rashatt. 'He usually lets us know if he is going to be away.'

'Quite so, quite so, Dr. Rashatt,' said the Provost. 'But, you know,' he said, addressing Philip, 'he's very … how can I describe him? He's very eclectic in his ways.'

'Idiosyncratic,' said Dr. Rashatt.

'Yes, that is a pleasant word. Let us call him that.'

'Or perhaps mercurial?'

'Yes, I like "mercurial" too. Let me make a note of that,' said the Provost, taking out a small blue spiral notebook and carefully selecting a blank page.

How Timmaya might be described was less of a concern to Philip than what might have happened to him. He saw Bogadan in every corner, under every bed, concealed in every cupboard.

'Do you think something might have happened to him?' said Philip as Provost and Assistant Provost attended to the entry of the new word.

'Well,' said the Provost, 'I suppose he could have accepted invitations to other wedding ceremonies. He is sociable as well as mercurial. Or he might have gone to get married again, or perhaps he is just recovering…'

'Recovering from …?'

'From other wedding ceremonies,' said the Provost.

'Or maybe he has gone on a course. He likes courses,' explained Dr. Rashatt. 'In fact, we all like courses, Provost.'

Philip felt that he too needed a course – stress management, Bogadan management, get-your-priorities-right management, see-the-woods-from-the-trees management.

'Yes, well, they do him no good in my opinion,' said the Provost, 'but I think he feels better for going on them.'

'So,' said Philip, 'has he been getting any peculiar phone calls, or has he perhaps seemed unusually nervous?' There were times when Philip confused the Downing Foundation with the Secret Service or Interpol. This was one of those times. His often doom-laden self imagined, if not Timmaya's head, then his bloodied body falling out of a locker in the Chemistry lab. 'I mean, there's been no one here looking for him, asking questions about him, behaving strangely …?'

The two paused and looked at each other, nonplussed.

'Only you,' said Dr. Rashatt.

'Oh,' said Philip.

'What a pity he isn't here,' said the Provost, staring wistfully up at the ceiling.

In a gesture of affection and reassurance, Dr. Rashatt tapped the back of Philip's hand. 'It's such a shame that he's going to miss your lecture, Professor Philip.'

'Lecture?'

It's a shame I never found out more about that foreign yobbee. He seemed so… pleasant. Cute even. No idea what his name is.

William? Harry? Archie? Oliver? David?

The truth is I'm missing Europe, and I'm missing Europeans. I went over to the Shangri-la to find Sylvie, but I think this afternoon must have been her language class afternoon. Too bad.

Instead, I found Mike and spent Happy Hour with him. He said, 'But yes, my dear, you must go. The world awaits you.' And then he added something along the lines of, 'It's awful out there but until you experience it for yourself you will never understand how life works. The outside world offers freedom and adventure, but also heartbreak and sorrow. To avoid all that, some of us just prefer to stay here.' I'm not sure I understood. In fact, I didn't understand. Then he said, 'Let me look into your cocktail and I will tell you your future.' So, I did, and he said, 'You will become a cultural attaché and represent your country overseas.' He handed me back my drink and said, 'Never fear. It's written in your Namisan Dawn. Just be patient.'

But I'm not patient. I'm afraid that I'll never leave here again. I don't have a job, and I don't actually need one, but what is my purpose? We all surely need something of our own.

Pappee and mammee *think I'm 'done.' They won't be forking out for more study abroad. I could apply for a scholarship. I've been told that* Imee *Felicitu's husbundee handles study bursaries at the Foundation. I might try him.*

Surely nothing can be written unless I write it myself?

*

'Just please to sit here and read, please. I will record,' said Imee Nattat.

'Read? What exactly? And why?'

From the main lecture room, Philip had been delivered into the hands of Imee Nattat – she of the henna-tinted curls – a long-term member of faculty, who ran the Phonetics department. Philip was still hyperventilating but more from self-satisfaction than from shock. He had realised that day that, when visiting foreign universities, it is always wise to come prepared with some learned presentation or other. On this occasion, some advance warning would have helped but, in the circumstances, he surprised himself by coming up with the rather clever lecture topic: 'London – my kind of town,' in which he guided his earnest listeners on a lightning trip around the neighbourhoods closest to his favourite public houses. His performance, he felt, was not far short of intoxicating. But now after his descent from that pinnacle of triumph, he was a little weary. *Imee* Nattat was asking only a very small favour of him as she guided him into a classroom, labelled 'Language Laboratory,' an area empty of students but crammed with gnarled wooden desks and sturdy, back-breaking chairs. The walls of the room were decorated with curled and crinkled images of Britain, cut from popular tabloids and broadsheets, and on each of five of the desks there sat a battered blue Coomber cassette player.

'Professor Philip, you will do for us a wonderful thing,' said *Imee* Nattat. 'You will give for us your voice as a model for all our students.'

Staring now at the desktop in front of him Philip prepared to read with feeling and conviction the 2009 Ikea catalogue.

'Starting from …?'

'Page one,' said *Imee* Nattat.

Time passes slowly and your throat grows dry when you reach your eighty-seventh Swedish catalogue label. Philip wondered to what extent *Imee* Nattat's students might profit from a description of a high pile hand-knotted rug that is naturally soil repellent.

'Language counts,' explained *Imee* Nattat. 'We owe much to the Ikea family for teaching us about numbers, colours and comfy corners.'

Philip was not the first. *Imee* Nattat recalled with pride the visits of earlier linguists.

'Professor Abercrombie of the University of Edinburgh.'

'He was here?' said Philip, looking around him as if to spy a coat and hat, a pair of spectacles, a half-eaten plate of haggis and turnip.

'Oh yes. He was here,' said *Imee* Nattat, a hint of one-up-womanship creeping into her voice. 'You know, we have a recording of him reading *The National Gallery of Scotland* catalogue. 'Of course, he is pushed on now. A very fine man he was too. And we also had Professor Henry Widdowson here. He too is a very fine man and he is also very tall. We have much to thank him for. Following his advice, all of our students now have a *portyfolio* of their work, as a result of which we are almost world-class, unlike the Oil and Gas Institute in Abu Nar, where none of the students keep a *portyfolio*. I trust that Professor

Widdowson is not yet pushed on and will enjoy the autumns of a thousand peacocks. He said he would return to us,' she said sadly, 'but we have not heard from him for many years. He read for us *The Times* Crossword for 17 June, 1987. He has very very wonderful intonation.' Her eyes glazed over as she remembered his magical rendering of the numbers up and down. And then she took note of where she was. 'Please, page four. Sofas, I think.'

The Provost's library tour came as a welcome release from extensive descriptions of home delivery and assembly. Between the book stacks, cockerels strutted while cats slept curled up on chairs. In a sheltered corner close to the Mechanical Engineering collection, a cluster of staff members were taking a break, picnicking at one of the study tables. They smiled and raised their glasses as Philip passed.

'As you see,' said the Provost, 'our academic community is very laid up.'

'Are they taking something for it?'

'For what?'

'For whatever they've got.'

'Food, I suppose,' said the Provost, looking in the direction of a learned professor who was eating a late lunch with a book propped up in front of him. As they passed, he turned a leaf of his book and brushed away the dead cockroach that fell from its pages.

Philip returned wearily to the hotel following his final tour … of the Chemistry labs, wearing protective sunglasses with Stars and Stripes lenses, a gift from the American Embassy. He was given a lift back to the hotel by Dr. Rashatt, who expressed the hope that Professor Philip would return very soon.

*

Sin greeted Philip heartily.

'Welcome again, my friend. I trust that one is well-travelled.'

From the kitchen came rhythmic hacking sounds as though someone was at work with a very large machete.

Sin fuelled Philip with *sneks* and more *tiga tiga*, while he described to him his plans for the future. He intended to attract foreign visitors by opening a spa and giving massages and beauty treatments. When he managed to remove the bats from the dining hall in the unused wing of the hotel, he would open it as an exclusive dining venue for tourists.

'Do you have many tourists?' asked Philip.

'No, not as yet,' said Sin, 'but I am sure they will come when the regularity of our PAST flights improves. If Namisa can do it, so can one. One will also offer a wide range of dishes here in the dining room – dishes like spaghetti bolognese, lasagna, and frogs' legs.'

A tiny grey frog jumped over Philip's feet as he said this.

'As you can see there is no shortage,' said Sin.

*

Back in his room, Philip made one last call on his mobile to Timmaya's home. His family had still had no word and they were beginning to worry. Philip was also beginning to worry. Unused budget would be lost and that would reflect badly on him. According to Alan, there were times when you were in trouble if you spent too much money and other times when you did not spend enough. If the scholarship did not go to Timmaya, then it would have to go to the other name on his shortlist of two. It was beginning to look as though Bogadan was even in control of the hand of destiny.

***

PART FOUR

WUNAMISA

29

HOME ALONE

After another gruesome night in the Coral Creek Beach Hotel, Philip flew back on the 7:30am flight that left at 9:00am. When he got home at 11:00am, Felicity – as was her habit – was already out at her Coffee Circle meeting.

Philip showered and then dressed for work. How refreshing to be back home in his little bungalow and find his clothes all neatly pressed and clean from the SnowWhite Dry Kleen Shop. This, at least, was one benefit of having Felicity around. She entrusted everything to Mrs. Katraree now, and the cleaning lady – also supplied by Mrs. Katraree – simply hung the clothes up for him in the wardrobe.

His thoughts were once again focused on the whereabouts of Timmaya. He had made a wasted journey. He remembered back to what Timmaya had said … that Bogadan could be vengeful. What could he deduce from the present situation? That someone had leaked to Bogadan that the scholarship money might be going to Timmaya? That Bogadan had intercepted Timmaya and

– God forbid – had somehow disposed of him? If he had indeed disposed of Timmaya, then did that mean he was a threat to Philip himself?

Philip glanced at the typewriter on the kitchen table and at the pages nibbled and shredded by Parrot. Parrot was standing on one leg eating a biro. He tipped his head and said in a dark deep voice 'Felicitu.'

Ah yes, Felicity. He had almost forgotten all about her. She was his wife, wasn't she? And yet they hardly spoke and they hardly ever saw each other. There was the small matter of their marriage still to be sorted out. He had been totally focused on the issue of scholarship and research grants, and she had been totally focused on her current project and her involvement in the Coffee Circle. She was lucky, he thought, that she didn't have his responsibilities. It hadn't even occurred to him to ask her what she was working on. How dreary and boring her life must be, he thought.

Standing in front of the hallway mirror, Philip brushed his damp hair into place as he waited for Ratni to come and pick him up. Only now was he beginning to look normal again after those two nights in the wilderness. He was clean and refreshed, clean hair, freshly shaved. He wore a crisp white shirt, his navy jacket, his beige trousers neatly pressed, his black shoes expertly heeled and shined, and last, but not least, his smart red tie.

Philip paused to think for a moment. Something was wrong. His smart red tie? He did not have a red tie, and yet there it was. He was wearing it. For a split second he thought, 'How kind. Felicity's bought me a tie,' but then another thought struck him. With trembling hand, he turned the tie over and saw the label.

Alone in the house with Parrot, the light dawned. Philip stared at the mirror, and his cuckolded self stared back. He had neglected Felicity, and in this period of his absorption in other matters – mainly the question of the scholarship – Felicity had found herself attracted to the very worst person she could possibly have been attracted to, and had drifted into a liaison with him. The very worst person Philip could have imagined had invaded his personal life. The evidence had been there all the time and he hadn't seen it or heard it. For surely Parrot's voice was also the voice of Bogadan?

'Naughty girl,' said Parrot in a dark and mellifluous tone. And Parrot's voice was also the voice of Jonathan and of Caroline, and of countless other unnamed women.

'Naughty boy,' said Parrot now in that distinctly female voice. 'Darling, darling.'

But whose voice was that, and where was Imee Nattat, Prapundar University's expert in Phonology now when Philip needed her? His ears burning with anger and indignity, he gaped at Parrot, the custodian of all secrets. The babbigall quivered slightly under his scrutiny, then opened and closed his beak in a standoffish parrot yawn.

More light dawned. Philip was dazzled with light dawning. What had been going on here? Bogadan and Caroline? Felicity and Bogadan? And what had been happening with Jonathan? What were Jonathan and Bogadan getting up to at Sleepy Hollow? This villain had systematically seduced all the Foundation wives and now Philip's own dear Felicity had fallen victim. The horror of it … the horror. Philip stood frozen in front of his reflection, blinking at the tie and gutted by the awful reality of its significance. He heard footsteps, then a creak and a rattle as the porch door opened and shut. It was Felicity, returning full of the joys of the Coffee Circle.

'Philip,' said Felicity, sweeping in through the door.

'Felicity,' said Philip. His cheeks glowing pink, his face stinging.

'You're back,' she said, putting down her bag.

'What's this?' he said, pointing to his tie, like someone in the throes of amnesia.

'It's a tie,' said Felicity.

There was silence.

'Yes?' said Philip.

'And it's red,' said Felicity. She raised her eyebrows.

'It is not *my* tie, Felicity.'

'Then,' said Felicity, 'why are you wearing it?'

'This ...' said Philip, flapping the tie in her direction, 'this is Bogadan's tie.'

'Well, you should jolly well give it back to him,' said Felicity, walking into the kitchen.

'My name's Parrot,' said Parrot.

'Naughty boy,' said Felicity.

'How did it get here?' insisted Philip. 'How did Bogadan's tie end up in my house?'

'Our house,' said Felicity.

'How did Bogadan's tie end up in my house, mixed up with my things, while I was away in Pundar?'

'I have no idea,' said Felicity. 'I don't know what you two get up to on your cocktail nights. Exchanging trophies and items of clothing perhaps? I'm a good wife. I don't ask questions.' She took out the *cha cha* bags and dropped one into her astrological mug.

'You have no right to do this, Felicity.'

'What?' said Felicity.

'What?' said Parrot.

'Betray me,' said Philip. 'You've betrayed me with my worst enemy.'

'Oh, for goodness sake, Philip, you've been reading too much Shakespeare.'

'We're practically diplomats, Felicity. You can't go around fraternising with the natives and bringing me into disrepute!'

'Yes, it's all about you, isn't it?' said Felicity. 'Never a thought for me. Don't forget that I'm doing you a favour. Let's face it, you couldn't have got the job without me. No wife, no job, remember? So, don't give me that poor-me routine. I'm the one who should be complaining.'

As their voices rose, Parrot hung upside down from his perch and added to the clamour. 'Stop it! Stop it!' he squawked.

'You lured me out here to the back of beyond, telling me how lovely it would be.' She slammed her mug down on the kitchen table and splattered hot *cha cha* all over her nibbled notes. 'I'm making the best of a bad job, Philip, I really am, and your red tie is the last straw.' She strode into the hallway and picked up her bag.

'Where are you going?' said Philip.

'I'm going to see my friend Mike,' said Felicity. 'What's it to you?'

'And who's Mike when he's at home?' Philip shouted after her. But she was already out on the porch with the door slamming shut behind her. Had he made a terrible mistake? He just wasn't very good at arguments. He felt as though he had just argued with his best friend and the idea of it filled him with immense sorrow. And as he wallowed – all too briefly – in the grief and emptiness of it, the door burst open and a shadow darkened the threshold.

'I here, boss,' said Ratni.

*

Ooops! I think I got the cleaning mixed up. In fact, I know I got the cleaning mixed up. I'm actually not very good at this. You'd think that I'd be able to get a few measly little name labels on the right clothes, but no. I got distracted and, well… chaos.

A few clients have been in and brought stuff back. It's not the end of the world. I mean, it's hardly going to be the cause of any family tragedies, is it?

*

Philip did his best to put on a brave face. Sitting in the Accounts office, hugging a cup of very hot sweet *cha-cha*, he could see that one of Alan's little stories was forthcoming.

'I offered Sylvie one of my biscuits,' said Alan, 'and guess which one she took?'

'Oh, I don't know,' said Philip, who was overcome by an intense weariness.

'She picked the *pikapika*,' said Alan, and then he roared with laughter.

Philip looked at Alan with disgust.

'What a miserable so and so you are!' said Alan. 'Where's your sense of humour?'

Philip thought that perhaps he once might have had a sense of humour.

'Come on,' said Alan, 'tell your Uncle Alan what the *bushkil* is. After all,' he said, 'a *kipkip* snake shared is a *kipkip* snake halved, *na na*?'

Bathed now in self-pity, Philip gave Alan a detailed and very sombre account of the events following his return from Pundar. Alan ate his doughnut and sipped from his mug of Namcafé as he listened. When Philip had finished, he folded his arms and sat waiting for Alan's judgement. If he hadn't worked it out as yet, thought Philip, he would get the picture now.

'So,' said Alan, 'first he squeezes you to make you give him the scholarship. Then he threatens to tell Bryant about you and *Imee* – should I say *Imeetinee* – Felicitu, and about how you were, let's say, economical with the truth. Heaven knows, Lady Downing won't like that if she ever finds out. And now, you discover that all along he's been canoodling with *Imee* Felicitu.'

'Well, he might be,' said Philip. 'I mean he probably is, but I suppose I could be wrong … though maybe not…'

Alan took another bite of his doughnut. 'Well, well, well,' he said between munches, 'Whatever. Your friend Ito Boy is messing with you big time.' He chewed and thought again. 'Well, do not fear, *Om* Pilip,' he said, 'your terrible secret is safe with me. Mind you, your terrible secret is not safe with Ito Boy… and he's walking all over you.'

'That's very reassuring, Alan,' said Philip. 'And what am I going to do about it? Am I supposed to sign all his papers and hand him over a big wad of cash? Timmaya's vanished off the face of the earth. Bogadan knows I'm expected to put the scholarship through before the end of the month.' Philip looked crossly into his cup and searched for a message in the *cha-cha* bag. 'I've a good mind not to sign.'

'Don't suppose you would ever do a *thingy* like that, would you?' said Alan, 'I mean, that's like retribution, *na na*? Isn't it?'

Philip thought for a moment. 'No, I can't say that I would do a *thingy* like that.'

'You know, it's like … out of character,' said Alan, wiping his fingers on his trousers.

'Out of character?' said Philip.

'A softy like you wouldn't do a nasty *thingy* like that. That's why it's out of character. That would make you just like Bogadan, *na na*?' Alan looked inside the paper bag for his chocolate brownie. He broke it into pieces with his thumb and forefinger and before sinking his teeth into one of the chunks, he said, 'Jonathan was a nice, reliable softy too. Bogadan liked him a lot … and Caroline as well, of course.'

Philip chewed at his fingernails.

'Want a bit of this?' said Alan, waving a wedge of brownie in his direction.

'No,' said Philip.

'I suppose he'll have Felicity writing his dissertations for him, will he?' said Alan.

Philip said nothing.

'Caroline was actually better at reports than dissertations,' said Alan. 'But Felicity, well, she's a writer, isn't she? She could add a bit of drama to his assignments. Plus, of course, she's a natural …'

'Language learner,' said Philip.

'There you go,' said Alan. 'Well, look on the bright side. You lose the girl – who you didn't really want in the first place – you keep your job, and you earn a lecture theatre. Sounds all right to me, *na na*? And Bogadan … well, he wins the girl, gets bags of loot, gets a new PhD, gets a helper through the Foundation, gets a professorship in Abu Nar, and maybe even gets his tie back. Sounds like a fair exchange to me, but then I'm only an accountant.'

*

Philip wandered back to his office. He took out the file marked 'Scholarship Shortlist' and reviewed the documents within. At the bottom of each page of Bogadan's application was a little yellow sticker that read, 'Sign here.' As if in a trance, he peeled off the stickers one by one. He delved into the bottom of the box file, marked 'Old Applications – Scholarships & Bursaries,' and pulled out the application for *Om* Trattat. He carefully stuck the stickers back onto each page of this weathered application. He placed Bogadan's application in the box file marked 'Rejected.' He put it at the bottom of the heap. He rather liked the feeling of putting Bogadan at the bottom of the heap.

That was enough for today. Everything else he would do tomorrow. He switched off his desk lamp and headed for the door.

*

Philip returned home that evening to an empty bungalow. Empty, that is, except for Parrot.

'Hello! Hello!' said Parrot. 'Kiss, kiss, kiss, kiss,' he said and dangled upside down from the beak-mangled window blind. Why did Philip not find that endearing?

On the table was a note from Felicity, nibbled around the edges. It read simply, 'I'm leaving. Your cleaning and your laundry are at the SnowWhite Dry Kleen Shop.'

This came as a terrible blow to Philip, who hadn't as yet had his supper. He looked in the cupboards for a tin of something to eat but found they were proverbially bare. Parrot climbed from the window blind to his cage, then stepped from his cage onto a tall kitchen stool, and then slid down one of its four chrome legs to the floor. Philip moved to the fridge. Parrot followed him, shuffling across the floor tiles as if with slippered feet. Philip opened the fridge door, and he and Parrot peered at the white emptiness within. Philip was so hungry he could have eaten a parrot. He looked at Parrot. Parrot stared back.

'What?' said Parrot.

There was a ring at the doorbell.

So, she was back, thought Philip. She was back repentant and full of remorse. Philip stepped over Parrot, strode into the hallway, and wrenched open the door. On the doorstep stood *Imee* Malitee from Number Sixty-Six, with what looked like a dish of hot food in her hands.

'*Om* Pilip!' she said evidently startled. 'I am looking *Imee* Felicitu. Where he is? I bringing food.'

'Not here,' said Philip.

'Not here?' said *Imee* Malitee with unmistakable dismay. 'He always here, excepting when is Coffee Circle.'

Over the months, *Imee* Malitee had developed a fondness for Felicity and she appeared at a loss now to understand why her friend had suddenly disappeared.

'Maybe she has *bushkip*?' asked *Imee* Malitee.

'Oh, yes,' said Philip suddenly remembering he must cover up her unscheduled vanishing. 'Her mother. *Imee* Felicitu has gone home to her mother.'

'Her mother, she is sick?' said *Imee* Malitee, her face full of anguish.

'Yes, she is not well. I mean, she is a little sick ... and ... her sister is getting married.' He put that in for good measure.

Imee Malitee looked puzzled. Philip winced at his error. One excuse, good. Two excuses, overkill.

'Her mother he is ill?' asked *Imee* Malitee.

'Yes, she is,' said Philip.

'And his sister. You are getting married?'

'No, I'm not,' said Philip.

'His sister getting married?' said *Imee* Malitee. She looked confused.

'Her sister. Yes, that's right,' said Philip.

'For us very strange,' said *Imee* Malitee. In Namisa, stop marriage, because mother sick bad omen. Mother sick big or small?'

'Small, yes, definitely small, very small,' said Philip.

'*Ah, jej*, good very,' said *Imee* Malitee, working her way towards the defining question. 'Then, when come back back Mrs Felicitu?'

Philip paused for breath. 'Felicity must help with sister's baby,' said Philip enunciating carefully. Namisans favoured pregnancies.

'*Ah, jef!* May sister have baby baby good good,' exclaimed *Imee* Malitee.

'Thank you,' said Philip, smiling and joining his hands in acceptance of good tidings.

Imee Malitee handed over Philip's supper, for which he was immensely grateful, and then she turned to go. But then, seeming to have a second thought, she turned back.

'Please,' she said, 'must-can take soon picture Mrs Felicitu, mother good, sister, baby baby to temple for special pray.'

'Most kind,' said Philip. 'Will certainly bring picture soon.' Yes, indeed, he thought, another job for Photoshop.

*

What's done is done, though. Some things you just can't reverse.

*

Philip had been like a brother to her. He was a pain, but then brothers often are. Hers was a protest of sorts – a Namisan *autumn-autumn* protest. She was doing it for Philip's own good. The day he realised he was self-centered, selfish, uncaring, and all the other adjectives under those headings in her Thesaurus, that would be the day he grew up. She was co-habiting with a little boy in short pants. He could barely make himself a cup of *cha-cha*, let alone prepare a complete meal – in that respect, she reflected, they had a lot in common. She was perhaps a little more resourceful than he was. She felt pity for him. He was out of his depth and in a foreign land.

If the truth were known, she herself had little to complain of. She had adapted. She had breached the language barrier. She had no living expenses. Her flat in London was rented out and earning her an income. She had writing space. She had inspirational material. She had new friends – her friend Mike the self-nominated anthropologist with the useful tips, her neighbours from Number Sixty-Two and Number Sixty-Six, and of course the Coffee Circle and her faithful mentor Mrs. Katraree. There was more solace here, more companionship than at any of the Saturday morning sessions at the Touchstone Bookshop. No, her defiance was principled. She had walked out in protest against poor treatment, lack of understanding, false accusations, and being taken for granted. She had fulfilled her part of the bargain. She had even taken a certain pride in ensuring that Philip's clothes were immaculately cleaned and pressed at the start of each working week. After all, he had to look the part even if he wasn't playing it that well. He was practically a diplomat after all. She had done more than she needed to, but she had gone unappreciated. If she hadn't looked after him, who would have? What he needed was a wife, but he wasn't yet trained up for the role of *husbundee.*

In the distance Felicity heard the hiss of the dry-cleaning machines and the hammering of the SnowWhite Sandal Repair Service and she felt greatly reassured to be in this haven of warmth, clean clothing and smart sandals. From the kitchen below came the promising aromas of a home-cooked meal overseen by Mrs. Katraree. Who better than her to tend to the heartbreak of a separation? Felicity's experience might now be added to Mrs.

Katraree's repertoire of human-interest stories and Felicity was more than happy to be the donor. Yes, she owed much to Mrs. Katraree and the Coffee Circle. Wasn't it here that her protagonist Flocky had met her mentor Katrina and wasn't it here that Flocky had met Charles?

Felicity considered Charles for a moment. He was not especially handsome – in fact, he was not handsome at all, but he did have a certain charisma. He was the kind of man who took what he wanted, a man to be respected and obeyed. He could be cruel and demanding. She rather liked that. His acquaintances were in awe of him. But beneath the tough exterior was a tender and mischievous heart, and the moment Flocky had met him, she had recognised herself in him. They were soulmates and sooner or later – it was only a question of time – destiny would draw their lives together.

*

For Philip, covering up Felicity's absence meant making the best of a bad job and doing the things that – by agreement or tacit understanding – Felicity did: the shopping, the tidying, the carrying of clothes to the cleaners. Fortunately, he still had use of the housemaid. At the appointed hour, though, a man presented himself at Philip's door in the place of the young woman who was usually there busily washing and dusting.

'I am Babli,' said the man. 'Mrs. Katraree she is sending me.'

'Ah,' said Philip, 'and have you by any chance seen *Imee* Felicitu?'

'I am coming to do cleaning,' said Babli. 'Where you like I start?'

Babli remained taciturn and there was no persuading him even to collect or deliver the laundry and dry cleaning. Philip's life had taken a turn for the worse. He took it that Felicity would be back and that this was a temporary state of inconvenience and discomfort. But there were no communications from that quarter, no text messages or phone calls or e-mails. Felicity had disappeared without trace and if the situation prevailed, he would have a deal of explaining to do. There had been raised voices followed by a disappearance. It wasn't looking good. Now he had two disappearances on his hands and, in the eyes of the uncharitable, this double absence had all the hallmarks of the work of a serial killer.

It was while he was on his way back from collecting his laundry and depositing his clothes – inexplicably impregnated with the odour of Pundar – at the SnowWhite Dry Kleen Shop that Philip met his Golden Star. There was no mistaking her – that silky nut-brown skin, those luminous eyes.

'Tanita!'

'Yes?'

'It's me. Philip. Wallee's friend.'

'Philip?'

'From the Camel Dance.' He stood transfixed like an enchanted idiot.

'I didn't recognize you. Philip.'

'No, I was wearing a skirt.'

'Of course.' She looked down. 'Philip…'

'Yes,' he said. In that moment, his heart lifted and he realised that while he missed Felicity's matter of factness, her common sense and her organisational ability, her departure had granted him his liberty. He had returned to his former state, a free agent, no longer bound by the ties of his arranged marriage.

'Yes,' he said.

'Philip, I think you've dropped your laundry.'

***

30

THE NAMISAN
AUTUMN-AUTUMN

The Namisan Government forecasts growth of up to 6.2 percent a year for the next five years. This increase of 2.8 percent is led by national investments in precious metals, and also in tourism infrastructure. GDP growth this year will be around 5.5 percent, partly premised on a 4.5 percent growth in the tourism and entertainment sectors, though up to now growth has been a great deal slower than originally projected (see Tourism, p.67). Investment in education and research supported by foreign donations is set to rise, promising a bumper year for education professionals and their institutions.

(Extract from 'The Economy,' (p.103) in *Namisa – A Traveller's Guide: from tradition to tourism and back*, **by Michael Robinson-Smith.)**

*

They had had word at TU in Wunamisa that in Prapundar the salaries were a great deal higher than they had been led to believe. Whoever would have told them that? Bogadan would have liked to know.

Imeetinee Fatt, Acting Head of Health and Safety, had taken the initiative and led a delegation of her Namisan university colleagues to meet with their Provost. It was an understatement to say that Bogadan was not amused by this development. He had always assumed that *Imeetinee* Fatt – Bindee to her friends – was a level-headed young woman, uncorrupted by the likes of Frank Gibson. But sometimes action is taken too late. He had not heeded his mother's warning, prior to *Imeetinee* Fatt's hiring, that this was a woman who might not toe the *liney*, and here was the proof. Furthermore, it had come to Bogadan's attention that *Imeetinee* Fatt had been borrowing books on the history of trades unions from the library, which Bogadan would now need to have removed and destroyed. For the good of all. He had to admit that his mother was unmatched in her ability to sniff out troublemakers. The faculty and staff were getting just a little too ahead of themselves. He'd have to look at in-service training provision too. Flower arrangement was fine and assisted the beautification of the campus, but who was the idiot who had encouraged faculty and staff to take leadership training courses? Bogadan had never before faced a situation like this. He could deal summarily with European expats and your average Pundari academic but in the business of dealing with his fellow Namisans, Bogadan was aware that he had to move cautiously to allay their fears and keep the status quo.

Assembled in the atrium of the administration building, the delegation waited while *Imeetinee* Fatt looked at her notes and cleared her throat.

'First of all, *Om Baadumba* Bogadan, we wish to thank you for seeing us today.'

'I am very happy to do so,' replied Bogadan. 'Indeed, we should be meeting more often. The Namisan staff and faculty are a very important element of TU and I want to be sure that they are *happy-happy* because happy staff are productive staff.'

'Thank you again, *Om Baadumba* Bogadan, for your kind words. We know that you are concerned for our well-being and we look to you as our father and, like a father, we hope you will provide for us and look towards the supplementation of our pocket money. As you know, it is some time now that we are not receiving our pay *increasements* and yet we are seeing many changes from day to day in the economic development of our fine country. What we are hearing is that in many places – government institutions, banks, private companies, excetera, excetera – staff are receiving *increasements* but we are still *waiting-waiting* and nothing happening.

'What we want to know is what happened to the money granted to us for *increasements* from the TUDI Project. It seems we have seen none of it and now it is many months since *Om* Wordswort authorised the TUDI payments for us. We are wanting to know why we are still not receiving our *increasements*.'

'Let it be known, *Imeetinee* Fatt, that we are currently reviewing our pay scales and expect to revert to you very soon. You will see significant changes to the organisational chart, to job descriptions and to your job titles. All of this is in accordance with the recommendations of the TUDI report. And you have no reason for fearing that Prapundari employees have better pay and benefits than you.'

'With the greatest respect, *Om Baadumba* Bogadan,' continued Imeetinee Fatt, 'we have heard that over there in Pundar, on average they are getting 20 percent more than we are.'

'Let me remind you, *Imeetinee* Fatt, that we are world-class and they are not, and this will be reflected in our revised salary scales.' Bogadan's eyelid began to twitch, and a bead of perspiration glistened on his forehead. 'And tell me please, *Imeetinee*,' he continued, 'who it is that is spreading about this misinformation about better pay and conditions in Prapundar.'

Imeetinee Fatt did not respond.

'Well, I am waiting, *Imeetinee*,' said Bogadan. Whispers were heard from amongst the members of the delegation.

'I cannot say,' said *Imeetinee* Fatt. Behind her, several members of faculty edged their way towards the exit.

'What do you think, *Imeetinee*, that I am here because I am enjoying the power of being in this position? *Na jej*, I am here because I am assisting the development of my country and I am taking pride in this. Here at TU we have the best of the best.' As Bogadan spoke, staff members looked at their watches and made their way out of the door.

Bogadan continued, 'Even we are having the cream of the Prapundari professors coming here. The culture that we are creating here it should be higher than they have at Prapundar. We have a different culture here. We have a different *graftee* ethic. You should know that people who worked at Prapundar are telling me, "*Om* Bogadan, in Prapundar I worked much less than here. Here you are *drudging* while there they are avoiding *grafty*." So, if you want avoiding *grafty,* you go there. If you make effort to be *drudging,* TU is paying you accordingly.' A few remaining faculty studied text messages on their phones and realised they were needed elsewhere. 'Do not come to me, *Imeetinee,*' said Bogadan, 'with your stories of *discontinence*. I suggest you tell me, without further smacking about the bush, who is *behindside* this *revolutioning.*'

Imeetinee Fatt raised her chin in defiance. 'The time has come for change, *Om* Bogadan,' she said. 'With me are Professor Timmaya and Professor Dwinndee. We will go forward with or without the faculty. We stand united.'

*

All this is very unexpected. It's all new to me. I think I may have got what I wished for. I'm not sure now that I know how to deal with it.

Where's Bindee when I need her?

*

From: ibogadan@tu.ac.nm
Date: 18 April
To: All Faculty; All Staff
c.c.: gsbogadan@tu.ac.nm
Subject: Message to the University of Trinamisa Community on the State of the Institution

Dear Colleagues

I. Now in this autumn-autumn semester it is time to reflect upon our accomplishments, our institutional goals, our aspirations. TU is only as good as the efforts of each individual member of our faculty and staff.

II. It was my mother Imee Baadeeyyumba Grace Shoon Bogadan who drew up the first TU statutes after obtaining a decree from the Government to set up what would soon become a world-class institution. We have developed rapidly from just an 'idea' – a mere twinkle in her eye – into a functional university. This autumn-autumn we can take pride in many other mylystones.

III. Mylystone achievements:

- Consolidation of our linkys with The Downing Foundation through conferral of a Fellowship of the University of Trinamisa on Om Baadumba Dr. Neil Bryant.
- The inauguration of the Sharwarmiyya Lecture Theatre in acknowledgement of the dedication and endless efforts on behalf of TU by Om Baadumba Professor William Sharwarmiyya of the Oil and Gas Institute, Abu Nar.

- The inauguration of our Lecture Theatre Number Two, dedicated to our own Jonatan Wordswort, who worked so tirelessly, together with his delightful wife Caroline, on the Trinamisa University Development Initiative (TUDI) before their untimely transfer to Tblisi.
- Recognition of high-achieving faculty through generous increasements. Yes, it is true that the University of Prapundar is said to offer a more competitive package, but let me remind you that institutions such as ours do not stay in front by following.
- Furthermore, thanks to the generosity of Imee Baadeeyyumba Bogadan, TU has actively provided assistance to many ailing faculty by helping them to return forthwith to their countries, or in the case of Namisan nationals by enabling them to avail themselves of the benefits of early retirement.
- The election of a new Acting Head of Health and Safety.
- The demolition of Building Three, and consequently the removal of a serious safety hazard, thus creating a safer environment for all faculty and staff.
- Finally, in the words of Imee Baadeeyyumba Bogadan, taken from her keynote address at the International Conference for Power and Innovation in Abu Nar, *Research and its Potential for Diversification: A Namisan Perspective*: 'Research, first and foremost, research. This is no time to play it safe by doing business as usual.'

- Let us then play it unsafe.

*

A celebration was imminent. Tanita, an Economics graduate from the University of Trinamisa, was home from Edinburgh, where she had completed an MBA at Herriot-Watt University, and from Paris, where she had perfected her French and completed a course in Political Science. All this without the assistance of the Downing Foundation. Her father, Beedee, Chief of Police for Greater Trinamisa, comprising Trinamisa proper and Wunamisa, had married into a wealthy and well-connected Namisan family. One of Tanita's uncles was a General, another uncle through marriage was Editor of the *Namisan Times*. Her cousins were equally well-placed. Her cousin Perl, for example, was a popular TV journalist at Nam-B, the official Namisa Broadcasting Company, while another cousin Flaik was, at 40, the youngest Director ever of NamTel, the Namisan State Telecommunications Company. Other cousins, uncles and aunties were either academics or worked in education.

It took several visits to the local GrikaGraka Café and to the Trinamisa Super Theme Mall branch of Starbucks for Philip to grasp the illustrious pedigree of his Golden Star. While she spoke, he gazed at her, intoxicated – or (in Namisan) *nitted* – with her beauty. Thus it was, that on their third or fourth meeting, emboldened by a tall NamLatte *nitted* with bulbi juice, he reached out and took her hand in his. It was a first in the history of Philip's love for women. And on the occasion that he did this, she fell silent and leaned forward fondly to cup his cheek in her hand. The Mall buzzed with activity, yet they heard nothing but the joyful hum of their own hearts.

*

Emerging from the Trinamisa Gallery, where she had just purchased a tiny but very expensive tub of Kipkip Eternity Creem, Tiki caught sight of the subsequent kiss and reflected that the man sitting on a wobbly chair opposite a raven-haired, delicately olive-skinned girl greatly resembled her colleague Philip Blair, Officer of Education and Culture. And in the next instant, she recognised that it was indeed Philip Blair, Officer of Education and Culture, and *husbundee* of the writer Felicity Blair, honoured guest of and regular contributor to the SnowWhite Dry Kleen Coffee Circle.

*

There comes a moment when you're looking into someone's face, wondering if they feel the same way about you as you do about them.

*

These were testing times for Bogadan, and even at the best of times he was not a very happy man when his mother came to stay at the villa. Granted, it was her home too, but he would have liked to think that the space was reserved exclusively for him. When she was there, usually driven in on alternate weekends from Wunamisa by Shambee in her gold Mercedes, Bogadan felt the need to confine himself to his room as though he were a naughty schoolboy punished for not completing his homework. He could not even count on his father's old study being vacant, for *Imee* Grace would take that over and use it as if it were Churchill's War Room, taking calls on her bling-encrusted mobile phones and making notes in her giant Oil and Gas Institute diary. She would load the armchairs with glossy bags of many shapes and sizes, inside which clouds of tissue paper enveloped her purchases ... negligees, peep-toe shoes, jingly beads, bracelets, body oils, face creams, perfumes. If he hadn't known better, he'd have said she was up to some kind of mischief.

The villa's sitting room, with its ornate green and gold brocade-covered furniture, would be occupied on most evenings by Grace, her sister, her sister's family, and a collection of clever friends from high places. Sometimes, as Bogadan crept up the stairs on his return from Happy Hour at the Sleepy Hollow, Grace would spot him and oblige him to join them.

'Ito*tee! Akeet oo jinganitalotta*,' she would say.

How could he refuse? He was the *pikapika* of his mother's eye. It was Ito*tee* this and Ito*tee* that.

'Ito*tee* is going to London to do his PhD,' Grace would say without ever having received confirmation of her son's hypothetical future. 'He's won an important scholarship – the only academic to do so in the whole of Namisa.'

But, when Bogadan and Grace were in the house alone, she would menace him, looking through his private papers for evidence of his activities, and examining his pocket diaries to identify appointments that he had not told her about. She would look in cupboards and in drawers to get a better picture of how her son was spending his time while she was in Wunamisa. He even found her once peering under his bed. But did she really think he'd be so stupid as to leave those magazines lying around for her to find? She had told him that she thought she had seen an insect scurrying underneath for safety, but no *bushkil* since she would make sure the maids vacuumed the room thoroughly when they cleaned the following day.

Bogadan wasn't entirely sure quite how low his mother would stoop. Theoretically, he was prepared for anything … except for her rummaging through the laundry basket. When, hot on her trail, he burst breathlessly into the laundry room, she had already pulled out one black satin sheet and was shaking it loose of the basket. She bent down, picked something up and then turned to him with a look on her face half of triumph and half of disgust.

'What is this?' said Grace, holding up a tiny blue sequined thong and dangling it in front of him.

Bogadan, always the master of originality, never missed a beat. 'Ah!' he said, 'I've been looking for that. It is for the departmental Christmas tree.'

'I am sure,' said Grace, 'that you must think I came down in the last waterfall. *Sheematipa*, Ito Bogadan!'

It appeared to Bogadan that the tide might be turning against him, as though some wretched Pundari witchdoctor must have waved a giant *okaly* leaf over his image and hissed an incantation. As if it were not enough that faculty and staff in Wunamisa were agitating for more pay and better conditions, now his *pappee*, that rumbling volcano that he had for so long managed to cool, was bubbling menacingly, threatening disaster before he could gather his valuables and run to safety.

***

31

GRIKAGRAKA'S REVENGE

When he came into the office the following morning Philip had the distinct impression that Tiki was giving him the evil eye.

'All right, *Imee* Tiki?' he said.

She remained silent with pursed lips and tapped away ferociously at her keyboard.

Philip made his way past the security guard's room and had the uncomfortable sensation that he was under scrutiny. The Foundation's minor employees looked up and then away as he passed. Or was he just paranoid?

In the kitchen, he prepared his first Namcafé of the day and carried it back carefully to his room. As he lifted the mug to his lips, Ratni lurched in through the doorway.

'*Om* Bryant, he want talk you,' he said.

'Oh, okay,' said Philip, relaxing into his chair.

'*Adoo, bis bis*,' barked Ratni.

Philip did not like his tone.

*

There's no such thing as love at first sight.
Is there?
You only see that in books or in the movies. It's just fiction.
Isn't it?

*

Bryant looked twitchier than usual. He was polishing his nose with his hankie and looking out of the window towards the bus station when Philip entered the room.

'Look, I'll come straight to the point, Philip. I've had a call from Grace Bogadan. She's asking about the scholarship and wanting to know why it's taking so long to process.' He turned to face Philip. 'So, why is it taking so long to process? I really don't have an answer for her. You see, Philip, if Grace is not happy then she calls Lady Downing, and if Lady Downing is not happy, she calls me, so that is why *I* need to know why it is taking so long to process this scholarship.'

'Bogadan's scholarship,' said Philip.

'Yes, that's what we're talking about here. Bogadan's scholarship. That's all. Just take care of it, will you? I don't want any more calls from Grace. It's bad enough dealing with the son without having to deal with the mother as well.'

Philip turned to leave.

'One other thing,' said Bryant. 'Some nasty *rumoreenz* floating around the office. Namisans can be very melodramatic, you understand.'

'Yes?' said Philip.

'Felicity … They're saying that you've been treating her rather badly, mistreating her in other words, and that now she's … gone missing.' He paused. 'I'm sure this is all traceable back to Ratni. In short, Philip, they think you've bumped her off. They're all saying they haven't seen her in a long while. Nonsense, of course. I must have seen her myself. When was it? Maybe last week. Or was it before that?'

'Oh,' said Philip.

'I take it she *is* in good health,' said Bryant. A muscle twitched in the vicinity of his cheek bone.

'As far as I'm aware.'

'Well, see if you can put her about a bit, will you? Tell her not to keep her light under a bushel.'

*

Philip returned to his office in the depth of depression. Not only had he had murdered his wife, but also his coffee had gone cold. Time to report to Finance, he thought.

'You see,' said Alan, his mouth bulging with croissant, 'you have to view this in perspective. There's a lot going on right now. It doesn't help that you might have murdered your wife and buried her in the garden.'

'Why do I get the blame for everything?' said Philip. 'What about *your* wife? We never see her, do we? But no one's accusing you of wifeicide.'

'Ah, yes. Well, actually, between you and me, I don't have a wife.'

'That's not possible. Everyone at the Foundation is married. It's a requirement.'

'Oh ho,' said Alan, 'look who's talking! You see, Philip, as you are only too well aware, sometimes we need to be a little resourceful in order to beat the system.'

'Can you keep it down a bit, Alan,' said Philip jerking his head towards Ronny's partition.

'He's out for the day,' said Alan. 'Gone to a wedding ceremony, all dressed up in his multicoloured turban and *shala kan*. I feel sorry for him sometimes, but really he only got what he deserved.'

'And what did he deserve?'

'A Namisan wife, that's what, and all her in-laws. You reap what you sow and all that.' Alan was in contemplative mode. 'You see, Philip, it's because of Ronny that you and me ended up married. Ronny and me – well, we were young and carefree when we first came out. But he would insist on fraternising with the natives. I told him, "Ronny, don't even think about it." But he thought about it and then he did it.'

'And then?'

'And then the Director of Residency and Foreigners' Affairs found out.' Alan paused. 'Well, he would do, wouldn't he? Because it was his daughter that Ronny was fraternising with. And now look at the fine mess we're all in with our Wedding Books and the like. After a bit of *wranglee-wranglee* with the authorities, Lady Downing had married status written into the job descriptions. The rest is history. I'll tell you about it some time.'

'So, Ronny married a Namisan.'

'He did, Philip. He did. But, I say to you today as I said to Ronny that fateful day, "Don't even think about it."'

Philip was thinking about it.

'If you marry twice, that's bigamy.'

'What? Even in Namisa?'

'Especially in Namisa.'

Philip folded his arms and considered how unfortunate was his lot in life.

'I hear,' said Alan, changing the subject, 'that Ito Boy's in a bit of bother over at the University.'

'Oh, how's that?' said Philip.

'The faculty and staff are agitating for more pay and better conditions. It does make one wonder what happened to the TUDI money. And, there are *spats* in Wunamisa.'

'What are *spats*?'

'Something like rioters.'

'And why are they called *spats*?'

'I don't know. Why is anything called anything? And there's more.' Alan looked grave. 'Your friend Timmaya, Philip … the police found him.'

A shiver ran up Philip's spine. 'Is he …?' Philip could not bring himself to say the words.

'Yes, I'm afraid so, Philip,' said Alan. 'He's …'

'Oh no,' said Philip, covering his face with his hands.

'In jail,' said Alan. 'Arrested for inciting the *spats* along with Professor Dwindee and Imeetinee Fatt. But don't worry. They'll be out soon. The Chief of Police will want to keep this quiet.' He paused for a moment, and then said, almost in a mumble, 'Don't want someone bringing in the Fellaship, do we?'

'Eh?' said Philip.

*

The Fellaship is an organization founded officially in 1951 by nursery school teacher Hamik Shoon, but which traces its origins back to the end of the twelfth century, possibly earlier. Accounts of the Fellaship are said to have been referenced in the lost manuscripts of Marco Polo. Based on a tradition linked to the legendary slaying of the Grikagraka by Fella Breekaya (see p.52), the group undertook to defend Namisa from foreign invaders. Shoon revitalized interest in the Fellaship with his series of children's books entitled, *The Tales of Fella*. Accused of attempts to indoctrinate and radicalize the young, Shoon was jailed by the authorities, but shortly after escaped and went underground, hiding it is believed in the Grotty Cave of the Nagapardar Region, from where he conducted a campaign of guerrilla warfare on those perceived to be enemies of the nation. In ceremonies involving the imbibing of *okaly* and similar intoxicating drugs, the more fanatical members of this sect would remove one of their own ears with a ceremonial blade known as an *atakrot*. Attempts at performing this rite under the influence often resulted in unfortunate mishaps according to statistics issued by the National Hospital of Soonamisa.

The Fellaship was not officially banned until 1961, shortly after Namisa had gained its independence from Britain. It is rumoured that Shoon lived out the rest of his days as a real estate re-seller in Dubai. Since Independence, there have been unconfirmed claims that the illegal redeployment of Fellas as spies and bodyguards in the homes of the governing classes is widespread.

Visitors are strongly advised not to stare or comment should they happen upon anyone they suspect may be linked to this sect.

(Extract from 'Officialdom – Linked Organizations,' (p.64) in *Namisa - A Traveller's Guide: from tradition to tourism and back***,' 18th Edition, by Michael Robinson-Smith.)**

Editor's note: this edition of the Robinson-Smith guide was recalled by the Ministry of Information and pulped. A handful of copies is still available from Amazon. The section on 'Officialdom – Linked Organizations' is omitted from subsequent editions. This section on the Fellaship now appears in 'Traditions and Legends,' p.67.

*

What I wished for was a man of principles, someone to lean on and believe in, a man who cannot be bullied, intimidated, someone who stands by his beliefs… He should be compassionate, honest… not too honest perhaps. Too much honesty can hurt. He should care for others, especially the underdogs. He should be fair. He should be a gentle person, not aggressive or nasty towards others. Someone who will admit his mistakes… because if he can admit his mistakes, it's easier to forgive him. But, I think, even if he didn't fit any of this, I would just throw my list away. Sometimes you have to make-do with what you have been given. That's what I think.

You know what? No need for Bindee. I can deal with this on my own.

*

Philip needed a break. Too much was happening too fast. He adjusted his computer screen so that prying eyes – he was thinking mainly of Ratni's and Tiki's – could not see from the corridor what he was surfing as they passed his office. Ratni strolled by much too often for his liking. Philip doubted that Ratni knew much about
NamisanNights.com
or
thewhatsupguidetotrinamisa.com
or indeed why he might be visiting those sites in the first place. He was finding it difficult to decide if he should take Tanita out for a meal, or take her dancing, or take her on a romantic boat ride. As a man out to impress his new date, he felt he had to pull out all the stops. Nevertheless, at times he was challenged to stay on task. As his cursor hovered over naughtynamisans.com, the phone rang. It was *Imee* Grace.

She addressed him abruptly and with the minimum of ceremony. '*Om* Pilip,' she announced, 'I am here in Trinamisa to attend to some family business. I wish to speak with you on a matter of some importance. You will kindly instruct your driver to bring you here to my villa … let us say at five o'clock this afternoon.'

A chill ran through Philip's body: up to now his day had been chillier than usual. Grace was angry. Very angry. He was certain that the only thing worse than an audience with Grace at this moment would have been an encounter with both Grace and Bogadan together. He paced up and down the length of his narrow office. He looked up at the clock. It was 4:15 pm. In forty-five minutes, he would be laid out as a sacrifice to the gods. He would be shredded and left for the birds to peck at. He could think of no means of escape. He was going to his doom under his own steam. Why would he ever do that? He had never aspired to martyrdom, and certainly not for the Foundation. If this was about the scholarship, and it could not be about anything else, then what was he to say? Would he recant or would he stand by his original decision?

He decided that he was very sorry for all he had done. He would definitely recant. He would tell Grace it had all been a terrible mistake. His pen had slipped. Well, perhaps not, but he would surely think of something.

He drove himself to Bogadan's villa. He could not bear the humiliation of being driven by Ratni and, anyway, Ratni knew far too much of his private business already. A security guard waved him in through the wrought iron gates, staring down in wonderment as he passed. He parked the green Cinquecento next to Grace's Mercedes. Mercifully, Bogadan's Lexus was nowhere to be seen. At the villa's gilded door, he was met by a tall, disdainful-looking man who wore a dark brown *shala kan* speckled with shiny satin threads, and a matching turban decorated, in accordance with the tradition, with a single red *babbigall* feather. The left side of his face was a latticework of pinkish scars and Philip had the impression – though he did not want to stare – that the man was lacking an ear.

In silence, the man directed Philip to what could only be described as an ante-room, sparsely decorated and windowless. And there he waited. And he waited. His palms grew moist and clammy, and his heart thumped against his ribs. A gold-plated carriage clock bearing the insignia of the Oil and Gas Institute ticked loudly from a bookless bookshelf. Philip stared first at the ceiling and then down at the floor, at an intricate mosaic, coloured in shades of blue and aquamarine. The legendary Namisan sea monster Grikagraka was shown rearing up out of the ocean bed, her great mouth brimming and frothing with the vile green blood of a row of bound Pundari warriors, who wailed and thrashed even as she snatched them from the rocky precipice that jutted out over the waters. Dismembered limbs … arms, hands, legs, feet cascaded down the cliff side as Grikagraka exacted her terrifying punishment on the hapless Pundari youths. But, there in the distance, approaching fast through the forest on his faithful *jimi* was Fella Breekaya, his *krot* reflecting the mauve light of a radiant sun, a sun which blazed violet right next to a pair of patent olive and black Prada shoes.

'Ah, *Imee* Grace, what a pleasure to see you,' said Philip ungrovelling himself from the horrors of Grikagraka.

Grace stood before him in one of her elegant twin sets, a row of signature pearls at her throat. '*Om* Pilip,' she said, coming straight to the point, 'what's this I hear about Itotee not getting his scholarship?'

'His scholarship?'

'Please answer my question, *Om* Pilip, I am not having the whole day waiting on you.'

'The scholarship … it all depends, you see, on …' Philip was sure it must depend on something.

'On what does it depend exactly?' demanded Grace.

'Education *pointeez*,' said Philip. 'Another candidate has more Education *pointeez*.'

'More? More than Itotee?' Grace glared.

Philip took this as the moment to admit his error. But as Grace stood there before him, glowing with indignation, the pitiful image of *Om* Trattat hugging his glass of Golden Lizard beer came into his mind, and he was filled with an unfamiliar emotion … that of compassion.

'More *pointeez* than Itotee?' said Grace.

'I'm afraid so. And that is why the scholarship was awarded to the other candidate and not to Bogadan.'

There was a fury in Grace's small brown eyes. 'When I spoke to you in Wunamisa, *Om* Pilip,' she said, exploding her Ps as she uttered his name, 'I explained to you how important this scholarship was to Itotee. I assumed we had an understanding.'

'*Imee Baadeeyyumba* Grace …'

'Yes?' said Grace.

'I am sure you must appreciate that *Om* Bogadan has…' Philip hesitated.

'Yes?' said Grace.

'That *Om* Bogadan has already received his scholarship many times over.'

Grace's brow crinkled. 'How so?' she said.

'*Om* Jonathan gave *Om* Bogadan the TUDI money, did he not?'

'He did,' said Grace, fingering the pearls around her neck. 'The purpose of TUDI was to ensure that staff and faculty at TU were supported and received the financial rewards that they deserved.'

'And yet, even as we speak, the faculty and staff are demanding pay increases.'

'I believe you are mistaken, *Om* Pilip. I myself authorised the payment of an across-the-board *increasement* that they all received.'

'No, they didn't,' said Philip.

'Impossible,' hissed Grace. 'It would seem, *Om* Pilip, that you are believing those who would wish to discredit us.'

For some absurd reason Philip thought of his Auntie Peggy at that moment and, taking her advice, he breathed deeply and straightened his shoulders. Then he spoke. 'When funds do not arrive at their destination,' he said, 'it may be because they have been misappropriated.'

Grace stared at Philip aghast. He stood his ground and stared back. Her eyes began to flicker unnaturally, and then she burst forth, 'How dare you make allegations of this kind,' she boomed.

Philip took a step back.

'You, *Om* Pilip, have been sticking your *nosee* into our business and arriving at very incorrect conclusions. You have abused our hospitality and maligned us. On what grounds can you say that money has been misappropriated? What nonsense is this you are telling me? I don't believe there is anything more we need to discuss Mr. Pilip.' And with that she turned to leave, but when she reached the doorway, she stopped abruptly and faced him. 'I assure you that Lady Downing will hear of this,' she said. 'Buba will see you out, Mr Pilip. Good day to you.' Her heels clipped away into the distance across the inlaid Grikagrakaesque floor. A door slammed.

Philip sat down on his gold-lacquered chair. What would become of him now? He imagined an incandescent Grace, seated in her oval office reviewing the facts. She would be making a number of very important phone calls. One would be to Neil Bryant, since clearly her earlier call to him had not had the desired effect. This one would sound the death knell for Philip's job. Another call would be to Lady Downing, who was holidaying in Bermuda, taking aperitifs with her celebrity house guests. Naturally, she needed to know what was going on while her back was turned. As Philip waited, in his mind's eye, he saw Grace pluck embossed business cards from her Louis Vuitton wallet, pick up the receiver of her special edition gilded NamTel phone – a present from her nephew – and key in the numbers of the great and the good to ensure that this one pathetic employee of the Downing Foundation would pay the price for his perfidy from here to the afterlife.

Buba, in a plaid sarong and an ochre-coloured *shala kan*, stood in the doorway and cleared his throat. He gave a not-very-low bow. 'This way please, *Om* Pilip.'

Philip rose and followed, his ill-spent life flashing before him. The early evening sun filtered across his path as he continued through an open passageway set in a bower of fragrant bushes. A cooling *autumn-autumn* breeze bristled through the leaves lifting the heavy blanket of heat, and a tiny bird with metallic-blue wings fluttered to the ground before him. Philip felt sorrowful for the loss of beauty. He blinked and, in a moment, the bird was gone, and then he thought that actually it was a far, far better thing that he had done, than he had ever done, and he thanked his English teacher Mrs. Lawford for instructing him in the profound truths of literature. As Buba waited in the atrium for Philip to catch up, Grace's voice echoed through the space from a room to their right. Philip stopped to listen.

'Hello, I need to speak to *Imeetinee* Fatt, Right now. *Adoo.*' A pause followed. 'Not contactable? How is she not contactable? Hasn't she got a mobile? She does not have one where she is? What do you mean by "does not have one where she is"? Where exactly is she, and what is going on there in Wunamisa?'

'*Akeet, Om* Pilip,' said Buba. '*Bis!*' And he led Philip towards the atrium, where he exchanged solemn glances with Grace's scarred and turbaned butler.

Buba pressed his palms together and inclined his head. '*Bungakrappa, Om* Pilip,' he said.

The butler, with his lip curled in an ugly sneer, pulled open the villa's heavy mahogany door and then slammed it with considerable violence the moment Philip had stepped outside.

***

32

THE *PLIGHT* OF SHAME

'You've rejected it?' said Bryant. 'Good God, Philip! Whatever possessed you?'

'I gave it to a more worthy candidate,' said Philip. '*Om* Trattat has more Education *pointeez.*'

Bryant slumped into his chair, shaking his head. 'Are you sure? Are you sure that Trattat has more *pointeez*?'

'Yes,' said Philip, though in truth he wasn't very sure at all.

'Otherwise,' said Bryant, 'we will suffer the consequences of your decision for years to come.'

For Philip, the Bogadan scholarship was past history. Let Grace do her worst. Anyway, her bark was worse than her bite. At least he hoped it was. He would stand by his decision. The beautiful Tanita would not want to keep company with a wimp. For now, his mind was focused on that evening's big event.

*

It's a lot to ask of someone, I know. It occurred to me that we've spent time getting to know each other and yet we still actually know nothing at all about each other. Not really. How is that? He's some kind of diplomat, but according to him 'not an especially diplomatic one.' He says he usually gets things wrong. I told him that was because he was new. I said there were bound to be a few hiccups at the start, and he said something about getting hiccups from too many Namisan cocktails.

I've told him about the time I've spent in France and the UK. That's about it. And now he's going to meet my family. Poor Philip, I'm really throwing him in at the deep end. I told him to bring his friends for support.

I also need friends for support. Dad has been called away to Wunamisa. Bindee is off the radar. Starting to get a bit worried about her.

*

'A party!' said Alan. 'But who's the lucky lady? So long as it's not Imeetinee Fatt. I saw her first.'

'You'll meet her tonight if you come with me,' said Philip. He and Alan were standing in the corner of the Downing Foundation garden, while Alan puffed at his cigarette.

'Careful,' said Alan, 'you're still married.'

'I'm getting a divorce,' said Philip. 'My wife deserted me and I'm having to bring up the *babbigall* on my own.'

'Yes, that's tough,' said Alan, 'but you must still wonder what became of her. You'll need to do a letter or something explaining that you've separated. Separation helps you keep your options open.' He took a puff of his cigarette. 'I suppose she could have gone back to London.'

'She's probably in some West London garret, beavering away at her novel now as we speak.'

*

And Felicity wrote:

Flocky could not express enough her immense gratitude to Katrina for providing her with a safe haven from Roberto's brutal schizophrenic nature. He could not help himself – that much she knew – though she was incapable of explaining this to her friend. She hated him and yet she loved him too. She forgave him for the mental trauma he had inflicted on her. Love and affection had restored her. Charles was there for her, by her side reassuring and supporting her. Bravely he had set aside his own troubles to help her resolve her own.

*

As Wallee's marriage ceremony and the Camel Dance had proved, Philip was not really a party animal, not – in any case – at a party such as this one. Yes, there were guests, a multitude of them, which fact gave Philip pause for thought. Here was a Namisan dynasty that had spread its roots through the most significant areas of society: the press, communications, the police, the armed forces, and academia. Thus, the occasion had more the flavour of a trade summit, if not an elite family gathering. The way these Namisans hugged and kissed indicated that most of them knew each other very well indeed. Philip realised he could soon be out of his depth and treading water. He was a foreigner and an outsider, and he was British to boot.

He had come with Alan that evening to the revolving golfball restaurant of the NamTel building for Tanita's graduation party. According to Alan, the founder of the Namisan State Telecommunications Company had been a fanatical amateur golfer – hence the golfball restaurant. The air resounded with Namisan pap and people hustled and bustled through the throng holding high their wine glasses. Alan quickly merged with the crowd, leaving Philip to fend for himself. The fact that Tanita had promised to introduce him to her immediate family and miscellaneous relatives filled him with both excitement and apprehension. He had put the trying events of the day behind him, or at least he was trying to put the trying events of the day behind him. He had managed to fob Bryant off with his story of Trattat's Education *pointeez*, though he wasn't sure how long that tale would hold up. Grace's ire was real and if she meant what she had said about contacting Lady Downing, his soujourn in Namisa could soon be over. But he had met the woman of his dreams and now, liberated from the yoke of marriage, he was a man on a mission. It was remarkable how desire could focus the unfocused.

In the back of his mind, though, Philip heard Alan's solitary voice reminding him of something – something about still being a married man. He told himself that, provided no one was there who knew of his circumstances, he was in the clear. Alan he could trust, but the others … He scanned the bobbing heads that filled the room and immediately spied Bryant, Ronny, and Tiki. Surely even Ratni could not be far. At that moment he was probably outside in Bryant's Mercedes rummaging about in the glove compartment.

Worse still, Philip noticed others too: invitees from Bryant's FFs, from the Medicals, from the G & Ts. All this was sure to complicate matters. He might be better advised to slip away now and go home before he was caught out. As he considered this, Tanita stepped out of the crowd. She was radiant in a gown of light-reflecting emerald satin with a spray of *babbigall* feathers positioned strategically at the plunge of her neckline. She looped her arm through his.

'There you are,' she said. 'I was worried you might have lost your way. Everyone's so excited about meeting you. I've told them you're practically a diplomat. The rest they can find out for themselves. You won't mind, will you, if they give you a little bit of a grilling? Let them be pleasantly surprised.'

Philip was keeping an eye open for surprises of his own and found some: Sylvie, Bernardo, Klaus.– Or was it Werter? And, the sleepy Lebanese and the cross-looking Pundari. Evidently there was a language school connection here, or perhaps an embassy connection, which was more likely. Philip gave them each an amicable nod and moved on, led by Tanita through the sea of guests. He was very speedily getting a grasp of the situation and an awareness of who he was dealing with.

'You must know just about everyone worth knowing in Namisa,' he said.

She laughed and squeezed his arm. 'There's someone very special I want you to meet.' She guided him towards the back of the salon where a familiar-looking man sat in the midst of a clump of Namisans. The man rose to his feet when he saw Tanita.

'*Om Baadumba* Dr. Towdi,' said Philip, bowing low. 'What a very great pleasure this is.'

Dr. Towdi looked confused.

'I'm Philip ... Philip Blair from the Foundation, one of your students from the Trinamisa School of Languages.'

'Yes, of course,' said Dr. Towdi, still a little blank. 'I'm very pleased you were able to come.'

'It gives me the pleasure of a thousand peacocks to be here,' said Philip. 'I don't know why I hadn't noticed it before ...'

'What?' said Dr. Towdi.

'The family resemblance. Your daughter looks so like you.'

'I don't have a daughter,' said Dr. Towdi.

Philip turned to look for Tanita, but she had drifted over to a group of women far to their right.

'Are you sure?' said Philip.

'At the last count,' said Dr. Towdi, 'I have one son and he is growed up and no doubt will soon have *kiddeez* of his own.'

Something was badly wrong here. Philip started to perspire. Tanita, he could see, was now carrying on a conversation with one of the women in the group. She was smiling at first but then her expression changed to one of extreme agitation.

'Dr. Towdi, excuse me,' said Philip. 'You are Tanita's…?'

'Uncle,' said Dr. Towdi. 'I am her uncle. I am the brother of her mother.'

'Who is …?'

'Mrs. Katraree. My brother-in-law, Tanita's father, is away at the moment in Wunamisa. They're having a bit of bother over there with *spats*.'

'So, he would be … the Chief of Police?'

'Correct,' said Dr. Towdi.

Philip watched as Tanita, her face contorted, turned towards him. And, as she stepped aside, he could clearly see the tall blonde woman who was standing next to her.

'And I'm guessing,' continued Dr. Towdi, 'that you must be the *husbundee* of the charming *Imee* Felicitu, who is a regular member of our Coffee Circle.'

'Correct,' said Philip.

'And you work at the Downing Foundation with *Om* Bryant.'

Philip was pale and speechless.

'So that means you must know my nephew Ito.'

Philip swallowed. He was conscious of a disturbance somewhere to his right. Could it be that someone was weeping? Wailing even. '*Imee* Grace is your …sister-in-law?'

'My sister,' said Dr. Towdi with some degree of pride. 'I have two sisters, Mitzee and Grace. One is a successful business woman, and the other is well-known for her contribution to educational development here in Namisa.'

'How wonderful,' said Philip, his voice faltering. The crying to his right rose in volume. The music stopped. A communal murmur filled the air. 'So, Tanita is Ito's ….'

'Cousin,' said Dr. Towdi smiling. 'Correct.'

The room had now become unnaturally hushed, except for Tanita's sobs. All eyes were on Philip. He approached the group of women and there he came eyeball-to-eyeball with Felicity.

'Philip,' she said.

'Felicity,' he replied, after which he pronounced a phrase that he remembered people often said in movies at moments like this. 'I can explain everything.'

'Philanderer, *imeetineeizer*, Blackbeard!' boomed Mrs. Katraree.

'Bluebeard,' said Felicity.

'Bluebeard, *jigolee* … adulterer … bad person.' Mrs. Katraree ran out of words.

Tanita raised her head from her mother's shoulder. She looked at Philip with reddened eyes, 'How could you?' she said.

'It's …' Philip searched for an answer. 'It's complicated.'

Cries of, '*Shematihut!*' and '*Sheematipa!*' came from the assembled company and followed Philip as he ran the Namisan gauntlet towards the exit. But on reaching the door, his way was barred.

'I shall expect, Philip,' said Bryant, 'to see your resignation on my desk on Monday morning.'

*

I can't write. I can't. I can't speak. I can't breathe. Give me time. Let me think. Stupid. Stupid. Stupid. Why? I mean…

Why?

*

Tanita hated him. Of this there could be no doubt. But in all sincerity, he *did* believe he could explain what had happened. And Felicity surely did not despise him so much that she could not or would not help him now in his hour of need – not just by supplying Mrs. Katraree with the correct vocabulary – but by reasoning with her and coming clean about their relationship. If Felicity really had met someone else – be it the mysterious Mike or the diabolical Bogadan – it would be in her interest to clear the air and reveal all.

When Philip awoke on Sunday morning it was to the insistent ringing of the doorbell and the tiresome cries of Parrot.

'Wakey wakey. Wakey wakey. Good morning.'

'All right!' said Philip, picking up Felicity's favourite hammer – the one she used when hanging pictures of her holiday home in France. Philip was on his guard now. He couldn't discount the possibility that Grace, or her sister, or Bogadan – the whole family, curse them – might send over a Pundari *bouncey* to rough him up. He raised the hammer and opened the door.

'Good morning, Philip,' said Alan. 'I bring you fresh croissants for your breakfast from the new Nambrioche bakery. And I bring you words of support and consolation.'

*

'First of all,' said Alan, 'you have been banned from all contact with Tanita.'

Philip put marmalade on his croissant and shared it with Parrot, who shuffled back and forth across the kitchen table between him and Alan.

'Tanita is grounded. The word on the block is that Mrs. Katraree was just a teeny bit too liberal with her daughter. All that mixing with foreigners has corrupted her.'

Philip sighed and so did Parrot.

'Needless to say,' said Alan, 'you are persona-non-grata at the SnowWhite Dry Kleen Shop. Things do sometimes get damaged in the cleaning process, as you are probably aware, so, if you have left any clothes there of late, I hope they are not expensive items.'

Philip added extra sugar to his coffee and stirred.

'As for Grace, she is telling everyone that they would have been celebrating Ito Boy's scholarship if it hadn't been for your mismanagement of his case. And, of course, you mismanaged it because you were so busy philandering.'

Parrot made a slurping sound as he watched Philip put the coffee mug to his lips.

'It's not that I'm negative, Philip, but I don't see a way out of this at the moment. So, I thought I'd come here this morning … and help you write your letter of resignation.'

'Mmm, lovely,' said Parrot.

*

Grace's home resounded with wails and the gnashing of teeth. She wondered at the wisdom of her sister Mitzee in sending Tanita to her for safekeeping at Villa Bogadan. But, a local tabloid had got hold of the story and the SnowWhite Dry Kleen Shop was currently awash with reporters. The girl seemed inconsolable, and Grace, who was normally imperturbable, added her niece's misery to her own growing list of concerns.

Following the catastrophic graduation party and the revelation that Tanita had been beguiled, if not seduced, by an adulterer – and a foreigner at that – Mitzee Katraree could be forgiven for removing her daughter from circulation. She had correctly anticipated that, in addition to the local media, the British rascal would shamelessly present himself at the SnowWhite Dry Kleen shop to contrive an assignation with Tanita.

Mitzee had learned all she needed to know about British men from *Imee* Felicitu and in discussions at the Coffee Circle. These accumulated insights had been passed on to Grace as cautionary tales. What had come to Mitzee's mind when deciding how to proceed with Tanita was the story of Gretna Green, a poor Scottish girl forced into marriage by a wicked Englishman against her parents' will. An heroic Scot by the name of Ben Nevis had assisted Gretna's escape through the jungle and, after suffering great hardship, she arrived on Ellis Island and thereafter in Hollywood, where she achieved fame as an actress and starred in two of Mitzee's favourite films, *Grand Hotel* and *Queen Christina*. That story at least had ended happily, but Mitzee was taking no chances with her own daughter's future by entrusting her to Grace. And, in Tanita's enforced absence, Mrs. Mitzee Katraree gave extended refuge to her own dear *Imee* Felicitu who, given the circumstances, showed remarkable fortitude and resilience.

After the disturbing encounter with *Om* Pilip, and her enquiries in Wunamisa, Grace had it in mind to initiate some investigations of her own. Bogadan had known full well that his mother was not adept at surfing the net. Indeed, she had had no interest in doing so … until now.

'Tanitatee,' Grace said to her niece in a moment of respite from her tears, 'are you familiar with this slurping the net business. I am just a little curious to see how it is working.'

Tanita dabbed at her still reddened eyes. 'Goodness, *Nantee,*' she said, 'that's rather proactive of you.'

'Today, one cannot afford to be left behind, and it would appear that slurping is very important and affords the discovery of much *informations.*'

'That is true, *Nantee*, but we usually say "surfing" not "slurping." "Slurping" is what we do when we drink our *cha-cha*.'

Disguising her intentions as best she could, Grace had Tanita search a few distractors.

'Ah, *jej*, this John Lewis *plight* is very useful,' said Grace putting on her Yves Saint Laurent glasses to survey the screen. 'And you say I can even buy *on-liney.*'

'*Jej, jej, Nantee.* Perhaps you would also like to see the *webplight* of Harvey Nichols?' Tanita's fingers flew across the keyboard typing here and clicking there.

'Impressive,' exclaimed Grace, removing her glasses and looking at Tanita in admiration. 'And what about the University of Prapundar? Do they have a *plight* too? It is good, I think, to see the competition.'

Grace replaced her glasses as Tanita Googled the University of Prapundar.

'What is this?' said Grace in dismay, '*Plight* in construction. What is this meaning?'

'They are working on it, *Nantee*. Maybe you can look at some other university just to get an idea of how they look.'

'Well, it is really not that important,' said Grace, 'but since you are here to show me, perhaps we should take a look at … the University of Oxford.'

As Tanita's fingers hit the keyboard, Grace changed her mind, 'No, on second *torteez*, let us look at the *plight* of the Oil and Gas Institute.' She fingered her pearl necklace nervously.

'Which one, *Nantee*? There could be many.'

'Well, perhaps the one in Abu Nar. I was there, you know, some months back. I was one of the keynote speakers for their International Conference for Power and Innovation. Perhaps we will find some *informations* about this on their *plight.*'

Tanita re-keyed her search.

Grace leaned in close to the screen. 'Oh,' she said, 'but it is very busy.'

Tanita saw that her *nantee* was confused. 'Would you like me to find you the *linky* to the conference?'

'Is this a *linky*?' said Grace, leaning in again towards the screen and pointing to the phrase, 'Communication and Cultural Understanding.'

'*Jej,*' said Tanita. 'Now look, all I have to do is *clicky* here and …'

Grace sat bolt upright and gave a gasp, as did Tanita.

'Goodness,' said Tanita. 'I had no idea that ...'

Grace waved her ring-embellished hand at Tanita bidding her to shush.

A colour photograph of Bogadan had appeared on the screen. Next to the photo were the words, 'Professor Ito Bogadan, Visiting Professor of Communications and Cultural Understanding.' Below this was a short biography, then another photo of Bogadan, a small, smiling figure in the midst of his OGI students. Beneath this image was a note which read, 'We give special thanks to Professor Bogadan for his unbounded contribution to the ongoing OGI research program.'

Tanita may well have noticed that her *nantee* was showing some signs of agitation.

'What is this little *liny* under the word research?' asked Grace.

'It means we can *clicky* here for more information,' explained Tanita.

'*Clicky, clicky,*' said Grace, her neck now grown red and blotchy.

Tanita clicked to reveal yet another photograph of Bogadan, standing with a book in one hand and his elbow resting on a bookshelf. The text under the picture read, 'Thanks to Professor Ito Bogadan, the Oil and Gas Institute has received research grants to the value of ...'

Grace pulled off her glasses, perspiration forming on her forehead, '*Shematihut!*' she exclaimed, '*Shematihut!*'

And it was thus that Grace Shoon Bogadan came to understand that her son was indeed channelling TU money into OGI, and was running not one department but two, and was collecting not one salary but two.

***

33

WHILE THE DINNER IS HOT AND THE KNIFE SHARP

Philip was indeed turned away at the doors of the SnowWhite Dry Kleen Shop. Babli was not big and intimidating, but he was assertive ... and Philip didn't much like the way he was wielding his dustpan and brush.

Back home he tried sending Felicity a text:
> pls help xplain truth 2 mrs k re us.

Seconds after he had pressed 'send,' a new message appeared in his in-box:
> om pilip i hearing bad thingeez but i am can helping u remedy situation. bog.

Philip gave a gasp of annoyance and pressed 'delete.' What was Bogadan thinking of? Hadn't he done enough remedying by now?

And there was the solitary insistent ringing at the doorbell.

'Wos up, Alan? Wos up, Alan?' said Parrot.

Philip opened the door for his friend, and strode into the kitchen, keying in another message to Tanita as he went.

Parrot squawked and flapped his wings. 'Darling, darling,' he said in his cutesy voice.

'What's up, Alan?' said Philip as he concentrated on his text. He glanced up. It was not Alan who stood before him in the kitchen doorway. It was Bogadan.

'*Om* Pilip,' said Bogadan, 'I can-helping you, and you can-helping me.'

*

'It is a tragic but all too common story. Your wife far from home and from her loving ones, and for this she was being too solitary. *Husbundee* at fault too. He was spending *alotta* times at cocktail bar of Shangri-La and in Sleepy Hollow Nite Club.'

'That's not true,' protested Philip.

'Hear me out, *Om* Pilip. So, *imee* not happy and is meeting another *om*. A very good *om*, very caring, very full of thoughts for her. This result in betrayal. Very difficult to trust *imeez* and *imeetineez*, thus in olden times, they are locked indoors and becoming very pallid. Pallid colour pleasing to the Namisan since sign of honest woman. Hence, *Om* Pilip, according to your excellent British law you are having to cast her out – in this case she is being casted out to our SnowWhite Dry Kleen shop – and then you are divorcing her. You are saying to her in a loud voice:

"You may go, wife, you may go, woman, you may forever go four times."' Bogadan sat back in his chair and smiled, 'There,' he said, '*bushkil* solved.'

'We would *never* say anything like that,' said Philip.

'What a lot of rot you talk, Bogadan!'

Bogadan raised an eyebrow. 'Believe me, *Om* Pilip, it is better to say it now while the dinner is hot and your knife is sharp. So that,' he continued, 'after six-month period of celibacy…'

'What?' said Philip.

'After six-month period of celibacy, according to *bunga* British law, you going to be free to re-marry, and you can-will marry my nice, very *smaartee* and *trikee* cousin Tanita. I will see for the visa requirements. Do not fear, *Om* Pilip. You will remember that my uncle Beedee, father of Tanita is Chief of Police and he have *alotta* relatives in Directorate of Residency and Foreigners' Affairs.'

'But that is not our law,' argued Philip.

'Nor ours. But I feel it is the decent thing.'

'Why are you doing this, *Om* Bogadan? What's in it for you?' Philip narrowed his eyes as if it would help him see inside this man's brain.

'You are my friend, *Om* Pilip. If I am not helping my *buddee*, who am I helping? In life we must to help someone, or we finish in the afterlife in the dark dank caves of Grikagraka with no Fella for helping us.' Bogadan's eyes had gone moist. He looked at Philip long and earnestly, like a man intent on expiating his sins.

Bogadan had at last done good. For, while Philip had lost a job, now through Bogadan's intervention, he would shortly be gaining a sweetheart.

'Oh and, Pilip,' said Bogadan, 'please call me Itotee.'

*

Didn't I write somewhere that your life can turn around very quickly, maybe even in a day? My life already has. Several times. It was the end of everything, and now it isn't. And all I had to do, all I did, was wait.

This is what I'm thinking. Sometimes all we have to do is wait. Wait until the boat steadies, wait until the tightrope stops bouncing, wait until the storm dies down, and just let the answers drift over to us.

Pappee brought Felicity to see me. I felt no animosity towards her. Why should I? Her story is a strange one. She and Philip were two people with a very particular agenda, each escaping from something minor yet of significance to them, each following an alternative option. There is always another route towards solving our problems but, mostly, we are afraid to take it. For that I admire them both and I think I understand Philip a little better than I did before. It's a story we will need to unravel for the sake of appearances, but just as there were options before, so there will be options now.

I'm wondering if all of us are escaping or trying to escape from something. My guess is that, just when we think we've lost it, whatever we're escaping from will show up later in the place we've escaped to. I suppose we need to turn around and face it or, otherwise, continue being pursued. But, then, what do I know?

So, now I have a new best friend. Who would have thought it? I don't read romances. I don't write them. That's Felicity's job. We agreed though that we both, in our own way, love the same man. Is that absurd or what? I see Felicity as a lone person rather than a lonely one. She is strong, though it was love or – at least infatuation – that weakened her. What she told me, and what I learned from her, was that there are moments in our life when we are driven towards bad choices and only by stepping away can we reformulate those negative experiences. It's all about needing to master the art of living.

I think I'm beginning to sound like a self-help book. It won't be the first time.

Good news for Nantee. *Felicity is going to help her write her book. Now Felicity is* Nantee's *BFF.* Nantee *says the book is going to be called* Jobs For The Girls. *Well, why not? Will there be a job for me, I wonder?*

Mike told me to be patient. I was, and I feel better for it. I sat in the garden at Nantee's *and practised being patient. And, while I was doing that, a tiny bird with luminous blue feathers fluttered across the tops of the flowers close to where I was sitting.*

Something I noticed, that's all.

*

Bogadan was foolish not to have noticed the change in Grace that evening, but this was no doubt because he was glowing with self-satisfaction at his resolution of the Philip and Felicity conundrum. He and Grace had travelled together in Grace's car, with Bogadan at the helm, to return Tanita to her mother. It had been a tearful homecoming, Mrs Katraree thankful that there was no lasting stigma adhering to the family and its reputation, and Tanita happy to resume planning an escape from the SnowWhite Dry Kleen business of which she would inevitably become CEO if she did not take action now. With what perplexity had

Tanita, Grace, and Bogadan downed the Namisan champagne offered them by Mrs. Katraree.

Grace was very quiet as her son drove her back in the car. Bogadan, on the other hand, hummed along to the strains of 'La donna é mobile' on his car stereo. Entering the lounge of the villa, Grace called for *cha-cha*, then turned to her son and said, 'And now, Itotee, I would like you to tell me about your research programme at the Oil and Gas Institute and about why the new lecture hall in Building 5 is dedicated to Dr. William Sharwarmiyya and not to Lady Downing. I would also like to know what happened to the TUDI funding and to the document I signed granting an across-the-board pay increase to all faculty and staff. And finally, I want you to tell me about Fliflee and your plans for the University's next Christmas party.'

Bogadan's warm olive complexion, paling under its rich exterior, turned to a troubled shade of khaki.

'I am waiting, Itotee,' said Grace. 'I am waiting.'

*

Philip noticed that in Bryant's office some of the pictures and certificates were missing from the walls.

'Take a seat, Philip,' said Bryant. On the floor next to Bryant's chair were two cardboard boxes. 'I won't be needing this,' said Bryant, pushing Philip's envelope across the desk. 'It is no longer necessary.' He looked embarrassed. 'I've had a communication from Lady Downing. It would be an understatement to say that she was most displeased to hear about your falsification of your marital status. However, she has acknowledged that your handling of the

Bogadan case, with its consequent revelations, has proved invaluable to the Downing Foundation. As you can imagine, it is of the utmost importance to keep this whole business as low key as possible. It could have been a scandal of immense proportions. We are fortunate in that Dr. Towdi's brother-in-law is Editor of the *Namisan Times*, that Beedee Katraree is Chief of Police and that Bogadan's sister Perl is a journalist with Nam-B. There were a few problems with a reporter from one of the tabloids, but Grace sent one of her people over to Media Village and the man's been spoken to. Information about the misappropriation of the TUDI funds is thus contained. Grace, although she would prefer not to admit it, is somewhat grateful to you for alerting her to the funding irregularities. But let us leave it at that. I understand that we will be undergoing some restructuring. I will keep you informed.'

*

'I'm not sure I can follow all of this,' said Philip.

'Do you think I can?' said Alan.

'Everyone's talking about it,' said Ronny from the other side of the partition. 'Bogadan was doing very nicely before you came on the scene, *Om* Pilip.'

'You see,' said Alan, 'everyone loves Namisa, but everyone wants to leave Namisa too. The only one who really wants to stay is Robinson-Smith because he has the monopoly on travelogues. We can't blame Bogadan for trying to do a moonlight flit. He was feathering his TOGI nest with golden *babbigall* feathers. The TUDI money went to TOGI and Grace knew nothing at all about the promised post that Bogadan was to take up there in exchange for the research money. Even Sharwarmiyya – he of the Building 5 Lecture Theatre – had been briefed not to mention it to her. This escape to Abu Nar was going to be Bogadan's break for freedom from his *pappee*.

'What about Bryant?'

'It happened on his watch. Do you suppose he didn't know? You were the perfect candidate. He threw you to the monster, thinking it would leave him alone and gobble you up. Lady Downing may have other plans for him now.'

*

Bogadan was true to his word. Philip found himself on the steps of the SnowWhite Dry Kleen Shop, a bunch of *bayseez* in hand for Tanita, *bayseez* picked by Babli from the flowerbed opposite the porch of the bungalow.

'Thank you,' said Mrs. Katraree. '*Imeetinee* Petee will put these in water. Now we may drink our *cha-cha* and talk of gardening and horticulturing in the UK, because I am often wondering why my flowers are not growing like in the Paddington Flower Show.'

'The Chelsea Flower Show,' said Philip.

'Are you sure?' said Mrs. Katraree. 'I don't like when people giving me incorrect *informations*.'

'I'm sure Philip doesn't want to talk about gardening, *Pappee*,' said Tanita. 'He's a diplomat. He doesn't know about things like that.'

'Yes, I can-am seeing that,' said Mrs. Katraree. 'We were never having this problem with *Imee* Felicitu, but since she is busy now *writing-writing* we must manage *outwith* her. We can be talking instead about diplomatic *thingeez*, like role of mother in chaperone meetings with daughter and prospective fiancé. In UK, for the example, how is this working?'

Philip looked into Tanita's eyes and she into his. Each noted the other's pained yet resigned expression.

*

When Philip and Bogadan resumed their meetings at the Shangri-La *Bi-Dillin*, Philip was aware that sooner or later Bogadan would be calling in a favour. With visiting rights established, he owed Bogadan one.

'My PhD,' said Bogadan, 'I think I shall do it in Edinburgh. I like the Scots.'

'It's cold in Edinburgh,' said Philip.

'Manchester, then.'

'Cold and windy … and it rains a lot.'

'Sussex?' proffered Bogadan.

'You could try London and just stay indoors all year if the weather doesn't suit you.'

'Well, I'm glad you agree,' said Bogadan.

After the restructuring, Philip had remained in his role as Officer of Education and Culture, but took over many of Bryant's networking responsibilities, like the FFs, the G & Ts and the much-loved Medicals. Bogadan was on all the honoured-guest lists. Bryant, they heard, was settling in well to his new posting in Katowice, though the harsh winters were doubtless a shock to his system after years of *autumns* and *autumn-autumns*.

'*Looka looka*, Itotee,' said Philip with some authority. 'I'm not at all clear what you would intend to choose as the subject of your research. Before you go any further at all, you will need to submit a carefully articulated proposal.'

Bogadan reached for his briefcase and pulled out a ring binder with a green Perspex cover. 'Do you mean a proposal like this?' Bogadan brandished the binder. He thrust it under Philip's nose like a magician forcing a card.

Philip snatched the binder from Bogadan's hand and read the title page:

Namisarpundar Cultural Traditions:
a PhD proposal by Ito Bogadan.

Philip was silenced as he turned and scanned the pages. Bogadan smiled at the waitress and pointed to their half-full and half-empty glasses. Then he took a cheroot from a small red enamel tin and lit up.

'Mmm …' said Philip, pausing here and there to read a line or a paragraph. 'Mmm…' He glimpsed up at Bogadan and then continued. 'Uhuh,' he said, turning more pages, his forehead tensed. He reached the final page, closed the file and placed it on the table in front of him. He sat back and tilted his head to one side.

'Well, Itotee, I have to admit that this proposal *is* extraordinarily well-written.'

Bogadan slipped one knee over the other, sat back comfortably in his armchair and puffed elegantly at his cheroot. His eyebrows were set in a nonchalant arc of pride. He gave Philip a gracious smile.

'Why,' said Philip, 'do I not think you wrote this?'

'Frankly, I do not care if you think it or not,' said Bogadan. 'The PhD grant applications come up for consideration in a month. I believe it might just be possible for your celibacy to be lifted by then.'

Philip sat upright. 'But I thought you said that it was final. How can you change it?'

'The ways of other societies are a mystery to us,' said Bogadan, raising his eyes to the ceiling fan. 'You see, if the ex-wife remarries, it brings redemption to her husband. This is a Namisapundar cultural tradition, by the way.'

'Felicity is getting married? To whom?'

'To me,' said Bogadan.

*

Philip and Tanita accompanied *Om* Trattat to the airport in Bryant's BMW. Felicity and *Imeetinee* Petee followed in the Cinquecento. For the occasion, Ratni wore a British officer's cap, which he had picked up near new for just a few *kolaz* in the Trinamisa Wednesday market. *Om* Trattat wore a brown suit and a new pair of Nike trainers, given to him on the occasion of his journey by Philip. Around his neck he wore a large beige luggage label, indicating his place of embarkation and his anticipated destination. Philip did not intend leaving any margin for error.

Tanita had been released from house arrest for the morning with a special dispensation from her mother, on the understanding that *Imeetinee* Petee and *Imeetinee* Felicitu – soon to be *Imee* Bogadan – would go too. Mrs.

Katraree was otherwise occupied with the Coffee Circle and, in the absence of *Imeetinee* Petee, Babli would take a break from his laundry deliveries and matchmaking activities, and occupy himself with replenishing the coffee cups and the plates of new chocolate *chipee* biscuits that Mrs. Katraree had seen advertised on TV in the commercial break after Pundari Big Brother. It looked to be a busy morning since the chosen topic was 'Morality in the Movies.'

Om Trattat had recently returned from a short visit home to Pundar, where he collected the necessary belongings and garments that would see him through his first winter of study in the frozen and hostile wastes of London. Some heavier items of clothing could be found in Pundar from time to time, since the early morning mountain chill warranted them. But there in Pundar, *Om* Trattat faced serious moments of self-doubt as a multitude of tiny Pundaris gathered around him for his suitcase-packing ritual. Having thrice removed a child, each one smaller than the previous one, from his baggage, he broke down in a crisis of sobs and wails. He had felt unprepared for the excess of cultural experiences that awaited him.

The departure from his post at the Trinamisa School of Languages was no less trying. Word had got out that *Om* Trattat's travelling bags might not be worthy of a PhD candidate. The combined efforts of multiple embassies resulted in the purchase of an A3-sized teddy-bear *cardee*, signed by all and sundry, and a complete set of Louis Vuitton suitcases, the acceptance of which represented something resembling a moral obligation on the part of the suitably overwhelmed recipient. More sobs ensued. *Om* Trattat's audience at the Trinamisa School of Languages assumed this was to do with his regret at leaving the school rather than his terror of the future.

'Let's take some photographs,' said Tanita when they reached the airport observation deck. Humid air wafted around them as they shuffled together in various poses and waited as Ratni pressed the camera button. After he had taken three views of the inside brim of his cap, Felicity confiscated the phone and sent him to buy the *cha-chaz* while the original poses were replicated and captured digitally.

'Let's take one of you with your plane in the background,' said Tanita, pointing in the direction of the waiting aircraft.

Om Trattat turned and froze. He gave an audible gasp. 'I am travelling KLM?' he said. 'I am not travelling PAST?'

'Your days of travelling PAST are passed,' said Philip, who had been waiting to pronounce those words for a very long time.

There was no response from *Om* Trattat. He remained immobile, staring out at the sun-bleached tarmac and behind it the rich green Namisan foliage and the purplish hills of Trinamisa.

'Are you all right?' said Philip.

Om Trattat's face seemed to quiver and crumple. Philip looked around desperately for assistance. '*Om* Trattat?' he said.

Trattat turned and looked at him. His face was distraught. Tears rolled down his cheeks and he burst into a wail of the kind that was becoming all too common these days amongst the subjects Philip had to deal with.

'I cannot! I cannot!' he cried.

'You cannot? What can you not?' said Philip.

Trattat raised his arms and grabbed Philip by the shoulders, then pulled him roughly into a tight embrace.

'I cannot thank you enough,' he sobbed into Philip's left ear, after which he cried profusely onto Philip's *shala kan*, that had been delivered freshly cleaned and pressed early that morning by Babli.

***

34

NEW TROPHIES FOR OLD

Philip looked up from the book and blinked, dazzled by the glow of the pages and the bright light streaming in through his office window. From Bryant's desk, from what was now his place of work, he could see across to a building site. There, scaffolding criss-crossed, and shunting cranes leaned in around the skeleton of a new shopping mall, set in the earthy foundations of what was to become Trinamisa's finest landscaped garden. Gone was the medieval battlefield of a bus station, gone were the shoulder-to-shoulder food stalls decorated with fairy lights and jangling with the muscular carcasses of the evening's communal dinners. In the foreground directly beneath Philip's window were the ever-verdant gardens of the Foundation, dense with trees and bushes in which chattering birds darted and fluttered.

From inside the room Philip had removed much of the original furniture and re-positioned the remainder, orienting the desk so that he could better appreciate the unchanging seasons from *autumn* to *autumn-autumn* and back again through the year. On the opposite wall, Lady

Downing continued to smile down upon the room's occupant, secure now in the knowledge that the Foundation was in the very best of hands. When he had left so hurriedly for his new posting in Katowice in Poland's industrial triangle, Bryant had left behind the sizeable golfing trophy prepared for him at his own instruction by Namisa Metro Sports. This Philip had passed on to his loyal driver Ratni, who was happy to obscure Bryant's name with masking tape and substitute his own, printed neatly on a sticky label by Tiki on one of her more obliging days.

Philip now had trophies of his own. Beneath Lady Downing's photograph, in pride of place on a highly polished mahogany side table was an octagonal crystal block that bore the crest of the University of Trinamisa, a sea blue circle bordered in ochre and black, with the golden ear of the young Fella in its centre. Engraved on its black Perspex base were the words:

In Appreciation

from the

RECTOR TU WUNAMISA

Prof. Imee Baadeeyyumba
GRACE SHOON BOGADAN

Some things, Philip reflected, did not change.

The side table also accommodated a most flattering collagen-pumped and Botoxed studio portrait of Auntie Peggy to whom Philip owed … something, though he could not bring to mind what. For her part, Auntie Peggy owed her makeover to the recent motivating stream of

Namisan and Pundari gentlemen who, sent to London by Philip for educational enlightenment, populated her front lounge and, in succession, occupied Philip's old bedroom under the perplexed and critical eye of Bruno the teddy bear. Philip had put away childish things, while Auntie Peggy took care to keep them on display.

In his three years and ten months of service – one year more than he had originally planned – Philip had lost a wife and gained … well … a wife. Tanita, so very *trikee* and *badee*, gazed out at him from the silver frame on his desk. It was not the pearl-white teeth, the dark shimmering hair, the moist nut-brown skin that entranced him. It was her extraordinary mind, though the teeth, the hair, the skin, and a great deal else were not without relevance in his estimation.

He gave a sigh of happiness and closed the book in front of him. He drew his hand across the pink dust cover on which was emblazoned the name of the author – Felicity Manning – and, beneath that, the book's title: *Love of the Two Hills*. A fluorescent sticker in the lower right-hand corner of the cover declared that this remarkable breakout novel was 'Winner of the Namisan Book of the Year Award, Best Foreign Language Literary Fiction Category.'

Philip, Tanita, and their good friend Mike Robinson-Smith had attended the awards ceremony. The judges had commended the book, saying that it worked on three levels. It was about a personal search for love and recognition. It was about the love between a man and a woman of mixed race. And, finally, all this was set on the backcloth of a location, the two hills of the title, which represented the memories and experiences that the place held for the protagonist who, through circumstance, had been estranged from her former life in Notting Hill Gate – hence the play on words in the title. Very ingenious, thought the judges. And so did Philip.

In 2009, the Namisan publishing industry saw the inauguration of an important cultural and educational initiative, that of the annual Trinamisa International Bookfair (TIBF). Inspired by the success of TIBF, the Pundari Booksellers (PuBoo) and the Library Association of Pundar (LAP) established the Prapundari International Festival of Literature (PIFL), also held annually in the Prapundari International Conference and Exhibition Centre with the aim of boosting the literacy levels of the local population, currently at 8 percent.

(Extract from 'Cultural Initiatives,' (p.242) in *Namisa - A Traveller's Guide: from tradition to tourism and back*, by Michael Robinson-Smith.)

[Editor's Note: As a point of interest, the Prapundar Office of Public Relations (POOPR) did warn the PIFL LitCommit about the dangers of ill-chosen acronyms.]

The film rights to *Love of the Two Hills* had been sold, and Namisa was set to become the centre of attraction for a new generation of movie tourists. Philip turned the book over to study the black and white photographic image of the new Felicity. Not a hair out of place, her eyebrows threaded into an aristocratic arch above her clear wise eyes, her generous lips parted very slightly in a smile, and around her throat a single string of glistening Namisan pearls, a present from her adoring mother-in-law Grace.

The inside flap of the dust cover carried this simple description: 'Felicity Manning, London-born author of *Love of the Two Hills*, is the University of Trinamisa's Distinguished Visiting Professor of Anglo-Namisan Literature.'

Bogadan at long last had taken the decision of changing the name of his department from The Department of Anglo-American Literature to The Department of Anglo-Namisan Literature in Translation, thus providing the perfect vehicle for Felicity's future literary activity. The decision to change the name of the department was also prompted by the fact that the American Embassy's Overseas Bursaries Department did not give Dr. Bogadan his requested post-doctoral research scholarship to Yale. This scholarship went to Professor Shimee Timmaya, the first Pundari to benefit from the award. This was a severe blow to Bogadan and a setback to his long-term agenda but, as Tanita commented, 'It is an ill *windy* that blows no one any good,' and 'When one traditional ornamental door closes, another one opens.' Philip had been privy to this information through his confidante Grace, his auntie through marriage, as if one auntie were not enough.

As Grace took pains to explain to Philip, Bogadan had felt for some time that the French were altogether more enlightened when it came to matters of culture and education, and fairer as regards the allocation of overseas funding in the area of academic development. There was a strong rapport between the two nations since they both had a long and illustrious history, which – as Bogadan was always swift to observe – was not the case with the Americans.

Bogadan had applied for the Yale Scholarship after spotting an advertisement in the Chronicle of Higher Education and, as he pointed out afterwards to Felicity, 'Those people at Yale. They are a rough sort.' Felicity agreed.

Now, on the eve of his and Tanita's departure for Paris, Philip was content that many loose ends had been tied up. He had not forgotten the significant contribution of Jonathan and Caroline's *babbigall* bird to this tale of triumph over adversity. These birds are known to live to a ripe old age, and when their time comes to *push on*, they take many memories with them to the grave, or to the dustbin, depending on how nostalgic an owner they have. In their privileged lifetimes they are, however, passed down like stories from generation to generation, and so it would be for that inimitable bird. Now lodged permanently with Felicity and Bogadan, and brought into the public eye through his metaphorical appearance in Felicity's novel, he was known in all Trinamisa by that unusual and exotic name, 'Parrot.' Over the years, Fliflee and her kind would become but distant voices on Parrot's beak. In times to come he would hear and repeat many a 'Stop it' and many an 'I love you' in his native Namisan, in Pundari, in English, and in the world's multitude of clever and colourful tongues.

Matured through his experiences of many Namisan autumns, Philip had enjoyed a brief but productive spell as Acting Director of the Foundation in Trinamisa, heralding in a new and glorious era of Medicals, FFs, G & Ts, and other relevant acronyms. Now he and Tanita were set to take up their new posts with The Downing Foundation in Paris – Philip as Assistant Director and Tanita as Cultural Attaché for both Namisa and Pundar.

In a surprise, but not altogether unintelligent, move on the part of Lady Downing, Alan was promoted up to the post of Director, with Ronny taking responsibility for the Finance Department and, additionally, the purchase of croissants from the new bakery adjoining the French Embassy.

A new and much-awaited Head of Education and Culture was flown in from Tallinn. Philip assured Lady Downing that for this candidate there would be no need to enforce the marital status rule. Furthermore, if Hugo Danvers – he of the pointy nose and coffee bean eyes – did manage to meet his soulmate in Namisa, he would be a far better person for such an alliance. Both Philip and Alan, who contrived to be otherwise occupied at the time, thought it most appropriate for Bogadan to meet the new arrival at Trinamisa airport.

*

Everyone has a story … including me. Our story is our guidebook to life. We just need to learn how to use it. As we turn the pages, some places become familiar territory. Others are left unexplored. The choice is ours.

*

A familiar *lingling* melody filled the air.

Philip saw a sudden look of concern spread across Tanita's face.

'*Pappee*,' she said, as if with a sense of resignation. 'Oh dear, what's up now?' She pulled her mobile out of her bag and put it on speaker mode. '*Pappeetee*,' said Tanita. 'We're just on our way to the Élysée Palace. We can't speak for long.'

'Tanitatee! Pilipitee!' said Mrs. Katraree. Her voice was distant but clear. 'You see I have a very good idea, but I need your advice. A second opinion.'

'Yes, *pappee*, we're listening,' said Philip.

'It's like this, my dears. Felicitee says that "No, it is not a good idea." But I am in two brains about it.'

'What's the *bushkil, pappee*?' said Tanita.

'This *yobbee* Mickee Robinson-Smith,' said Mrs. Katraree, 'as you know, he is having all the monopoly on our country. It is cultural appropriating and I don't like it.'

'He's been doing it for thirty years or more, *pappee*,' said Tanita, straightening her dress in the mirror. 'You should really have said something earlier.'

'*Ah jej jej*, but you know I have been *busy-busy* – the Coffee Circle, the new SnowWhite Book Club, the Women in Namisa Association … But now I am thinking to fix this.'

'Okay?'

'You see, I am cogitating to write *A Traveller's Guide to Namisa.*'

Philip stopped tweaking his tie and looked at Tanita.

'Many people around the world will be buying this book,' said Mrs. Katraree. 'What do you say?'

Tanita looked at Philip. A moment of mutual visualization passed between them.

'I don't think so,' said Tanita. 'No.'

'No?' said Mrs. Katraree. 'Are you saying I should not be writing this book?'

'*Na jej!* said Philip. 'It is a very good idea, *pappee*, but *na jej!* It will be a *workee* and a half. Take my advice. Leave it for some other *drudging* person to write. You are already making a contribution to this world, as we all should.'

A moment passed before Mrs. Katraree replied.

'Correct,' she said.

'Correct,' agreed Philip.

The End

Author's Language Notes

Since Namisan is one of the lesser-known world languages, for the benefit of readers an *Essential Glossary of Namisan (Namisan-English)* compiled by Michael Robinson-Smith is included in this volume. For ease of use, all Namisan words and derived Pundari words are identified in italics within the text.

It should be pointed out that prior to the establishment of The Union for the Preservation of the Namisan Language (UPNaL) in 2003, many words were incorporated into the language from foreign sources. Here they have been designated as 'loan words,' though strictly speaking they are words with a foreign origin that have been Namisatized. They therefore retain the flavour of their borrowed origins with uniquely Namisan usage and pronunciation.

As a reliable guide to pronunciation the author recommends the excellent introduction by the Pundari academic Baadliyya Trattat, PhD: *Introducing Namisan Pronunciation.*

No guidance is provided on issues relating to grammar. As multiple verb forms are provided in the glossary, readers may deduce their own basic rules relevant to an understanding of the text. For a full grammar rationale, we await the publication of Professor Shimee Timmaya's *Namisan Grammar Explained: A Pundari Perspective.*

To readers curious to learn more about Namisan and Pundari cultural issues, we recommend *Namisapundar Cultural Traditions* by Ito Bogadan, PhD, with acknowledgements to Im Baadeeyyumba Grace Shoon Bogadan, Felicity Manning, and the Author.

Students of Namisan will find *A Traveller's Guide to Namisa* helpful in expanding their knowledge of the Namisan language and in enabling them to acquire mastery of Basic Namisan.

The Author, 2020

Essential Glossary of Namisan

Developed and compiled by Michael Robinson-Smith as part of the Namisan Language Heritage Research Project commissioned by the University of Trinamisa.

Namisan – English

(NB. All words are provided in transliteration.)

Acception (n.) – acceptance
Adoo (adv.) – now
Ah jej! (emphatic affirmative response) – All right! Oh, yes!
Ah jej jej! (emphatic affirmative response) – Yes, indeed!
Akeet (imp.) – come
Alotta (det.) - many
An (pron.) – I
Annee (pron. f.) – I
At (pron.) – she
Atakrot (n.) – sharp ceremonial knife, traditionally employed by members of the Fellaship.
Atoo (pron. f. pl.) – they
Autumn (n.) – The Namisan season that is roughly equivalent to summer in the western hemisphere, but which relates also to the end of our spring and the beginning of our autumn. The weather in the *autumn* season

is hotter and more humid than in the *autumn-autumn* season (See below). [For further details, readers are advised to refer to the volume *A Meteorological History of Namisa and Pundar*, published by the Society of Meteorological Sciences (SMS), 1994.]

Autumn-autumn (n.) – The Namisan season that is roughly equivalent to winter in the western hemisphere but which relates also to the end of our autumn and the beginning of our spring. The weather in the *autumn-autumn* season is exceedingly hot and humid. However, the Namisan *autumn-autumn* is mild compared to the Namisan *autumn*. (For further details, readers are advised to refer to the volume *A Meteorological History of Namisa and Pundar*, published by the Society of Meteorological Sciences (SMS), 1994.) [Editor's note: The famous Shakespearean line is normally translated thus: 'Now is the *autumn-autumn* of our *discontinence*.']

Baad (adj. masc.) – clever

Baadee (adj. fem.) – clever

Babbigall (n. Ital. loan word) – parrot

Bassee (adj.) – simple

Behindside (prep.) – behind

Bi – two

Binso (n.) – winter

Bis (adv.) – quickly

Booting (n.) – dismissal

Bouncey (n.) – gangster, bouncer

Buddee (n.) – brother (but can refer to both males and females)

Buddeeitee (n.) – my brother

Bulbi (n.) – lizard native to Namisa and Pundar; also, a Namisan sauce made from liquidized bulbi combined with cow's yoghurt
Bummer (n.) – shit, (also explicative) Shit!
Bunga – good
Bungabai – Goodbye (informal)
Bungagogo – Welcome (lit. good come)
Bungaoomumba (adj.) – (lit. good and excellent), super
Bungaj (adv.) – quite
Bungakrappa – Goodbye (lit. goodbye to you)
Bushkil (n.) – problem
Bushkilat (n. pl.) – problems
Busy-busy (adj.) – very busy
Cara-cara (n.) – snail
Cardee (n. sing.) – (greetings) card
Cardzat (n. pl.) – (playing) cards
Cha-cha (n.sing.), cha-chaz (n.plu.) – tea, teas
Chick chick (n. Eng. loan word) – chicken
Chikoko (n.) – rat, native to the Namisapundar Region
Chipee (n.) – chip, as in 'chocolate *chipee* biscuits'
Coffee (n) – coffee
Comba (v.) – you beat, you win
Combi (prep.) – as
Credee (n.) – credit
Da – three, not a propitious number in Namisan culture (NB. Every effort has been made to exclude references to this number in the Namisan edition of this volume.)
Dillabinso – hill winter
Dillat (n. pl.) – hills
Discontinence (n.) – discontent
Divorcee (n.) – male divorcee

Divorceetee (n.) – female divorcee
Divorcement (n.) – divorce
Drudging (adj.) – (excessively) hard-working
Drumsters (n. Eng. loan word) – drummers
Easy-easy (adj.) – simple
Etset (adv.) – et cetera
Felicitatious (adj.) – felicitous
Fellaship (n.) – secret Namisan sect, supposed to be followers of Fella Breekaya. The organization was banned in 1961.
Fi – one
Galley (n.) – gallery
Gogot – (I) have come
Goo (vb.) – tell
Grafty (n. coll.) – graft, (hard) work
Happy-happy (adj.) – exceedingly happy, when one is very pleased with oneself
Hela (n.) – iron
Huhu (det.) – that
Hura (n.) – pungent, evil-smelling fruit native to Namisa and Pundar
Husbundee (n.) – husband
Husbundeez (n. pl.) – husbands
Hut – him
Im (n. f. sing.) – Form of address for women, both married and unmarried, roughly equivalent to 'Ms.' This is a recent addition to the Namisan language (c.2019), thanks to the work of the Women In Namisa Association (WINA), established by Im Felicity Manning and Im Mitzee Katraree. There is still some inconsistency in the adoption of this title: a woman

demanding the title *Im* in Namisan will still expect the title 'Mrs' in English, for example.

Imee (n. f. sing.) – married woman (also a term of address)

Imeezat (n. f. pl.) – married women

Imee Baadeeyyumba – form of address (lit. clever and excellent woman – rarely used.)

Imeetinee (n. f. sing.) – an unmarried woman

Imeetineeizer (n.) – womanizer

Increasement (n.) – (pay) increase

Informationz (n.) – information

Init (pron.) – it

Iz – if

Izni combali, jingali – If you can't beat them, join them

Jej sheema! (coll.) –What a shame!

Jid – there is

Jiggee (n.) – dance

Jimi (n.) – camel

Jinga (v.) – you join

Jigolee (n. Ital. loan word) - gigolo

Jinkooran, jinkooranipa (formal) – thanks, thank-you

Jinkooran alotta – many thanks

Joga (n.) – joke

Joga joga (v.) – to tell a joke

Kappi shay (v.) – (you) know

Kiddee, kiddeez (n.s., n.pl.) – child, children

Kipkip (n.) – species of snake native to Namisa and Pundari

Kooka – One hundred

Kola (n.) – kola – smallest unit of Namisan currency

Krak (v. imp) - go

Krips (n. pl. Eng. loan word) – crisps

Krot (n.) – ceremonial hammer, ancient weapon of war
Kureeoserz (n. pl.) - onlookers
Kwa kwa (n.) – traditional Namisan dish made from monkey liver
Lakati (adj.) – married
Li (pron.) – them (after a verb)
Liney (n.) – line
Linky (n.), linkys (n.pl.) – link(s), (Internet) link(s)
Lingling (n.) – Namisan stringed instrument played traditionally with a wooden comb-like plectrum or *plekut*. (Also used as an adjective to describe a type of traditional melody.)
Looka looka! (coll.) – look here!
Mammee (n.) – daddy (term of endearment)
Meetz (n. pl.) - meetings
Mumba (adj.) – excellent
Mumbatipa (coll.) – Good on you! (lit. excellent on you)
Mylystone (n.) - milestone
Na (negative particle) – not
Na bunga – not good
Na jej (emphatic) – No, definitely not
Nalakati (adj.) – unmarried, single
Nalungaseesee – Let us reunite
Na na? – (tag question) Isn't it?
Najid – there is not
Nappy (n.) – rest, break
Ni (negative particle) - cannot
Nit (pron. masc.) – we
Nitted (coll.) – drunk, intoxicated
Nitt (vb.) – lace
Nittee (pron. f.) – we
Not-a-thingy (coll.) – nothing

Off (adv.) – away
Ogat (n.) – horse
Okaly – species of tree native to Namisa and Pundar
Om (n.) – man (also a term of address)
Om Baadumba – form of address (lit. clever and excellent man)
Omzat (n. pl.) – men
On-liney (adj.) – method of purchasing goods on the Internet
Oo (conj.) – and
Outwith (prep.) - without
Pa (pron. masc.) – you
Pa kappi shay (vb.) (2nd person masc. sing.) – you know
Pa'at (pron. masc. pl.) – you
Pa'atee (pron. f. pl.) – you
Pa'ee (pron. f.) – you
Pala (adj.) – hot
Pappee (n.) – mummy (term of endearment)
Patter (n. Fr. loan word) – paté
Pikky-up (n. Eng. loan word) – pick-up truck
Pitti pointeez (n. pl.) – Smart Points
Plight (n.) – (web)site
Preepree (n.) – type of tree native to Namisa and Pundari
Prittee (adj.) – very plain, ugly
Pushed-on (coll. Eng. Loan word) – passed away, dead
Revolution (vb.) – revolt
Right-right (adj.) – correct
Rumoreenz (n. pl. Eng. loan word) – rumours
Sah sah (coll.) (sometimes written 'sahsah') – very true
Salami (n. Ital. loan word) – highly spiced Namisan sausage

Salati – Hi there! (informal salutation)
Samat – Savoury highly-spiced Namisan snack
Sanddij (n. Eng. loan word) – sandwich
Sanddijez (n. pl. Eng. loan word) – sandwiches
Scratchee (n.) – scratch (as in 'up to scratch')
Scuses (n. pl.) – excuses
Searching-searching – searching (intently)
Shala kanz (n. pl.) – traditional shirts worn on special occasions
Sheematihut! – Shame on him!
Sheematihat! – Shame on her!
Sheematipa! – Shame on you!
Sheematipa-at! (masc. pl.) – Shame on you!
Sheematihutoo! – Shame on them!
Shorty (adj.) – short
Sibee (adv.) – exactly
Smaartee (adj. f.) – clever, intelligent
Snippeez (n. pl.) – snippets (Eng. loan word)
Spidee Snapper (p.n.) – aggressive spider-like insect, red in colour, native to Namisa
Sun Vole (p.n.) – small parasitic insect, similar to a ladybird, that burrows its way under the bark of trees, most commonly the *preepree*
Sutti (adv.) – slowly
Sutti sutti (imp.) – Go much more slowly!
Taffee (pron.) – enough
Thingy (n., Eng. Loan word) – thing
Thingeez (n. pl.) - things
Ti (prep.) – on
Tika tika takeena (coll.) – Go for it!
Torteez (n. pl.) – thoughts
Toto (n.) – hello (semi-formal greeting)

Tototipa – hello (lit. hello on you: semi-formal greeting reserved for strangers)

Traka (vb. imp.) – strike

Tree – four, a propitious number in Namisan culture, but not in Pundari culture (NB. This number is not included in the Pundari edition of this work.)

Trikee (adj.) – beautiful

Trikitz (n. pl.) – seeds, resembling acorns

Tu (vb.) – do

Ullullah (n. masc.) – bull

Undersidewear (n.) – underwear

Up (vb. inf.) – have

Upa (vb.) – I have

Ut (pron.) – he

Utoo (pron. masc. pl.) – they

Vexy (adj.) – vexing

Wa (modal vb.) – will

Wadd (n. sing.) – valley

Waddat (n. pl.) - valleys

Waiting-waiting (coll.) – waiting a long time

WINA – Women In Namisa Association: see the entry for 'Im'

Withinside (prep. Eng. loan word) – within, inside

Workee (n. Eng. loan word) – job

Writing-writing (coll.) – writing a lot

Wun – five

Yellibellee (n.) – banana

Yobbeez (n. pl.) – youths

***

Printed in Great Britain
by Amazon